PRAISE FOR JOURNEY MAN

ESH Leighton's debut novel *Journey Man* is both gritty and glittering, corporeal in detail and cosmic in consequence. Itself a kind of mythical place for every artist, NYC serves as a capable portal through which Leighton thrusts a world-weary protagonist we can all recognize ourselves in. This book is sexy, slick, and one hell of a ride.

—Amy E. Casey, author of *The Sturgeon's Heart*

In her clear, meditative style, ESH Leighton has teased apart the best elements of gritty urban fantasy and vibrant ancient mythologies, and whipped up an incredibly addictive odyssey that explores the complexities of life, death, and purpose. *Journey Man* is one of those delicious, deeply compelling stories driven by raw and interesting characters that keeps you musing for months after finishing.

—Nix Damon, author of *Moira and Earth*

Leighton's genre-bending novel has myths, monsters, murderers, and muses, but at the core is something intimately human - the desire to figure out who we are. Once you start reading, you won't put the book down. The world building, the characters, the plot; all of it sings. Much like The Artist in the novel, Leighton has made something beautiful, dark, funny, and unique.

—Elison Alcovendaz, author of
Lovers, Exes, Soulmates

For a debut novel, Leighton writes with the same strike-of-a-match brilliance as the old school authors. The authors for whom readers loyally search bookstores, digging for their favorite work like papered treasure; the stories that have never been told except between those rare covers—unduplicatable, irreplaceable, unparalleled. Prose as familiar yet edgy as the scratch of a turntable's needle on vinyl, stark as fluorescent bulbs, and dreamy as cigarette smoke. I see *Journey Man* becoming such a title to uncover and Leighton the name to scour for.

—Stephanie Escobar, author of *Mercy of the Crow*
and *A Song Beyond Walls*

ESH Leighton's *Journey Man* is a witty, gritty journey that breaks the boundaries of fantasy storytelling wide open. It follows the story of Savage, a seemingly ordinary man who is anything but ordinary. This story is for the creative soul - a fun and compelling artistic experience in book form, packed with strikingly visual passages, philosophical ideas, and the most inventive characters I've read in a long time.

—Annie James Thomas, author of
The Boy Who Brought the Sea

JOURNEY MAN

A NOVEL

journeyman (*noun*): a skilled worker who has successfully completed an apprenticeship to an experienced artisan or craftsman.

ESH LEIGHTON

Hardcover ISBN: 979-8-9877268-0-8
Paperback ISBN: 979-8-9877268-1-5

Text copyright © 2025 ESH Leighton
Book Cover Design by ebooklaunch.com
Book design by Evenstar Books
Typeset in Palatino Linotype
Titles in Raincheck by Taylor Penton
Stock images from Vectorstock.com

Published in 2025 by Extra Extra Publishing House.

This book has been rated

RED

under the Extra Extra Publishing House
Scaled Content Ratings.

It has been determined by the publisher this book contains
a LIBERAL amount of content that may include, but is not
limited to:

Mature language or expletives
Sexual references or innuendos
Substance abuse or exposure
Graphic depiction of blood, bodily harm, or injury; self-
inflicted or otherwise

Extra Extra Publishing House encourages all readers to
practice autonomy in consuming books suited to their
comfort and preference. This scale was developed to aid
navigation of ever maturing themes, tones, subtext, and
story elements.

For more information on our books
please visit our website:

ExtraExtraPublishing.com

for William,
my person

. . . everything comes together and adds
one knot more to the thread of life,
nothing, nothing remains in your memory
of the savage sea which summoned up a wave
and plucked a shrouded apple from the tree.

The only thing you remember is your life.

—FROM *BIRTHS* BY PABLO NERUDA
TRANSLATION BY ALASTAIR REID

PRELUDE

The man in white has been searching for so long. Months and hours and lifetimes. And now, he's found him.

The Artist is sitting at a sushi bar, a plate of untouched fish and rice in front of him. He sketches in a notebook, hunched over his work.

The man in white pulls a cell phone from his pocket, dials, and lifts the phone to his ear. "I've found him," he says. "The Artist. I've found him." He hangs up and places the phone on the table before him.

The man in white wears a titular white suit, pressed and modern. He appears young, thirty-something. But appearances can be deceiving. His blond hair is cropped and parted like a midcentury adman.

A bell rings over the door as it opens, and the servers and sushi chefs cry out *"Irasshaimase!"* The man in white has his back to the entrance, but he knows who walks in without looking. He prepares himself mentally as he realigns his wireframe glasses over his nose.

The man in black approaches his table. He wears a hoodie over his bald white head. He has no eyebrows, and the shadows under his eyes and cheekbones conjure to mind the image of a skull.

"Hey friend," he says enthusiastically, his words twisted with his affected Eastern European accent. "He'd better be fucking here. I was busy. *Big* busy. Make-the-world-spin-round busy."

"What, trying to reverse its axis?" the man in white asks flatly as he rubs his thumb over his nails.

"Ha, maybe." The man in black grabs the paper sushi menu and fills out his selection of rolls, dropping the pencil on the table with a flourish when he's finished. "Where is he?"

The man in white gives a subtle nod to the Artist sketching at the sushi bar. The man in black turns to look.

"You're sure?"

"I would know," he says. "It's him." He draws in a deep breath. "Can't you smell that?"

The man in black pulls down the hood of his sweatshirt and inhales. "Oh, yeah," he chuckles. "I haven't smelled that in a long time."

"It's weak, a shadow of what it was." His eyes flick back from the Artist to the man in black across from him. "It's been a long eon," he sighs.

"But it smells like . . ." The man in black breathes in again, trying to grasp the scent.

". . . creation," the man in white finishes.

"Inspiration," the other corrects.

"Mm, both."

The men watch the Artist at the bar, silent for a long while. A waitress drops spiraled rolls of fish and rice at their table, but neither seems to notice.

The man in white hadn't given up. The Artist, as they refer to him, is tall, with broad shoulders he hunches over as he sketches. His black hair falls over his eyes, which he repeatedly pushes back. He grunts as he scratches at his facial hair, a charcoal pencil between his fingers. He's irritable and magnetic. Just like he always was.

Is it time? the man in white wonders.

Is it possible? the other thinks.

They look back from the Artist and catch each other's eyes. It's been a long life. The men know each other backwards and forwards, but they are not friends. The man in black smiles his sardonic smile, only one side of his mouth curled up, only half a Cheshire Cat. "What do you want to tell the others," he asks, "about our buddy there?"

"Nothing," the first says. "Not yet."

"Good. It's been a long time since we had a secret."

"Devlin, we've never shared a secret."

"Necessity breeds strange bedfellows." He takes a piece of sushi roll in his fingers and eats it in one bite. "Delicious," he says with a full mouth.

The man in white arcs one unamused brow at Devlin. "I'm not hungry."

"Why are you okay with this? I mean, I'm not here to look a gift horse in the mouth, but you know what this means for me, that we've found him. You know what that means I'm going to do."

"Going to attempt to do," the man in white corrects as

he glances back to the bar. The Artist is rising from his chair, extending to his full height and stretching his back. He's taut as a bow. "I think he's changed."

"I think you're wrong."

"Time will tell."

"It looks like your time just ran out," Devlin says, nodding toward the subject of their debate.

The Artist walks to the door, and the man in white catches his gaze. His eyes drink in the sight as he stares at his friend from so many years gone.

But there's no flicker of recognition in the Artist's eyes. An uncomfortable smile crosses his mouth, forced under the man in white's intense stare. The Artist nods and utters a soft, uncomfortable "Hi" as he walks past and out the door, the bell ringing in his wake.

"Holy shit," Devlin says, swallowing another bite. "Did he recognize you?"

"No," the man in white says. He wished he had. "No, he's forgotten everything."

PART I

THE HERMIT

ONE

If Savage had created the world, he'd have done everything differently.

There's nothing beautiful or worthy about the task that busies his hands. He's culling baby mice, using a sharpened pair of shears to cut their heads off their bodies, one after the other in an endless parade of tiny pink corpses. He's been a lab tech for years, but his heart never seems to harden. He winces with each snip of the shears.

Savage culls the animals in a tiny genocide of the rodent race because the lab doesn't need infantile mice. No study currently requires the animals, so they must be killed. Culling the rodents bothers Savage enough, but his canine audience is making it worse. The dogs are watching him from plexiglass cages, their needy eyes like brown puddles begging for fresh rain.

"I'm sorry," Savage says to the mice. "I'm sorry," he looks up and says to the dogs. There's a spaniel, a pit bull mix, and one that looks more wolf than dog, with a brindled brown coat and upturned ears.

The last of the mice whimper in the plastic container on the counter. They beg for a mother they'll never know, wriggling in the confusion of freshly bestowed life.

He looks down to his gloved hands, black with death. They shouldn't be black, they should be red. They are red. But Savage is colorblind. Red and its cousins: pink, orange, and purple, are lost to him. The infantile mice, so pink in birth it earned them the official name "pinkies," wash out tan to his inept eyes.

It's so late in the night, it's become early again. *Four o'clock?* he wonders. Probably five now. Time is lost under the constant fluorescence. Savage knows he works the night shifts because he's responsible for the tasks deemed unworthy of daylight. There are no windows here. No one needs to witness death as it haunts these rooms.

A plastic name badge clipped to the pocket of his scrubs reads *Savage, Ryan* and features his picture. He looks uncomfortable and fidgety even frozen in the photo, his black hair disheveled and swept off to one side, his eyes staring down the camera. He once had a girlfriend who said he looked electric. She had bestowed the word on him like praise. He took it as an insult.

The wolfdog mewls at him.

"What?" he asks.

She scratches at the plexiglass. When he doesn't move, she barks at him, frustrated.

He sighs and closes his eyes. "Dog," he says to her, "I can't."

She falls quiet and cocks her head at him. The room is silent save the hum of air being pushed through the HVAC system and the snipping of the shears.

He doesn't want to look at the dogs anymore, so he hurries to finish. All the mice are dead and their whimpers run quiet. He disposes of their tiny bodies in a double layer of plastic biohazard bags. Biohazard-red to everyone's eyes but Savage's. He puts the bag, heavy with death if not in weight, onto a large rolling cart and makes his way to the lab's incinerator. Here, the freshly born bodies will retire to ash. He loads the bag into the drum of the incinerator, locks the latch, and turns the machine on. In a fiery whir, everything inside is swallowed down the throat of the beast.

When he was fresh out of school, he used to think he could parlay the experience gained from being the lab bitch into drawing medical diagrams for textbooks. Perhaps not the most rewarding work, but he would be paid to be an artist—something most creatives can't boast. That goal seems undesirable now. He imagines creating a detailed drawing of the human muscular system, a form with no eyelids, skin flayed open, staring out as if perplexed or frightened from a glossy page onto the likes of some Connecticut med school douchebag, who's cursing to himself because he can't get the damn thing down pat. Savage swallows in mild disgust.

Art school. So long ago, now. He would stay up all night, buzzed off a bump or two of cocaine stolen from some bullshit party, and paint. He was incendiary. He'd blast Bowie—"Life on Mars," "Sound and Vision," and "Changes,"—and paint until his hands cramped and his fingernails separated from their beds. His creativity used to crackle and spark and keep him up at night. But the cocaine probably helped.

He still lies awake at night, but not from cocaine nor creativity. The spark doesn't live in him anymore. You can't wring juice from an old orange peel. It's insomnia. Chronic, gnawing insomnia. And he still sketches. His idle hands can't help the habit. But he's just a man who doodles. And fuck that word very much, but *doodling* is the only way to describe what he does anymore. His brain used to hum with creativity. Now it's a dull Edison bulb flickering in someone's basement.

Back in the room with the dogs, the she-wolf is scratching maniacally at the bottom of her cage. When she hears Savage enter, she stops and sits down in a huff. The pit bull and the spaniel are panting at the sound of her panic.

She whines at him.

It hurts. It hurts in places he didn't think could hurt anymore. His conscience. His humanity. He's bleary eyed and exhausted. And something in him breaks.

"Fuck," he says.

He opens the lockbox on the wall where the keys to the cages are kept. He's cursing to himself over and over "Fuck, fuck, fuck" and he doesn't hear the door to the lab open.

"Oh shit, I'm sorry man," someone says. Savage jumps. It's a member of the janitorial staff—he wears the appropriate beige coveralls. He must be new because Savage doesn't recognize him. He's a bit younger than Savage, mid-twenties, short with a sparse mustache. He rolls in a yellow mop bucket. *Caution!!/¡Cuidado! Wet floor/Piso Mojado.*

"I didn't mean to get in your way," the man says. "They told me to come in here and start breaking down for the night? I dunno, it's my first day."

"No worries, you just startled me," Savage says, closing the lockbox. "I get so used to being the only one around most days."

The man crosses the room, hand outstretched. He has words tattooed on his face by someone who never should have been given a tattoo gun. The letters are indecipherable. Two smudges, one over each eyebrow.

The wolfdog starts barking again. She paws at the floor of her Plexi kennel, digging, digging, trying to escape.

"Jesus Christ, what's her problem?"

"You must've startled her too, I guess," Savage answers. They step into the hall, closing the door on the barking.

"I'm Oscar." He glances at the name badge dangling from Savage's pocket on its retractable cord. "You're Ryan?"

"Everyone just calls me Savage, my last name." They shake. Oscar's hands are warm and dry.

"Cool, cool man. Why is that?"

"There were a bunch of Ryans growing up, so that's how they distinguished between us, I guess?"

"Oh nice. Hey, I like your tattoos, man." Oscar points to the sleeve of tattoos on Savage's arm, the rendering of tarot cards inked down his skin. Death. The Sun. The Hanged Man. They're the classic, old fashioned tarot, in inks of blue and yellow, red, green, and black. He couldn't see the red ink, of course. But it was included to have the piece stay true to the original art.

"Thanks," he replies.

"I have some ink, but none that good. I've got this"—he lifts the sleeve of his uniform to reveal a quarter sleeve of a goat-headed man in gray scale. "And I got this shit on my face

I've gotta get removed," he laughs. "Man, I was a stupid kid."

Savage shrugs. "We all do stupid shit."

"Yeah, man, but I put that shit on my face! You know how hard it is to get a job with shit on your face?" He laughs, and Savage feels himself returning the smile. He shakes his head a little. How strange it must be to be that good-natured.

Oscar sighs. "I was lucky to get hired here," he drops his voice a little, "but can we take a smoke break? I've been here, like, hours and I could use a little pick-me-up."

"Sure, there's a spot around the back of the building."

As they make their way down the hall, they trigger the motion sensors on the fluorescent lights. Every time Savage walks under them, they click to life. He imagines them being roused from sleep with a drowsy *What? I'm awake.*

"This place is just a bunch of blank doors. I can't tell them apart," Oscar laughs.

Outside, on a slab of concrete at the back exit, Oscar takes out a pack of Newports. It's half full of cigarettes, with a few pre-rolled joints placed inside. He pulls out one of the latter, lights it, and sucks in, the tip of the joint blazing orange in the night. He offers it to Savage, but Savage shakes his head.

"It's your stuff, dude. Smoke it down a bit." He's quiet for a moment. "Shit, I thought you meant you wanted a cigarette."

"Nah," Oscar says, his lungs tight with smoke. "It's not that kind of night." He laughs as he exhales. "Shit's legal now, anyway."

"Yeah, but . . . they're kind of tight asses around here with that kind of thing. Medical facility and all."

"True . . . just like me. Gotta be shipshape. I'm my own medical facility," Oscar laughs.

"What do you mean?"

Oscar glances at the door a beat, makes sure they're alone. "I got a little bit of everything. I supply certain, uh, *products* to those in need."

"Oh yeah?" Savage wonders if his supply includes sleeping pills. "What kind of products?"

"Little of this, little of that." Oscar hands the joint to Savage, and this time, he takes it.

"Like prescription stuff?"

"Maybe. Sometimes. What do you need?"

"Sometimes I have trouble sleeping..." Savage shakes his head and trails off. He's not usually one to air personal issues to strangers. Or friends. He takes a drag off the joint and hands it back to Oscar.

"I think I can hook you up."

"Yeah?"

"Yeah, I'm not sure if I have Ambien or anything right now, but I can check." Oscar stubs out the joint on the concrete.

"Ambien doesn't usually work well for me for some reason."

"No worries, sometimes you've got to boost that stuff with something stronger."

Savage waves him off. "We can talk details later. Wouldn't want you to get in trouble on your first shift."

"I'm pretty sure this job's a joke, man. I haven't seen anyone other than you in like, hours."

"That's usually how nights like this go."

They head back inside to the white room where Oscar abandoned his mop bucket.

The wolfdog immediately starts barking again as the fur on

her back bristles, and she commences trying to escape, pawing furiously at the plexiglass. She keeps looking to Savage and barking at him, like she's judging him for not understanding.

"I'm gonna get outta here before that dog gives me a migraine," Oscar calls over the noise as he wheels his bucket out the door.

The dog quiets. She looks at Savage, appraising him, cocking her head back and forth.

"I know, I know," he says. "But I can't. I'll lose my job."

She barks, once.

He sighs.

He locates his personal effects, pockets his phone and keys, and pulls his hoodie on over his scrubs. The wolfdog is whining and mewling in excitement. Grabbing a plastic leash off the wall and the key from the lockbox, he goes to her kennel and cracks it cautiously. She pushes out and places her paws on his shoulders—she's a big beast—and quiets, looking him straight in the eye. She barks once and darts off to the door.

He slips the lead around her neck as she calms and opens the door wide enough for both of them. She's off like a shot, pulling at him with her canine strength. He runs after her, not given much other choice.

They dart past Oscar, who's mopping the end of the hall under the green glow of an exit sign.

"Hey, what are you doing?"

"Sorry man!"

Savage opens the exit and as the dog pulls him out into the night, he hears Oscar behind him. "Where are you going?" he yells.

"I don't know," Savage mutters to himself.

In the parking lot, the dog stops, turns her big pretty head back to him and woofs softly.

"What now?" he asks her.

She turns away from him, slips the lead, and disappears into the night.

Sometimes, when he still had a car, Savage would drive for hours at night, headed nowhere but away. Away from Las Vegas. Away from the din and glimmer and lights. He would drive until he could see the stars again, the crest of the Spring Mountains holding back the glare from the city like water in cupped hands. He'd stare up at the lonely sky—the Milky Way like God's ejaculation over a canvas of blue—and pray to no one and nothing for something to change.

"Please," he'd implore, not knowing what it was he was begging for. "Please."

But that little luxury—of leaving the city, of freedom, of starlight—is gone. He had to sell the car when the cost of maintaining it became something unmanageable.

The sun begins to rise over mountains scorched like the tired breasts of a Nevada woman, tan and wrinkling in the crevices. He pulls out his phone as he waits for the bus and googles Nevada wild canines. Coyote. Brown Wolf. Neither are quite right.

Exhausted, Savage boards the bus and slips into a seat near a window. The events of the night are catching up with him. The weed he smoked with Oscar. The thrill and adrenaline of releasing the dog. The depression that that likely cost him his job. And losing the dog. He lost the fucking dog. He lets his head droop against the window of the bus, and his vision grows fuzzy.

But some movement on the sidewalk below catches his attention. It's the dog. The wolf. The coyote. He snaps to attention and sits forward.

"Hey," he says more to himself than anyone.

In a city full of peculiar people, the dog is looking up at the most peculiar man Savage has seen in a long time. The man looks like an amalgam of a hobo, a street magician, and Walt Whitman. He wears a deep blue jacket—white stars embroidered on the shoulders and down the lapel—and a broad brimmed Stetson, navy with tired gold tassels. His trousers are striped and faded, wide around his feet like someone cut off the bottom of a stilt walker's costume. The morning breeze tosses his frayed whiskers about his face. He has something tucked under one arm, a small box of some kind.

The dog glances away from the old man and stares straight up at Savage.

Would-be-Walt follows the dog's gaze. He gasps and drops his box, its contents scattering to the sidewalk.

Savage springs up, apologizes to the bus driver, and scampers down the stairs.

"Hey!" he calls to the dog and the man.

The man is scrambling for his belongings, shoving them unceremoniously back into the box. They appear to be small vials, some black, some white. The bus hisses and puffs and pulls away from the stop as the dog and the old street man break into a run.

"Hey, wait!" Savage darts after them.

The man keeps one hand around his possessions, the other holds fast to his hat. He glances back over his shoulder at Savage, eyeing him with a discernible fear. The man and dog turn a corner and Savage follows in pursuit.

"I just want to make sure the dog's okay," he utters to himself in frustration through his hastened breath.

When he follows them around the corner, the old man and the dog have disappeared into the desert morning, like they were never there at all.

TWO

What a cruel morning. "Bullshit," Savage says to no one. Since his bus left without him, he heads to the bar.

His favorite watering hole sits a short walk from work. It's a typical off-strip Las Vegas joint. *Clover's*. The misappropriation of the apostrophe has always perturbed Savage. It should be *Clovers*. Unless the proprietor was named Clover.

He ruminates, once again, on the likelihood of anyone actually being named "Clover" as he passes through the tinted double doors. There is a big, wooden U-shaped bar with video poker machines every second seat.

Lainey is behind the bar. Her name is Magdalena, but the name doesn't suit her. She tries hard to be the cool-girl, and there was never a cool-girl named Magdalena. She wears a loose flannel over a worn cotton band tee-shirt, cropped to expose her midriff. She's Coachella couture.

Lainey isn't Savage's girlfriend. Savage doesn't want a girlfriend, especially not a cool-girl girlfriend. But they've slept together on more than one occasion, and he can summon an image of what she looks like naked from memory, not imagination.

"Hey." Her face lights up.

"Hey," he replies. He situates himself on a barstool away from the only other patron.

She yawns. "You want your 'yoush?" She's already reaching for the bottle of Bulleit.

"Yes, please."

Savage is painfully aware of how attracted to him Lainey is. He can smell it coming off her. He's tall and fit, and despite his cheap clothes, "electric" face, and quiet nature, he still draws women. He chalks it up to the fact that he has become the *ungettable-get*. Women want Savage because he doesn't react. He's too tired and too broke to summon the will for anything, courting a cool girl included. And no woman has ever made him summon the effort. It's the perfectionistic quality of his nature to always seek some great, gilded creature that doesn't exist.

Lainey passes him his rye under the green glow of the mock-tiffany lamp. Lana del Rey pours her soupy, bluesy voice from the speakers.

He sips his drink, letting the whiskey glide past his teeth and swim over his tastebuds.

"How was your day, dear?" she says, faking Florence Henderson.

"Mm, kind of shit. I'm pretty sure I lost my job."

"Oof, really?"

He hesitates. He doesn't want to tell her about the dog.

Or the escape. Or the weird man who disappeared into the morning.

He shrugs. "I'll find out soon enough, I guess."

"I was thinking of you the other day, my little sleepless buddy."

"Oh?" Savage has spent too many mornings at this bar waiting to slip into stupor or mania. Whichever arrives first.

"I saw this article. 'How to fall asleep in under a minute' or something. I'll send it to you." She grabs her phone. It's plugged in by cable to the sound system, and static crackles over the speakers as she types on her screen with chipped, blue nails. "Something about how controlled deep breathing is supposed to counteract overactive adrenaline. Like meditation or something." She looks up and smiles.

He appreciates the thought, but his issue isn't small enough to be rectified so simply. No blue light before sleep. Have white noise in your bedroom. Warm milk. Lavender. Breathe. He's tried it all. This is chronic insomnia. *Manic* insomnia.

"I'll give it a read. I'm sure it will help." He smiles back and looks into his glass. But there's no reprieve at the bottom for white lies.

"I'll text it to you because I can't DM you, Mister-Too-Cool-for-Social-Media."

"I'm definitely not too cool. If anything, I'm far less cool than you."

She's looking down and fidgeting with her phone. The cable crackles over the speakers again.

His own phone buzzes on the bar, and a text blinks across his screen.

Here you go, Mr. Cool, followed by the link.

A small group of patrons walks in, and Lainey wanders off to greet them.

Savage wonders why he comes here. He can drink at home for far cheaper. He debates which is worse: being around others and wanting to be left alone or being alone and wishing for the noise of another human.

He pulls out his moleskin sketchpad and a pencil and begins to draw the bottles behind the bar. Maker's Mark. Four Roses. Basil Hayden. Tullemore Dew.

"You want another whiskey?"

"I should switch to something lighter. You still have Strongbow on draft?"

"We switched it out for some berry cider, locally brewed," she says as she polishes the rim of a pint glass. "I guess we're trying to sound the dog whistle that only hipsters and foodies can hear. Want to give it a try?"

"Sure."

Lainey pours him a pint before tending back to other customers.

On the radio, Dave Matthews is crooning, asking the bartender in the song for another drink. Savage smirks at Dave's analogous request. He assesses his latest doodle as he sips his too-sweet cider. A hand claps him on the back.

"Damn, dude. You should do that professionally." It's Oscar, tattoo faced and smiling. "Seriously, you're a fucking *artist.*"

"Oh, hey." They shake hands. "What're you doing here?"

"Yeah, it's weird. This is like the closest bar to work. I've never even been here before." Oscar looks down at Savage with a frown. "Dude, that shit was crazy. What the hell happened with that dog? I know I'm new, but I'm pretty sure you're not supposed to let the animals loose. That's like some PETA shit, right there," he laughs.

"Yeah, not my finest hour for my career. I fully expect to get fired when they find out."

Oscar looks down at him. "You're just sitting here alone with your pink beer, man? That's sad."

"It's pink? Oh." Savage looks at the pint glass. "I couldn't tell. I'm colorblind."

"Really? It's like a bright pink beer, man." He sits down next to Savage and gives Lainey a wave. "Can we get two shots of Don Julio?"

Savage shakes him off. "No man, no tequila for me."

"Well then, let me get you another pink beer. Just in case you do get fired." Lainey sets down a shot of tequila and another pint of cider. Oscar takes his shot. "So, you can't see any colors?"

"No, I just can't see red . . . or shades of red. Like pink." Savage rubs his lead-stained fingers into his eyes. He can feel bags beneath them, big as Samsonite suitcases.

"You look tired, buddy."

"I am. I am always fucking tired, man."

"Is it the graveyard shifts? You could probably switch to days?"

"No, it's not that. I'm just an insomniac."

"Savage, the colorblind insomniac."

"That'd be me." Savage lifts his glass in a mock toast.

Oscar gestures to Lainey. "Another one, please? Can I get a lime this time, too?" He turns to Savage. "Well, good news, buddy." Oscar glances around. He leans in. "I've got some sleep meds for you."

"Ambien?"

"Nah, some knockoff. *Ambivalen.* Supposed to be strong as shit." He takes a plastic baggy out of the pocket of his jacket and passes it to Savage under the bar. "Give that a try. Let me know. Oh, and take my number so you can call me if you want more or whatever." Oscar gives Savage his number.

"Thanks man. What do I owe you?"

"Nah, it's just a couple pills. Try 'em and if you want more, we can talk about price then."

"Seriously?"

"Yeah. It's called good faith. I got faith in you, man."

Savage pulls some cash out of his wallet and leaves it on the bar for Lainey. "In that case, I'm going to catch the bus, get the hell home, and crash out."

In his apartment, Savage pours himself a glass of whiskey, drinking it in small swallows. He pulls out his sketchpad and leans over the counter on his forearms. He stares at the blank page, tapping his pencil against his forehead. But his mind wanders, and the page stays blank.

Savage's parents died when he was fourteen. Car crash, shit happens. His first experience with insomnia accompanied his grief. For nearly a year, the bells in his head were tolling, trapping him in a buzzing bronze stupor. He was lucky to sleep two hours a night.

His parents are a sore spot he tries to avoid revisiting.

He does upon occasion for the sweetness of the guilt, like an inflamed tastebud on his tongue he can't help but drag along the inside of his teeth. He revels in the guilt of being the last of their little triad to have survived. At fifteen, his grief had dulled to a more bearable flavor of pain. The insomnia, too, had eased. Its intensity titrated down to a mere hum at the back of his consciousness like the hissing of lighted neon.

In his reverie, Savage has mindlessly sketched a rough depiction of the star-spangled stranger, the man on the street who found the wolfdog. He has captured the look of fright in the eyes of the Whitman lookalike, his brow shadowed by his drooping Stetson, the ivory box clasped to his chest.

"Hello, Old Walt," he says to the sketch.

He uses the rest of the rye to take the pills Oscar was kind enough to gift him. He puts the glass in the sink, where its only companion is the glass from last night's whiskey.

He takes off his shirt as he drags his half-drunk body to the bathroom. He gazes at his weary reflection in the medicine cabinet. It's a window into the side of Savage that feeds on ugliness. Loneliness. Anger. Where darkness hides, Savage can hear it and smell it and sense it. Some unbridled part of him sniffs it out like a fox and drags it back to his hole to feast on later.

He averts his gaze, his drunk mind wandering to the wolfdog and wondering where she is, and leaves mirror-Savage to sort out his own through-the-looking-glass mind. To wonder about his inverted life and to think of the mirror-wolf in the backwards desert.

Savage is in his grandmother's garden. Somehow. He doesn't question it. Dreamers seldom question the stuff of dreams. He stands before the birdbath, which has grown large enough for him to sit on the edge and bathe his feet in the cool water.

The would-be-Walt walks into the garden, looking particularly Whitman-esque. Savage waves at him as though he's a pal. An uncle, a mentor. Old Walt looks better than he did in life. His star-studded jacket and navy Stetson are free from desert dust, and his gray whiskers are neatly seated about his face.

"Savage," the man says, as he joins him at the lip of the giant birdbath. He rolls up his striped Victorian circus pants to the knee, and places his bare feet in the water, sighing.

"Y'know, I've been with you a long time," the man says. "Possibly the longest."

Savage nods along, complacent in that way of dreams.

"I'm not supposed to be here," Walt says, leaning into Savage's ear in a conspiratorial fashion.

"No?" Savage asks.

"No. But I've used the last of my virility here, with you. To warn you. Because you're special."

"I'm not special." Even in his dream state of pliability, Savage feels the need to correct this fallacy.

"Oh, but you are, child, child." The old man says it like a lullaby, rocking softly, slowly. "I did my best to protect you. To protect you, child, child." He sighs again.

"Thank you," Savage replies, his tone earnest.

The sky is darkening in the distance. The cotton candy clouds are swirling in on one another, creating a bruise in the heavens.

Old Walt grabs Savage by the arms, twisting his body so they're face to face. Savage shifts, uncomfortable under the man's intense gaze.

"Child. *Child.*" It no longer sounds like a lullaby. Walt's yellowing fingernails dig into the skin on Savage's arm, drawing blood. It would sing red in another's eyes, but Savage's eyes are lacking. Even in a dream, he knows no red. Black runs down his biceps over his sleeve of tattoos.

"You mustn't—" the man starts.

A thunderclap fills the space around them, a tantrum of the gods. Savage shutters at the noise. A gale sweeps over them as the temperature drops, the wind raging like a banshee.

"What?" he calls out over the storm.

"You mustn't—" the old man tries again, raising his voice over the wind. It rips through Nan's garden, uprooting the blooms from the earth and tearing the leaves off the trees. A tornado of flora swirls around them in angry eddies.

"*You must not—*" the man screams, but a cyclone touches down from the sky and swallows the old man whole, like a fly on the tongue of a toad. Savage gasps, his heart in his throat. One moment he was there and the next . . . nothing. No Walt.

The thunder roars again like an incensed creature. The old man must not be sitting well in the belly of the beast. *Good,* Savage thinks. He hopes Walt fought going down.

He stares up into the storm. The clouds swirl furiously around one another, forming a shape. A face? No. A skull. A skull that snaps its jaw open and shut at Savage like it's threatening to consume him next.

"Come and get me, motherfucker," he taunts. He's not afraid. He's angry. The message the old man spent his last "virility" to deliver was interrupted by that damn storm, and the frustration of conversation-interruptus has left him indignant.

The sky begins pelting down a hail so furiously, it slices through the skin on Savage's face upon impact. He doesn't shy away despite the pain.

"You'll have to try harder," he yells to the storm.

At this, the skull in the sky laughs. It's a terrible laugh that fades into thunder.

I WILL, the storm says back.

A huge hailstone decks Savage in the face, and with a blink, the lights go out on the dream.

In the living room, the sun peeks through the gaps in the blinds. The sleep meds must have kicked in faster than Savage anticipated. He's shirtless on the couch but never got around to taking off his jeans or making it into bed.

What a weird fucking dream. He wonders about the real Old Walt. Where he's at and if the wolfdog is still with him. He hopes so. Maybe they became friends. He shakes off the last of the dream—it's fading now, anyway— as he walks into his room and turns on the TV. He cues up an episode of *The Joy of Painting* with Bob Ross. Bob's dulcet tones will banish his adrenaline and lull him back to sleep. He spreads himself out on his white sheets like molasses on wax paper. As he settles in, the bed starts to tilt. Slowly, subtly, like the world has gone a little crooked. Then, the bed pitches up at a ninety-degree angle and throws him onto the floor. He falls with a painful thump and curses, confused.

He snaps into consciousness, back on the couch, in his jeans, in the odd and uncomfortable position. The getting up, the white sheets, watching Bob Ross—it all was a dream, just a boring one.

Once again, he gets up, and peels off his jeans. His big feet get caught, tangled in the legs, and he stumbles, falling to the floor. *Through* the floor. Endlessly falling down, down, down. He wakes again, on the couch, in his jeans, contorted in the same awkward position.

"Well, shit." His thick self is catching on to what's happening. Savage is stuck in one of those damn dream loops. He knows he's unconscious, very likely on the couch, in his jeans, in an awkward position. It's been a while, but this used to happen all the time during the last bad bout of insomnia.

If it weren't enough to be a perpetual insomniac, life, it seems, has thought it amusing to give him another sleep issue—continuum dreams. He's researched them, if Wikipedia constitutes research. False awakenings. Most people will experience one at some time or another, the waking from a dream into another dream. But Savage's screwy mind sees fit to propagate an endless loop of these dreams. Each time he wakes he is certain for a moment he is experiencing real life. He sets some arbitrary goal for himself—today it's getting from the couch to the bed—one he will likely be unable to reach, and he's doomed to live in the continuum forever. No hyperbole. When he finally wakes to the world of the living, he's sure he's spent an eternity in the loop. Years upon years at least, like some sort of boring, personal *Groundhog Day*. But he's no Bill Murray. And there's no clever plotline to move the story forward. No Ned Ryerson for comic relief. No Andie MacDowell to fall in love with. No lesson to learn by the end of the movie. Only the terrible desperation of either attempting to achieve the goal at hand or to wake himself up.

He wakes, he falls.

He wakes, he can't touch anything, like he's a ghost.

He wakes, walks to his bedroom, and discovers his naked ex-girlfriend spread out on his bed. She yells at him for walking in on her exposed, even though this is his room in his apartment.

He wakes, he puts on Bob Ross. Bob scolds him for not taking his art seriously. "You've got to make some changes, friend," Bob says in his whisper-quiet cadence. "Beauty is all around us. You just have to look for it, Savage."

And on.

And on.

When he finally wakes, he does not go to his room. He does not take off his jeans. He does not watch Bob Ross. Instead, he heads to the kitchen and pours a glass of water, to assure himself that the cycle is actually broken. Today must have been twenty years in the loop at least. Twenty lifetimes. Twenty days? Twenty minutes. It's fading now, even as his heartbeat slows, and the sweat begins to dry from his chest. The terror of the loop is subsiding, and he knows this is actual consciousness. Sweet, stale consciousness.

Someone knocks on his door. He fetches the shirt he'd

abandoned on the couch and answers.

"I don't believe it."

It's the old street man, whom he's come to think of as Old Walt.

"Savage," the man gasps, his voice hoarse and straining for air. He draws ragged breaths and grabs Savage by the shirt.

Savage instinctually removes the man's hands from him. "What—how do you know—"

"Please?"

"Please what?"

Old Walt's eyes bore into him.

In that moment, the veil of space seems to fold into itself. Savage falls into the man's blue eyes, in deep as a submarine, as if they were boring into his very soul. There are answers in there. Truths swirling in the sea of his eyes like fish on the line. The eyes blink once. Twice. And the man collapses.

Would-be-Walt lies dead across Savage's threshold. Eyes wide, fingers and arms contorted at peculiar angles, like rigor mortis and a stroke hit him in one shot. Savage kneels and shakes the man's shoulders firmly.

"Shit, shit."

The old man's star-spangled jacket lies open, revealing a street-tanned chest covered in wiry gray coils of hair. On a cord of leather tied around his neck lives an ancient key. As Savage shakes him, there's no response but the clacking of the man's teeth against one another.

"No, no, no . . . c'mon man." He checks for a pulse on his wrist. His skin is like yellowed, curling paper and is warm to the touch. "Shit, shit. You can't be dead. C'mon man . . ." But there's nothing to find on the man's wrist but a tattoo of a black crescent moon mirrored against a white one.

He reaches into the pocket of his jeans for his cell phone, but he must have left it inside somewhere. The ivory box catches his eye. It's sitting on its side near the fallen man, lid still intact. Instinctively, Savage reaches for it. It's made of a heavy, dark wood, but the cover is of ornately carved ivory. He tries to open it, but the cover is locked tight.

Savage glances back to Old Walt, his eyes glazed over. He spots the key on the leather cord and carefully fishes it out of the pillowy bed of chest hair. The man's tan skin is flecked with gold, catching in the light as Savage moves the key on its cord.

"Sorry . . ." he mumbles, feeling like he's violating the old man's privacy. But curiosity is as strong a drug as any.

He inserts the key and twists. The mechanism pops inside. He lets the key fall back to its owner's chest and cracks open the box, its gold hinges squeaking in protest.

The box contains neat rows of vials of sand, fitted into a deep blue velvet backing. "What?" Savage says, as he pulls out a vial. It must be some new street drug. Or something. When Savage shakes the contents, they swirl like whispers in a bottle.

He closes the box, intending to inspect it at a later moment, and realizes the man is gone.

Vanished.

The corpse he knelt beside has managed to disintegrate into thin air like water through a sieve.

Savage searches around himself, like he's lost his keys and not the body of a deceased man.

With not but a whisper, the box Savage holds in his hand

whisks out of reality. Savage is left with nothing. No thread of proof of what has transpired. He blinks into the morning.

Somewhere in the distance, a wolf howls a long, lonely note.

Savage is waiting for Oscar at Clover's.

The last time he slept was the hour he dreamt of Old Walt and the storm. That was three days ago. One hour of sleep in three days. He rubs at his eyes, feeling the tickle of his lashes beneath his fingers. Sleep keeps calling to him, her siren song some elusive melody he can't quite remember.

He called Oscar and said the meds didn't work. The janitor-turned-pharmacist offered to provide Savage out with something "stronger."

Savage sits, head heavy in his hands, his fingers gripping his dark hair like if he pulls it all out, it might answer his problems.

I am a savage, he thinks in his bleary-eyed mania.

It's past midnight. All the evening barflies are leaving in groups of twos and threes, disappearing like players in an Agatha Christie novel. And then there were none.

He once read somewhere that the natural circadian rhythm for humans is twenty-four hours and eleven minutes. Yet another way the world is one giant erroneous screw-up. Of course humans would evolve to need eleven more minutes when there is no possible way to make the earth slow its spin.

Lainey isn't working tonight, a fact he's thankful for. The

bartender sets a rye in front of Savage, one big rock floating inside like a tiny iceberg.

"Hey, buddy." Oscar arrives and pats him on the shoulder.

"Hey." Savage looks up. "I like how you make it sound like we're old friends."

Oscar smiles and shrugs. "Who knows, maybe we are? In a past life or some Buddhist shit like that." He sits down and orders a beer. "So, that stuff didn't work?" he asks, his tone hushed.

"It kind of did. It helped me fall asleep, but then I had a bunch of fucked up dreams and woke up after about an hour."

"But you did fall asleep?"

"Yes."

"I'm no doctor, but it sounds like they *are* working, they're just not working enough. Some of those sleep meds work better when you piggyback them with something else. You want to sleep, man, you take some K with 'em, and you'll sleep through the fucking apocalypse."

Savage squints, incredulous. "You want me to take ketamine?"

"I got some I could sell you right now, and you could go home and sleep and feel great in the morning."

Savage is quiet for a moment, as he rubs his thumb over the lip of his glass. "Do I snort it like coke?" he asks, still looking at his drink.

"You can, but it lasts longer if you, like, put it into a drink and take it. You want it to last all night, so you should drink it. It's pretty safe as long as you don't overdo it." Oscar passes Savage a little bag containing a white powder and shows him how much to take.

Savage palms the bag. The plastic grows slick with sweat in his hand.

Oscar orders another beer and, when the bartender walks away, he says, "I've got a bunch of packets of that Ambivalen, too. You'll need some more."

They're quiet for a moment.

"So, did you get fired?"

"You know, I just assumed I did and never went back in." Savage laughs without humor.

"Well, at least you're a good drawer. I was thinking about that drawing you did the other night. You're really good. Like *really* good. You should do something with that. Better than killing a bunch of sad little creatures."

"It's true. It would be better. But I wouldn't know where to start."

"Sometimes, you just gotta start where you are."

When they've finished their drinks, Savage covertly passes Oscar the money owed under the bar.

"I think that'll work for you, buddy," Oscar says. "I know it will. Let me know how it goes."

Savage stands and threads his long arms through the sleeves of his hoodie. "I will. Thank you. Really. I appreciate it."

"See you on the other side." Oscar gives a little wave.

It's late, and busses run infrequently in Vegas, so Savage is due for a long walk home. His insomnia is like a weight tied to his feet, dragging him down through the pool of the ordinary. He is Virginia Woolf, with rocks in his pockets. Or was it Sylvia Plath? No, Plath was the oven, Woolf was rocks in the river. He always inverts their suicides.

Poor Plath. Poor Woolf.

He gazes up at the starless sky. His mind wanders to the dream from the other day. The sky . . . the sky had swallowed the old man whole, he remembers now. But there's no storm in this sky. The desert night is as clear and empty as a bell jar. That was Plath.

He passes the stretch of the walk home by the abandoned construction site. The houses were half built and discarded during the housing bust of the recession. Years later and the houses are left vacant and partially complete. It's the unfinished part of Vegas—the part that tourists don't see. A streetlight flickers out above him. The night is dark and lonely.

There's a soft scratching sound off to his left. He glances to the street. Walking alongside him, about ten feet away in the middle of the abandoned road, is the wolfdog.

Savage perks up. "Hey," he says to her quietly. "Hey, I know you." He's positive it's the same dog. She has the same brindled brown coat and upturned ears and humanistic look to her eyes.

He walks to her slowly, crouches his posture, and outstretches his hands trying to be unthreatening.

She looks up at him and furrows her canine brows.

"How did you end up here?"

She woofs.

He makes it to the middle of the road and kneels beside her.

She woofs again, softly.

"Hey, hey, girl. It's all right." He pets her behind the ears and takes her face in his hands. "Where did you run off to?" he asks.

She looks at him intently, cocking her head. It's dark—he can hardly make out any detail—but her eyes are so human, he wants to cry for some reason he can't quite understand.

She tilts her head back and lets out a long soft howl.

"Howlin' at the moon, huh?"

But there's no moon in the sky. It's a new moon. She sits up, at attention.

"Now, how am I gonna get you home ..." He stands up and scratches at his facial hair.

The wolfdog howls again.

Something in the night howls back.

She stands up, spooked, and looks at him once more before taking off into the night. She heads for the dusty hills beyond the vacant housing lot.

"Wait!" he calls to her. "Damn it."

But it's no use. She's gone, and he is alone again. Not even the moon to keep him company.

It's ten the next night, and Savage hasn't had a minute of sleep in over twenty-four hours. But what he wouldn't give for twenty-four hours and eleven minutes.

He appropriates the proper amount of ketamine into a glass with water and uses it to take the dose of Ambivalen. He gets into bed, lying on top of the blankets. He tosses and turns on his flat IKEA mattress. Fucking Swedes. Some things shouldn't come in an eight-by-ten-by-two-foot box, and a mattress is one of them.

The desert wind has begun to rage in full force, whistling through the cracks in his cheap windows. He waits for sleep to overtake him.

Blissfully, it does . . .

. . . but he reawakens a short time later.

"Fuck," he curses his insomnia, eyes still closed.

He's awake.

He's awake, yet again.

When he opens his eyes, the first thing he sees is the color red.

THREE

Savage lies on his back, pillow under his head, looking up toward the ceiling. A red swath of fabric covers the top of a four-poster bed like a scarf on the throat of a great headless creature. This is odd. This is not where Savage sleeps. His shitty IKEA bed doesn't boast four pillars with lush red fabric draped over them. His bed is made of pressboard and laminate, not this ornate mahogany. There's amber lighting that feels soft and sweet in his eyes like honey would feel in his mouth. Thick red and gold tapestries cover the walls. The curtains drawn over the windows are shades of scarlet, as well.

His breaths come slow and relaxed as he marvels at the beauty that is this crimson and mahogany and amber. He's captivated by the side of the spectrum previously unknown to him.

There's salt in the air, as if the ocean is nearby.

He takes a deep, appreciative breath. The air tickles on the way in, like there are feathers in his nose. He looks down and sees a beautiful head of blond hair. She's face down above his chest, gently rubbing her teeth over his left nipple. He blinks in confusion and motions to push her away. But his right hand is occupied. Another blonde is sucking willfully on his fingers.

"What the fu—"

"Shh." A third blonde head appears, rising from between his naked thighs and pressing her finger to his lips.

Lefty lifts her eyes to meet his, and Righty is smiling now, his thumb between her teeth. They are gorgeous. Gorgeous and identical. They have ample lips and hips and breasts and are clad in pink feathery lingerie. They smile, and each blonde crookedly bites her bottom lip in tandem, as if on cue.

They take their time, working over his body like it's a temple, and they are there for nonstop, devout worship. They make his skin burn and his body sing in a way he cannot recall feeling before. Come to think of it, he can't remember much of anything right now.

Righty and Lefty take turns at his mouth, fingering the length of his dark hair. Sucking on his ears and lips and chest. They rub their hands over him softly and drag their fingernails over his skin. And Center—ah, sweet, sweet Center—keeps her focus on his groin. Sometimes Righty helps. Sometimes Lefty helps. Sometimes all three of them are there, a mess of lips and mouths and teeth loving him slowly and steadily. The smell of jasmine and seawater swells in his nose. They work him over in a blissful state of confusion for what feels like hours. When he finishes—when they're finished with him— his back arches, and he stifles a shout between clenched teeth.

They pass his seed around between their mouths all the

while looking at him with eyes wide as saucers.

He's crippled from exhaustion, barely able to lift his head. He feels like consciousness is a curtain, closing and opening repeatedly on the theater of his mind. He loses the battle and slips into an exhausted and comfortable sleep.

Sometime later—how long, Savage can't tell—a loud banging comes at the door of the red room. The lights are extinguished, and there isn't much visibility.

Bang. Bang.

A voice follows.

"Open the door! I know you're in there, you skanky succubi."

The blonde triplets have been resting and reveling in Savage's many nooks and crannies. They pull away at the sound of the voice, rising together.

Bang, bang, bang.

"You know damn well you can't keep me out here forever. Open this door, harlots!"

The door crashes open. The women scamper like spiders. Like crabs. They rush to put on robes, muttering anxiously amongst themselves.

A figure walks through the room, casting open the curtains and letting in a weak, gray light. Savage rubs at his eyes in confusion.

The man is visible now. He has reddish brown hair that falls to his chin and a patchy graying beard. He wears dark clothing, a charcoal jacket, black gloves, and a dissatisfied expression. His jacket has a high collar, almost clerical in style. But this man is no priest.

"I don't care if you have one of your freaky clients in here," he says to the women as he throws open the last set of curtains. "I know Devlin gave you something. Something you shouldn't have. You're going to tell me what he gave you, and then you're going to give it to me, *now*."

He turns and faces them, looking at each of the triplets with disdain and disgust. When he casts his gaze to Savage, he blinks incredulously.

"*What*." It's not a question but a detonation. He looks to the women. "What the hell is he doing here?" He points with a gloved finger. To Savage, he barks, "What the hell are you doing here?"

"I don't, I-I-I don't know how to answer that." Savage motions to get up, but he's become acutely aware of his nakedness. He sits back down and covers himself, cupping his hands over his groin with a soft clapping sound, his lanky legs hanging over the edge of the red bed.

"Do you know who I am?" the man asks.

"No, sir." The "sir" might be overkill, but it feels appropriate in the moment.

"How did you get here?"

"I honestly don't have the slightest idea."

To the triplets, the man says, "What the hell did you do to him? Was this Devlin?"

"The Knave gives us many orders. We only comply," the women answer, in unison, as if they have one voice and one brain and three mouths.

"Get him his damn clothes."

The women scamper again.

The man continues, "I don't know what you did to get your hooks in him, but find someone else to suckle, you freaking sirens . . ."

They fetch Savage his clothing. He notices in the gray of the morning, they aren't as alluring as they seemed the night before. Their eyes are bloodshot, red vines growing over the white, framed by twisted black lashes. Broken capillaries line their cheeks. Their teeth slightly overlap one another in the front, which their dry lips snag over when they move their mouths.

The man doesn't leave to allow Savage to dress, so he turns toward the wall and pulls on his jeans. He pulls his tee over his head and slips his shoes on his bare feet. When the man gestures for him to follow, it doesn't occur to Savage to refuse. The man's authority is daunting. They make their way to the door, and he mutters an insult to the women indecipherable to Savage's ears. They hiss in response.

Outside, they are in a shitty apartment building. A gold C7 is pressed crookedly on the red door. Savage follows behind the man. They descend chipping stairs, walk through the lobby of an old building, and exit to a cold street. Flurries are drifting to the sidewalk.

"Wha—" Savage looks up in confusion. "Where the hell are we?"

"Brooklyn."

"What? What the fuck . . ."

"That's the least of your worries, kid."

"But I was just in Vegas. Now I'm in New York? How the

hell did I get from Vegas to New York with no memory of getting here?" The words come out in a rush.

Savage follows the man around a corner to an alleyway. Overhead, a subway clatters along a green track. The man pulls off one black glove with his teeth and lays a hand on Savage's bare arm.

"What are you doing?" Savage asks.

"I needed to check something. How're you feeling?"

"Uh, cold?"

"And?" The man squeezes his arm a little.

"Creeped out?"

"K. Nothing else?"

"No?"

"Good." He re-gloves his hand, wiggling his fingers to realign them beneath the fabric. "What do they call you?"

"Savage." At this, the man laughs. "It's my last name," Savage mutters defensively. "Who the fuck are you? What the hell is going on?"

"They call me Bishop. Those delightful little vixens hooked themselves a human, though I don't know how exactly. What's the last thing you remember?" Bishop starts walking again. Savage follows.

"You mean before the triplets were all over me?"

Bishop stops. "Did they have sex with you?"

"No, not exactly. I mean, we didn't have actual sex . . ."

"Just oral? Little seamen mongers." He answers his own question.

"Yeah, how do you know that?"

Bishop walks again, turns a corner. "Because those creepy little harlots are succubi. We tend to call them 'sirens' in my circle, because of their preoccupation with seamen. Haha, little pun."

Savage shivers in his light tee shirt. Bishop glances back at him. "Yeah, I'll bet you're cold. You're not really dressed for late New York winter." He squints at something over Savage's shoulder. Then his eyes grow wide and his nose flares. "No fucking way."

"What?" Savage glances behind him but whatever was there has turned a corner, evading his gaze.

"One problem at a time," he says, swallowing what looks to be a mouthful of anger. He turns back to Savage. "Let's get you in the car and get you warmed up." He pulls keys out of his jacket pocket as he tries to sound lighthearted, but there's an underpinning of haste to his words.

Savage stops. "Look dude, I don't know you. I don't know how the fuck I ended up in Williamsburg, or wherever we are."

"Ha, no, do you see any complacent millennials or artisanal bagel shops? This is Brighton Beach."

"Whatever, I need to not be in New York. I need to be home in Vegas, or else I need to sober up from this trip from hell."

"Sober up? You took something?"

"Mm . . ." Savage balks.

"Spit it out."

"Sleeping pills and ketamine."

"Hell, Alice. You didn't find a K-hole, you found a rabbit hole."

"What does that mean?" Savage shakes his head in confusion.

"It means you've stumbled upon . . ." Bishop hesitates,

finding the words. "The world of gods and monsters, so to speak. Being three thousand miles away from your depressing little life in Vegas should pale in comparison to the fact that you just got seamen robbed by succubi. Actual, *mythological* succubi." He pauses, looks out over his shoulder in the distance, a plume of breath exiting his nostrils in the chilly air. "And if it weren't for this reaper having separate business to attend to with those little creepers, you'd probably be getting it stolen again."

"Reaper?"

"For lack of a better term."

"Is that, like, Brooklyn slang for a 'repo man'?"

"No, like the Grim Reaper. Like *this*." Bishop grabs at Savage's arm and points to his tattoo, to the tarot card representing Death. "Like Death."

"You're fucking high, man."

"No, that'd be you that ventured into the world of illicit drug cocktails, not me."

"I may be stupid enough to have mixed drugs, but I'm not an idiot. And I think I'm about capped out on all this talk of succubi and reapers."

Bishop cocks his head heavily to one side. "Look, there's only two ways a mortal should be capable of seeing me. A" — he holds up his index finger — "I'm about to reap your soul, or B" — he sticks out his thumb — "I will it to be so. So here." Bishop winks and blinks out of sight with a little swirl of black smoke. One moment he's there and the next, he's not. Like the lights that flicker in your eyes when you rub them too hard for too long. There's only empty space where he was standing.

"What the fuck?" Savage says to the nothingness.

Bishop blinks back in and cocks his head to the other side, smiling somewhat unpleasantly.

"Does that mean I'm dead? Did I overdose?"

"This isn't the afterlife, kid, this is Brooklyn. And I can assure you, those are definitely not the same place."

Savage stares at him, incredulous.

"Look, will you just get in the car? I'm not going to let you die. It is the *very definition* of my job to make sure only the souls that are supposed to depart are reaped."

"*Reaped*?"

"Yes, it will be a reap-free day for you. Unless you should step in front of a bus or something . . ."

"Yeah, I'm not getting in . . ."

Bishop laughs. "Oh, c'mon. Look, it's such a sexy car. Get in just so you can say you rode in one."

Savage glances at the car parked on the street next to them. It's a black classic car, shiny and pristine. "What's that, an Olds?"

"Damn straight. 1968 Oldsmobile Toronado, to be specific. Original owner, right here." Bishop taps on his chest.

"And you park it on the streets of New York."

Bishop unlocks the driver's door. "I have my ways of ensuring its safety."

Savage sniffles, his hands stuffed in the pockets of his jeans, his shoulders shrugged up to his ears contorting away from the cold. Bishop gets in and leans over the passenger seat, looking up at him with a smile, like a pedophile with promises of puppies or candy. "Please?" he says. The cold wins out over trepidation, and Savage slides into the passenger seat.

Inside, it smells like sandalwood and leather and old

cigarettes. When Bishop starts the car, B. B. King plays on the stereo. The reaper accelerates, throwing the car into motion like he's hurrying away from something.

"So, this is real," Savage says after a moment. "I'm really in New York City."

Bishop affects a thick, Brooklyn accent. "If you can make it here, you can make it anywhere." He gesticulates with both gloved hands and laughs.

"I don't even know how I made it here."

"I'm not too sure about that, kid. Seems like you lucked upon some strange magic." He flicks on the windshield wipers as snow flurries gently brush over the glass. He navigates the city traffic and narrow single-lane streets with haste, gliding past delivery trucks, slipping into the oncoming lanes of traffic, passing as seamlessly as a shadow.

"Where are we going?"

"First and foremost, away from the sirens and their Brighton Beach brothel—say that three times fast. I have some personal business to attend to in the city, so I figure you can keep me company for a bit until you sober up."

"What do you mean, 'the city'? I thought we're in the city?" Savage looks out the car window at the storefronts and apartment buildings, brick and mortar and concrete abound.

"Local colloquialism: 'the city' refers to Manhattan proper. If traveling from the outer boroughs to Manhattan, that means you're 'going into the city.'"

"New York City."

"No," Bishop laughs. "No one here calls it that. If I impart no other New York wisdom upon you, let it be this: it's just New York. Or 'Manhattan' if you mean Manhattan. Or the

Boroughs: Brooklyn, The Bronx, Queens . . ."

"Staten Island?"

"We don't even need to bring that up. There's literally no reason anyone ever has to go to Staten Island. Ever."

Savage studies him. Bishop's face is likable and warm if not all together pleasant. When he smiles, he's like a sallow Santa Claus, if Santa was younger, thinner, and sarcastic. And had shaved sometime in the last month. Savage runs his fingers over his own scraggly facial hair, his lips twisting from their permanent pout into a smile, despite himself.

"You think I'm still tripping?" he asks.

"I'm not going to leave you unattended to find out."

They drive in silence for a bit.

"So, those were actually succubi or sirens or whatever?"

"Indeed."

"Why were you so angry when you saw me with them?"

"Let's just say you don't look like their usual clientele."

Savage runs his fingers over the red detailing on the interior of the car. "It's so weird . . ."

"What? Is something wrong with my car?"

"No, no. Your car's just fine." Savage smiles again. "I've been colorblind to red my whole life, and now I can see it for some reason."

Bishop doesn't answer, only furrows his brow.

Savage looks at his sleeve of tattoos. He's fully able to see the scenes rendered on his arm for the first time. Now he gets why the artist demanded using red. He rubs his thumb over the tarot characters who live on his skin.

Like this, Bishop had said. *Like Death.*

The Oldsmobile passes over the Brooklyn Bridge,

flanked by glorious structures on both the Brooklyn and the Manhattan sides, like giant stone and metal pieces of a jumbled three-dimensional puzzle. The sun sets over the Hudson, illuminating the Statue of Liberty on her little isle in a brilliant blaze of yellows, oranges, pinks, and reds. The green of Lady Liberty's gown against the sunset is remarkable.

"Is your whole world view being blown by the full color spectrum right now?" Bishop asks, nodding over his left shoulder out the window.

Savage squints into the sunset, breath caught in his throat. "Yeah." He nods. "Yeah, it is."

When they arrive in the city, they head uptown to a street where half the signs are in English and half are in Korean. They pass piles of trash bags on the sidewalk, hollering street vendors, and cultural chaos as Bishop pulls the Olds into an underground parking structure. When they get out, they take the elevator up through the sub levels to the 13th floor of the building.

As they ascend, Bishop warns, "Prepare yourself. This is probably going to be a little overwhelming for you." The doors slide open to reveal a scene unlike one Savage has ever known. A gasp catches in Savage's throat. Bishop sighs before getting off the elevator. ". . . or a lot overwhelming."

If Savage's world of color was blown open before, it's now reassembling itself into a new manic kaleidoscope completely foreign to him. But he suspects it would be foreign to any human.

It's a party. A lounge. A hall of opulence. The walls and floors and furniture are in varying shades of magenta and orange and fuchsia, with ornate wall hangings, feathered pillows, and floating balls of light. It looks simultaneously retro and futuristic and other-worldly. The room is vast, far larger than the narrow building should allow, somehow stretched beyond the limits of physics.

There are pockets devoted to smaller gatherings with couches and cushions circled intimately near one another. It looks like the inside of Genie's bottle. It looks like an ashram. It looks like Studio 54.

"Welcome to the Quantum Club." Bishop gives a nod, encouraging Savage to follow. They make their way through the room. The music is something Savage has never heard before. It's quick and rhythmic, sensual and insane. The occupants of the party glance to Savage occasionally, cocking their heads or covering their mouths in surprise.

"I feel underdressed." Savage straightens out his thin, white tee-shirt and runs his hands through his unruly hair.

"Don't worry. If they're looking at you, it's not because you're not rocking coattails."

There's entertainment, of sorts. A beast with the shirtless body of a man and the head of a dog blows fire toward the ceiling and howls in delight. Beautiful half naked beings dance on pedestals and float from the ceiling, executing aerial acrobatics with lush fabrics.

One such creature, naked with red and gold skin, swings in a giant birdcage suspended overhead. She has feathers instead of hair and is a manifestation of every hue previously unknown to Savage's colorblind eyes.

"Hey, you," she calls to him.

He cranes his long neck skyward. "Yeah?"

"Twenty pounds of ashes if you let me out of this cage."

"Don't," Bishop says.

As they continue to make their way through the crowd, Bishop nods here and there to others. Occasionally he offers a casual salute, but he walks with determination. He's all business. They approach one of the intimate corners of the party. Four individuals are gathered on a long, velvet couch, curved around a low glowing table.

"Felicity, Felicity, just the muse I need to see," Bishop says as he claps his hands and rubs them together. He speaks to a beautiful auburn-haired woman. She is styled like Brigitte Bardot or Raquel Welch, with teased hair and winged eyeliner. Her mouth pouts like that of a tiger.

"Already, Bishop?" She tilts her head, disinterested and unamused. "You may as well become my dog, you're in my lap so often."

"What can I say, it helps me trudge through my desolate existence."

She blinks her cat eyes softly and slowly, with determination, as if to illustrate the magnitude of her indifference.

"Can't you see I'm conversing with the Oracles?" She gestures deliberately with long, pink fingers to the women she sits between—two identical beings with cottony puffs of white hair and eyes without irises or pupils. Contained within their naked skin are nebulas and galaxies, black holes and star systems, that subtly undulate in the dark.

"I see that, yes."

"And?"

"And you want me to come back later."

Her gaze falls on Savage. She cocks her head, dramatically. Savage swallows, dumbstruck by her beauty in a room full of so many beautiful things.

"And you've brought a companion? No, surely not a human?"

Bishop shrugs.

"Tsk, tsk, Bishop, what would the Ancients think of this?" She smiles her pursed lips. "I'm intrigued now. Have a seat."

Bishop and Savage settle on the couch opposite her.

"I need some vials."

"Oh, let's save business for later, Bishop. We have company." She speaks to Bishop but looks at Savage.

Bishop sighs loudly and leans back on the pink velvet.

"What's your name, stranger?" she asks.

"Savage," he answers.

"Indeed, you are." She folds her bare legs over one another. They're so long they could almost wrap around him twice. She turns to the man in the circle, the last guest at their private party. "Reve, darling, why don't you help illuminate this conversation?"

Reve is a handsome man with gold-flecked dark skin. He's clean-cut with tired eyes, and when he tilts his head, gold specks catch the light. With a "Certainly" he pulls something from the inside pocket of his jacket—a fluffy, pastel substance, not unlike cotton candy. He pats it down into a disk and rolls it like a joint. "Felicity," he says as he proffers the multicolored cigarette.

As she puts it to her lips, the dog headed man approaches, snaps his fingers which ignite into a flame, and lights it for her.

"Mm, thank you, darling."

"My pleasure," the dog replies in a throaty growl as he licks his chops and walks away.

Felicity pulls a long, deep drag off the joint and exhales a pink smoke. She passes it to the oracle on her left, who partakes and blows out blue. The oracle passes it to Savage.

"None for him," Felicity castigates. "I don't care to see what the inhalation of pure lucid dreams would do to him."

"Dreams?" Savage questions.

"Yes. Reve here is one of the most talented Sandmen there is."

"Sandman?" Savage questions Reve. "You're a fucking sandman."

Reve nods.

"So, you make people sleep?"

"And dream, yes." Reve has a subtle Latin accent, his words coming out less like speech and more like a purr.

"Huh, well I have a fucking bone to pick with you."

"Oh dear, we seem to have an insomniac in our midst," Felicity instigates.

Bishop places his hand on Savage's shoulder, as if to quell the coming diatribe.

"No, no. I want to know. I want to know why I haven't been able to sleep properly for years."

"To that, I cannot speak." Reve calmly responds to Savage's rancor. "I'm afraid I am not your sandman, child."

"Care to speculate?"

"Perhaps you've done something to inadvertently alienate your own sandman?"

"Like what?"

"It could be any number of things, but alcohol abuse for one. Excessive dependence on electronics is another example. If you have an imp of anxiety lurking around you, they tend to scare our kind off."

Felicity takes another deliberate drag off the joint and exhales yellow smoke into the middle of the conversation.

"Reve, it's Reve, right?" Savage leans forward, his forearms on his thighs.

Reve nods.

"Reve, will you do me the favor of hunting down my sandman and telling that motherfucker I will happily blow him for a proper night's rest? Please. Pass that message along." A rogue lock of hair falls into his face and he pushes it back, frustratedly.

Reve doesn't answer.

"This is the most worked up I've seen him," Bishop says, flatly. One of the Oracles passes the joint to Bishop. "No, it's okay. That dream stuff doesn't do anything for me. I need something a little stronger. No offense," he says to Reve.

"None taken. I'd expect nothing less from a reaper."

"And I won't take offense to *that*." He turns his attention back to Felicity, who is luxuriating in her dream high, leaning back onto one of the Oracles and running her fingers through its white hair. "Not to hurry this little get-together, but has it been long enough to talk business now?"

"I don't need any of your death sticks, Bishop," she says, dreamily. "It's a small clientele that requires them, and I'm afraid I've got a full inventory at the moment."

"Alright, what would you like to trade?"

She focuses her eyes back on Bishop and sits up. "I want a

private audience with the stranger."

"Yeah . . . I don't know. He already got molested by succubi today."

She scoffs. "I take offense at that. I'm not a thing like those little sirens. Anyway, I wouldn't deign to touch him. I fear he'd implode into a manifesto or an epic poem if I did. Just shudder away into art from pure inspiration."

"Mmk, well . . . that's gotta be worth, like, ten vials."

"Two."

"Cut the difference and land on five?" Bishop shrugs.

Felicity sizes up Savage with her gaze. He wants to protest at being objectified as a form of trade, but he's intrigued and bewitched by her. He'd like nothing more than to lay her down and fill her voids.

"Deal." She turns to the Oracles and Reve. "You don't mind my darlings?"

Noiselessly, they leave.

Bishop turns to Savage, putting one hand on his shoulder. "I will be right there." He points to a bar of sorts, where a winged man is ordering a cocktail. "That Mothman needs to answer some questions, anyway." He stands. "Five minutes," he says to Felicity, holding up all five fingers on his gloved hand.

"And five vials," she replies.

Bishop leaves them.

Felicity watches Savage silently as she takes a final drag off the dream cigarette and exhales indigo. The pastel smoke hangs in the air. It smells so sweet, it sticks like sugar in the back of Savage's throat when he inhales. "Would you care to join me?" She pats the cushion next to her.

He would. He does.

"You're an artist," she says. It's not a question.

"Yes."

"Not a musician . . ." She leans forward and stubs out the dream into a pile of sparkling ash. "Perhaps a sculptor? But there are few of those left these days."

"I sketch."

"Mm." She nods. "And paint?"

"I used to. I used to paint a lot. And take photographs . . . Not so much anymore."

"That's a pity." She studies him. "But I suspect you would succeed at any art form you set your mind to."

He balks at the compliment. "I-I don't know how true that is."

"I do." She studies him another moment. "Why are you here, Savage?" She lets the *S* of his name hiss in her mouth for an extra beat, like she's tasting it. Like a memory. Like a reverie.

"I don't know."

"You don't know?"

"I don't know how I got here. I'm not even sure where *here* is, exactly. It seems I did too many drugs, and now I'm partying with the Grim Reaper, and Mr. Sandman, and—"

"A muse."

"And a muse." He nods.

Savage glances over to Bishop. Whether Bishop is arguing with the Mothman or jesting with him, Savage can't discern. Felicity lets her attention flick past his shoulder. The music subsides, and a tall, thin creature steps to attention. The guests stop and watch as the creature takes one impossibly slender arm and drags it across its thin midsection. A beautiful stringed music emits from the beast, hollow and rich at once. Haunting and fulfilling. Many of the guests begin to stomp lightly, or pat the tables, or clap their hands in an intricate rhythm that complements the music. *Bum-ba-da-ba-bum, bum-ba-da-ba-bum.*

Savage turns back to the muse. If he had it within his ability to cherry-pick every detail and create a perfect woman, Felicity would be her. He has never been so attracted, so drawn to anyone before in his life. He feels hungry, ravenous, thirsty for her presence in such an intense and immeasurable way, it makes him dizzy. He reminds himself he does not know her. *She isn't even a fucking human, you maniac*, he thinks. He takes a sharp sniff in to clear his head, but the room is full of so much olfactory magic, it has little effect.

He clears his throat. "So, if I have a sandman, do I also have a muse?"

Felicity thinks for a moment. "Perhaps. You exude talent. I would assume our kind would be drawn to you. But there is something interesting about you, I can't quite figure out." At this, she leans in and runs her fingers over the lock of Savage's hair that keeps falling into his eyes. He folds into her wrist and catches her scent. It's heady and floral, fresh cut roses and white wine. "I've never known a human in our world," she says, "one who could see and converse with our kind like this. It's intriguing." She tucks his hair back, running her fingers over his ear as she does. Despite the warmth of the space, his skin immediately bursts into goosebumps.

"I feel pretty fucking un-intriguing in this room." Her smell and touch have given him a rush, and the words are thick in his mouth.

She smiles. "What, this?" Her eyes scan the room. "You must understand we adore your kind. You give us purpose. Our world exists because *your* world exists. All this mayhem, all these pretty monsters" — she gestures around them — "are for you. You complex, beautiful, poor creatures."

The cello beast finishes its performance, and the guests clap and offer praise. Felicity shouts *"Brava"* and turns back to him. "But an artist . . . in my humble opinion, artists may not make the world go 'round, but they sure know how to appreciate the spin."

"Is that why I'm so," he stumbles over his words, "why I'm so drawn to you? You're the muse I've been chasing my entire life."

"That would be logical." She leans into him again. "But I was never one for logic." She rubs her perfect nose lightly across his chest. She looks up at him through the comb of her thick black lashes. "Mm," she sighs, "you are redolent of craft and skill. You smell like . . . an awakening."

His breath catches. He hesitates, knowing that if getting semen-robbed by a succubus was off limits, kissing a muse likely is as well. But he, too, was never one for logic. He gently takes her chin in his hand and tilts her mouth toward his. He pauses, staring at her face for one perfect moment, seeing nothing that isn't her, and brings his mouth to her lips.

They barely touch. A world flashes before his eyes. A world of color and memory. Of dream and creation.

She pulls away, like she has been shocked, long fingers covering her mouth. And just like that, whatever window was cracked into a deeper side of this already deeper world opened and slammed immediately shut.

For a moment, the veil of her perfect composure is lifted, and she looks at him, eyes wide, brows creating a little crease of concern betwixt them.

"You, my darling, are no ordinary artist."

With this she regains her composure, so visibly it's as if she has merely powdered her nose. She sits back into the couch, straightening her gown, and pushing her long hair over one shoulder as Bishop returns, apparently unaware of the kiss or the strange current of energy that is buzzing between them.

"Alright, children. Time is up. My vials, if you would," he says as he extends an open palm to Felicity. She fetches five small leaf-shaped vials, full of an opalescent liquid that catches the light and bounces it back in a rainbow of colors. Bishop churns them in his hand before dropping them into the pocket of his cleric's coat. They clank together like little bells. "Now, how 'bout a little felicitous fellatio?" he asks, wagging his eyebrows with sarcasm.

"Go, Bishop, and take this savage with you before I cut you off from my inspiration for good."

"Worth a try," he jokes, starting for the door. "Always a pleasure, my dear."

As they make their way back through the room, Savage looks back to the beautiful muse sitting alone in her opulent booth. Her hand is covering her mouth, and he could swear she is crying.

INTERLUDE

The Knave, clad in darkness, works his way through the streets like a whisper.

He feels good. He feels great. Things are on track, and the satisfaction of nearly achieving his goal is a high that sings in his veins like—like what? Like a siren? He laughs at this. Yeah, like a siren. Or three.

A mist hangs over the blue streets, so dense it pools like soup around his ankles. The sun is about to rise topside. But down here, the dawn gives way straight to dusk. Nightfall reigns.

He sucks in a jubilant breath of predawn air. It smells like extinguished fire and dead things. It smells like home.

He kicks up the mist as he hastens his stride. The creatures of the blue are hiding from him in their reverence. They will not come unless they are called, which is how he likes it. This morning, he needs no company. He needs time to plot and to think. This is the long game. The pieces are all set on the board, and all he has to do is wait, making minor adjustments as he goes. But he feels confident.

He feels good.

He feels great.

On a street bench, the Knave spies a familiar tuft of gray and white hair sitting beneath a tired old Stetson.

He grimaces at the disturbance.

"What are you doing here?" he calls to the back of the man's head. "Why haven't you moved on?" The Knave's voice has an affected accent. Eastern European.

"I've been hiding from the Bishop," the old man says, sounding calm if a little insane. "And I came to find you, you old fop."

The man doesn't turn his head to address the Knave. This angers him. He clutches his hands into fists, and the tattoos on his fingers fade under the pressure.

"You will speak to me with respect in my domain," he growls and walks around the bench to face the insolent old soul. The sandman looks as tired as ever; death has brought him no respite. His soul hangs thinly in the morning, not quite transparent . . . faded. Faded and graying.

"I lost all respect for you when you silenced my soul. I won't be silent any longer. *Leave that child alone.* Let him sleep."

"I think that's the problem, old man. The dude can't sleep. He's an insomniac. Thanks to you."

"I did my best. It's not easy working for a soul such as his. And then those sleeping pills overloaded me. Killed me dead."

"Thankfully. *Finally,*" the Knave amends.

The sandman contorts his aged face in anger. "As long as I was living you would not get to him."

"But you're not living anymore. So move on, man. Go find your afterlife. Or not. Just get the hell out of my domain."

The sandman's face falls, and he suppresses a little smile. "'Get the *hell*'? Is that a pun?"

"What?" The Knave barks. "What do you want? Why are you here? You're going warn me some more? Just do it and get it over with so I can get on with my existence." He scratches his bald head and looks out into the distance, feigning disinterest.

The sandman stands, leaning heavily on the arm of the park bench for support. His wrist trembles beneath him, threatening to collapse. "It won't work," he says, pointing a finger from his free hand in the Knave's face. "You may think you know his soul, but I know his dreams. We may not be perfect, but his sense of duty and distaste for abandonment will outweigh his perfectionism."

"So, you say."

"So, I *know*. I have faith. I have faith that child will come to his senses. No matter what you do to him, or how you try to sway him. He's grown strong over the years."

"You don't know what you're talking about, old man. You're behind the curve. Thanks for the advice and for ruining my morning. You're a persistent old sonofabitch, I'll give you that much. But you're wasting what little is left of your essence. Your replacement has already taken over, and that dude has far looser morals than you ever had. Too late, end of story. Yours anyway. My stars are aligning. Ta-da. The end." He stops, sniffs in sharply. There's a change in the air. The change of arrival. He can smell the reek of life and death arriving as he breathes, that sick smell of sandalwood and cigarettes.

He has two choices. First, he can stay here, stick to his

ground and assert dominance—it *is* his realm, after all. But staying put will invite questions. Questions he's not willing to answer, and the lack of answers will lead to an argument. Option two, he can bounce. It may come off as weakness, but only if the reaper can sense his leaving. And since this entire world smells like him—it is made of him, crafted of his very spirit—he may be able to pass into the blue undetected. In a split second, he decides. He elects to leave.

"Dasvidaniya, old man. Better luck in your next incarnation."

The old sandman tips his hat at this. The Knave feels mocked, but there isn't enough time to bring down his wrath. Besides, this sandman will be naught but a memory in no time at all. Better left to the reaper to call him home or whatever the hell it is he does.

Shit. He's taken too long in his indecision. Bishop is blinking into existence right as he is blinking out. They catch each other's eyes in the moment they both inhabit the same plane.

"Goddammit, Devlin."

He hears Bishop call after him, as he himself, fades away.

Indeed, Devlin thinks, smiling. *Indeed*.

FOUR

Awakening to his room in Vegas is almost as disorienting as "waking" to the red room in Brighton Beach. That dreaming without sleeping. This is different. This is stale and sour, waking to a world drained of everything interesting.

Savage is still in bed as if nothing happened. As if his world wasn't blown to beautiful and insane bits. It's brown and black, gray and green. The depressing colors of his life. He feels like he visited Oz and tasted technicolor, and now he's back in sepia-strewn Kansas.

He swings his feet out of bed to the floor. His foot slips on something as he presses it down into the hardwood. The ground is littered with paper. He stoops to the floor and brings to his face what appears to be pages ripped from his moleskin. But they're not blank. They're sketches.

There are drawings in pencil and ink and charcoal, each depicting the same figure, over and over. Felicity. Her pouting mouth, the curve of her cheek, the length of her neck and fingers and legs. Some are full portraits, some only pieces of her. A few capture her whole body, some only her face.

There is one sketch depicting the moment she held his gaze as he walked away, her hand over her mouth, tear halfway down her cheek.

Twenty, thirty sketches of the muse, all crafted without any memory of doing so.

"She was right," he thinks out loud. He may not have dissolved into an epic poem, but he did split away into shards of inspiration by obsessively, unconsciously sketching her. Over and over and over.

Savage gathers all the papers from the floor, assembling them into an uneven pile on his bed.

Only one captures something other than Felicity. He holds the sketch up for further examination. It's a hooded figure with a jagged skull for a face. Beneath the picture in block letters issued of his own hand reads CHAOS.

Sanity is a delicate and beautiful thing. Like a reliable vehicle escorting its driver safely from one place to the other, it's a finely tuned machine liable to break down when an object is thrown into the motor. Right now, Savage feels like the automobile of his mind is running on flat tires with misfiring cylinders. He cleaves to the memory of when it ran smoothly and fears it's only a matter of time before the damn thing explodes.

He's walking at dawn, trying to clear his mind. The March

morning air is still cool. Vegas hasn't yet turned into the sultry naked beast she'll be come summer.

He stops at a park a short walk from his house and sits under a stucco gazebo, situating himself at a picnic table. He removes a tired moleskin sketchbook from his back pocket, but it's only habit. He doesn't want to draw. It's like he overdosed on inspiration, and his well is empty. He's in need of a fix. He rubs his fingers over the frayed edges of the missing leaves along the crease. With a deep sigh, he drops his pencil. It rolls off the table to the ground. His head falls into his cupped hands, and he closes his eyes, unable to muster the will to do something as small as fetch an errant writing utensil.

How does he go back to being a person? How can he pretend that there is nothing more to the world, when he knows otherwise? It's been three days. Three lonely, quiet, horrifying, sleepless days. He fears for his sanity. He fears for his body. If he deigns to take the drug cocktail again, what if it hurts him? What if it kills him? What if—worst of all—it doesn't work? The fear catches inside him like a vice on his lungs.

"*Fuck*," he calls out to the morning.

He wonders if he flew to New York on a plane like a normal human if he would still be colorblind. Red lost to him just like it always was. If he got on a 747, traversed the skies, touched down in Newark or JFK or Laguardia, hopped in a yellow cab or an Uber or a Lyft and commanded his driver to take him to the street in midtown where the English turns to Korean, would he find a hidden soiree dripping in voodoo and mythology and witchcraft? *Probably not*, he thinks. *It's not the destination so much as the mode of transportation.* And no earthly mode can take him where he needs to go.

It's done. It's not his decision to make. It never really was. He runs back to his apartment, abandoning his sketchpad in the park where it lay.

"Alright, sandman," he says to his empty home, "if you're there and you have any say in the matter, let me wake to the muse and not the sirens."

Ketamine.

Ambivalen.

Sleep.

New consciousness?

Consciousness.

He wakes in a patch of grass.

Wet grass.

Cold, fucking wet grass.

But there is a glory to this grass because it belongs to the world of the others. Its coldness and its wetness are sublime.

He sits up. He's outside a large ornately carved gothic gate. It's massive and time-worn and rusty brown in hue. Biblical figures are carved into its peaks, and it looks like a clock tower and the facade of a church at once. A little road leads under it, allowing access to what appears to be a park.

Fuck. I overshot it and landed in England, Savage thinks, as he stands and dusts the sprigs of dead winter grass from his clothing.

As he approaches the arch, he sees an unmanned guard

post. He glances past and realizes he's not in a park but a cemetery. Melancholy and magical. Great mausoleums are situated along the hills.

A plaque at the gate reads:

THE GREEN-WOOD CEMETERY
Has been designated a
NATIONAL HISTORIC LANDMARK
Brooklyn, NY
National Park Service

Not exactly what he had in mind, but New York nonetheless.

Alone in the city he doesn't know, Savage ventures into the cemetery without much inspiration of what else to do. He finds himself in the heart of the grounds, intrigued and lost in the great maze of headstones and mausoleums. A heavy drizzle plagues the city. It's a dreary day in the bedroom of the dead.

Nothing appears to be amiss. If not for the change in locale and time, he wouldn't even be sure he'd tapped the rabbit hole. Whatever snow had accumulated on his last visit has melted.

He's on the hunt for red. There's an abundance of earth tones, browns and grays and greens. But finally, a bouquet of poppies nestled in an urn catches his eye, red as cardinals. He sighs in relief.

Savage kneels before the grave, studying the blessed color of the flowers and the headstone they sit before. Cora Weaver is interred here, and her epitaph reads, *I am not free.*

"What a weird thing to have on your headstone . . ."

Savage utters as he stands.

He walks on, hands in his jean pockets. His shirt is damp, and he shivers against the storm.

Savage almost doesn't see him. He's a man—*creature, monster?*—with the enlarged head of a crow. He wears all black and is almost lost among the shadows. He stands off the path, next to a graying tombstone. He remains still, head cocked and posture crooked as he watches Savage make his way through the graves.

Startled, Savage's brow twitches in confusion.

"Hello?" he calls out.

In a blink, the crow-man is just a crow flying off among the sodden trees.

"And goodbye, I guess," Savage says. He nods to no one and continues to make his way through the vast cemetery. Rainwater creeps from the strands of his hair into his eyes and down his collar. He rakes his fingers through his hair and blinks away the rain like someone else's tears.

He comes to a break in the graves and discovers a little lake. It has a fountain spraying water skyward. Park benches are situated around it, some beneath the shade and protection of low-hanging trees. Here, he sits and seeks shelter.

Across the lake, Savage sees Bishop before Bishop sees him. The reaper has a cigarette hanging from his mouth. Black smoke curls into the air around him like ink in water. He's unrolling his sleeves and pulling on gloves. Eventually, he spies Savage on the bench.

"Ah." Bishop tosses his hands up. "Eureka!" He walks around the lake and sits beside the human. "Couldn't stay away, huh?"

"Not so much." Savage shivers, the damp morning pressing against his exposed arms. "I should've worn a coat this time."

A little sardonic smile flicks across Bishop's lips as he sucks on his cigarette. The filter is red and the shaft ink black.

"It was really hard to return to life as it was," Savage says.

"I can only imagine."

"Once you know, you can't unknow. Y'know?"

"I know."

Savage gazes out over the water. Under the surface, orange koi fish dart around in search of food. "How did you find out I was here?" he asks.

"My associate told me."

"The crow dude?"

"That'd be the one. Name's Rook. He said a peculiar looking human was lurking in our territory."

"Bishop and Rook? Does that mean there's a Knight and a Queen?"

"Ah, don't ask questions you don't really want the answer to, kid . . . it's more of an in-joke than anything."

Savage nods without understanding. "Why did he think I was peculiar?" he asks. "I feel like I look like a normal person . . ."

"There's sort of a smell about you. The scent of awareness, I suppose."

Savage remembers what Felicity said about him. About how he smelled of craft and skill and art.

Bishop taps off the ash into his glove and dumps it into the deep pockets of his coat. He ejects a deep sigh. "Also, you talked to him. So that kind of gave you away." Bishop turns and squares himself to Savage. "Do you have a death wish?"

he asks with unwavering eye contact. "You're going to kill yourself mixing sleeping pills and, what was it, ketamine?"

Savage nods.

"Yeah. 'Course it was. You're playing with fire. I should know. I've seen it many, many, *many* times. A million times. *You can't do that.* You don't want to die, kid. It's not your time." He takes another drag, careful to blow the smoke away from Savage.

"No, I don't want to die. That's not it." Savage runs his fingers through his damp hair, frustrated. "It's–it's like I just said, I can't unknow. How am I supposed to go back to life like it was? Bishop, I'm not telling you this to make you feel bad for me or anything, but I have nothing. *Nothing.* Nothing to look forward to. Nothing to get me out of bed in the morning. No calling. No vocation. And I know it sounds weird, but I feel like I'm supposed to be here. Like being with you . . . you and Felicity, knowing this world exists . . . that's my calling."

"Oh, kid . . ." Bishop lets out a thoughtful sigh and leans back against the bench. "I don't know what I'm supposed to do with you anyway. To the best of my knowledge, this is the first time this has ever happened . . . that a mortal came into our world. You're not supposed to go back to unknowing because you were never supposed to know in the first place," he pauses. "You really don't have anything to go back to?"

Savage laughs. "Yeah, I forfeited my shit job. I hate Las Vegas. My parents have been dead since I was a teenager. I don't have a car or a cat or a dog or even a fucking fish. I can't sleep at night . . ."

"Okay, okay. Picture painted. You're depressing me. You're depressing *even me*, and you have no idea what depressing shit

I see every day. You want to be here? You want to hang out with these monsters? Why don't . . ." He rubs a gloved finger over his beard. "Why don't you come be my apprentice?"

Savage opens his mouth. Closes it again. He feels like the koi fish in the water. "You want to teach me to kill people?"

"Jesus, I don't *kill people*. I reap their souls. It could be a way you could stay here, among my kind, and you wouldn't have to screw around with drugs anymore. I'd give you a job. A vocation. Teach you a trade. One day, you can be a reaper all your own. I've been doing this a long time, and it's a lonely business. I like Rook just fine, but the guy's not a big talker. I could use the company . . . and the challenge, to be honest. And I can show you . . ." He pauses thoughtfully, gesturing in the air like he's literally grasping for the words. "I can show you exactly how beautiful this universe is."

"Is that how reapers are made? Is this normal?"

"Kid, this is so far outside the realm of normal, you have no idea. No, reapers aren't *made*. But it's moot. You can't go back to not knowing, like you said. And it's the only thing I can think to offer you." He turns to face Savage. "But you have to promise, *no more ketamine bullshit*. It's dangerous, and lazy, and stupid. And you may think I don't know you, but you don't strike me as any of those things."

"No," Savage says, "I'm not. I just wanted to sleep."

"The first time," Bishop corrects.

"Yeah."

"But *this* time . . ."

"You're right. I wanted to come back."

"Well, you're back now, Dorothy. Welcome to Oz."

Savage thinks about Bishop's offer, and wonders if he has

the stones to help the reaper claim souls. To eventually reap souls on his own. Somehow, he doesn't think it'll be the same as culling laboratory animals. "Can I think on it?"

"I expect you to."

"It doesn't make any fucking sense to me, but it's something I'd like to consider."

"Don't trouble your mortal mind about the minutiae." The black smoke swirling out of the reaper's nose paints him as a cheerful dragon. "But part of why you're back is for the muse, I assume."

Savage's silence is an admission.

"Damn artists, always chasing the muse." Bishop stubs out his black cigarette and pockets the butt. Savage scrutinizes the action, squinting in confusion. "What," Bishop says, "you want me to throw it into the lake? All the fish would die. First lesson, whether you accept my offer or not: necessary reaper gear. You need your smokes." He holds up a jet-black pack of cigarettes, the box unlabeled. "And your gloves." He fans out his fingers.

"What, no scythe?"

"You know," Bishop turns to him, "it was a bitch to carry around."

Savage chuckles and shakes his head.

They stand and walk through the cemetery. Bishop extends his arms, palms out, feeling the breeze as if he's a farmer tending to his crops. But his harvest yields headstones in lieu of corn.

"Lesson two—still useful even if you *don't* become a reaper—what's the point?" Bishop asks. "What do you see?"

"Uh." Savage regards the space. "Headstones, mausoleums,

asphalt, roads . . ."

"No, no, no. Look. *Really look.*"

"Uh . . ." Savage scrutinizes his surroundings. "Dirt?"

"Well, that's closer. Birds, squirrels, trees, mosquitos, dragonflies," he rattles off. "Even here, in this silent place amidst this city that breeds cacophony like rabbits produce spawn, *death* breeds *life*. This spot of death teems with life. In the plants and animals. In the insects and organisms that break down the bodies and allow them to return to dust. Edvard Munch once said, 'From my rotting body, flowers shall grow, and I am in them and that is eternity.' *That is eternity.* It's all here. It's all balance. The great balance. It's eternity."

Savage thinks a moment and looks around. The rain has stopped. The ancient ground grows in crooked hills. It's quiet and beautiful, and Bishop is right. There are living things all around them.

"I haven't been to a cemetery since my parents died," Savage says quietly, his wet hair falling into his eyes.

"I know. It's all over your face, kid. Tell me what you miss about them."

"They were my parents, I miss everything," Savage says. Glib. Angry.

"No, tell me *what* you miss. I love the intricacies of life. I so seldom get to appreciate them in my line of work. Give me something potent. Give me something small. Something real."

Savage sighs and thinks for a minute before answering. Water is still dripping from the trees and dropping into puddles around them. "My mom had corkscrew curly hair. I thought her hair was the most beautiful thing. I remember sitting in the backseat behind her when she'd drive with the windows down and watching all those crazy curls blow in the wind. The strands looked like people dancing."

Bishop smiles.

"When I got older," Savage continues, "I got into darker artwork. I learned about Joel-Peter Witkin and Andres Serrano when I was about thirteen. I was drawn to this dark, *dark* photography. So much of their work is violent and so fucking creepy but my parents never judged. They didn't try to shield me from it. And they weren't scared like other parents might have been. No . . . Dad just bought me a camera." Savage shrugs.

Bishop has led them off the beaten path a little as Savage ruminates. They are standing in front of an old family plot. Here are buried a husband and wife: *William Harold Lockwood (1869 - 1924)* and *Adeline Sarah Lockwood (1872 - 1935).*

"That's weird, those are my parents' names. I mean, not exactly, not the full name, but the same first names . . ." He falls quiet.

Bishop is looking at Savage, but Savage's eyes are cast down to the graves. Bishop gives him a minute before uttering, "It's okay. You can say it."

"I'm still angry," Savage replies, quietly.

"I know. And that's okay." Bishop takes a big breath in and looks out over the trees. "Anger is part and parcel. If you weren't angry, I'd be concerned. But you have to work through that anger, kid. It's time."

"Fuck, I thought I was past this," Savage says, sniffing in sharply to stifle his emotion. "They were all I had. They were all I'll get. I didn't have siblings. I didn't have anyone. I'm alone. They died, and they left me *alone*. They didn't deserve to die."

"No one deserves to die. You *get* to die. It's a privilege. It's a reward."

"What?" Savage's deep voice breaks, his mouth thick with saliva he's forgotten to swallow. "They were rewarded by having their bodies broken when their car folded like a tin can beneath the wheels of a semi? That's bullshit, Bishop."

"You think death is this violent act where your body is betrayed, that it mars your spirit somehow. It isn't. They aren't angry that they died, Savage. Only the living harbor anger about death. The dying don't even remember it."

"Were you there? Was it you?" His eyes are stinging now.

"No, but I know what happened. I know how it always happens. It's like birth. There's this confusing, horrific, glorious moment of coming through the canal to a screaming mother, and she's right there to comfort you afterward. That's what we're like, the reapers. We're the comfort that greets you upon death. We're mothers to the dying. Midwives for the end. We birth you onto, well, onto the next part."

Savage swallows hard. "What's the next part?"

Bishop thinks a moment. "No. Not yet, kid. There's a lot of emotion and feelings, *human* feelings, you've got to work through first. You'll get there. *We'll* get there. Just not today." He puts his gloved hand on Savage's shoulder. "I'm so sorry the loss of your parents caused you so much grief, but I'm not sorry they died. I think you'll learn to accept their death when you realize what a beautiful thing death actually is."

Savage lets his eyes drop to William and Adeline's graves.

"It's okay to be angry," Bishop continues, following

Savage's gaze to the headstones. "It's not okay to stop living because the people you love died." He lets the words sink in. "C'mon, let's get out of here."

They make their way back through the cemetery and under the big, gothic archway. Bishop's Oldsmobile is parked on the street next to a bakery, a plume of steam rising from the building into the cold, wet air. The world smells like warm bread. Even inside the car, Savage can still smell it.

Night has fallen on the city. It wears the darkness like a blanket tucked in at the corners. Bishop is about to conduct a meeting. They are in an elegant room with a high, carved ceiling. Chandeliers reflect off the wood of a large, polished table at its center. Assembling around the table is the motliest of motley crews Savage has seen.

There's Bishop, with his black gloved fingers and unkempt head of reddish hair. There's Rook, the silent crow-faced reaper. Next to Rook is a reaper with a face like a doe. She has wings made of birch tree branches and sits on the edge of her chair to avoid crushing them. Another reaper. She looks like a stone cemetery statue, gray and white and black with moss growing over her shoulders in little green colonies. Perpetual black tears stream down her face.

Across the table from the reapers is a beautiful woman with long dreadlocked hair. Little silver and gold rings are strung throughout her locs with bits of abalone shells. She emits an aura of warmth. It's not like she's a kind soul, which she may be, but like her dark skin is glowing under its own volition. Like she exudes sunlight through her pores. She watches Savage with an unwavering gaze for several moments at a time. Every time he catches her eye, she neither smiles nor releases her stare. He drops his gaze, weary under the pressure of her warmth. He wonders what she is. His best guess is life incarnate.

The pair of Oracles sit on either side of her, their sightless white eyes unblinking in their nebula-strewn skin. Next is a creature Savage can only assume is some embodiment of time itself. He's straight backed and entirely white. His skin and eyes are so light, they're almost translucent. His long white hair is gathered behind his head. He blinks once a second, precise as a metronome, and has a large tattoo of an hourglass on each of his forearms. Impossibly, the tattooed sand within appears to slip through.

Rook leans his beak into Bishop's ear, but if he speaks, the sound is indecipherable. Bishop pulls something from his coat pocket. It's one of the leaf-shaped vials that he bargained for with Felicity the night at the club. He pulls the tiny cork from the top and sips down half of the inspiration.

Savage sits off to the side, in a leather chair in the corner of the room. He wishes he had a sketch pad with him. The magnificence of the creatures assembled here is a sight he's sure he'll never experience again. He catches bits of the guests' conversation. They all appear tense and talk in curt tones, but not the earth woman. She appears to be calm and thoughtful. Or perhaps her mind is otherwise preoccupied. She's staring at him again. He looks down to his hands under the tension of her gaze.

Bishop explained Savage will not get to be privy to the meeting. "Sorry, kid. This is sensitive, make-the-world-go-round kind of stuff," Bishop had said. "Just policy, I'm afraid."

Last to arrive is Felicity. She wears a floor length, mint green dress (a shade they once offered for telephones and convertibles in the mid-sixties) with a slit so high, Savage can almost see god. He stands when she enters, though he doesn't know why.

She cocks her beautiful head. Her long brown hair is back tonight. "Bishop, you brought the savage again. Found yourself a pet, have you?"

Bishop throws his hands up in defeat. "Kid can't stay away from me, clearly. I must be just that fascinating."

She leans into the earth woman's ear. They converse for a moment and Felicity nods. They both look to Savage. He sits back down as he watches them, nearly missing the chair in the process. The woman smiles, and Felicity laughs and nods again.

"What's so funny?" he mutters to himself. He combs his hair back with his fingers, and it immediately falls forward again.

Felicity approaches him, her heels clicking against the hardwood floor. "Alright, come with me, you." She extends her hand.

Bishop interjects, standing. "Whoa, whoa, where are you going?"

"Don't worry, I'll take good care of him." Here, she winks one set of long lashes at Bishop.

"No, no—" Bishop starts.

"The last time we all met to discuss the matter at hand, it

took *several days* to reach any kind of conclusion, if I recall. You're going to make this man, this *human*, what, sit out in the hall? For days?" Her hand is still outstretched, but Savage fights the urge to take it in his own.

"Yeah, but I—"

"Talk to Ray, it's her insistence."

The earth woman's face curls into a gentle smile.

"Bishop, he's a dynamic spirit. He needs stimulation," Felicity censures.

She reaches for Savage and tugs him from his seat with a gentle hand, guiding him to the door.

"Keep the stimulating to a minimum, please," Bishop calls.

She smiles over her shoulder and continues toward the exit.

"Felicity! No stimulating at all, actually!"

Outside, they walk with long, casual steps. It's late, and the air is cold now that the afternoon storm has subsided. The streets of New York are more desolate than Savage has seen portrayed in films. No merry crowds bustling at crosswalks and down avenues. The air smells like an odd mixture of trash and warm honey from a nearby cart selling roasted nuts.

"Why are you back?" the muse asks as they walk.

"It was hard to stay away." He pushes his hair back again as he watches her slender legs do their delicate walk. He looks up. "I was living my greatest fear—a mediocre existence doing a shit job and talking to no one. Where every ounce of art within me was dead. Or dormant." He is quiet for a beat. ". . . and then I talked to you."

"Hm," she sighs and stops for a moment. "We did more than just talk though. Didn't we?"

"Yeah. Y'know, I drew you in my sleep that night." He swallows, thickly, and debates continuing. "I see you every single time I close my eyes. You've permeated the picture show of my mind, and it's amazing . . . Amazing but not as good as the real thing."

She smiles at him, her pretty pink lips pursed. "You're not really drawn to me, you know. You're just getting high off the inspiration I exude. You like the idea of me, Savage. Not me. One day, you'll find a muse of your own kind."

"Somehow, I doubt that is true."

At this, she looks away and continues to walk, passing him by a few paces. She turns her long neck and glances back at him like a swan in a lake, a little smile playing at her lips.

They arrive at a beautiful building, with great white steps leading up to its entrance.

"Have you been here?" she questions.

"No, I've never really been to this city before. Not in my real life, that is."

"The Metropolitan Museum of Art." She starts up the steps. "Follow me. You'll love this."

"I'm pretty sure it's closed?"

"Think outside the box, darling," she replies.

He follows.

She opens the great doors, even though he's sure they were locked. The lights in the center hall are dimmed, and she brazenly walks past a night guard. She turns her back on the man in the uniform and presses her finger to her lips in a mocking hush. "Shhh . . ." she says in jest, as the guard is clearly unable to see or hear them. They make their way into the museum like shadows among the art.

She leads him to the left through the work of the ancients, Greek and Roman statues, most stark white, some dark gray. There are tall pillars flanking the room, casting it as Greek as The Parthenon. A headless, armless statue catches his eye. It's ruddy brown from age, and the color and the shape move him.

"Mm, the good old days," she says, looking at the piece.

Savage's interest is piqued, but he doesn't reply. Not yet.

She walks on. "Back when we were not just believed but *worshipped*. The Greeks may not have had everything right, but they were a hell of a lot closer than the fools of today." She drags her fingers gingerly along the display cases.

As she walks, she begins to speak in a tongue Savage surmises is ancient Greek. She recites a long verse, and Savage revels at the sound of her voice, how she slopes and moves through the words like a song. Greek sounds like conception on her tongue. When she finishes, she looks at him, and laughs, softly. "It is the opening lines of the Odyssey. *'Muse,'*" she says in English, "*'tell me of the man of many wiles, the man who wandered many paths of exile after he sacked Troy's sacred citadel. He saw the cities—mapped the minds—of many; and on the sea, his spirit suffered every adversity—to keep his life intact, to bring his comrades back.'* That's my favorite version, the Allen Mandelbaum translation. I've been enjoying the art of the rhyme, as of late."

"So, you were alive for this? Alive in ancient Greece?"

"No. Even muses don't last that long. But some incarnation

of me was. The cycle spins itself onward, and I am here, in this time, to help fill the walls of this museum and every one like it with the art of the modern age."

They continue on. She leads him through the ancient art of the Americas to the contemporary art. Streetlight floods in through the large glass panes that cover half the sloped ceiling. In the low light, the colors of Savage's contemporaries still manage to flood his eyes. Pink. Red. Purple. Black and yellow. Aqua and forest green. He curses the blindness that has afflicted him every other day of his pitiful existence but is thankful that for tonight, he can see color.

"So, is this your favorite place in the city?" he asks her.

"No." She smiles like she's keeping a secret.

"It seems like it would be."

"While I love art, I love artists more. I'd rather be around the creating than the creations."

He nods. "Sound logic." He waits for the answer to the unasked question, but she isn't going to give it without prompting. He folds. "So, what *is* your favorite place?"

"I have many and few. Some secret. Some not so secret."

"Alright, be evasive. Don't tell me."

She smiles at him again and turns back to the paintings. "The Rose Reading Room in the public library on 5th Avenue." She concedes after a moment of silence. "It's a manifestation of great creation, and it's the setting of great creation. Writers and students gather to work. Tourists peek in. All under a pink painted sky."

He follows her to the Pollock on display. *Autumn Rhythm (Number 30).* Likely his most famous work, it's enormous and remarkable. They appreciate it for a minute, before she says,

"Some people are so judgmental of the modern abstracts. To me this is like jazz. Like an orgasm. Unpredictable. Symphonic."

The windowpanes cast shadows on her face. She's immersed in the painting, her eyes traveling along its lines, darting like hummingbirds. She's a work of art unto herself. She's The Velvet Underground's "Oh! Sweet Nuthin'." She's Klimt's *Goldfish*. She's Neruda's "Eleventh" and Dvorak's *Seventh*.

Savage walks in front of the painting, looks at her intently for a moment, breathes in her scent of wine and roses. She tilts her head to one side. It could be a question, an admonition, an invitation. He doesn't bother wondering. He sees her like she's pure, cool liquid and he's dying from lack of drink. When he kisses her, she lets him, and she tastes even better than she smells.

FIVE

Savage wakes to his cheap, IKEA mattress once more and forces a grunt out through his nose. This fucking room. This fucking city. He blinks his eyes. An intense fire rages in his head, a headache to end all headaches.

"Oh my god," he says to no one. The effects of the most severe hangover he has ever known push into his every bone and flood out through his every pore. He runs his hands through his hair, and his fingers find something wet.

"What the shit?" He brings his hands before his face. Red, but only that black-red his broken eyes are capable of perceiving. *Blood?* He sits up so quickly, his sore head sends the room in spirals.

This time, this awakening, there are no sketchpad papers littering his floor. Around his room are canvases of assorted shapes and sizes. They depict Felicity's superb face in varying degrees of abstraction. They lean against the walls like an audience who watched as he slept.

He hasn't painted in years.

He steps into the bathroom and studies his face. It's not blood on his head but paint. He has smears of the stuff across one of his cheeks, over his furrowed brow, and congealed in his black hair.

He walks to the kitchen. More paintings are strewn about his apartment. Near the sink, he sees tubes of acrylic paint laying haphazardly atop one another. There are reds and oranges and purples here, colors he would never bother using as they evade his vision. Brushes still coated with paint are in the sink, the acrylic making its way down the drain in spirals of color.

Painted on a canvas as tall as he is, the *pièce de résistance* rests against the front door, barring entrance or exit. It's a pop-art depiction of Felicity's face. She's biting her finger, eyes cast down. The comic book feel and bold lines distinctly channel Roy Lichtenstein and his Ben-Day dots.

He pushes his hair off his face. "Fuck." He keeps forgetting he's covered in paint. He looks down at his hands, the hands that took it upon themselves to create while he slept.

He assembles the pieces. Some are brilliant. It's tragic that this is his best work because he won't take credit for it. The drugged, unconscious body he left behind just regurgitated the art he sensed coming off Felicity. Nothing more.

Many of the pieces are still wet. Gingerly, he places them out of the way to let them dry.

He washes his hands and the brushes that line the bottom of the sink, pulling the caked and clotted pigment from the bristles. He thinks about Bishop's offer. He's not sure he can be a reaper, but he knows that he can't stay here in the limbo that is his life. *Half living is half dying, as they say . . .* do they say that? Did he just make it up? It's true. He feels ancient, the repetition of his life marching over him, like he's buried beneath it all as it passes by overhead. And even though this life is a crypt, he is alive. And he's never felt half so alive as he does in the company of the reaper and the muse.

He dries his hands and grabs a grinder, a small pipe, and a jar of bud from the counter. He steps out to the patio off his living room. There's a single plastic chair and an old table with a crusted ashtray and a lighter on top. Savage isn't much of a toker, but sometimes a good joint can help clear his mind. He grinds some of the weed and loads it into the pipe. He takes a deep inhale and sets the pipe on the table.

It's quiet out, early morning in the desert. The streetlights around his apartment complex are blinking off as daylight approaches. The sun rises over the mountains in a glorious scene of dripping colors Savage's eyes cannot appreciate. Las Vegas may be a tragic filthy city, but dawn and dusk are pure art. The sky over the city is changing like someone is peeling away the curtain from the heavens.

This all could be the diluted ramblings of his drug addled mind. A severe side effect of the ketamine and the Ambivalen. A vivid series of dreams. There's probably no muse. No fucking reaper. Not likely. He laughs, mirthlessly. "You're a fool," he tells himself.

But there's a simple way to prove his insanity. Or, less likely, his sanity.

He takes another small hit off the pipe and pulls out his phone. He googles where Pollock's *Autumn Rhythm* resides. Google answers: The *Metropolitan Museum of Art in New York*

City. He googles The Met. The museum's website offers a map of its premises. Off to the left of the main entrance is the ancient Greek and Roman wing. Then the ancient American room which leads to the contemporary art. He nods to no one.

"K, well . . ."

He searches Green-wood Cemetery in Brooklyn. It's a scenic and historic location, so there are many pictures generated in an image search. Most of them show the great, gothic archway at the entrance on 25th Street. Green-wood's website allows an online search of those interred on its grounds. He queries Adeline Lockwood, and the site provides the precise location of her grave.

He nods again. One last thing. Google maps, street view. He pans across the street from the cemetery. Here is a bakery. "Baked in Brooklyn," it's christened. As he knew it would be.

Savage waits. And waits. And waits.

But he's never been known for his patience.

Days pass. A week. No Bishop. *Did he forget?* Savage wonders daily. Hourly. *Did he change his mind?*

In the cemetery, Bishop had made Savage promise not to use the ketamine and Ambivalen anymore. But how was he supposed to communicate his decision? He wonders how much longer he can wait before the banality of life drives him to break out his stash. To break his promise.

I bet he changed his fucking mind.

Sleep wanders into his life whenever it finds the time

and deigns to visit. He's tired and anxious. He's starting to worry about money. About living. If he's not going to become a reaper, if he's not going to follow that vocation, it might be time to start looking for a new one. The thought alone of returning to work at the lab is so odious and anxiety-inducing, it makes him want to vomit.

Eight days.

Eleven days.

Eleven and a half.

He definitely forgot.

He's walking home from his favorite sushi place where he can always afford some sashimi and rice for cheap. The Zen environment is usually calming to his nerves but not tonight.

He thinks about that last night he spent in the otherworld. With Bishop. With Felicity. She didn't just indulge him by allowing him to kiss her. She kissed back, and she tasted like she wanted him as much as he wanted her. Her pointed tongue felt like it was probing his talent. Her fingers tried to scrape through to the bone to find where he kept the art inside him. But she had stopped him. He would have laid her down on the floor of the museum and tasted every part of her. He would have held her and pressed her into him to absorb the magic she exudes. But she had stopped him. She had stopped them both.

Being a reaper might not be the thing that calls to him most, although if he's being honest with himself, the idea is becoming more intriguing by the day. But it's a way to facilitate staying in that world. If he accepts, he will be able to stay in the layer of the universe that is spread over this one like a crazy technicolor dream. It's more than a possibility. It's the only option.

At home hiding in his cupboard, the supply of ketamine and the packets of Ambivalen reside in front of his cans of soup, like little blemishes on an Andy Warhol print. They're calling out to him from the darkness, tempting him. He tries to mute their noise. He promised Bishop not to use them, and he has every intention of keeping his word.

If Bishop would just show up already . . .

Twelve days.

No sign of the reaper keeping up on his end of the bargain.

He drifts off to sleep on the couch, the TV flickering colors in the dark.

He experiences a continuum dream where someone is knocking at his door, and he can't manage to answer. Knocking, knocking, knocking.

Knock, knock.

Who's there?

I'll never know.

He wakes from his latest bout of dream spirals, shaken and sweaty. He grabs his phone from the coffee table and ignites the screen to check the time.

5:12am.

It took less than twenty minutes to drift off. But he spent an eternity attempting to answer the damn door of his mind.

He picks up the remote from the arm of the couch, his body weary. On the TV, unrest is beginning, and protests are breaking out, with flaming effigies and tear gas. *A little mental preparation for what's to come,* he thinks. He wonders if this is what he will be subjected to if he accompanies the master of the macabre. *Maybe . . . but only if the reaper shows his face again.*

A bottle of Bulleit, half full, stands sentry on his coffee table next to a few sketchbooks of varying size. He reaches for the whiskey and pours a good portion into an old glass. He can taste the desert dust that has accumulated at the bottom and regrets not rinsing it out first.

His gaze falls past the television to the canvases stacked against the wall. Felicity's stunning face looks upon him from those paintings, the beauty not originating from the artist, he's sure, but the source.

Savage picks up one of the notebooks from the coffee table. He flips to a blank page and begins to sketch by the light of the television, ruining his eyes by the moment. He throws back the whiskey and pours himself another. The perfectionist inside him analyzes the state of the world and judges every bit of it. This world, this ordinary world, is also plagued by demons and wickedness. Voices, too loud, abusing their native tongues with the stupidity of their remarks. Sacrifices made for naught. Soldiers soldiering on to line others' pockets, already overflowing but demanding more. Humans can't figure out how to coexist, it seems. His mind wanders to that first night in the club, to those varied beasts in every color unknown to man. He remembers how they coalesced into one giant magic prism.

Anything is better than this. Better than watching this world peel itself and disembowel itself and light itself on fire over and over. Better than hiding in his apartment, sketching monstrosities by the light of the television. Anything. Even helping a lonely reaper collect souls.

He thinks back to the cemetery, when Bishop first proposed the idea. They got distracted talking about death.

And grief. His parents. His anger. But he never agreed. He never assented.

"Shit." He throws his sketchpad and pencil back on the table and half runs, half stumbles to the kitchen.

He knocks down the cans of Campbell's reaching for his stash. He grabs his glass of dusty whiskey, and mixes in a dose of K with a lead-stained finger.

He uses the mix to swallow two of the Ambivalen pills.

He winces at the familiar sting of whiskey and sighs out a breath of fire.

The rest goes down easier.

He sits back down on the couch and lies on the cushions. He stares up at the swirls in the drywall on the ceiling.

"Come on," he whispers.

He snaps his eyelids shut, like a kid on Christmas Eve willing it to be morning.

He thinks of the cemetery.

He thinks of the club of creatures.

He thinks of Bishop. And Rook. And the veritable round table of sundry souls.

He thinks of Felicity.

He thinks of Felicity.

"Come on . . ."

The sun is already up in New York.

It peeks its yellow head through the thick gauze curtains of the room Savage finds himself in.

He sits up, drowsily, smacking the living shit out of his head on something.

He curse-shouts in pain.

He's woken up underneath a table.

"The fuck?" he asks himself, his tongue heavy in his mouth.

The table is huge, and he has to crab-walk sideways to get out from under it, knocking over a chair in the process.

He grasps the arm of the chair, using its support to stand. The floor swims beneath him.

He recognizes the room now.

It's the meeting space where Bishop conducted his "make-the-world-go-round" business. It looks different in daylight, all the opulent chandeliers extinguished and the chairs vacant.

"He-hello?" Savage calls. His head feels like a marionette too heavy for its strings. "Helloooo?" he says to no one. He hiccup-burps and swallows back a throatful of bile, a clenched fist at his mouth.

He tries to make his way to the exit, but he can't remember which way Felicity took him when he was here before. He shuffles around, his feet numb things beneath him that fail to react to his will.

Something catches his drunken gaze. The paintings Savage made of Felicity are leaning against the wall in stacks of canvas.

Strange.

"Are you tired of vacuuming being such a *chore*?" someone asks.

"Wha?" He spins around.

It's his TV. His TV from his living room, on his entertainment unit, sitting next to the leather chair he sat in the other night.

And it's talking to him. "Do you spend *hours upon hours* vacuuming your house? And forget trying to vacuum stairs! *What a pain!*" the infomercial says.

He's dizzy and nauseous.

His sketchpads are here now, stacked atop the polished wood of the round table.

And his bottle of rye, open, the little cork stopper at its side.

He draws in a ragged breath, his lungs rattling in protest.

Something's wrong. Breathing is hard. He blinks his eyes to clear the confusion. It doesn't work.

Then, there's the dog. The wolfdog. She's sitting at attention on his couch, which is now also in the meeting room in New York. Somehow.

"How did you g-get here?" he asks.

The dog doesn't reply.

He stumbles, catching his foot on the leg of one of the chairs. He falls down on all fours.

The wolfdog whines at him, as if displeased. Or perhaps concerned.

"I got it, I got it," he tells her in a thick voice, ignoring the fact that it's illogical. It's all illogical. He hiccups again and suppresses the need to vomit, shuddering under the weight of his nausea. His breaths are coming with increasing difficulty.

He heaves and spits repeatedly on the shiny wood floor. The whiskey he drank earlier calls from his esophagus like a demon, all fire and fury. He gasps. Heaves and gasps, heaves and gasps again. His hand finds the mess of soured saliva, and he slips down completely, smacking into the hardwood floor.

He moans. In pain. In distaste.

The wolfdog howls. It's a screaming moan, like a woman,

like a banshee. The sound is painful in Savage's ears. The howl echoes through the room, an entity unto itself clamoring for the exit.

Savage rolls into a fetal ball, covering his ears and cowering from the cramping pain in his stomach. Water drips from his nose. The lights are going out on the room, and he realizes his eyes are rolling back into his head.

A form appears over him. Whether it exists in New York or Las Vegas, Savage can't tell. He doesn't even know in which city he exists. The form issues a quick slap across Savage's face, and he glimpses the culprit. His face is right before Savage's, his eyes obstructed by sunglasses with purple lenses.

He paws at Savage, pulling at his shirt and shaking him.

"Enough with the sleeping pills," the man says into Savage's face.

"S-sorry." He hiccups, and his stomach turns again. "Oh god . . ."

"Are you trying to kill us both?" the man in the purple sunglasses yells.

The wolfdog howls again, somehow louder than before. Screaming, screaming.

Savage moans once more, and the lights dim completely on the scene. His mind surrenders to the confusion and the pain of the moment.

"What the hell?" Bishop is shaking him awake. Savage can only moan in response. He opens his eyes to the reaper's face above him. He glances around. They're back in Savage's dim apartment. The wolfdog and the man in the purple sunglasses have disappeared.

"Okay, up you get." Bishop helps him from his supine position on the couch.

Savage rolls over and vomits onto the floor, near the reaper's shoes. The whiskey burns more coming up than it did going down.

"Yup, there you go. Get it up." Bishop's hands clap Savage on the back like he's burping a babe. "Not your time, kid. Not your time."

Savage gasps in deep, ragged breaths. Bishop helps him sit up on the couch, propping him up like a rag doll. The reaper stands and walks around the corner to the kitchen, his long gray coat trailing him like a shadow. Savage hears the tap running.

Bishop returns with a glass of cool water, and he hands it to Savage. He sits gingerly on the edge of the coffee table. "What happened?" he asks, his eyes blistering with either concern or judgement, Savage can't be sure.

Savage takes a long sip of tap water. He can taste the minerals and chemicals from the desert, but it soothes his throat on the way down. "It's been like two weeks . . ." he replies with a rough tongue.

"What?"

"I thought you forgot about me."

"Christ, I forget how impatient humans can be."

"I wasn't sure." He takes another sip. "I wasn't sure if you knew that I agreed. I didn't know how to find you. To tell you I agreed."

"Ah." Bishop nods. "It didn't have to be a written contract with a signature and a handshake. I know what's in your heart. I had to make sure you were mentally prepared. The transition isn't going to be an easy task."

"Then why did you offer it to me?"

The reaper takes a long breath, his lips pressed together in a line of concentration. "I see something in you. A little of me in you and a little of you in me, perhaps. Because I'm lonely, and you're lonely. Because misery loves company, as the saying goes."

Savage looks down to his sleeve of tattoos. The inked Grim Reaper is rendered as a hooded skeleton upon a white horse, wielding a scythe, a raven on his shoulder for company.

Bishop follows Savage's gaze. He points with a long, gloved finger. "I've already got Rook." He points to the raven. "Maybe you're my white horse, the light to my dark."

"I'm nobody's light." Savage laughs without humor.

"We'll see about that," the reaper replies.

Savage flushed the rest of the ketamine with Bishop standing watch to ensure.

"Can I keep the sleeping pills?" he had asked.

"Why? I'm going to hunt down your sandman and put that sleepy bastard to work. You won't need the pills. Once you're fully transitioned, you won't even really need to sleep anymore. Ditch 'em."

With a bit of hesitation, Savage had emptied the foil packets one by one into the toilet as well.

"Now flush."

And he did.

"Why won't I need to sleep?"

"I dunno, I don't. The other reapers don't."

"But they weren't once humans."

"True. It'll be a learning process for both of us. We'll see I guess?"

Bishop had given him express instructions to let several days pass to allow the residual effects of his near overdose leave his system.

And now, three days later, déjà vu. He's on the couch, sketchbook propped on his knee, and pencil drooping from his right hand as he dozes.

He doesn't notice the late-night news has turned over to early morning infomercials. *Are you tired of vacuuming being such a* chore? *So much of your day taken up, constantly wrestling with the mundanity of your existence?* the television seeps into his subconscious.

"Kid? C'mon, kid. Kid!"

"Wha-?"

"Wake up. You've managed to depress me again." Bishop grabs the remote from the coffee table and turns off the TV. "Better." He chucks the remote onto the couch.

Savage rubs his eyes.

"I'm sorry," he says, as he sits up and stretches the stiffness from his crying body.

"It's time."

"Time for what? To go?"

"Yeah, grab your toothbrush, buddy, and whatever human stuff you may need." He sniffs in sharply as he looks around Savage's apartment. "Jesus, this place is grim."

"You don't get to use that word," Savage calls as he walks down the hall to grab some essentials.

"That's how you know it's true. I'm the authority on the grim."

Savage packs his necessary earthly belongings into a gym bag.

"Are these all Felicity?" Bishop calls from the living room.

"I can't be held responsible for what I painted while I was asleep," Savage replies as he walks back into the room.

Bishop is smiling, thumbing through the canvases.

"You really are quite the artist."

"That's what they tell me." Savage walks up and pushes the paintings away from Bishop, back against the wall. "Just leave them, I was high and asleep."

"Right, sure." Bishop waves his eyebrows.

"Seriously. So, will I be able to come back?"

"Huh, I hadn't thought about that. I suspect you will for a while but not indefinitely. Get what's important."

"Nothing's important," Savage says.

"That's sad."

"Mmhm."

"*Grim*, some might say."

"Stop."

"You'll get used to it, my friend." Bishop claps his gloved hand onto Savage's shoulder, and in a swirl of darkness and smoke, they dissolve into the night.

PART II

WHEEL OF FORTUNE

SIX

"Alright, kid. I think I should start you off with something nice and simple."

It's deep in the night in middle America.

Savage and Bishop stand before a house with a flat roof. The paint on the trim of the windows is chipped with age. An old red Ford is parked in the driveway, sporting a dented Kansas plate, and the lawn is unkempt and patchy, with dead leaves accumulated in the corners of the yard. Somewhere down the street, an old engine turns over.

Savage closes his mouth in a hard line, taking in the scene before him. It reminds him of everything, and it reminds him of nothing. He could be anywhere. Main Street, USA.

Breath accumulates in little clouds of condensation every time he exhales. He looks to Bishop. The breeze catches the ends of his reddish hair and tosses it over his forehead. No fog comes from the reaper's lungs.

"Sometimes the things I see . . ." Bishop runs a gloved hand over his hair. He starts again. "My existence is my own. I walk this path because I chose to. But a reaping like this is likely one of the best you can ask for. This old woman says goodnight to her life every lights out. She's ready, now." Bishop takes his gaze from the house and focuses on Savage. "This one will go a little slower than some others. There's more time to process in a death like this. Less reaction and more deliberate action, if that makes sense."

It doesn't, but Savage nods anyway.

"Rules," Bishop continues, "I need you to stay completely silent. No talking. No questions. *No noise.* No gasps or sighs or yawns, yeah?"

Savage is about to agree verbally but stops himself and only nods.

"Catching on already, I like that. When we go in, stay a few steps behind me. I don't know exactly how this is going to go . . . and here I thought I'd seen everything. Time to shake it up, I suppose."

Bishop takes a moment, closes his eyes and centers himself.

The reaper's eyes move beneath his lids like he's having a vivid dream. His breath hitches in his throat. Surprise. Discovery. His eyes stop their wandering, he lifts his lids and calls out a name.

"ROSIE."

When he speaks, his voice is different than Savage has heard it before. It's different from any voice he has *ever* heard. It's deep. Authoritative. Unworldly. The hairs on the back of Savage's neck bristle.

With a blink, they're inside the house in a long hallway with wood paneling and crooked pictures lining its walls.

The photos must be of Rosie's family. A couple on their wedding day circa the early nineties. A man with a mustache like Freddie Mercury. A woman with hair permed like Jessie Spano. Two kids posed in front of a JC Penny black background in matching blue and white outfits.

They walk down the hall to the staircase. Savage feels the thick carpet beneath his shoes, muting his footsteps as they climb.

In the bedroom of the sleeping woman, it smells like the past, stuffy and tired and lingering. A cocker spaniel wakes, lifting her head from a worn round cushion on the floor. She tilts her head at them but doesn't bark. The woman sleeps beneath a great patchwork quilt, her hair spread out around her head like a gray ocean.

Savage glances past Bishop and sees the woman's face. A small smile plays at her lips. She's sweet even in sleep.

Bishop takes off his gloves and rolls his sleeves to the elbow. He pulls out one of his black cigarettes, flicks open a silver lighter, and ignites the tip with a dark red flame. He inhales its fumes deeply and stands for a moment observing the sleeping woman. This is the most like the quintessential Grim Reaper that Savage has ever seen Bishop look. In the low light, he's a wraith, all darkness and smoke.

Savage stays near the door, willing himself to fall into the shadows.

The dog looks up at him with sad eyes. She rises from her cushion and scratches at his legs, emitting a low whine. The white of age has overtaken the tawny fur around her brows and whiskers. He can't shush her or acknowledge her. He looks back to Bishop, but his back is turned to Savage.

The dog whines again. Savage kneels and takes her in his arms, holding her there as they watch together, a little audience for the reaper in the theater of the dying.

Bishop takes another drag. This must be why Felicity referred to them as his *death sticks*. At the edge of the bed, he leans over the woman's sleeping face, exhaling his black smoke around her head like a storm cloud. Savage squints into the dark and sees the woman's body collapse, releasing every ounce of tension. The stress of living. As a sigh escapes her lips, Bishop takes the woman's hand in his own. He holds it firmly, his grasp both careful and firm, full of affection and concentration. He pulls her spirit from her body like he's peeling off the tired top layer of an onion to reveal the lively purple orb underneath. He pinches his cigarette between his lips in exertion.

The spirit splinters and comes free of the form.

The body falls to shadow, the soul to light.

Bishop stands, stubs out the end of the cigarette with a naked finger, and pockets the stub. Rosie is beside him. She's a tiny woman, standing shorter than five feet. She looks relaxed and not at all surprised. Bishop offers her a hand with a smile.

"Where are we going, Rosie?"

"Hm . . ." she sighs. "The beach. Under the stars."

Bishop smiles again and glances over his shoulder at Savage.

In another breath, they are on the shore of an inky black ocean, a million stars glowing above and reflected onto the water. The sand is like crushed graham crackers beneath their feet, damp and golden. Savage still holds the spaniel. She's settled into his arms but remains alert.

The air is humid and briny in his nose.

Bishop is still holding Rosie's hand. She looks up, smiles at him, and gives his hand a little victorious shake. Bishop laughs. Together they walk into the water, but somehow it doesn't saturate Bishop. Rosie's white nightgown flows and pillows around her like a jellyfish. When the water reaches her chest, Bishop turns to her and says something Savage cannot hear. He kisses her on the cheek.

The dog looks up at Savage and whines. He gives her head a scratch with one hand and ruffles the hair on her chest with the other one. In the water, Rosie takes a deep breath and submerges herself. Bishop watches for a minute as she swims in the moonlight toward the black horizon. He says something in an ancient voice with an ancient tongue Savage can't understand. It might be a prayer or a salute or a poem. Savage thinks it's all three. Bishop places his hand on his chest and bows his head.

The spaniel mewls again.

Bishop turns and walks up from the water. It moves around his legs, still not penetrating the fabric of his trousers. He unrolls his sleeves and pulls his gloves from his pocket, and he notices the spaniel for the first time.

"Damn, we'll have to go back to Kansas to drop this little girl back. Unless . . ." He takes the dog's face in his hands. She whines again. He removes her from Savage's hold and sets her on the sand, her tail wagging. "Go on, Tillamook."

The dog runs into the water and paddles out, eager to follow her master, until Savage can no longer see her. Until she succumbs to the waves of the impossible ocean.

When Savage lost his grandmother, whom he called Nan, his family flew to San Diego to be present for the funeral. When they visited her house when she was still alive, they usually drove. But for the funeral, they flew. Savage was six. He remembers the stewardess giving him a small, plastic 747 to calm his nerves on the flight, and he remembers thinking he was a little too old to be pacified with cheap plastic toys.

The wake was at Nan's cozy home. The guests smoked and drank and chatted amongst themselves in the front room. As the youngest mourner in attendance, Savage didn't know what to do with himself. The smoke from the lounge deterred him from staying in the house. There was idle chatter, peppered with the occasional chuckle, and there was far less talk of Nan than he thought appropriate, even then. Even at six. He let himself out to the backyard, into Nan's miraculous garden. She cultivated a myriad of species of roses, pruned and adored. Even in the weeks leading to her death. Even with the cancer in her bones and lungs, she tended to the garden for as long as she could.

Savage wore a little black suit, bought especially for the occasion, with dress shorts in lieu of pants to allow comfort in the balmy summer. He wished they were pants; he felt silly wearing shorts. He sat on the stone step, scratching at the dirt with a long stick, and cried to himself. Little bits of silent grief fell for his beloved Nan, who always came to visit for his birthday in late October. But not this year. There'd be no Nan this October. Halloween would always remind him of his grandmother. She with the quick and witty tongue and the papery skin that showed the veins underneath like wandering blue rivers. Every year, she'd help him craft a costume and stitch magical things from nothing, even when he wanted to be something hard. Even the year he wanted to be a Teenage Mutant Ninja Turtle.

The young Savage approached his grandmother's rosebushes. This bloom looked black, so he knew it was red to the rest of the color-sighted world. He took the girth of the petals in his fingers and pulled, plucking the entirety of the blossom from the bush. He squeezed the flower in his little fist, the silky texture of the petals not unlike Nan's skin.

"Nan," he said into his angry little fist, he said to the rose. "Where did you go?"

"Sweetie?" his mother called from the kitchen through the screen door. He didn't answer, closing his eyes and willing time to reverse. "Ryan?" his mother called. She brought him out a dish with a butter cookie. He didn't eat it. He kept it in the pocket of his stupid, black shorts because it came from Nan's kitchen and therefore was a piece of her. He managed to get it all the way back home with only minor damage, where he kept it in his room until the ants found it and carried it off in minute bits until it was as though it wasn't ever there at all.

Savage seldom thinks of the stale butter cookie and the Teenage Mutant Ninja Turtle costume, but he allows his mind to wander to them now, in Bishop's quarters.

Inside Green-wood, inside a mausoleum marked for a family named Smithe, is a grim reaper's expansive and secret lair. The tomb is at the back of the massive cemetery in an infrequently visited corner. It was built into a hill beside an ancient tree, the graying roots of which are exposed and stretched out like a bony hand. An iron door, green with age, bars the entrance to the bodies of the Smithe family, or so the public would think. The outside appears to be an average sized crypt. But inside, the reaper has manipulated physics to accommodate an ample living space, the majority of which is devoted to a lavish sunken living room, its walls lined with bookcases. Identical black bound books line the shelves.

In keeping with the model of his beloved Olds, Bishop's home bears a midcentury modern aesthetic, with a low backed, wrap-around charcoal sofa and swanky chairs. Here, Savage sits in front of a conical red fireplace, where an ever-burning fire merrily chews through logs like the spirit of Christmas incarnate. Early Miles Davis emits somewhere from a turntable.

Savage has his head heavy in his hand, and Bishop has left him to percolate and meditate on his first reaping.

When the record comes to the end of the second side with a whir and a scratch, Bishop reappears and sits near Savage.

"How are you hanging in there?

Savage shrugs.

"You're thinking about a grandmother, perhaps?"

"How did you know?"

"Sweet old lady like Rosie . . . if you had a grandma you were bonded to, logic would dictate you'd be thinking of her, now."

"Yeah."

"How old were you?"

"Six."

Bishop nods. "What are you working through?"

"When you asked Rosie where she wanted to go . . . it doesn't seem like everyone would have the same transition-place."

"No. They don't."

"I'm wondering what my grandmother's place was."

"Somewhere that brought her peace and happiness in life."

Bishop watches Savage for a moment in silence. He exhales and claps his gloved hands on his knees before standing. He approaches a shelf and retrieves a book. Riffling through the pages of the first book for a moment, he abandons it, replaces it, and retrieves another. This time he finds what he searches for and returns his attention to Savage.

"Would you like to see it?"

Savage looks up through his black brow. He's forgotten where the conversation left off. "What?"

"Your grandmother's gateway."

Savage thinks a moment. "Nan won't be there?"

"No, she passed through a long time ago. But these places are never forgotten. Not by our kind. They're sort of like . . . collectibles."

Savage wrinkles his nose.

"Sorry, *collectible* isn't the right word." Bishop scratches his face. "Somewhere between *shrine* and *memento.*"

Savage pauses. "And I could visit Nan's?"

"Yes, you can. I think you ought to. Work through your humanity so you can start to work towards eternity."

"Okay." Savage stands. "I can do it."

Bishop takes a moment to center himself, eyes closed like he's sorting through a mental maze. Then, in a flutter and a blink, they're at Nan's gateway.

It's her beloved garden, as Savage knew it would be. A big pregnant moon hangs in the sky, the rosebushes cast in shadow. The stone pathway that leads through the breadth of the yard is flanked by hollyhocks, peonies, and sweet William. It's quiet, and a light breeze stirs the perfume of the jasmine that climbs up a trellis by the patio door. The moonlight is so bright, the colors are visible even in the dark. A fat bougainvillea bush drips its magenta blooms over the back fence. It's Nan's garden in a way Savage has never known it. Every one of her ambitions and every fecund summer night manifested into one moment, displaying the full spectrum of color he never got to experience when she was living.

Savage searches at his feet for a twig. When he finds one, he sits on the stone step at the backdoor of the cottage. He scratches into the ground a sketch of Nan, her face smiling and kind. Tears slip down his face, but he is comforted by their presence. It's a catharsis. Somehow, it's good to know his grief for Nan is still within him. The grief itself is part of her. A part he gets to keep, even though the rest of her is gone. Even now.

"While we're figuring out this transition, I enlisted a little help." It's later that night. Bishop is pouring himself a glass of some brown libation from a crystal decanter.

"What do you mean?" Savage asks.

"Well, I'm going to need you rested until—or if—you reach the point where you can operate without sleep. 'Til you move past humanity. I can't have you all bleary eyed and sleepy and . . . insomniac-y."

"*Insomniac-y?*"

"For lack of a better term."

"Yeah, being *insomniac-y* is no good," Savage chuckles.

Bishop sits across from him on the sectional. There's a reading light behind his head so he's bathed in a halo of warm light. "I looked into it, and I don't know what you did to piss off your sandman, but that guy is like a rumor. I'm not sure he actually exists." He scratches a gloved finger over the stubble on his chin and takes a sip from his glass. "So, I asked Reve for help."

There's a knock on the iron door of the mausoleum.

"Ah, perfect timing."

"Reve?" Savage repeats.

"Yeah," Bishop says as he stands to answer the door. "You remember him from the Quantum Club?"

"Yeah, I remember."

Bishop opens the door and from the shadow of night, the sandman enters with arms folded, looking calm and perpetually bored.

"Bishop." He nods, the gold flecks on his cheeks catching the light. He looks to Savage. "Hello," he says flatly.

Savage gives a small, unenthused salute. "Hi."

Bishop welcomes him into the living room. "Reve, can I offer you some liquid courage?" He swirls the liquid in his glass. "It's really courage." He winks to Savage.

"I don't imbibe when I'm working, I'm afraid," Reve says.

"Why would you need courage?" Savage asks Bishop, stifling a yawn.

Bishop shrugs. "To face my lonely existence?"

"I thought that's why I'm here."

The sandman cuts to business. "Shall we begin?"

"Wait, right now?" Savage says.

"That's the idea."

Savage yawns. "Well, that's good timing, I guess, because I'm really fucking sleepy all of a sudden."

"That'd be the sandman in the room," Bishop answers. "Let's get you some rest and get you feeling better."

Savage turns to the sandman in the corner. "Can I make a request?"

"What would that be?" Reve emerges from the shadows a bit, so half his face glows from the flames in the fireplace and the other is lost to blackness.

"I get these terrible fucking dreams."

"Nightmares? I have no control over the content of your dreams, I'm afraid."

"No, they're not nightmares. They're more like loops or dream spirals. In the dream, I think I wake up, and go about my business, but I'm still dreaming. Then I realize I'm dreaming, and something weird will happen. The details don't seem to be important. Then I'm back waking up again. But not really. I'm only dreaming I'm waking, over and over. And the dreams feel like they last forever."

"Continuum dreams? Those are rare indeed . . ." The sandman stays quiet for a moment. He uncrosses his arms and places his chin into his cupped fingers. The sleeve of his cream-colored suit comes down a bit, revealing a tattoo Savage can just make out in the low light. "I cannot think why your sandman would give you the continuum dream," Reve continues, "unless it is your own subconscious trying to reconcile your insomnia. I'm not sure. I will, however, make certain to give you no such dreams while you are in my charge."

"Cool, that's all I want." Savage's face twists into another wide yawn, like that of a child. "Hey, what's that?" he asks through his yawn, pointing to the corresponding spot on his own wrist as he snuggles down into the couch.

"This?" Reve asks, looking down at his wrist. "It is the mark of my kind. The mark of the dreaming mind and its duality." He pulls the sleeve of his suit down over the mark, concealing it from sight.

Savage isn't sure, but he assumes the mark is a tattoo of twin crescent moons, one ebony, one ivory. One he's seen before, and recently. But he's too groggy to examine the thought further.

"Alright, go to bed, kid," Bishop says, taking a throw blanket off the edge of the couch and draping it over Savage's long body. He squeezes his shoulder. "Sleep tight."

Savage falls into a deep and resounding sleep that feels like dipping into a warm, black ocean.

He dreams of nothing.

Savage wakes in the morning to the smell of bacon and coffee. He stretches and yawns as he sits up.

"Wakey-wakey, eggs and bakey," he hears Bishop call over the sizzling of bacon in a pan.

"G'morning," he says drowsily. "Oh my god."

"Everything okay?"

"Yes. For once, *yes*." Savage stands and reaches his long arms toward the ceiling. He feels rested and alive, invigorated and renewed. The morning sings in his nose and ears and paints him a new man, the sleep a baptism for his spirit. He lets out a contented sigh. "That's the best night's rest I've gotten in—no, that's the best night's rest I've *ever* gotten."

Bishop glances at him as he plates the food. "Ha, that explains the screwy thing that's going on with your face. Your mouth is like . . . contorted, and your eyes are all squinty. It's weird."

"Hush."

"Really. You should go look at yourself in the mirror. I'm not sure you'd recognize yourself."

Savage sits at the small dining table off the kitchen. "Wait . . ."

"Hm?" Bishop asks.

"There wasn't a kitchen before."

"No. I didn't need one 'til today. You gave me a reason to expand for the first time since the 1800s." He places the plate in front of Savage. "I have no idea if any of this is good or even edible. But I couldn't say 'wakey-wakey eggs and bakey' without actually having eggs and bakey. And I *really* wanted to say 'wakey-wakey.'"

Savage bites into the scrambled eggs and gives a thumbs up.

"But wait, there's more." Bishop grabs a French press from the counter and depresses the plunger. "I was kind of praying you wouldn't need the caffeine, but I thought the smell of coffee would be comforting." He sits at the table and lets Savage eat for a moment. "There is also a bathroom, now, but please don't think too hard about how I made the plumbing work."

Savage snickers. "Thank you."

When he finishes his meal he says to Bishop, "So, I've been thinking about yesterday. And . . . what about my parents? What were their gateways?"

"You sure you're ready to see that?"

"Might as well get all the heartache, all my humanity, out on the floor and trudge through it at once."

Bishop stands and approaches the many shelves of black books. He pulls one out. It takes him two, three, four tries. "Ah," he mutters. He snaps the book closed.

Savage hears the faint chords of a song begin. As the volume increases, he recognizes it. "Fuck," he says flatly. It's the opening of "In My Life" by The Beatles. It was his parents' song. "Are you trying to kill me with grief? Is that the goal?"

"According to their reaper, it was playing at the gateway. And you wanted to 'trudge through all the heartache,' remember." Bishop winks one eye, then closes them both.

He lets most the song play out before—
Blink.

Savage is on a mountain at dusk, just as the sun is setting over the peaks. The melody of "In My Life" is echoing through the trees.

The air is cool and crisp. He stands at the entrance of a cabin, door ajar. There is a big quilt covered bed and a fireplace. The walls are wooden, and big windows display a view of the mountain the cabin is built into. Trees upon trees upon trees. The back door is open, and a great orange sun is setting, filling the room with its radiance.

"This must have been their honeymoon spot," Savage says without prompting. "Mt. Charleston," he explains.

"It's no real place." Bishop shakes his head. "It's a representation of a place or time that brought them peace. This is closer to how it existed in their memories than how it exists in reality."

Savage walks into the cabin. It smells of peppermint and pine. He runs his fingers along the footboard of the wooden sleigh bed. "But it was the gateway for both of them, right?"

Bishop's face cures into a gentle smile. "Yes. It's worth noting that not all married couples, even ones who die at the same time, have the same gateway."

"They didn't die at the same time," Savage says, quietly, his gaze intent on his fingers as they play along the wood. "My dad died on impact, and my mom . . . she died in the ambulance on the way to the hospital."

"I'm sure your pop waited for her, kid."

Savage walks to the back door. The sun is impossibly big and impossibly orange, a giant shining disk that paints the trees in a golden glow. Savage goes to step out the back.

"No," Bishop starts.

Savage doesn't hear him.

A blink, and Bishop is in front of him barring the door. He is backlit, his face lost to the shadows. "Savage, no. You can't go through there."

"I want to know. I want them to know. I want to see them. I want to tell them I'm okay. Am I okay? Fuck." He stifles a sob.

Bishop clasps him by the shoulders, speaking into his downturned face. "I know. I know, kid. More than you'll ever understand, I know. Your grief is my grief." He shakes his shoulders, lightly. "I'm sorry for your loss. I'm sorry you were put through this."

"I would say it's not your fault, but . . . ." Savage lets out a half laugh.

"Yeah, yeah. I know."

"It wasn't you this time, either?"

"No. Not me."

Savage sighs.

A blink, a flicker. Back to the mausoleum. Bishop pulls a vial of inspiration from his pocket and downs the last of the contents.

"What do you think, should we go hunt down a muse and bug her for a spell?" He wags the vial back and forth in his fingers. "I think it'd make us both feel better."

Savage nods. "I think you're right."

In the Toronado, Bishop starts the engine with a smooth purr.

"Why do you drive when you can be anywhere you want to be whenever you want to be there?"

"Because I like getting around in style." The reaper slides on a pair of sunglasses and waggles his eyebrows above the frames.

Savage lets out a chuckle.

"Well, I'll be damned if I ain't already. The kid can *laugh.*"

"Yes, I am capable. It's just you're not that funny."

"Lies. I'm hilarious."

Bishop twists the volume knob. Blue Öyster Cult is on the reaper's playlist today.

"'Don't Fear the Reaper?' Now you're just being cliché."

"Hey, this song is about me, kid. If there was a song called, 'Don't Fear Savage, the Grumpy Insomniac Artist,' you'd be all *over* it."

They drive north through Brooklyn, passing over the Gowanus Canal.

"Wha-what's wrong with that water?" Savage points out the window to the peculiar green water of the canal. "Is this some weird side effect of my colorblindness or something?"

"You're not trippin', dude. That color does not exist in nature, but your eyes ain't lying. Just never go swimming in the Gowanus . . . unless you want to end up with gills." Bishop mouths *"radioactive"* comically.

They turn along the water, to a stretch of New York quieter and less congested than Savage has yet seen. Bishop slides the Olds along the curb and parks on the empty street. They get out and zigzag on foot through the alleys between the brick buildings for a bit. Many have large, open windows displaying artist studio space. Some are occupied by their craftsmen; some are vacant with giant canvases stored along the walls of the rooms.

In a gray, modern building, a young man is working. He has a clay-stained apron tied around his middle, and there are bits of artistic refuse in his beard. He works diligently, hands coated, deep in thought and creation. Felicity sits on an unused artist stool, her long blush colored dress brushing the floor. Her legs are crossed, posture attentive. She looks like she's listening to a silent symphony, her eyes closed in deep meditation, lips set in a serene smile.

Bishop and Savage stand at the window and watch the man work and the muse muse for a minute.

Felicity shifts and opens her eyes. She smiles a little to herself and shakes her head before exiting the building to greet them. "What a pair you two make."

"Wanna hang out for a bit? We could use some cheering up," Bishop says.

"Does that mean you're out of vials?"

"Yes, but that's not the point. Your company is requested." Her little smile grows.

"Alright." She concedes. "But I'm not going to spend the rest of this glorious day in that desolate cemetery you call a home."

"Let's give the kid a good New York meal. If that doesn't show him the purpose of life, I don't know what will."

Bishop drives them into the city, up to The Village. Savage looks out onto the quaint tree-lined streets and thinks he's never seen so much brick in his life, and if he has, he's never been able to appreciate the majestic, rusted color.

"Hey," he says. "Red. I can see red."

"Yeah, you could before? Remember the sunset?" Bishop asks.

"Yeah, but I was high and stuff . . ."

"Maybe it's the muse." Bishop gestures to Felicity in the passenger seat.

"Maybe it's the reaper," Felicity retorts.

"Nah, color seems more like your arena . . . I hate navigating this godforsaken neighborhood," Bishop says as he loops through one-way streets. "South of Houston, and the grid goes to absolute shit."

Felicity's laugh sounds like bells.

They pull into a spot on Bleecker. "Whomever you bribed to always ensure parking for this beast, I'd genuinely like to meet," she says as she gets out, giving the hood of the Toronado a little pat.

"Indeed. The gods of parking are fickle, fickle beasts," Bishop replies as he closes his door.

They approach a little hole in the wall Indian food place, crafted to look like an old train-car, with metal siding lining the roof and old-fashioned sconces. The walls are red and the lights low.

"Ah, my friend," the owner says to Bishop as they enter.

The man gives him a hug. "You must be losing weight, I have not seen you in over a week."

"A problem I intend to remedy tonight. I even brought friends," he gestures.

"Yes, please, sit." The owner motions to a table at the front by the window. He hands them menus. "You have beautiful friends," he says, winking to Bishop.

"He's not talking about you," Bishop shakes his head at Savage, and Felicity laughs.

The owner brings them water and drinks on the house, and Bishop orders a smorgasbord for the group.

"Wait," Savage says, "you didn't have a kitchen."

"You are correct, sir."

"But we're about to eat a ton of food."

"Yes."

"So, if you eat, why didn't you have a kitchen?"

"No one *needs* a kitchen in New York."

"What?" Savage laughs.

"Hey kid, just because I don't *need* to eat doesn't mean I don't *love* to eat." Bishop gives his gut a loving pat.

People walk in droves past the window of the restaurant. Smoking cigarettes. Walking dogs. Arm in arm with friends or lovers. Hands full of packages. On their phones. Yelling obscenities.

A middle-aged couple stops and reads the menu posted outside the window, muttering to themselves. The man shakes his head, and they walk on to eat elsewhere.

"Idiots . . ." Bishop admonishes. "No finer meal in all of Manhattan," he mutters.

The food arrives in silver serving bowls and on big hot

plates. Chicken tikka masala and lamb vindaloo. Saffron rice and shrimp tandoori. Bloated poori and crispy samosas.

It's the best food Savage has ever tasted. The chicken is so tender, he cuts it with a spoon.

"How have I never eaten here?" Felicity exalts as she dips a piece of naan into the sauce on her plate. "The food is inspired."

"And here I thought I was going to get shit from the muse for not bringing the kid to some four-star, Michelin-rated, blah blah bullshit joint." Bishop stabs into the puffy poori with his fork, deflating the bread and ripping off a corner.

They talk and laugh, and Savage feels like he's in good company for the first time in a long time. Maybe ever. The spices are round on his tongue. He can taste the heat, but its comfortingly spicy. Satisfyingly spicy. Like his palate and stomach have been cleansed by the time the meal is finished.

After eating, they sip warm chai. Felicity swirls her cup like she plans to divine something from the leaves. "Did you and Ray get the Devlin situation sorted?" she asks.

"In front of the kid?"

"Come, Bishop. If you are going to have him accompanying you all over creation, you don't have to keep him in the dark. At least not totally."

Devlin. The day Savage met Bishop in the red room of the sirens, he was shouting about Devlin.

"I'm doing more than just keeping him company," Savage says.

"What do you mean?"

"Meet my new apprentice." Bishop gestures with gloved fingers.

She turns to look at Savage, eyebrows arched in surprise.

"Who's Devlin?" Savage asks.

The reaper sets down his tea. "We were having a perfectly nice dinner, and you have to open this can of worms."

"The can was already open, darling, you're just placing one on the hook." She runs her fingers through her silken hair.

"Ugh . . ." he grumbles. "Devlin is the devil?" Bishop grimaces and makes the statement a question.

Savage blinks, deliberately. "What." His tone is flat and unamused.

"Yeah, sorry kid. See? Life was simpler before you knew that."

"Bishop," Felicity reprimands.

"I mean, he's not really the devil. All that Christian-Satanic-Lucifer-Demon-fallen-angel-BS is so far from the truth. That paints him in a far more sinister light than is warranted. He's an emotional grifter. He's chaos. He's . . . the undoer of the done . . . and he sort of thrives on evil and discord," he adds the last part in hurriedly, like he's hoping Savage won't notice.

Savage remembers the sketches from his first night down the K-hole—a score of sketches of Felicity and one of something else, something sinister. *CHAOS*, it said. *Bishop had only referred to Devlin by his name that day*, he thinks. *How did I know?* He takes another sip of tea.

"The Devil's name is *Devlin*?" he asks.

"Well, yes and no. It's a nickname I gave him, kind of a pun. He'll put the Devil-in ya."

Savage blinks, unamused.

"It's just because I refuse to refer to him as 'the Knave' or 'His Darkness' or 'The Prince of freaking Shadows' like his little sycophantic groupies. Sometimes, I call him 'Dev.' He really doesn't like that one."

"So, what's wrong with him? I mean, aside from the obvious. What's 'the situation'?"

"He's . . . let's just say he's become dissatisfied with his position in the scheme of things."

"And now he's . . . satisfied?"

"Not so much."

"I don't think I want to know what satisfies the devil." Savage grimaces. "What does he want?"

Bishop and Felicity share a loaded glance.

"What?" Savage asks.

"He wants to remake the world."

"He—what now?"

"Yeah, I know, tough times," Bishop remarks.

"He wants to *remake* the world. Like, remake it. Rebuild?"

"He wants to tear it apart. Arguably, rebuilding could be the next step, I suppose."

Savage sighs. "Well . . . there's a lot to improve upon."

Bishop and Felicity share another look.

"His motives are not perfectionistic or to better your home," Felicity explains. "If the world is remade, Devlin thinks he's entitled to all the souls who populate the world now."

"To do what, exactly?"

"We're not sure. That's part of the problem."

"Oh. Well, fuck," Savage responds.

"Yeah, exactly. Even though I haven't figured out his motives yet, no good would come of it, that's for damn sure." Bishop takes a pinch of fennel seeds from a silver dish the owner dropped with the check and swallows it with a sip of tea. "Don't worry about it, it's not going to happen. He's crafty, but he doesn't have the power to pull a job like that on his own. Which is why he's being such a pain in the ass right now. He's like a toddler throwing a tantrum. But his tantrums have a little more kick than a two-year-old's."

"So, I guess that means the situation hasn't really been handled, then?"

"I'm working on a solution, kid. Don't you fret."

The sketch of the hooded figure lingers in Savage's memory, acutely now, like a fresh nightmare. Bishop's promise brings him little comfort.

INTERLUDE

It is deep in the night, or early in the morning depending on perspective. The hours are small and tender and yawn like razor-toothed kittens. This is the hour his kind are most potent. They hang in the air. They're like aromas that can be tasted or sounds that can be felt. They're silent and surreptitious. They roll in like fog.

Remy looks in upon the sleeping human, his new mark. His new mark that nearly ended him after only a few weeks.

He's in the Bishop's quarters, but the reaper is nowhere to be found. Remy wouldn't dare enter the crypt if he sensed his presence.

The human sleeps heavily, a blanket twisted over his body with one lanky leg exposed. It's the restful unadulterated sleep that can be given only by one of Remy's kind, by a sandman.

He emerges from the shadows, straightening the lapel of his amethyst suit.

Though he sees no sandman present, he can recognize the

signs. He's like an architect walking into some else's building; he sees the supports and foundation and design choices, though the layman wouldn't.

He leans over the sleeping savage, inspecting the art of the sleep. It's a natural sleep, no more pills, thank fuck. Remy isn't sure how much of that he could sustain. The kid killed his last sandman with those sleep-forsaken things. Of course, the old man was just that: old. On his last legs. But rumor has it this sleeper has killed a dozen sandmen. A score. His whole life, he's spent overloading them, one after the next, as they dropped like flies in napalm.

But Remy is wiser. Wiser and not alone. That's a good start.

Remy takes in a deep sniff. No dreams. The man's sleep is pure unconsciousness, this much he can tell.

"What are you doing?" a calm voice inquires.

Remy jumps.

Reve, his bored-faced associate, has appeared behind him.

"Checking on my charge, clearly. Though it seems I've no need to," Remy tries the playing-stupid defense, "as you are attending to him? Did I miss something—was he reassigned to you?"

"I'm doing the reaper a favor. He needed a sandman, and you were nowhere to be found."

"The dude's got weird sleeping habits. I've had some difficulty adjusting to his rhythm."

"Surely you've worked with night shift workers and insomniacs before?"

"Yes," Remy replies, pulling his purple tinted glasses from his face, and rubbing the corner of his suit over the lenses. "It's not that. He's an odd one, that much is clear. But I don't know why exactly . . ."

On the couch, the savage lets out a heavy snuff from his nose, like he's commenting on Remy's assessment. Like he's judging.

Remy's lips curl in fear or perhaps disgust.

Reve is watching Remy watch the man. "Well, there's not much I can do about your lack of work ethic," he says. "It's not as if we have a superior."

"Why are you telling me this like it's something I don't know?"

"You seem to need reminding." There's that *dumbass* subtext again. "Might I encourage you to check in on your other charges a little more frequently?"

"And this one?" Remy gestures to the sleeper.

"Consider him reassigned."

"I—" Remy stops himself. If Reve wants to take the insomniac, he can have him. Remy has already achieved the main task assigned to him. The Knave will just have to accept that he's been replaced and can't play the spy . . . though that's not a conversation Remy looks forward to having. But the thought of not having to deal with the savage and his volatile sleep habits anymore is a reward worth the castigation.

Reve crosses the room to the chair by the fireplace. He sits, gingerly, like he's avoiding getting wrinkles in his suit.

Remy runs his hand over his cropped beard, the gold flecked hairs catching the light. "Well, I might as well run my rounds if you're staying with this one." He's eager to leave. If Reve is here at the reaper's behest, that's a good sign. Remy wants to report back the news, both good and bad, and get on with his night. As much as the Knave has given him, he's still unsettled by his company. Best to tell him quickly and get out.

"Yes, I'll be here," the dark-skinned sandman replies to the light. "I was given a job, and I intend to do it."

Remy replaces his glasses on his face. "Don't have too much fun." He waves casually, waggling his fingers. "Tata."

He slips into the night with the shadows.

He hopes he came across as ignorant. Arrogant. Some combination thereof. He doesn't need Reve to trust him, but he doesn't want to seem untrustworthy, per se. He thinks his feigned stupidity got that point across.

Now, to the depths of the world, to the blue streets the Knave haunts.

SEVEN

A fire crackles in the den of the reaper. Savage and Bishop are a half an hour into a game of chess. A handful of captured pawns and some better pieces stand sentry from the sidelines of the board. Savage moves his mahogany knight in an unsuccessful attempt to pin Bishop's queen.

Bishop had suggested they play after their last reaping of a middle-aged man who passed from a heart attack alone in his home. Slowly, slowly working Savage's tolerance up from the most placid deaths to ones more violent. This one was a bit of a shock to Savage's system. It was the first sudden death he'd witnessed.

"You're thinking too little, kid. Chess is the long game." This is their third game, and Bishop has already beaten him twice. But Savage does feel better. Stretching the muscles of his brain and the quiet interaction have brought his heart rate down to a reasonable pace. The panic in his lungs has subsided.

"I guess I tend to get caught in the here and now," Savage says.

The coat that Savage has been wearing on reapings is draped over the arm of the couch. Savage didn't want to wear the same kind as Bishop, his gray one with its clerical collar. "I don't want to be your clone." Savage had insisted.

"You couldn't be my clone even if you wanted to. You're like seven feet tall."

So, he'd decided on a simple black overcoat over a black tee, despite Bishop's insistence that his "uniform" didn't need to be black. But the black had felt right.

"I have a question," Savage asks after a moment of quiet gameplay.

"Shoot."

"Why can't I talk or make any noise at the reapings?"

"You don't have the reaper voice yet."

"I don't understand."

"In the moments leading up to their death, the only thing the dying should hear from a reaper is their own name. It comes to me like . . . kind of like inspiration. Their name, their gateway. They already exist. I just tap into them when that moment of dying approaches. And if you were to speak, your human tongue still intact, I think it would be monumentally confusing."

"Hm." Savage ponders.

"I don't really know what would happen, honestly. As I've mentioned many-a-time, these are unprecedented circumstances. But I'm not going to find out, so it's best that you keep quiet until it's time for you to reap. *Check.*"

Bishop has Savage's king cornered.

"Shit." He makes a last-ditch effort to save the game as Bishop chases his futile king around the board for a while.

"And checkmate."

Savage hangs his head in defeat. "I surrender."

"You're getting better," Bishop says.

"Ha, you don't need to pander to me."

Bishop shrugs. "You are. Every day, you're getting better. Opening up those big baby browns." They reset the board. "Here." Bishop hands him the ivory bishop piece.

"Yes, you're the bishop. I get it."

"No, ass. Take it."

"Why?" Savage asks. He examines the piece, rubbing his thumb over the diagonal slit in the armor on the faceless head.

"For you. If you need me."

"I'm not sure I get it."

"I'm not always here. I can't always be with you. But if you need me, call me."

Savage blinks a moment in confusion. "What, talk into it like a phone?"

"No, Jesus, just touch it or hold it and think of me, and if you need me, I'll be there."

"That's sweet."

"Shut it."

"No really, I'm touched. I'm feeling a duet coming on." Savage hums the opening lines of "Islands in the Stream."

"So, now I'm Kenny Rogers?"

Savage shakes his head. "I'm Kenny."

"Pfft," Bishop scoffs.

"You're one hundred percent Dolly."

"Lies."

"I've never met another person who made me think to myself, 'If Dolly Parton were a scruffy, middle-aged dude . . .'"

"*Middle-aged?*"

"Middle-aged . . . *ish?*"

"You know, you're coming out of your shell kid, and I'm not sure I like it."

The tunnel smells of oil and stale urine. Savage recognizes they stayed local, this time. The New York subway system greets them as they blink into existence at the scene of the pending death.

They're at the end of the platform, where the discolored yellow tile gives way to the tunnel the trains emerge from. Here, a red sign sways in an unseen breeze, reading *STOP! Do not enter or cross the tracks.*

Red. When did he start taking red for granted? It crawls in unnoticed at every corner now. Here on this sign, there on the woman's red lips as she stumbles toward them.

There are only a few people scattered at the stop, waiting for a late-night train. But the young woman clicks her too-ambitious heels past the others over the yellow safety dots that line the edge of the platform.

She's a few yards away from Savage and Bishop now, and she thinks she's alone. But for the reapers in the shadows, she is.

She's eighteen or maybe twenty. Her face is rivers of mascara and despair. She wears a jacket of faux yeti fur, pale pink and fluffy and opened to reveal the tight dress underneath. Savage wonders how she isn't cold in the New York night.

She lets out a strangled sob, a sound so pitiful it reminds Savage of a dying animal.

"Why?" she asks no one. "Why?"

Savage remembers asking unanswered questions to invisible deities. Now, he is one. He's the one who listens.

The girl is pulling at her pink-dyed hair by its roots. She's lit from within with anguish and anger.

Bishop's hands are bare. He lights one of his black cigarettes and lets it hang from his lips, never dropping his gaze from their target.

Savage isn't sure he's ready for this. But he knows what's coming.

They wait.

She stumbles onward.

She's nearly at the end of the platform, where they stand. Where the train will come to meet them shortly, an old and expected friend.

The girl squats down in her misery, her bubblegum pink head in her hands. She lets out another scream of frustration and rubs the heels of her hands over her eyes like a crying child.

Savage hears it before he sees it. The train is coming. Waves of electricity scamper down the third rail in whispering whines. He hears the rumble, feels the deep vibrations emitted from the belly of the beast. Down the tunnel, the lights of the subway appear like animal eyes.

Savage's heart thumps in his chest. *No, no, no,* he thinks. He's second guessing everything. The other reapings were mostly peaceful and quiet. The souls went out like lone candles being swallowed by the darkness.

But this?

The girl cannot see them, and he cannot stop her.

She looks up from her hands, resolute. Her decision has been made.

Bishop says her name, in his deep and resonant voice. His reaper call. The voice that makes the hairs on the back of Savage's neck stand sentinel.

"MARINA."

The train approaches with a *clack-clack, clack-clack*. It stirs the air at first in a breeze and then in a gust, the wind pressing against Savage's nose and ears and eyes.

The girl hiccup-cries once more and stands, the wind whipping her hair around her face. She lets her heels fall off her feet. Her breath is shallow.

No, no, no . . . Savage repeats in his head. He's trembling in fear and impotence, his heart beating wildly beneath his broad chest. He stifles the urge to cry out. Tears well in his eyes, and he fights to remain silent.

The events unfold simultaneously in slow motion and in the blink of an eye.

When she spreads her arms out, her yeti coat falls from her shoulders to her wrists. In that moment, her face falls, and the peace of letting go overtakes her.

Bishop jumps to the rail. He stands, facing the train, pulling his bare hands from his pockets, cigarette pinched between his lips. As the girl leaps from the platform, Savage sees the eyes of the rail conductor grow wide in panic and shock as he pulls the emergency brake. It will be too late.

In that instant, Savage hopes the girl and the conductor will reach a better outcome. But he knows better.

The train lets out a squeal and a hiss as the operator attempts to stop.

Bishop spreads his hands out like a doctor helping a woman birth a babe, ready for the catch.

When the impact throws the girl back, Bishop has her in an instant, cradling her spirit in its violent finale.

Savage stifles a sob, looks down, and misses the rest.

Blink.
Flutter.
Flash.

The girl's gateway is a canyon, orange and brown and gaping.

A misted over sun denotes early morning, the rays long and the shadows longer. Bishop has gifted something unique to the girl. Not including the dormant gate of his parents, this is the first Savage has visited with music. A deep voice wails over tinkling piano notes. Savage doesn't recognize it at first, but it comes to him. It's Anohni's tragic ballad, "Hope There's Someone." In a late-night conversation in a dark bar, a fellow barfly had once described this album as the saddest in existence, and Savage had listened to it after.

It seems a great gift for the reaper to give the young woman this song, and Savage knows it must be of significance to her. But it kills him a little. It kills him right along with her. It's too goddamn perfect. He hopes if Marina ever wondered, like the writer of the song, she can now relish in the fact that she is not alone in death. That there is someone there to accompany her in the darkness.

Savage watches Bishop comfort the girl's spirit. She transforms from crestfallen panic to acceptance. Calm. Her breaths slow. Bishop holds her head in his hands, soothing her, speaking assuring words right into her face. The mascara streaks are fading. As the beautiful voice reaches a crescendo and the piano notes become fast and agitated, the tears flow backward and erase like reverse time-lapse footage.

She's nodding. She hears him.

But there's no reversal of Savage's tears. They flow down his face and drop to the desert floor beneath his black shoes.

The song builds and swells.

All around them, the chorus of voices echo in a haunting harmony.

It takes everything within Savage to contain himself, to stay silent, but breathing is work. Air comes into his lungs in stifled and shuddering bursts as he submits to his emotion. He's a grown man but he stands alone and vulnerable as a child. It's everything he can do to remain soundless.

He watches as Death enfolds the girl. She craved his company, and he abides in ample form. Her pale fingers spread out over Bishop's dark coat as she returns his embrace.

As the song comes to its end, hand in hand, Bishop and the girl walk to the edge of the canyon.

Jesus, not again, Savage thinks.

They look at each other and nod. Both are smiling and calm. They jump from the edge and out of Savage's sight. He doesn't see what happens when they leap, whether they float or drop like stones. He only knows that they are gone. He's left alone in the gateway of the girl, in all its orange splendor.

He lets his sobs free of his chest and gasps.

"Fuck," he says to no one.

He palms his face. Rubs his crying eyes. He feels like he is trapped forever in this moment, in the terrible beauty of it. The chords of music are still resounding in his ears. The sun hangs unnatural and unmoving. And the desolate canyon spreads out before him, so like the hole inside that is splitting him in twain.

There is nothing.

"*Fuck,*" Savage calls out, his voice echoing and ricocheting through the gateway. He's a lone splotch of black ink on the cracked desert floor.

But the moment ends, and Bishop appears beside him. Savage could swear there are remnants of tears in Death's own eyes.

"Hi friend," he says as he gives Savage's shoulder a pat.

Savage doesn't respond for a moment. "That was," Savage takes in a big gasp of air, sniffs his tears back, and steadies his voice, "that was beautiful."

Bishop nods. "Thank you."

"It's strange. I have a hard time finding that level of beauty in the world, and I didn't expect to find it here."

"I want you to remember that," Bishop says, squeezing his shoulder. "It's very important you remember that, okay?" There's a gravity to the reaper's voice.

Savage doesn't question him. "Okay."

Green-wood hangs its trees overhead like curtains for the privacy of the dead.

Savage is kneeling against the trunk of one, graves scattered nearby. He has his sketchbook open against his knee as he captures the scene before him on the pages within.

Bishop has left him to his own devices, off handling Bishop-only business, and Savage is using this time to process.

Savage has witnessed the reaping of a woman in a sudden car crash, distracted by her own reflection in the rear-view mirror, and that of a construction worker who'd fallen to his death. He's seen an old person slip in the shower and a single man choke on a chicken bone alone in his apartment. But the subway suicide has stayed with him the longest.

She was a fucking kid, he thinks as he sketches the little white headstones that stick out from the ground like nubby teeth chewing the morning. Bishop had told him afterward that it was a privilege to age. He thinks of the young woman and how she abandoned that privilege. "To live a life" Bishop had said "rich and full of mistakes and anger and knowledge and heartache, and hopefully, *hopefully,* some joy: it's a privilege. Not everyone gets sixty, seventy, eighty years. Some get robbed. Some rob themselves. And you were almost one of them. That young woman chose to give it up. And she'll never know what a gift time is."

Time. It used to feel like the machine he was trapped in but now . . . he feels it stirring in his cells. It moves through his blood and bones. He feels some ancient connection to the universe deep within him. He wonders what will happen to his mortality now. Will he still experience the gift of death, or has he sacrificed that with his new vocation?

Questions for another day. He closes the sketchbook and stands, breathing in the crisp morning. He slips the book into the big pocket of his overcoat, his fingers brushing past the ivory bishop piece. He marvels for a minute at the sun rising over the tops of the trees before he turns back to the pathway that leads to the mausoleum.

Savage once visualized himself as an agent of death; all the hours spent in the lab waiting for the go-ahead from management to cull assorted species of rodents on any given day. But now . . . he sees the lack of grace in how he handled this task. Death is Bishop's art. His creation from destruction. It's the vessel with which he creates his beauty. Savage was just a pied piper without a flute.

A cockroach scampers past his feet on the dirt pathway.

Savage hasn't earned his gloves yet, hasn't handled an actual reaping. But Bishop says he should be ready soon, which seems an outlandish thought. How will he eschew someone to the afterlife? How will he know how to craft a gateway? He doesn't even know what happens after the gateway, what the afterlife looks like. Savage shakes his head at the thought.

Another cockroach crosses the path in front of him.

Then another.

A fourth.

Savage glances to the grass that borders the path. He gasps in disgust. "What the shit?"

A mound of the insects is moving like a brown boulder beside him.

Down at his feet, they are closing in around his shoes. He jerks his head back up, and the entirety of the graveyard around him is crawling and undulating like a brown sea with millions of cockroaches.

There's a terrible clicking as the insects quiver over one another, each struggling to get to the top of the heap.

They are crawling over his ankles and up the legs of his pants. They make their way up his body, up the length of his coat.

He shoves his hand into his pocket and fetches the bishop chess piece.

"Bishop! Bishop! Fucking Bishop!"

No answer.

He grunts in frustration and tries to brush the insects off him, but they are everywhere. He runs over their blackness, each footfall landing with a sickening crunch.

The creatures are climbing up the headstones and monuments, up the walls of mausoleums, up the trunks of trees.

"*Bishop,*" he yells as he runs, the piece still clutched in his hand.

He sees the mausoleum marked Smithe and runs for it at breakneck speed. He has to reach through a tangle of antennae and legs to access the handle to the great iron door, brushing his long hands over the many shells. He pushes his way inside and slams the gate shut behind him.

The moment he flicks on the light to the quarters he shares with Bishop, the reaper appears.

"What, kid?"

"Cockroaches. *Fucking cockroaches,*" Savage gasps.

"What?" Bishop looks confused.

Savage grimaces and opens the door to show the reaper what has become of the world outside. But the cockroaches are gone. "Wh-what the hell . . ."

"You called me for a bug? I'm not your exterminator. Well, I'm sort of *an* exterminator. Just not *your* exterminator." Bishop chuckles at himself.

"No, Bishop, not just a bug. Swarms of them. Millions of them. *Everywhere.* Trying to consume me. Trying to consume everything. But they're all fucking gone now."

"Ahh . . . that's not so good." Bishop is serious now, poking his head out the door and scanning the grounds.

"What? What's not so good?"

Bishop closes the door. "Cockroaches. They're sort of Devlin's domain."

"What does that mean? Devlin wants to kill me with roaches?"

"No, not kill. Just freak out. Or spy. Probably both."

"What, why?" Savage shakes his head. "Why does Devlin even care about me? Or even know who I am?"

"Dunno. I try to avoid getting too far into the head of the devil."

Savage sits on the couch, still catching his breath. He clears his throat. "Speculate."

"He probably knows you're my apprentice-slash-wingman-slash-friend." Bishop checks under the coffee table, under the couch. "Probably jealous. Our kind aren't supposed to have contact with humans, which is a rule he's definitely tried to bend on many occasions, to no avail." He lifts the cushions on the couch, checking under each one. "But see, you're not just any human. And I didn't find you, you found me. The particulars of how are still fuzzy to me, but hey, I've got a laissez-faire mentality when it comes to the living." The reaper sighs, accepting the absence of any roaches inside, and drops the last cushion back on the sofa. "You ready for a reaping?"

"Now?"

"I can't very well leave you alone, and that was what I was doing before the cockroach catastrophe. It's probably what I should resume doing now. These are delicately timed events, see. You might as well come." Bishop turns to Savage and looks him squarely in the eye. "I have to warn you though. We're not in easy territory now."

"What does that mean?" Savage asks, his back stiffening. "Worse than the girl and the subway?"

"Yeah." Bishop nods. "Worse."

EIGHT

A woman is crying on the ground. Her wrists are fettered to handles bolted into the concrete floor, and her fists are tied closed around two wooden staffs. She's naked, save for a piece of purple cloth draped around her groin and hips. Her mouth is gagged, and her eyes are wide with terror as she tries to glimpse the man in the mask.

The man isn't looking at her; his hands are busy with a different task. He's humming to himself under his breath as he situates a large green wreath around her body. His hands are covered in black latex gloves, and he wears two masks: a tight black ski mask that covers most of his face, and a bone white mask with brown rams' horns covering his eyes and nose and forehead. His lips and nostrils are all that are visible.

Savage feels his heart jump. *Jesus Christ, what've I gotten myself into,* he thinks. He thinks but does not say.

He looks around. They're in a garage, or perhaps a storage unit. There are no windows, and one of the walls houses a large rolling door. There isn't much here. An old table. A small ladder against one of the walls. An intense heat is coming off three large lights which are pointed down at the woman's naked form.

Bishop has been studying the scene intently. He looks angry, his nostrils flared, as he paces slowly, following the man in his circuit around the woman.

The man in the mask finishes placing the wreath around her body and stands erect. He's tall, broad-chested. Much larger than the petite woman on the floor. Savage knows the man likely had little trouble subduing her.

The masked man claps his long hands together like he's satisfied with the task and exhales. He raises his finger in an *aha* motion and grabs a black trash bag from the nearby table. From within, he withdraws a grisly surprise—the head of a cow, bloody and dripping.

The woman's eyes go impossibly wider, and she tugs at her restraints, whimpering. The masked man places the cow's head below the woman's left foot, outside the perimeter of the wreath. She grunts and tugs, but it's futile.

The masked man takes out another treat—the head of a bobcat. Congealed blood drips from the beast as he places it to the right of the woman's feet.

Bishop takes in a big breath and glances to Savage. He nods to him, checking in. *Are you okay?* his eyes ask.

Savage gives a quick nod. He's not sure he's okay, but there's nothing he can do about it. He's as impotent as a shadow, fettered by the very thing that enables him to bear witness to the crime.

Bishop removes his black leather gloves from his fingers,

one by one.

A glimmer of hope crosses Savage's mind. He doesn't know who they're here for. Perhaps the woman will break free and attack the man. Perhaps they're here to reap his heinous soul, and she'll be saved. Perhaps.

The man places a taxidermic eagle's head to the right of the woman's own. It looks like it was ripped from its body long after it had been stuffed. The woman begins to hyperventilate at the proximity of the man. He leans over her, his masked face a foot from hers, and lifts his finger to his lips. "Shhh . . ." he hushes. Spit has soaked the gag at her mouth, and she takes in a deep, rasping inhale.

The man goes back to the bag for one more item. He pulls from its depths a dismembered human head. The head once belonged to a man with long blond hair, and the masked man holds it by the flaxen strands. The woman screams beneath her gag and yanks at the manacles on her wrists. They won't budge. They cut into her skin, and her wrists begin to bleed.

He places the last head to the left of the woman's face, so the four heads surround her like the corners of a frame. The man nods again, satisfied.

When he pulls the knife out of its holder on his belt, Savage pushes his fist into his face to keep from speaking. Or cursing. Or crying. He pants behind his hand, his knuckles pressing into his nostrils and lips. Something in him breaks, and he feels everything inside him, every single emotion, turn to hate. To anger.

He glares at the man in the mask.

Fucking coward, he thinks, *you can't even show your fucking face*. He takes a step toward the soon-to-be murderer. He studies his clothing, the shape of his mouth beneath the ski mask, his dark eyes. *You fucking Zodiac knock-off,* he thinks. Savage is disgusted at the pitiful creature before him. Disgusted, but oddly drawn in, like a moth to a flame. But Savage is smarter than a moth, and he knows contact with this flame means death. The man sniffs in from behind his mask, swallowing down some snot at the back of his throat. His breath is quickening. He's excited. He's in his own fucked-up land of make believe, and it's making him high.

Bishop lights a cigarette with his silver lighter. He kneels beside the woman. His face drips with empathy. He's not focused on the masked man anymore, but Savage can't draw his attention away.

Bishop lays down on the floor next to the woman, ear to the ground, focused squarely on her as she lies drowning in her terror.

The masked man straddles the woman's thighs. He holds the knife in both hands.

"**TERRA**," Bishop exhales in his reaper voice.

When the man raises the knife for the first blow, Bishop places his bare hand onto Terra's naked belly. Her soul breaks free as the masked man plunges the knife into her body. Bishop took her a moment early and spared her the pain.

In a blink, they're gone. Off in a swirl of smoke and shadow and onto Terra's gateway for safe escort to her afterlife.

Savage blinks in confusion. He's still here. Still in the garage with Not-Zodiac and Terra's naked body.

The killer stabs her again. And again. And again.

Savage should be concerned as to why he is still here, why he wasn't whisked away with Bishop at the passing like in every other reaping he has attended. But he's entranced. He winces with each blow of the knife to the dead woman's body.

Savage counts twenty-one times. Fucking overkill.

By the end, Savage is shaking. In fury. In shock. He can't discern one emotion from the other at the moment.

After the twenty-first blow, the killer stands. He's sweating and breathless. Depleted. He rubs his fingers under his mask over his brow and wipes the sweat away. Savage leans in for a glimpse at his face, but the killer moves too fast.

Savage, in his rage, is fascinated. *Who the fuck do you think you are?* He eyes the man, stalking him like a puma eyeing prey. How entitled of a man to think he has a right to someone else's life.

The man situates Terra's body, moving her feet a little to straighten her, repositioning the purple cloth about her waist. When he's satisfied, he grabs the small ladder from its place against a wall. He props it open below Terra's feet and takes an old 35 mm camera from the table. Savage recognizes it as an Olympus Pen. The man loads film into its chamber and clicks it shut. He climbs up the ladder and looks down to the scene, snapping a few pictures.

Good god, Savage thinks, disgusted. The man climbs down, inches the ladder over, and climbs back up, starting anew. When he's finished, he climbs down again and replaces the ladder. He turns off each of the lights.

In a coil of shadow, Bishop reappears. He's squinting at Savage, dubious. Maybe angry. Savage's eyes go wide. Bishop gives him a distinct *What-the-fuck?* look.

Savage shakes his head and shrugs. *I don't know,* he silently replies.

The man hits a switch on the wall, and the big garage door draws open.

Now re-gloved, Bishop takes Savage's hand within his own and they blink away from the murder scene.

"Kid," Bishop starts. "What the ever-living hell was that?"

"You tell me."

"What?"

"I'm just along for the ride," Savage says. "I have literally no idea what I'm doing or how to control anything. I'm completely at your whim."

They're walking down the worn pathway to the Smithe mausoleum. The sun is setting, casting long shadows around the cemetery.

"All I know is one minute we're at the death, and the next, here I am at Terra's gateway with no Savage anywhere in sight."

"I don't know what to tell you. I'm sorry."

"Look, I know that was a lot," Bishop says, turning to Savage. "I *know*. That was a reaping of the most violent and shocking kind. It doesn't get much worse than that." He sighs. "Maybe it was just a shock to your system?"

"Well . . . yeah, it was shocking," Savage says, throwing his hands up in confusion.

"Aside from the obvious, was that different for you in some way?"

Savage thinks. "Yes. Normally I'm fixated on the dying. But

this time . . . I haven't seen someone take someone else's life before. It took everything within me not to react. To not will myself corporeal and kill the killer before he could hurt her."

"Maybe your fixation on the killer pulled your attention from the reaping and kept you there." Bishop sighs again, blowing his breath out through pursed lips. "Try and focus on the dying next time. Even if someone is taking their life."

Savage nods. "I'll try."

When they reach the mausoleum, they discover the raven-headed reaper, Rook, sitting in the grass, his big eyes like obsidian marbles in his crow head.

His black suit looks out of place in his current position, his legs splayed out straight like a bored toddler, propping himself up on gloved hands.

"What's up, little Rook?"

The great crow cocks his head, speaking silent words only Bishop can hear.

"No, I don't know," Bishop replies to the inaudible question.

He unlocks the door of the tomb. Rook stands and dusts off his suit as they enter.

The two reapers sit in the far corner of the large sectional sofa.

Savage busies himself by looking at the bookshelves filled with their identical occupants, walking his fingers over their spines. He doesn't pull any of the notebooks out. He's not sure he's allowed.

The killing is flashing before his eyes in surreal detail. *Why*, he wonders, *did that look familiar?* Something so obvious is evading his mental grasp, like déjà vu or a forgotten dream.

He walks over to Bishop's collection of vinyl. The reaper has an expansive assortment, with an entire wall of shelving devoted to it. He clearly prefers jazz and blues, but there's a fair amount of classical, and a lot of classic rock. Pink Floyd. Lynyrd Skynyrd. The Who. Savage pulls out Led Zeppelin's *Three* to peek at the cover before sliding it back into place.

Bishop and Rook seem to confer without words, although every so often, Bishop exclaims something audible.

"What? . . . no, no, no . . . that's not part of this . . . dammit . . . alright, alright, alright. I'll go talk to her." He turns to Savage, calling across the room. "Wanna go to Greece?"

"Uh, sure? For a reaping?"

"Not exactly. Not yet."

A loaded moon hangs low in the sky over an ink black sea. Its reflection is as brilliant as the moon itself, so there are two moons this night. Savage finds himself walking a dusty road along the harbor in Crete, following Bishop's dark silhouette as they make their way up a hill.

"Stubborn. Ass. Muse," Bishop says to himself with each step. "She's done something with the space around this place to keep me from narrowing in on her exact location," he mutters. "Absolutely *inspired* . . ."

"How'd she do that?"

Bishop shrugs. "I dunno. But if it were time for her reaping, it'd be a different set of circumstances. No one can hide when their time comes."

Savage doesn't mind. He has a moment to enjoy the new locale. The night blanches the Grecian landscape, turning it shades of black and gray and white. Giving it a sameness only night can bestow, as if it is any other place he has been. Though Greece is new to him—hell, he's never crossed an ocean before—it feels familiar in that way that night always feels familiar. He pulls a deep breath into his lungs. It smells simultaneously new and ancient, dusty and ripe, and Savage wishes he could see it in sunlight, wishes he could marvel at the colors of another country with his newly opened eyes.

At the top of the hill, they approach a form in the darkness. As they come closer, it becomes clearer: a large throne, carved of stone and crumbling. They draw nearer until Savage can make out the details of the radiant creature who sits upon it.

She emits a small glow in the low light, vaguely purple in the darkness. Her dark arms rest on the throne, and the top of her corkscrewed hair is coated in dust. Her gown is faded from age, riddled with tears, and fraying at the seams.

As they approach, Bishop stands before her. Savage follows behind a bit, not wanting to interfere with whatever this is.

The muse's head is held high with its crown of dusty hair. Her eyes are distant as if looking to something far in the past or future but seeing nothing of the present. Not seeing Bishop as he stands before her.

"Verity," Bishop says softly. He leans in and places his gloved hands on her shoulders. "Verity," he says again, at eye level.

"It is not the time nor the place for your company, Dark One," Verity says to Bishop, eyes still distant, tone flat. "But my time in your domain fast approaches."

"Do you know why I've come?" he asks.

"The muses, my daughters, my sisters, they worry for my wellbeing. They fear I have gone too long without seeking any sustenance or sound."

"Mmhm," he says. "That seems like a valid concern."

"They bring me scraps . . ." she says weakly. "Little morsels of art and music. Just enough," she sighs. "Just enough to keep me. To force me to stay myself and not to turn to darkness." Her eyes still look past Bishop, unfocused. "Do you know why I have starved myself all these centuries?"

"No," he says. "I don't."

"I have been fasting. I have deprived myself of the mediocrity of the modern world to wait for the new renaissance. I became learned in the ways of the Oracles. The divining spirits bequeathed unto me the ability to glean facts from near and distant futures. With this gift, I had a vision of a world so replete with sound and glory, even the untrained eye or ear would orgasm in exaltation. But that rhapsody appears to have been a farce.

"We are arriving at our end, Dark One. We have spent these many eons allowing this beatific universe to swirl around itself, and it is fast approaching its descent into the void." She takes a deep breath. "I have fasted too long and now I lack the energy required to make any changes to the fate of our known land."

She speaks with such reverence for language, it's as if she folds the words into origami with her lips and teeth and tongue. Savage is certain at any moment she'll exhale, and a small paper crane will fly free of her mouth.

Verity blinks, arduously, for the first time since they have been in her presence. Bishop leans closer, his nose inches from her face.

"I fear for you," she says to Bishop, seeing him for the first time. She lifts her hand to the reaper's patchy beard. "The souls of the dead will not be yours to ferry to their destination." Her eyes are tearing up, her once flat voice now charged with emotion and breaking. "I fear for you, Ancient One. I fear the Knave will succeed, and this land, all your work, will have been for naught." She blinks. Great dams of tears burst and leak down her face, taking a coat of dust with them as they go. She shudders as she inhales.

"Who's there?" she asks, glimpsing Savage's shadow in the moonlight for the first time, sniffing the night like a wolf. "Wh-what strange art is this?" She breathes. "You taste ancient, child. Your faculties are like none I have ever known."

"Thank you?" Savage responds, daunted.

She gasps. A look crosses her face that is caught somewhere between epiphany and guarded fury. "It is not a compliment. It is an obligation. I cannot tell for how long you have sat as idly as myself, but it smells like millennia." She spits the words at him. She straightens and extends as she speaks to him. "You have the capability to use your potency for the good of your kind as well as my own, and you must do everything that is within your power to rage your art into the coming night. This is not a request. It is a fact I foresee as plainly as I see your naked lack of esteem.

"When you wake from your resounding slumber, your position in this universe will be made clear to you, and you will have to adjudicate whether your dalliance with the world of the fleshed was enough to remind you of the beauty you have created and are capable of creating, still.

"For it is your past self you have always passed judgment upon, when it should only be your future."

Savage opens his mouth to speak but words fail him. He doesn't know how to respond to her outburst, and Bishop looks back at him, eyes wide with surprise.

"Verity?" he says, turning back to her.

She blinks, heavily now, like she is staving off sleep. "Yes, Ancient Bishop. You may return to reap my soul, but it is not this night and not this time. I have found the virility to pursue another endeavor and another day. I have few ambitions I shall enterprise to complete in this life. The first of which is to appreciate the full moon's cautious dance on the sea."

At this, Bishop nods. "I'll meet you at another night and another time, my friend," he says to her as he starts back down the hill.

"Pilgrim," she calls to Savage.

He and Bishop both turn back to the crumbling muse on her crumbling throne.

"You have the ability to reconcile your past. It lies in your future."

Savage says nothing but takes these words with him like a sack of rocks to carry on his back, all the way down the hill. All the way home. All the way.

NINE

"What do you think of artists like Joel-Peter Witkin and Jan Saudek?" Savage asks Felicity.

"I see value in all art," she replies.

They're seated across from one another at one of the chess tables in Washington Square Park, but they're not playing. Savage warms his hands with a coffee he bought from a cart near the entrance, and he's studying Felicity as she studies a street performer.

"That's not an answer," he says.

"It is entirely an answer," she says, eyes flicking to him from the street performer. She arches one manicured eyebrow at him.

The performer is a woman, face painted white with large blue tears down her cheeks. When someone places a tip in her bucket, she springs to life in slow, silent performance, like a marionette without strings.

"It's a bull-shit-muse-answer. Of course, you see value in

all art. That's, like, your job description." Savage takes a sip of coffee.

Felicity tilts her head at him.

Savage has been left to his own devices, once again. The murder was a lot to take, and he has discovered wandering the streets of New York helps him process. He'd accidentally discovered Felicity here in the park, as if his natural compass has her for true north.

"I want to know how you feel about it, personally," he says. "Does that kind of macabre controversial photography appeal to you?"

She draws in a big thoughtful breath. "It's not my favorite."

"Aha. So, you have favorites."

"Of course, I do. I told you that. I told you how much I loved the abstracts when we were looking at the Pollock . . ." Her voice trails off. Savage remembers Pollock and his *Autumn Rhythm* and how it played silent witness to their intimacy. "Why do you ask?"

"I—" Savage stumbles over how to start. "We were at a reaping the other day. A murder." He shakes his head as the memory chases goosebumps over his skin.

"Murder isn't my forte," she says.

"I know. But the murderer . . . he positioned the victim in a very, *very* specific way. Like he was trying to convey a message. Or, more . . . like he was crafting a diorama. And when he was done, he photographed it."

Felicity looks from the white-faced woman to him and grimaces. "That's unsettling."

"Yes." Savage nods. "It was. It is . . ."

A child walks up to the performer's bucket and places a

dollar within. The woman mutely smiles and plucks a flower from behind her ear, offering it to the little girl, who claps with glee.

"The thing is, I always loved that kind of dark, unsettling photography, like Witkin. Like Saudek. It resonated with me. I ended up becoming more of a sketch artist and sometime painter, but I had a whole period in my teens where I was really into photography like that."

"So, what are you grappling with?"

"I'm not sure."

"Savage, enjoying dark artwork isn't the same as a murderer photographing the scene of a crime."

"That's not what I mean . . . of all the reapings to witness . . . of all the murders, it just seems odd that that was my first one. One that seemed like it was specifically crafted to appeal to my aesthetic."

"Witnessing your first murder would likely stay with you regardless."

"That's not everything."

"Oh?"

"The way he positioned the woman's body, the props he used . . . it all seemed very familiar. It took me a couple days, but I figured out why." He pushes back the sleeve of his coat, revealing his tattooed forearm. "These are tarot cards," he says.

"I'm familiar. The major and minor arcana have spawned a great deal of wonderful artwork."

"The murder . . . it was staged to look like *The World*. I mean, *The World* tarot card. I don't have that one tattooed on me, but that's what he was going for." He lets his coat sleeve fall back over his arm. "The woman's name was *Terra* for Christ's sake. I think he chose her on purpose because she was earth. Her name literally meant earth."

Felicity stares at him intently, biting at the inside of her lips. Savage finds she's especially beautiful when concerned. "It's just coincidence, Savage."

"Her name?"

"No, the entire tarot card vignette."

"Yeah . . ."

"Like I said, the arcana have inspired a great deal of artwork, but clearly, they've also inspired some madness. The tarot doesn't belong to you."

"I know."

She places her hand on his. "You can't own that man's mania. Just because he shares some similarities. He's not you." Her long delicate fingers gently stroke his skin.

He squints at her. "How did you know what I was thinking?"

She slides her fingers from his. "Just . . . what you said. The inference was clear."

"I know he's not me . . . but he feels so close it's . . . unsettling. I don't want to be in his head."

"Then don't be in his head." She stands and moves her long auburn hair over one shoulder. "C'mon," she says. "Let's go."

"Where?" He tosses his coffee cup in the trash.

"It looks like it's going to be a beautiful day, and you haven't seen the High Line yet."

The street performer finishes her dance and stands still once more.

Nighttime in The Village smells like baking waffle cones and rotting garbage, freshly lit cigarettes and cheap weed. Felicity had abandoned him after an afternoon spent wandering the High Line. She claimed to have to tend to one of her artists, but Savage suspected she was instilling a boundary. Like she was enjoying his company too much and needed a break to clear him from her head, to wash the taste of him down with something else. Something mild.

The whole neighborhood feels like honey, dim and lit with amber lights. The city has gotten cold, and Savage turns his collar to the early spring night. He zigzags back and forth for blocks until he finds what he's looking for.

The sign over the awning of a little shop reads, *Familiars: New Age Shop & Fortune Telling*. Chimes ring overhead when he opens the door.

A woman in her late forties is leaning behind the counter, her face in a book. "Hello," she says warmly, tipping her head up.

"Hi. Uh, do you sell tarot cards?"

"Sure do. There's a handful of different options over on that shelf. We're sold out of that Wild Unknown brand that's so popular right now, but I do have one of those dope David Bowie decks left."

"Actually," he steps toward her, "I'm looking for a classic deck, with the original art." He pulls up the sleeve of his jacket, exposing his tattoo. "The Rider-Waite deck."

"Rider-Waite-*Smith*," she corrects. "History has ignored

the female POC artist for too long." She steps out from behind the counter and pulls a deck from the display. "After all these years, it's still the go-to standard when it comes to tarot," she says, handing it to him.

"Thanks," he says, taking the deck and rubbing his thumb over the yellow image on the front. "This is all I need."

The woman takes the deck in hand and walks to the register. "I could break these in for you?"

"You mean a reading? It's okay, I really just need them for the artwork."

"C'mon, it's bad luck to have a set and never use them for a reading." She glances at the silver watch on her left wrist. "I'm closing soon, anyway. I wouldn't even charge ya for it."

Since Savage has time to kill, he shrugs and acquiesces.

The woman goes to the door and turns the sign from *open* to *closed for a reading*.

She reaches her hand out to Savage. "I'm Terra."

Savage goes cold.

She senses his sudden shift in energy. "What did I say?" she asks, her hand still outstretched.

"Nothing, nothing." He shakes his head. *Just a coincidence.* "I just met another Terra is all."

"Oh, ha." She waves her hand at him, turning to the little table at the back of the shop. "I meet other Terras all the time. Once you hear it once, y'know ... what do they call that? Bader Meinhof?"

"What?" he asks, following her lead and sitting at the table.

"Y'know, the Bader Meinhof Phenomenon. When you hear a fact or name for the first time and then hear it over and over again. Most people in my field would call it *synchronicity*."

She breaks the seal on Savage's new cards and tosses the plastic film away. "Here. Shuffle."

Savage takes the proffered cards and absentmindedly shuffles them between his hands.

"You visiting?" she asks.

"Yeah . . . indefinitely, it seems."

"Well, welcome. Don't let the world at large put the wrong idea in your head about New Yorkers. We're mostly pretty decent people."

"I came from Las Vegas, so I'm used to living in a tourist-trap city."

"Mm." She nods, taking the deck from him. "Then I suspect we'll see lots of change and transition in your spread. But you probably already know all about that." She gestures to his arm where Death, The Sun, and The Hanged Man live.

Savage shrugs. In truth, he didn't get the tarot tattooed on him because he was familiar with the practice or because he believed in divination. He got it because the art was compelling to him. Because the characters who lived in the deck called to him like old friends. He feels somewhat silly for misnaming the deck and not realizing he was omitting the artist before.

"Alright, let's see what we've got." She flips over the first card. It's blank. "What . . ." She flips over another one. Blank. A third. Blank. Her eyes go wide, and her hands freeze over the cards.

"Is the deck misprinted?" Savage asks.

She looks up at him through her heavy brow. "You need to leave."

"What? I'm sorry, did I do something?"

"Take these with you and go."

"But I haven't paid for them."

She draws in a deep breath, like she's furious or terrified. "Look, I don't know what you're playing at or who you are, but the only other time I've seen anything like this was when I tried to give a reading to those glassy-eyed freaks on Cornelia Street."

"What glassy-eyed freaks on Cornelia—"

"*Leave*," she yells. "Get out of my shop."

Savage scoops up the cards and flees. The chimes ring over head as he steps out into the night.

He walks a bit, looking back over his shoulder at the shop until he can't see it anymore. He's back at Washington Square Park where he started his day. He flips over the cards in the deck as he walks, one by one. They're all there. The swords and wands and cups. The knights and queens and pages. The Hierophant. The Fool. The Chariot. None of the cards is blank, not one.

"What the fuck . . ." he thinks aloud.

He stands under a streetlamp and shuffles through until he finds The World. It features a naked woman wrapped in a length of blueish purple fabric, a staff in each hand. She's surrounded by a wreath with the heads of a man, eagle, lion, and ox at each corner. Savage swallows hard, thinking of the murder. The number of the card is twenty-one.

The killer had stabbed Terra twenty-one times.

The block near the park is quiet. He glances up and spies the large white arch at the center of the square, lit from underneath and glowing in the darkness. He walks onward, placing the deck back in its box and pocketing it.

The park is calm, its daily allotment of visitors already

reached. A couple walks a corgi. A teenager rides a skateboard through the center of the square.

The hairs on the back of Savage's neck stand upright. He's being watched. With all the madness he's adapting to, he's not sure if it's friend or foe who stalks him now.

He glances over his shoulder and spots the twin white cotton-candy heads of the Oracles sitting side by side on a park bench. He suspects they were there before but only made themselves known to him in that moment. He crosses the park to them.

"Are you the glassy-eyed-freaks on Cornelia Street?" he asks them.

The Oracles don't answer. Or blink or look at him. They look past him. They look *through* him.

He takes the deck of cards from his pocket. "Can you tell me why these turned blank when someone tried to give me a reading?"

Neither oracle takes the cards. They don't even look at the deck.

One begins, "Your future is—"

"Unknown," the other finishes.

He looks down at the cards and replaces them in his pocket. "Isn't everyone's?"

"No," they reply in tandem, taking turns after that.

"Others make decisions and their futures change."

"Malleable."

"Moldable."

"Your future is—"

"Unpredictable," they say together.

"Unprecedented."

"Unknowable."

"What does that mean?" he asks, tucking a wayward strand of hair behind his ear. The night seems to darken a shade or two.

"We cannot predict what we cannot predict," they say. They're holding one another's star-spotted hands.

Savage sighs. He doesn't know what to do with that.

"It will become clear to you in time," one says, answering his unasked question.

"It is only unclear to us."

"And the rest of the universe."

Somehow, this doesn't make Savage feel better.

"A gift," Bishop says. He passes Savage a pair of black leather gloves across the table of the diner they're eating in.

"It's time?" Savage asks.

"I think so. You finished your BLT, yeah?"

He hadn't, but his appetite ran away the second he saw the gloves and understood their implication. "It's now?"

Bishop nods. "Now."

"I don't . . . I don't know what to do?"

"It's okay, don't overthink it. It's not a pretty scene—it'll be a double reaping—but that means I'll be right there with you for the other soul."

Savage takes a breath and nods. "Okay. Let's go."

A swirl of smoke and the pair leaves naught but a memory in New York.

They reappear miles and miles away. A different time in a different climate. The sun is so bright, it mutes out everything else for a moment until Savage's eyes adjust.

A man and a woman are naked, each tied to their own gnarled tree. The trees are about five yards apart, and the pair are angled so they face one another.

Joshua trees, Savage thinks flatly. They must be somewhere near his old life in Vegas. Savage knows Joshua trees are only indigenous to the Mojave Desert. The sun is high in the sky, and a thin sheen of sweat coats the man's brow and upper lip.

They are both gagged, and the man is struggling against his bonds, fighting to free his hands. His feet kick under him, stirring a cloud of desert dust.

The woman is unconscious.

A third figure is at a nearby parked car, his head buried as he rummages in the popped trunk. There is nothing but Joshua trees for miles, their strange spindly arms outstretched to the desert sky like hands in hallelujah. The man at the car finds what he's looking for, stands, and turns back to the couple. His head is covered in a black ski mask with a white ram demon mask over the top half of his face.

"F—" . . . *uck*, Savage starts to say but finishes mentally. He bites down hard on his lips.

Bishop turns to him, eyes wide. He shakes his head, silently communicating, *I didn't know.*

Savage shakes his head back at him. *It's okay.* He needs to overcome his preoccupation with this killer. He needs to focus on the dying and not the murderer, and there will be no better exercise in that practice than with the same killer who stole his attention before.

The Tarot Card Killer's hands are once again covered in black latex gloves, and Savage knows what those terrible hands can do. They are black holes at the end of his arms, those hands. Things that steal and swallow.

Cradled within his hands, the masked killer holds a large coiling green snake, pinching it behind its diamond shaped head. The snake holds its mouth agape, frozen in anger from being handled in such a manner.

Savage doesn't know what kind of snake it is, but he suspects nothing good can come of this. He runs his gloved hands angrily over his head, unused to the feel of the leather gliding over his hair.

Bishop gestures to the fettered man and then to Savage. *You take care of the man,* he means. Then he nods to the woman and puts his hand to his own chest. *I'll take the woman.*

Savage nods, understanding, and walks over to the man, kneels beside him. He can smell his terror. It's metallic and robust at once, like blood and body odor, metal and salt.

Focus on the man, focus on the man, Savage repeats to himself. He studies him. His hair is wavy and brown, his eyes blue. He's young, early twenties. Maybe not old enough to buy booze, yet. Not old enough to die. The least Savage can hope to give him is a peaceful transition.

The killer approaches the unconscious woman and lays the snake over her naked body. She stirs under the animal's weight.

Fucking focus, he tells himself.

Bishop kneels beside her. He removes his gloves and pulls a cigarette from the pack.

Fuck, Bishop didn't give Savage any of the death sticks. He feels around in his pocket and finds a pack of the black and red unlabeled cigarettes live there, next to a lighter, and the ivory bishop piece. He sighs. At least he's prepared in one way.

The woman rouses to the snake coiling its way over her breast. She gasps in terror and tries to wriggle out from under it. She lets out a muffled scream and twists her body from under the reptile, trying to throw it from her. The snake, already incensed, doesn't appreciate her movement. It hisses, recoiling its face from the woman's. She screams through her gag again, and the snake strikes at her with venomous fangs, once. Twice. She cries out in pain and terror.

The young man pulls, pulls, pulls against the ropes that bind him. He leans all his weight against his wrists, hoping something will break and his hands will slip free. He grunts in pain.

The Tarot Card Killer looks from the woman to the man, cocking his head, perturbed. He shakes his head in silent admonishment.

Bishop exhales a breath of black smoke into the woman's face as he places his hand on her cheek and says, "**EVE**."

Eve's spirit and the reaper curl away into a ring of smoke and are gone from this plane.

Right, Savage thinks. *Our turn next.*

The killer is staring at the woman's dying body. Savage sees him take the same old camera from a pocket and kneel to take a picture. When the killer stands, he goes back to the trunk of the car and removes a large plastic bottle before returning.

Savage realizes it's a bottle of lighter fluid.

Don't look at that fucker, look at the kid, Savage thinks. The young man is sobbing quietly under the acceptance of the futility at trying to escape.

The killer begins to squirt the contents of the bottle over his body. The young man squints as some of the fluid gets into his eyes, blinking hard from the burn.

Savage fights his anger, knowing anger isn't the emotion that will help him now. *The man, not the killer,* he thinks. It's empathy. He needs empathy. He focuses. He sees the young man. He looks *into* him, like opening the cover of a book and starting to read the pages.

It starts as a blur. Conjoined images fold over one another, fading and clashing. And then it clicks like a kaleidoscope, the manic crystalline colors of life. The moments that make up the minutes that make up the days, spinning and swimming around one another before Savage's eyes in utter brilliance and clarity. He *sees* Adam. His life. His everything.

Childhood. Adulthood. Elementary school teachers and high school bands. First dates and first kisses, grandparents' funerals and watching *Rick and Morty* on the couch. Cooking fresh trout over an open flame in the woods and masturbating quietly in the shower. Taking molly and getting the flu. Getting lost. Feeling seen. Fighting. Fucking. Swimming pools. U-haul trucks. Airplane sickness bags. Dust clouds. Anger. Fear. Exhilaration. Failure. Mercy. Hubris. Infatuation. Joy.

Savage takes in a deep breath, overwhelmed, buzzing. Like he's shot up with the strongest drug he's ever taken. And it's life. It's all of life in a fraction of a second.

He knows. He knows the man's spirit, his everything. And he knows his gateway. Savage has been there with him every step of the way, twenty-one years of living and breathing folded up into one precise instance and injected into Savage's very soul like heroin in the bloodstream.

Adam. The young man is Adam.

And Savage is Adam.

They are one and the same, two sides of the same coin. There is nothing to question because he knows every ounce of Adam as much, if not more, than he knows himself.

The Tarot Card Killer stalks over to Adam, dark eyes beneath the hollows of the mask.

Savage gazes at Adam's face, a few feet from his own, and calmly takes a cigarette from the pack, puts it to his lips, and lights it. He pulls the glove from his left hand, places it into his right pocket. He inhales the black smoke from the death stick. It doesn't taste like tobacco, or weed, or any other plant one could roll in paper. It's sweet like reprieve. It's like a cool fog rolling into his lungs from a morning on the ocean. Both something rotting and something living, at once.

He sees the fear growing wide in Adam's eyes, and he knows: he's the only one who can make it better.

The killer lights a match.

Savage exhales into Adam's face as he taps into a part of himself that, minutes before, did not exist. "**ADAM**," he says. His voice new and ancient.

He places his hand on Adam's boyish face the moment the killer throws the match. They are gone before the fire takes.

"What is it?" Adam asks. He points to a waterfall. It looks like Kauai, but it's better than Kauai. Painted in broad, impressionistic strokes, green and fecund. If Van Gogh had made it to Hawaii, it would have looked like this. The colors swirl where the waterfall meets a glassy pool. The sunlight reflects and refracts in splendid prisms, casting almost tangible rays. Adam and Savage are nestled into a mountain alight with life. The birds and insects sing, and it sounds like jazz.

Savage looks to the waterfall as it meets the great pool of jade beneath in a gentle melodious splashing.

"Home," Savage says.

Adam nods. "Do I go alone?"

"You're not alone."

"But . . . can you come with me?"

Savage doesn't need to think. "I can."

Adam looks a little apprehensive. Not scared, he'll never be scared again. But cautious. He was a cautious person in life, and it's carried over to death. "What happened to the woman?"

Savage is confused for a moment.

"The woman with the snake?" Adam clarifies.

Savage had assumed they knew each other. That she was the Eve to his Adam. But he realizes now the killer had only chosen them like he chose Terra: for their names alone. He needed the lovers to be Adam and Eve, just like The Lovers card of the major arcana. Biblical references seep into all of art, even the art of the occult, the art of the tarot. Adam and Eve, strangers in life, became tied together in death.

"She's in good hands," Savage says. He thinks of Bishop's hands, his strong pale hands. The instruments for his art. Savage realizes how literally true his statement is. He amends, "She's in the best hands of all."

Savage gestures to the water, and the men wade in. It's the perfect temperature, like amniotic fluid. Like the womb. Adam swims out, pushing the water away from him in quiet ripples. Savage follows, but the water doesn't saturate him. It moves over his body like satin over silk.

When Adam looks back to Savage again, his eyes are calm.

"Thank you," he says to Savage.

"Thank you," Savage replies.

"On the count of three?"

Savage smiles. "Sure."

"One," Adam counts.

"Two," Savage continues.

"*Three.*"

Both man and reaper take in a breath of air, though they know it's unnecessary, and dip below the surface. Savage feels Adam slip through the gateway like a finger through a crack.

Onward.

Onward.

When he opens his eyes to the afterlife, Savage takes in a sharp breath.

There is only blackness.

A black void.

Nothing.

TEN

How long Savage stays in the void, he cannot know. There is no time here. He cycles through the emotions. Shock. Denial. Anger.

He spirals through grief deeper than any he has ever known because it does not belong solely to him. He grieves for the world. He grieves for mankind. He grieves at the giant flaw in the system. And he realizes the void isn't the flaw, the lack of an afterlife isn't the error. *Life itself is.* The mistake, the happenstance, the mystery that led to life was only a glitch in the system. It never should have existed. The world should have remained lava and rock, dry winds blowing over continents not forgotten because there was no one to remember them in the first place.

There must be an afterlife. What the ever-living fuck is the point of it all if there isn't? Why spiral onward into forever, generation after generation, if there isn't some link in the chain connecting the after with the before? With the during?

What's the point of the gateways if they lead nowhere? Why not let life snuff out like match-ends if the souls are damned to nothingness?

He holds onto the void because it helps him keep the anger on his tongue, tart and burning like overly ripe citrus. He's not sure he knows how to get back, but he doesn't dwell on it. It doesn't matter. There's no point. There is only the end of everything, and Savage bathes in its blackness because there is no point to anything. He seethes in perpetuity.

"Kid," a soft voice says.

Savage has no room for voices in the void. Fuck that voice.

"Kid," the voice says again, more firmly. "*Savage*. It's time to come back now."

Bishop looks like he always does, his long dark coat with its perpetually popped collar. His scruffy hair that doesn't know whether to fall to the left or the right. His kind and broken eyes.

"Wh—" Savage says in a voice he'd forgotten he had. "Why did you come?"

"I let you process for a bit, but we're not meant to stay here."

"*Here?*" he scoffs. "Where is here?" Savage knows nothing but his anger and everything else feels forgotten and foreign.

"The in-between."

"In between," Savage repeats.

"In-between life and death."

"I thought that was the gateway."

Bishop nods. "Yes."

"This isn't the gateway."

"It is. It just doesn't have its soul anymore."

Savage looks around. Where there was nothingness, there is a waterfall. And a small teal pool. Green trees with twisted roots and branches that blow in a soft breeze. A sky so blue it looks like it drank the ocean. The Van Gogh-gone-to-Hawaii painting that was Adam's gateway.

And Savage exists. He has long hands and legs and feet in their black shoes. He wiggles his fingers. He runs them through his hair and feels the corners of his deep-set eyes. He feels the scruff of his facial hair. "I forgot myself."

Bishop gives a small half smirk. "You did." He claps him on the shoulder. "No worries, it's understandable."

But Savage thinks of his grief. His anger no longer has flames underneath it, but it's still simmering. His face falls, beleaguered by the same unadulterated emotion of a child. "There's no afterlife? That's such bullshit, Bishop. That's such bullshit." Silent tears streak down his face.

Bishop gives his head a soft shake. "No, Savage. There most certainly is."

Savage's breath catches in his throat.

"Reapers just don't get to see it."

"But . . . why?"

"It's not for us."

"Adam's okay? I got him there safely?"

Bishop smiles. "You did great." He turns his face to the breeze. "I mean, just look at this Savage. Damn, if I didn't know you were an artist before . . ." He leans down and runs his fingers through the wild grass growing about his feet. He picks up a rust-colored stone from the bank and rolls it in his hand. "It's so fully actualized. So tactile, so fragrant . . ." He sniffs in. "And the birds . . . is that—is that Coltrane?"

Savage nods.

Bishop laughs. "Good god, kid . . . color me impressed."

"I don't know if I'm cut out for this, Bishop."

Bishop thinks a moment. "I don't know if you are either. I've never molded a reaper from a human . . . let alone an artist. But I think it's important. Scratch that, I *know* it's important. You're meant to be here. You're meant to be doing something bigger. I don't know if you ought to be doing this. But I'm impressed, regardless."

"Beddy-bye time, kiddo," Bishop says as he opens the door to the Smithe crypt, letting Reve into his quarters.

"No. Wait, wait, wait," Savage says, sitting bolt upright from the couch where he had been sketching, dreamily. "I have questions. I have so many questions, and whenever he's here for longer than thirty seconds, I knock the fuck out and don't get to ask."

A hesitant smile crosses Reve's face, like he's unfamiliar with the sensation of being amused. He cocks his head at the barrage he has entered to. "Yes?"

"The tattoos. On your wrist." Savage yawns. "Fuck, it's happening already. The tattoos on your wrist. The duality of sleep, or whatever it was you called it. That's a sandman thing, yes?"

"Yes."

Bishop sits at the other end of the sectional, across from Savage, intrigued by the conversation.

"I—" Savage yawns again, sinking into the couch. "*Fuck*." He sits upright again and smacks his face on both cheeks. "A man died outside the door of my apartment. In Vegas. Not that long before I met you all. He was old and looked like Walt Whitman, and he came to me in a dream to try and give me a message."

Bishop's brow furrows. "What are you talking about?"

"He told me he used the last of his virility to visit me, but he was swallowed by my dream before he could tell me what he came to say."

Even Reve looks intrigued now.

"Did a sandman die recently?" Savage asks.

"Yes," Bishop and Reve say at the same time.

Savage is slinking in his seat again.

"Can you turn off the sleep juice for a minute, Reve?" Bishop asks. "I'd like to know more about this."

"I'll try," Reve purrs, stepping down into the sunken living room and joining the other men on the couch.

Savage sighs. "That's a little better, thank you." He leans forward, pressing his forearms to his knees. A rogue lock of hair falls into his eyes. "Do you know what he was trying to tell me? Why he died?"

Reve and Bishop look at one another. "Bishop?" Reve asks.

"I'm not entirely sure. Sandmen, muses, reapers . . . they're not immortal. Their life span is not like that of a human's, but nothing lasts forever."

Savage nods. "Felicity mentioned something about that."

"Right. His time had come, as it comes for all."

"But why? Why did he make himself known to me? That has to be against the sandman code or whatever."

Reve nods. "It's against the rules of all myths. We're not to interfere."

Bishop shakes his head. "I'm sorry, Savage. I don't know what to tell you."

Savage feels like Bishop is being cagey, but it seems uncharacteristic of the reaper he has come to trust so implicitly. Bishop and Reve are looking at one another, their gaze laden and charged.

Savage swallows. "What aren't you telling me?"

Bishop shrugs, sighs, and drops his head to a gloved hand. "A lot," he says, his gaze squarely directed at the floor.

"*A lot?*"

He looks up. "Please trust that I will always tell you everything I can. And if I'm not telling you something, it's not my choice."

"I'm more confused now than I was before."

"I know and I'm sorry."

Savage studies his friend. His mentor. "You'd tell me if you could?"

"I would."

"Will you tell me at some point?"

"In time, you and I will talk like old friends, and there will be nothing secret between us."

Savage lets his lungs empty the entirety of their contents. "I trust you."

Bishop's lips curl into a slow smile. "As well you should."

"Not to interrupt," Reve says, "but midnight approaches . . ."

"Oh yeah, pumpkin time," Bishop says, standing. "We'll let you get on with your work. I know you've got places to be and dreams to weave."

Reve nods placidly, and Savage already feels his consciousness unspooling like a thread.

He lays back on the couch and nestles into a cushion. His eyes fall closed.

Bishop throws a blanket over him, and he starts to drift off . . .

"Did you know Walt was his sandman?" he hears Reve ask.

"Yeah. I knew he went rogue, but I didn't realize he manifested himself to the kid."

Sleep, oh sweet, glorious sleep, she who had evaded Savage for so long. *Wait just a moment*, he thinks, *just one more moment . . .*

"Curious, why do you always call the savage one 'kid?' It seems . . . improper."

"Term of endearment, I suppose."

"I have charges, you know," Felicity says. Her hair is braided in a crown around her head, and Savage thinks she looks like poetry incarnate. She bats her long lashes over her light eyes.

"I'm aware. So do I now, y'know." He tucks his pencil behind his ear with lead-stained fingers.

"Yes, I've heard. Word on the street is your gateways are masterpieces to behold."

"Bishop talks too much."

"I wouldn't expect anything less."

"From me or him?"

"Both." She laughs.

"Whatever. I still get personal time. Man's gotta eat, artist's gotta art." He closes his sketchbook. "And I didn't find you this time, you found me."

"I *happened* upon you."

Savage is sitting in an archway of the Cloisters, one long foot up on the wall, the other casually dangling to the stone floor. He was sketching the gothic architecture and the sweet, cloistered garden in the center that gives the place its name.

"Well, I *happened* to be exploring the beauty of the city. It's not my fault if you and I are drawn to the same places," she says.

He sits up a little, pulling his foot in toward his body. Felicity sits opposite him, leaning against the other pillar of the archway. They're quiet for a long moment, each studying the flowering little garden. Springtime is alight in the quiet den of the city, igniting the space in pinks and yellows and greens. The air is charged with the smell of an incoming storm.

"They're calling him the Tarot Card Killer," Savage says.

Felicity flicks her eyes to Savage. She says nothing.

"The cops, I mean. Or the press. *'Tarot Card Killer' Stalks Sin City: Three Dead Confirmed.* I saw it on the paper the other day. I called him that, 'The Tarot Card Killer,' in my head. When I put it together, what he was doing. I'm glad someone else figured it out, too." He's holding his sketchbook to his chest, pressed there with one long hand, as he gazes out to the garden. "The last one was 'The Lovers.'"

"What do you want me to say?" she asks.

"I don't want you to say anything." He looks at her. "I just want to stop thinking about it."

She inches closer to him. "Then stop thinking about it." She breathes in, absorbing the air around him. "It's changing you."

"I know."

"Then tap into something that makes you feel like you."

"That's why I'm here. That's what I'm trying to do. It's not working."

She tilts her head at him, sadness creeping into her eyes. She reaches for his hand and rubs her fingers over the backs of his. "Artist's hands . . ." she says under her breath.

"Reaper's hands." He jerks away in realization. "You can't touch my hands. It's not safe. What if I—"

"Reapers can't reap my kind. Not just any reaper, that is. And they're not reaper's hands." She shakes her head and takes both his hands in her own. "They were formed to make art, not death. No matter what Bishop is trying to turn you into." She breathes in sharply, like she abruptly changed her mind, and leans back against the other pillar.

The rain starts in a gentle burst, the drops slapping against the walls of the garden. She gazes out from their shelter of the archway to the sky.

Savage takes the pencil from behind his ear and begins to sketch. Her eyes flick toward him, and she leans back, relishing in his art as it washes over her like water.

He captures her perfect cat pout. Her cheekbones. The coils of hair that have broken loose from their braid at the nape of her slender neck. Her eyes and ears and mouth and décolletage. Her everything. He smooths over the charcoal with his fingers, and it feels electric, like he's touching her skin and not the rendering of it.

Her eyes close and roll backward gently as a small moan escapes her lips.

He flips the page, starts over, sketches faster. He captures the little *v* between her brows, and the tip of her tooth as it skates over her lower lip.

The rain awakens the soil, drawing out its earthy springtime magic.

He flips the page.

He draws the gist of her, half her gorgeous face, one set of lashes.

He turns the page.

He draws her whole form, the length of her. Her long legs and slender hips.

He flips the page.

He draws her hands, their long nails, the single opal ring on her middle finger.

He flips, he draws. He flips, he draws.

She moves, gently undulating in the rhythm of his art.

He casts the sketchbook aside, leans forward, and takes her pale face in his carbon-coated hands. When he kisses her, she moans against his mouth and wraps her hands around his wrists.

His heart races against his ribs like it's threatening to break free of its cage. Nothing, *nothing* tastes as sweet as the muse. He could swallow her. He could swallow her whole.

She breaks free, pulling back a little, and whispers his name against his lips. It never sounded like music before, never sounded like a goddamn symphony.

"No, *Savage*," she repeats, firmer.

He exhales, "Yes?"

She pulls at his wrists enough to get his eyes in front of hers, inclining her head to the right.

Someone clears his throat.

"This is clearly inopportune timing," the reaper says.

"Fuck," Savage says, looking to Bishop. He coughs, clearing the desire that sticks in his throat. "Whassup?"

"Oh, nothing, I was just looking for my little source-peddling muse here, seeing as I'm out of bottled inspo. But I'm obviously interrupting something." He's got a sarcastic smile on his face, his eyebrows so high on his forehead, his hairline is threatening to swallow them. "I can't begin to tell you what a bad idea this is."

Savage sits up. "Hey—" he starts to protest. To explain he doesn't need to explain himself.

"He's right, Savage," Felicity interrupts. She stands and smooths out the length of her gown, rubs her thumb over her upper lip. "I have some inspiration for you, Bishop, let's go talk trade details." She hooks her hand through Bishop's arm.

He looks back to Savage and grimaces, apologetically. "I'll see you back at the crypt, yeah?"

Savage nods. "Yeah."

He hears the muse's heels clicking away as she and the reaper leave him.

Savage looks to his sketchbook where he'd tossed it. Its pages are open to the rain, the storm eating away at the pencil recreations of the muse, one drop at a time.

ELEVEN

Something inside Savage stirs, like someone is calling his name from the other end of a long hallway. A reaping. *His* reaping.

He's sitting with Bishop at their favorite diner in South Slope. They're situated at a booth at the back of the restaurant. The waitress has just dropped off their food, and Bishop is biting into his pastrami on rye.

"Shit, I think I've gotta go."

"Whaddya mean?" Bishop asks, his mouth full of sandwich.

"I mean I gotta go. It's time."

Bishop swallows, his eyes lighting up. "A reaper call?"

Savage slides across the red vinyl of the booth, grabbing his long, dark coat. "Yeah, I think so."

"Your first solo call. I'm a proud papa."

"Nope, nope. You're still not my dad."

"Let me have my moment."

"So, how do I do this?" Savage asks, standing over the

table. "How do I, y'know, *get* there?"

"Focus on the call, almost like you're trying to lean your ear into it to hear it better. But your *internal* ear. Your mind's ear. And you should be whisked to the scene. I'll be on standby if you need me. You've got the bishop piece. Use it if you need it."

Savage nods, trying to shake his nerves.

"Alright, I can do this." He makes for the door and calls "Bye" over his shoulder.

Before he makes it through the doorway of the diner, he's stepping into another place, miles away. For a moment he is nothing and nowhere, before becoming something, somewhere again.

Savage squints to make out the scene before him. The room is dimly lit and smells so heavily of gasoline, it burns his nose. His eyes adjust. He's in the living room of an apartment, a purple couch in front of a television and velvet-seated barstools at the breakfast nook. It looks familiar.

Savage feels like he's been here before.

He looks out the open window. The lights of Las Vegas cast a gaudy glare. A man in dark garb is lifting the unconscious body of a young blonde woman. Her head lolls over the man's arm, her face soft and pretty if not unique.

Savage realizes why the place looks familiar. He has been here before.

The unconscious woman is Lainey, the bartender from his

favorite shithole bar in Vegas. And this is her apartment, a hipster high-rise in the downtown district, a stone's throw from the El Cortez Hotel.

Shit. His heart explodes in his chest. *Shit, shit, shit.*

Lainey's hair is pressed over her face, blond strands sticking to her eyelashes and lips.

The man in the dark clothing looks over his shoulder to the window. Half of his face is covered in the bone white ram's head mask.

Savage shoves his hand in his pocket and grasps the ivory bishop piece.

Bishop, Bishop, Bishop, he thinks. He cannot do this. He cannot reap someone he knows. He cannot handle another of these killings.

The Tarot Card Killer hoists Lainey's body to the window, trying to maneuver her through its opening. She's heavy with unconsciousness, and her limbs are limp as a rag doll's.

Bishop appears like a whisper, his face twisted in concern.

Savage points to the killer. Lainey's body is halfway out the window.

Bishop rips off his glove with his teeth, running to the killer and his victim.

Savage hears Bishop say her name "**MAGDALENA**" as the killer lets go. Savage's own gloved hands fly to his head, flinching with the realization of his once lover's murder as he hears a sickening thud resounding in the night.

His breath is coming in unruly bursts, and he feels himself breaking. *No,* he thinks this and only this. *No.*

The killer turns on his heels and grabs a lighter from the countertop. He holds it up, thumb on the spark wheel, but he pauses before lighting it. His dark eyes flick to Savage.

Savage straightens at the weight of his gaze.

The killer isn't looking through him, he's looking *at* him. He sees him.

"Savage," he says, his voice thick and muffled by the ski mask.

Savage's blood goes cold.

"You could have saved her, you know."

"What?" Savage barks.

"You could have saved them all." The killer inches toward the door of the apartment, keeping his eyes on Savage. "You're not a fucking reaper." He laughs. It's a manic laughter that starts deep in his chest and bubbles out his mouth like foam.

"I am."

"Do you know what 'Magdalena' means? *Woman from the high tower.*" The killer answers his own question. "How convenient that she lives on the twenty-eighth floor. *The Tower,* Savage. It's too perfect. You know you're not a reaper."

"*I am,*" Savage reasserts, his voice an angry growl.

"No. You're not. You're not a shadow. You had it within you this whole time to save them, and you didn't. You're no different from me." He's circling Savage, slowly, slowly.

Savage trembles with anger. "I'm not the fucking same as you."

"Aren't you? Tell me you're not just the tiniest bit curious how the photographs turn out. Tell me you don't find this all hauntingly beautiful. I set up a camera on a long exposure timer down on the street," he says. "Let's go look."

"We're. Not. The same," Savage asserts.

"Oh," the killer says, stepping forward, "but we are."

Anger burns in Savage's nostrils. He makes a grab for the killer. He's prepared to throttle him, to take his face in his hands and break it over and over. But the killer flicks the lighter and the fumes from the apartment ignite before Savage has the chance.

"What the fuck, what the fuck?" Savage screams as he finds himself back at the mausoleum. The flames didn't hurt him—they didn't have a chance to before some self-preservation trip-switch within him engaged and escorted him away from the scene before the explosion.

Bishop isn't back from the reaping yet, and Savage paces maniacally until he returns.

The reaper swirls into the living room in a curl of black smoke. "Hey, what happened there?"

"Where do I fucking start?"

"Okay, okay. Calm down." Bishop pours a glass of some brown liquid and hands it to Savage.

"I don't need fucking courage."

"It's whiskey, dude. I thought you could use a glass."

Savage looks at the glass and downs the pour in a single gulp. "Firstly, I knew her. I *knew* her. I *fucked* her. More than once."

"The victim?"

"Yes. Her name is Lainey . . . was Lainey."

"Seriously? What are the odds—"

"High," Savage interrupts. "That fucker has been planning

this whole thing."

"What fucker?"

"The fucking 'Tarot Card Killer.' He can see me, Bishop. He fucking *talked* to me."

"Wait, wait, wait—"

"I don't know how it's possible," Savage says, answering Bishop's not yet asked question. He slams the glass down on an end table and sits on the couch, burrowing his hands into his hair. "Someone is fucking with me, Bishop. In a major way." He looks up. "I've been talking to Felicity about how those murders have stayed with me because," he thinks for a moment, "because if I were going to be a serial killer, I would be him."

Bishop sits down. "Okay, first, I understand you're reeling, but you need to calm down."

Savage grunts.

"No, really hear me," Bishop continues, "try and calm yourself down. This sounds like someone *is* fucking with you, Savage, but it's not the 'Tarot Card Killer' or whatever that asshole is calling himself. It's Devlin."

"Devlin's fucking with me?"

"This killer has to be working at Devlin's behest. It can't be coincidental."

"Why would Dev—"

"Shh," Bishop interrupts. "Do you hear that?"

Savage listens. It's not a sound, it's a call. A reaper call.

"A call? Why are we both getting the same one?"

Bishop's face falls. "We're not. We're both needed."

A man with a dream and a machine gun is stalking the inhabitants of a mall, somewhere deep in the middle of the country where people still frequent malls.

Bishop and Savage stand and wait.

Bishop looks to Savage, his face apologetic. *Had I any choice,* his face says, *we wouldn't be here.*

But there is no choice.

Reapers are subject to the whim of humans, and humans are fickle creatures. This evening, the man—he with the dream and the machine gun—decided to put his plan into action. The one he's been working on for days and days and weeks and months and maybe even a year. His pet project. His idea that was more than just an idea. His life's work. His magnum opus. And today, he's decided, it's time.

Savage braces himself against the coming terror.

He should turn to Bishop and request an out. *Not now.* He needs to think. To process what has happened. *Let me go home,* he implores mentally. But he catches sight of Bishop, and the reaper's face stills his mind.

Bishop is brimming over with emotion. Furious and frustrated, he's near tears, raw emotion streaking his face. He's more animal than man, more instinct than form.

The energy of the mall is so charged, the air almost sparks around them. Electric panic. Manic terror.

Savage and Bishop are near a diamond shaped apex of corridors. A large nonsensical sculpture of a giant golden ball teetering on the edge of an obelisk sits at the center. Mall art.

Machine gunfire echoes from somewhere down to their right in a terrible popping. Of the many terrible things Savage has heard in his life, it is by far the worst. Instinctually, he ducks his head and covers his ears and the back of his neck. But he remembers himself and drops his hands. Bullets can't harm him. He's a shadow, he is the night, he is the darkness that precedes the light.

But what if the Tarot Card Killer was right? Do I have the power to stop this? He swallows his confusion. But something derails his train of thought before he can begin to spiral.

Running down the corridor come creatures so ugly and horrific, Savage knows they exist not in the world, but on their plane—the plane of gods and monsters. The beasts chase the gunfire like an echo. They are like dogs and hyenas and demons. They scamper on all fours awkwardly, their legs not quite in rhythm. They're cackling and slobbering, reveling in the terror. They proceed the man with the gun—his parade. His opening act. His entourage.

"Hellhounds," Bishop mutters.

They rush around the space and sniff out terror from where it hides in fissures and cracks.

For a moment, all is quiet.

Savage dares to take in a shuddering breath. He feels a fire igniting inside. Some rage is catching like kindling within him, and the flames are being fanned.

Here's the man of the hour. He's young and ugly, not because of how he looks, but in his spirit. His soul is grimy as a sewer. He holds his gun, almost lazily, smacking it with his right hand against his left with casual regard.

The patrons have fled, but the stink of their fear remains.

They've sought refuge in stores, under clothing racks and benches. Behind registers. In fitting rooms. They're fleeing through the back doors of stockrooms. They are mostly gone.

Mostly, but not all.

The shooter walks past a candy shop, the sweets overflowing from wooden barrels. He cocks his head and fires into a GAP. Screams emit from everywhere, like the building itself is crying out in horror.

He approaches the courtyard where Savage and Bishop stand. He fires off short bursts here and there so casually, Savage feels the embers within him burst into a raging blaze.

Bishop's face is tight, jaw clenched beneath the scruff. The other agents of death blink into existence like old TV sets, curling in with the same smoke that accompanies Bishop when he travels. The reapers locate the dying and begin to usher them onward through their gateways.

The shooter squats and tilts his head to spy someone hiding beneath a bench. He murders them with a squeeze of his trigger, before straightening and continuing his hunt.

Savage's fury tastes of copper. His head and body thrum with its power. He thinks the hatred will burst something inside his brain. His fists clench, his nose flares. When the shooter approaches, he swears in his rage he will be able to make himself corporeal again, to rip this man to shreds and throw the pieces to his hellhounds. But Savage notices Bishop's hands. They're bare as the shooter grows close enough to touch.

Savage removes his own gloves, though he's not sure for whom his hands are meant.

"THOMAS," Bishop says, his voice deep magic.

From somewhere, a shot is fired at the mass murderer. It hits him from behind, and pitches him forward, like he has caught his foot on an uneven floorboard.

The new shooter—the good shooter—is a police officer in a tactical vest. He cradles his gun like it's an extension of his hand. He takes quick precise steps, approaches the man, and shoots again.

Bishop kneels and snarls. He takes the hand of the murderer and rips the soul from the body with so much force, his face twists in exertion. Around them, the hounds howl in either anguish or delight, Savage cannot tell. Thomas' soul looks terrified and barren, but he and Bishop disappear before Savage can see the emotion on his face evolve into anything more.

Around him, Savage hears the shuddered breathing of the dying. Lungs are collapsing in a panoply, like an orchestra warming up their instruments before a performance. A final performance.

Savage sees Rook and his big crow head, as he takes the soul of a middle-aged woman, who lies in her death like a pool.

He cannot hear his call anymore.

He doesn't know whose soul he's here to ferry onward because all he can hear, all he can smell and taste and feel, is his own wrath. It echoes inside him like a great brass bell.

Savage shakes his head and stifles an angry sob.

What a fucking world.

A stifling claustrophobia bears down on him, and something in him snaps. He's over it. He's over the reapings and the darkness. He's pressed down upon by a weight he was never meant to bear. He's being suffocated by death.

Something brushes his leg, he looks down and sees one of the hellhounds, sniffing at him curiously.

"What the fuck do you want?" he yells at it.

The hound reacts to his voice like it's been slapped.

And it's the end of his rope. The levee breaks.

Savage calls out in fury with a voice he has never heard, an unintelligible shout breaking from his lips past his saliva coated teeth. It's the voice of his deep self. It emits from the base of his soul and calls to the hellhounds. They stop their mad chase around the mall and look at him with countless sets of eyes. He takes his guttural call and casts the beasts out. It's a howl of rage. A howl of power. The hellhounds cower and scamper away in fear.

Some of the reapers are staring at him with perplexed faces and bare hands. Whatever has happened, it wasn't commonplace. Not even among this company.

He feels himself shuddering, teetering, like he's a vessel brimming with water and poked full of holes. He fades away from the mall, out from under the cloying smell of death and rage.

A pop sounds in Savage's ear drums.

He's somewhere else entirely. Somewhere new.

A densely furnished apartment lays before him. A glance out the giant arched windows reveals the lights of the Chrysler building, so he's back in New York. There is a huge marble fireplace, ornate pink chairs, and an abstract rug over the black and white tiled floor. An ivory chandelier is suspended over a polished coffee table, and art hangs everywhere, mismatched and curated in a mélange of lavish disarray.

Billie Holiday's version of "As Time Goes By" emits from an old phonograph, its brass horn like a gilded lily.

There's a fire in the hearth and a muse on the sofa. She lies long and lean, her head propped on one hand as the other thumbs through the glossy pages of a book of photography. Her gown is sleeveless and cut high over the throat.

"Savage?" Felicity asks, as she tilts her head to him.

He's not sure how he found her. There was no reaping to call to him. No Bishop to help escort him. And space folded on itself in a way he's never felt before.

She catches sight of his face. "What's wrong?" she asks and sits up, swinging her legs off the edge of the couch.

"This whole fucking world."

"What happened?" She stands and approaches him. Her graceful brow furrows in concern.

"Look," he says, "I just saw about a dozen people get murdered by a shooter with an Uzi, and before that a woman I used to date got murdered by that Tarot Card psychopath who confirmed that he is, in fact, in my head and plucking out the worst of me to enact. So, I don't need any coy cat-and-mouse crap right now." He shakes his head. "I don't know why I'm fucking here. I don't know why I'm in this room. I don't know why I am the chosen apprentice for the Grim Reaper. I don't know what the point of life is in this disgusting world that repeatedly lights itself on fire like a masochistic phoenix. What's the point? What's the fucking point?"

She places her hands on his chest, below his collarbone, above his racing heart. She says nothing and pulls him into her. Her eyes close in a reverie of rapture, eyelashes fluttering as she breathes in. She emits a tiny sigh of delight.

"Don't do that. Don't start what you can't finish," he says.

Her eyes pop open and stare up at him, charged and feline under her dense lashes.

He has nothing gentle left in him as he takes her head in his hands, a fistful of perfect auburn hair, and opens his mouth over hers. With one hand, he pulls at her hip, crushing the fabric of her dress into a ball of silk. She moves her mouth with his, their breaths coming in spastic gasps. His other hand moves from her hair, gliding over her breast, down to her stomach. His hands move to the roundness of her backside, and he lifts her, pushing her body into his.

With a burst of arousal, he picks her up completely and places her on the couch. He kneels on the floor before her and slides his hands up her dress. If possible, her skin is smoother than the silk of her gown. She sits forward and pushes her face into him, her hand on the back of his neck. She presses her forehead against his. "Savage," she says. Maybe she meant it as an admonishment, but she revels in his name like it's honey on her tongue.

His eyes still on hers, he reaches upward and places his fingers inside her.

She lets out a gasp followed by a cry. "Savage." She tries for self-control but emits a moan. "I can't, Savage. Stop."

He pulls back. "It has to be like this?"

"You don't understand," she starts.

"No. I don't." He leans into her, looking into her eyes as he cleans the remnants of her from his fingers with his mouth. She moans again at the sight.

The Billie Holiday album finishes, a whisper and a click

emitting from the turntable over and over. *Whir, click. Whir, click.*

"I can't," she says.

"*Why?*"

"I can't," she repeats, her only reply.

He stands in frustration. "Please. *Please.* Explain to me why not. I'm so tired of not getting answers to my many, *many* questions. Everyone is so fucking cagey around me. Well, guess what, honey? You all invited me into this manic world. The least you could do is enlighten me."

She shakes her head and brims over. "Savage," she says through her emotion, "it's not my choice."

"*What* isn't?"

"You're a human."

"That's not fucking it, and you know it."

"I—" She's interrupted by a knock at the door.

She stands and lets out a big breath. She straightens her gown and pads to the door of her apartment with bare feet.

Bishop lets himself in, springing into a dialogue Savage misses the first bit of because it began before the reaper entered.

"—her time, but this is going to result in a shit show, as you well know because whenever one of your kind perishes, a multitude of Devlin's finest come to snack on the leftovers—" His eye catches Savage standing by the couch. "Whoa, again?" His eyes flick back and forth from Savage to Felicity. "I thought you went back to the mausoleum, kid."

"After you left me to watch the people of the mall of middle America perish, somehow, I ended up here. I didn't even know 'here' existed before now."

"You didn't go get him?" Bishop asks Felicity.

"Not me," she responds. "I don't think I have that power even if I wanted to."

"Okay, well. That's odd. And we should have a conversation about the ethics of reaper-hood at some point, but I'm afraid there's no time. We have business to attend, and it's best if you come with. I'm not going to leave you alone until I figure out what the hell Devlin's up to."

"Bishop, I can't. Something weird happened at the mall, and I couldn't hear the call. I don't think I could reap someone now, even if I wanted to. The killer and that shooting have fucked with my head." He rubs his fingers over his temples.

"It's not a call, not for you anyway, so that's the good part. But the shit's about to hit the fan so pull yourself together, and you can choose to examine your fucked up head after."

"What's going on?" Savage asks.

"It's Verity's time."

The muse, the reaper, and the man who has lost his calling. They're exhausted. Distraught. Crestfallen. Each with their own burdens to bear.

The color is drained from Bishop's face. Savage wonders what his own face looks like.

He's a mess of emotions. Too much. The guilt at Lainey's death. The weight of the atrocity. The confusion of what happened after the shooting, when he cast the hellhounds away using a voice he had never heard. And the sexual frustration of being so near Felicity's folds and shape without being allowed to explore them . . . it all has sent him into mental spiral.

They're in Greece again, approaching the foot of a great ruin, all crumbling pillars and empty space.

Felicity looks overwrought. Her eyes flit back and forth, seeing nothing.

Savage looks back to Bishop. The reaper reaches into his pocket and manifests one of the silvery vials of inspiration. The bottle is almost empty, but he tips his head back and pours the last drops down his throat. Felicity notices and taps him gently on the arm as she produces a fresh vile as if from nowhere.

"You're a peach," Bishop says to her as he removes the cork.

"I don't understand why one of the other reapers can't claim the old muse," Savage says to Bishop. "You look like you could use some time."

"'Some time' is an understatement," Bishop sighs. "But this isn't like a human reaping. It's a special event when one of the other kind perishes."

"So, send a special reaper."

"I *am* the special reaper." Bishop downs the inspiration in one swallow and casts the empty bottle aside. It skips over the dirt and disappears.

Savage thinks about everything he's seen Bishop do, how he has his gloved fingers in every inch of this other plane. How everyone seems to know him. He realizes Bishop is more than he'd been led to realize. He's an authority.

Savage steals a sidelong glance at his friend. The reaper's

russet hair falls around his eyes, and he scratches at his stubbly beard. Bishop suddenly looks as ancient as the ruin.

They follow a group of tourists to the precipice. The travelers speak in assorted tongues. They're pointing in excitement as they eke their way to the monument.

"What are we going to do with all these people?"

"Watch," Bishop says. A strange look comes over the tourists' faces, one by one, like an echoing emotion they all experience. They look uneasy, distressed, confused, lost. Over and over, the look crosses their faces, and they walk off, uncomfortable. "They're all experiencing a bad feeling right about now. Or remembering something else they should be doing. Or feeling a little ill. It's like a pheromone I emit that wards off the living. Those fated to continue living, that is. How do you think I keep people away from my car? It literally smells like death."

Verity has summoned the last of her strength to stand betwixt the pillars of the ruin. All around her, muses gather, crying and cloying to the crumbling steps. But Verity holds her head high, her mane of coarse curly hair flanked by the sun. The columns cast striated shadows on the assembly of muses, blotting out half the group in great black bars of darkness. Pollen and dust motes spiral and dance in the afternoon air.

Felicity makes her way up the stones and kneels near the dying deity.

Though the tourists have left, others are beginning to approach. Savage thinks Bishop's death scent has worn off before he takes a closer look at the new visitors.

"What the hell?"

"What?"

Savage nods over Bishop's shoulder.

"Ah, yeah. I told you to expect a shit show, kid."

The creatures approaching are gaunt-faced, crooked jawed, and impossibly tall. Long black garments hang over their hunched backs. They look like a coming onset of ugly ashen heads propped on black draped pillars. As they grow closer, Savage realizes they aren't eight-feet-tall—they're hovering a foot or so off the ground.

"What in god's name are they?"

"Vampires. Damn scavengers."

"Shouldn't we drive them off somehow?"

"Nothing we can really do."

"Stakes or garlic or something?"

"Nah, that's bad mythology. Unfortunately, this sort of thing draws their kind like moths to the proverbial flame."

A full crowd is forming. Approaching from all directions are sundry creatures of varying color and shape and talent. The Oracles appear from nowhere, hand-in-hand, and stand on either corner of the ruin. They angle their sightless pale eyes toward Verity.

Reapers arrive, some Savage recognizes and many he doesn't. Rook stands by his identical counterpoint. She wears a pressed white suit and has the head of a dove.

A group of ageless people, their skin brown and creased, join the crowd. Male and female, each has silken white hair that flows down their backs. They clasp their hands as if in prayer.

"Who are they?" Savage asks Bishop, nodding in the direction of the praying folks.

"*White Hairs.* Empaths. They're like walking Pandora's

boxes. They hold all the emotions of humanity."

A few of the hellhounds have found their way as well, and they scamper through the crowd sniffing, snarling, and drooling.

The vampires have dispersed themselves around the group, sticking out like big black-clad thumbs.

Bishop removes his gloves, rolls up his sleeves. He ascends the steps, directly in front of Verity, his dark garb juxtaposed to the pale stone of the ruin. He stops when he is a few steps from the muse.

The group is silent, except for the occasional yelp from a hellhound or sob from a muse.

Verity raises her hands.

"I am not a martyr so do not weep for me, my sisters," she says to the muses. They lift their pretty heads to hear her words. She's trying to keep her voice even, to keep the emotion buried deep within, but Savage can hear it attempting to break its way out. "As the embers of my fire stir the last of their heat, the cockles in the heart of another begin to warm. This is a treacherous time for our kind. The fate of the world, I fear, is in peril. This magnificent spinning universe is approaching its quietus.

"But I sense a sliver of sanguinity among all this darkness. Put your faith in the right souls, and it will serve you well, my friends . . . my friends and my enemies. I will see you all in another life."

At this, many among the group bow their heads or kneel to the ground.

The vampires open their terrible, crooked mouths, in an asynchronous chorus of unhinging. Their jaws hang open and ready like many hungry snakes.

Verity reaches her hands to Bishop.

"Ancient Dark One. My friend. I am ready for you now."

He smiles at her and lifts his bare white hands to meet her dark, cracking pair. They lock in together and embrace this way for a moment, like family, like love.

"VERITY," he says.

With a crack like an explosion, they disappear from this world. A sonic boom ripples out, blowing back the long hair of the empaths and stirring the gowns of the muses. The crowd flinches and bows their many heads against the wind. Savage squints his eyes to the dust.

The air settles, the sun dimmed by a purplish haze. In the dusky light, pieces of raw ideas float like bits of ash raining down from a fire.

The muses, tear stricken and mourning, open their pretty hands, and face the sky to absorb the last of their great sister. Felicity makes her way down the steps but keeps her eyes and head skyward as she catches the ideas in her palms.

The vampires tilt up as well. They inhale deeply and suck the unfermented inspiration in their gaping mouths, pulling it from the air like water down a drain.

The White Hairs throw the vampires angry glances as they attempt to catch bits of the ash in their upturned hands. When the storm subsides, they approach the muses and give them the pieces as if they are adding to a collection plate at church, bowing with solemn faces and uttering words of condolence.

Savage makes his way through the dispersing crowd. The vampires leave when there is nothing left to be sucked from the air.

"I'm sorry for your loss," he says to Felicity as he meets her at the bottom of the stone steps.

"Thank you. Even deities grow weary of our lives of un-living. We too crave an end. I only wish she had sustained herself more. Instead, she lived a depleted life waiting for the next renaissance."

He wants to take her hand in his own, but he refrains. She's trying to instill a boundary, and he's trying to respect it. Together, they sit on the stones and await Bishop's return.

A return which never occurs.

INTERLUDE

The moment Bishop pulls Verity's soul to her gateway, it all goes to shit.

They were swept away in the wind of the sonic wave. It pulled them from Greece to the gateway like kites in a storm, spinning and swirling before touching back down. The gateway is an exact echo of the scene in Greece—they left the crumbling ruin to arrive at its ghostly replica. But the earthly sun hasn't followed them, and the ruin is cast in an eerie purple light. A purple the color of Verity's very soul.

The old muse sighs. She lets the weight of life go. "Onward and upward?" she asks.

"Indeed, sister. Keep on keepin' on," Bishop replies.

Where the sun once existed in the real world, there is now a chasm into the cosmos, a break in the sky exposing the underbelly of the universe. Bishop and Verity turn to face the void, hand in hand.

"There, Dark One?" she asks.

"There."

"For once, words fail me." She laughs to herself.

In a blink, she is transformed from the dark and aged muse into a white heron. White, save a blueish gray streak over her eyes.

A screaming echo emits from somewhere far away, over their heads, like the faint whistle of a bomb being dropped. Odd. This is a sacred and silent space. Any sound should come from Bishop's own hands, crafted of his own mind.

Bishop glances skyward. High in the atmosphere, hooded black clad creatures are falling from the sky, like giant man-sized raindrops.

"Fuck," Bishop says, a word he is not wont to use, but if the shoe fits . . .

The heron that is Verity looks up to him, her eyes widening in a way that betrays her true self.

"Go," Bishop says to her. "I'll handle this."

The bird hesitates, spreading its wings and folding them again.

"*Go*," he demands.

The heron takes flight in a flutter of feathers and makes for the hole in the universe.

Bishop watches as her form shrinks into the sky and hopes her aim is true.

As the black clad creatures near the ground, they right themselves, and fall to a crouch around him. Two. Then four. Ten. Fifteen.

"Is this necessary?" the reaper asks. "Can't he just send a message to me like everyone else?" The hooded demons surround the reaper, closing in. "Like, 'Hey Bish, what up?

Can you swing by my place? Need to chat.' That would suffice."

The demons stay mute.

"I would *answer*." Bishop drops his tone to a condescending level, like he's talking to toddlers. "It's funny because 'Bish,' while short for Bishop, is also slang for 'bitch.' Dual meaning." He risks a sideways glance to Verity's form. She's nearly at the chasm. "You battle-born have zero sense of humor," he says flatly. *Fly, fly*, he prays. He can only hope Verity makes it through before whatever is about to happen happens.

One of the demons places a hand on Bishop's shoulder, making a grab for the reaper. "Hey now," he protests. The others immediately follow suit. They are a mass of hands grabbing at every piece of the reaper, trying capture him. To take him by force.

"This is a *sacred space*," he shouts, all hint of humor gone. He attempts to fight them off, shaking his arms and legs from their grasp. He kicks and punches, but the demons are faster and stronger. Hatred incarnate. Anger embodied.

The heron calls in the distance, squawking in protest of Bishop's attack.

The battle-born turn their heads to the noise, and Bishop seizes the opportunity.

He takes the only weapon in his arsenal, his bare hands, and forces them under the hood of one of the creatures where its face should be. The thing emits a hiss like steam escaping a kettle as its hood falls back. There is no head. No face. Only a swarm of some buzzing insects, somewhere between flies and hornets, swirling in a tightly clustered mass.

Bishop lets out a moan of disgust and presses his hand into

the swarm. The insects buzz in fury and scatter like marbles on a tile floor before reassembling into the vague shape of a man's head. The hum vibrates in Bishop's ears, rattling his brain against the cage of his skull.

But mercy: in the distance, he glimpses the snow-white heron as it passes through the void. Verity has made it to the other side.

With her, she takes all the purple, all the color, from the space. The gateway is unbalanced, no muse left to give it art and life. They're left in black and white, the sharp contrast of the creatures against the barren land and the clouded sky. The in-between.

The creatures knock into Bishop as he ducks and fights, stands and ducks again. He evades their grasp, but he can only hold them back for so long.

He's done with this nonsense. "Fuck this noise. **ENOUGH**," he yells in his basal, ancient voice. His divine voice.

The demons are lifted by a great unseen hand and thrown back, simultaneously. They fall in a black ring around the reaper. They struggle to their feet and right themselves.

The reaper straightens the lapel of his coat and brushes the hair out of his face. He cracks the knuckles of his bare hands. They rush him again. He lets out a great animal cry and once again knocks them back. "I can do this all day," he jests.

The creatures' black hoods and clothing fall away where they stand, exposing their true forms—black clouds of swirling insects.

"Ugh." Bishop grimaces in disgust.

The insects come together to form one, large tornado of flying darkness.

The tornado amasses, growing taller and wider until it towers over the reaper.

"Shit."

The insects descend and envelope him.

He protests, his pale hands covering his face as he turns away.

They force themselves around him and swallow him whole.

TWELVE

On the steps of the ruin, the reaper who was once a man and the muse he has fallen for sit and wait. Neither speaks. Their quiet contemplation is beginning to evolve to worry.

They allowed time for Bishop to reap the muse. But the day grows old and the shadows long, and Bishop has not reappeared. Savage unbuttons his coat to allow reprieve from the warm, Greek evening. Felicity sits beside him, her long gown a puddle of color around her. He spies the moon as it rises on the Greek horizon, a silver coin in a pool of sunsetting gold.

They sit so close their littlest fingers touch between them. To the passerby, they look uncomplicated. Just a man and the woman he loves. They could be lovers on a honeymoon.

But, ah, how it feels. It feels complicated. His mind and body are drawn into her. He's the moon rising on the hill, and she's the earth they sit upon. He's caught in her orbit.

As the minutes pass, he becomes less concerned with what

will become of him and Felicity and more for what has become of Bishop.

"How long does it take?" she asks after time. Too much time.

"Not this long." He shakes his head. "I've only seen human reapings, but I imagine reaping a muse shouldn't be much different or take much longer . . ."

He'll return, Savage tells himself. *He'll come back in all his sarcastic glory and make some wry observation about the proximity of the human to the muse.*

As if she could sense his thoughts, Felicity pulls her hand away and tucks it into her lap.

"Savage?" she asks. "You know. You know we can't do this."

"Can't do what?" He knows, he's just not willing to say it.

She shrugs her slender shoulders. "This." Her voice is small, the cracks between pavement stones. A thumbtack under a bare foot. "We can't continue. My kind isn't supposed to interfere with humans. It's forbidden."

"I'm not a human anymore," he starts, "or, not only a human."

She looks at him, that little crease appearing between her eyebrows. That disquieting one that betrays her concern. "I'm not sure what you are exactly, Savage. But I know we cannot be involved. It's too volatile for muses and artists to have any relationship other than the one intended."

"I think these are extenuating circumstances."

"That's an understatement."

"Screw the rules. Who's going to enforce them? Who's going to reprimand us?"

The look she gives him is inscrutable. "You have a limited view of the universe. Just because you've been given a window into the depths—"

"A *window*?"

"—don't be foolish enough to presume you understand this world." She stands up, the folds of her dress falling like rose-colored water. "This is my existence, Savage. My *life*, for lack of a better term. You've been romping around as a reaper for a month, and you're already prepared to break the rules. But this is who I am and what I do. I am not foolish enough to risk the design of the world because we're currently caught in a loophole."

"This isn't just a loophole. We're down a fucking *well* of the unknown here, Felicity. Who knows what rules apply?"

"I do."

He looks down, frustrated, his dark eyes staring into nothing. He's finally found something worth fighting for, but this isn't the fight he wants to have. He lets the quiet wash over them and looks up at her. "I won't force you into anything."

She lets her shoulders fall.

"I don't want to threaten your livelihood," he continues, "and I'm certainly not going to pressure you into anything you don't want to do." He stands, gazing down at her. The energy between them is palpable, even as they argue. "But I know I'm not crazy in thinking you feel something for me, too."

"Of course, I do," she replies. Her eyes flick to the sunset. "I love all artists."

"I thought I was no ordinary artist..."

The sky slips from orange to magenta to purple in that

sweet, confused spectrum of dusk. From the crumbling remnants of the ruin, a hooded figure approaches. As it nears, the dark legs and bare feet of a woman show with each stride.

"Who's this?" Savage asks, nodding his head to the woman. Felicity turns her head and snaps to attention the moment she sees the figure, their predicament cast aside.

The woman removes the hood of her cloak to reveal a head of thick, dreadlocked hair. Her face is somehow warm and welcoming without smiling.

"Ray," Felicity says as she bows her head.

"Yes, child, I am here." Her voice is wine and bonfire smoke, smooth and sooty. She has a thick accent, but Savage can't place it.

Felicity lifts her head and embraces the woman.

As she and Felicity release, Savage remembers where he'd first seen her. It was his second sojourn into this other world of secrets and magic. The day of the gathering to discuss the "make-the-world-go-round" business Bishop had described.

"I don't think we've been officially introduced," Savage says to her, remembering the way she had bore her gaze into him.

"But we know one another, Savage. Savage in a strange land."

"Right." He nods. "We met at the gathering that day. The roundtable meeting."

"That was not our first meeting."

"No?"

"No, Savage. It was a different time, a different plane . . . but if you think on it, I'm sure you'll remember." She folds one hand under her chin, resting her head upon it as she waits for recollection to come to Savage. Her wrists are tattooed with vines. The tattoos move, subtly, as if they are growing over her arms.

"I'm sorry, I don't remember."

"At your job where you worked with animals. You felt guilty for having to kill them. You talked to me. You released me."

Savage is mute, his eyes wide with confusion. He shakes his head.

"And again, in the desert by the abandoned houses as you walked to your home."

"Wh—"

Ray cocks her head to one side, piercing his eyes with her stare. The way she had before, when she was a wolf and times were simpler.

"The wolfdog?" He goes quiet for a moment. "Why were you following me as a wolf?"

"To protect you. Something far more insidious was stalking you. I merely did my following in the open."

Despite the warmth of the night, a chill washes over Savage.

"What else was following me?" he asks, his voice deep and soft and wooden.

"The same thing that has taken our friend on this night."

"What's happened to Bishop?" Felicity asks, fear stricken.

"Devlin, it seems, has tired of our agreement. He's taking matters into his own hands."

Savage finds himself back in Brooklyn. Back, but somehow not. He notices the sudden silence before his eyes adjust. In a bluish haze, bits of ash are floating from the sky like a gray snowstorm. There are no cars. No people. It's empty and hollow.

New York is constantly ebbing with noise, it breathes and moves and rasps like a giant dirty lung. But this Brooklyn lies before them silent as a tomb. The shops and delis are dark. There are no lights in the windows of the apartments, that warm and constant glow that thrums through the city is missing. That feeling whenever you're alone, you're never actually alone. Except for Felicity and Ray beside him, Savage is painfully aware he is now alone.

The dim streetlights emit an anemic, gray glow, everything is sickly and hushed. Wrong. The city is a colorless specter before his eyes, a visual echo of the New York he has grown to know and love. It reminds him of before, when he couldn't see red, and the world was lusterless and dull.

"Where are we?" he asks the women.

"Under," Ray replies simply. Ominously. She lets out a great sigh.

Without asking, Savage knows what she means.

Ray seems to glow in the night. She's a faint golden glimmer amidst the endless blue dark. She draws her cloak closed, the whites of her eyes stark against the gloom.

He glances at Felicity and notices tears are in her eyes. "Are you okay?"

"Such a shame," she says as she extends her hand to the falling ash.

Savage feels his fingers twitch to reach out to her, but he stiffens and keeps his hands to himself. "What's wrong?"

"This." She gestures to the falling drift. "Verity."

He looks to the sky. The ash floats down so slowly it's almost suspended. Where it eventually falls, it pools around their feet in dusty puddles.

"It's what remains of her inspiration."

"It ends up here?" Savage asks. "That doesn't seem right."

"It's the lost bits. The soured pieces. The muses take what we can, but we cannot find it all. The sky will cry with her all over the world. It's imperceptible on the human plane, but we can see it here."

In the distance, something howls.

"This is as close as I could bring us without alerting Devlin of our presence," Ray says. "He may still know . . ."

"Wait." Savage stops them, reaching for the chess piece in the pocket of his coat. He had forgotten. "Bishop, c'mon. C'mon . . ." he says. He holds the piece at eye level and mentally focuses on the reaper.

"Savage one," Ray says, cupping her hands around his as they hold the piece. The tattooed vines twist about her wrists. "He cannot answer."

"How do you know?"

"Bishop gave you this. A piece of him to help you connect to him." She shakes her head. "I don't need a talisman. He lives within me and I within him. I am the piece. And I can feel he's somewhere he cannot leave. Distraught. And bound." She drops her hands from his, her eyes full of dew.

"Who are you?" he whispers.

"I am everything Bishop is not. I am life itself." Savage places her accent, then. She sounds like everyone. She is from everywhere, all at once. She turns away from him, continuing. "Come, we must hurry."

They traverse the abandoned streets, their footfalls resounding in strange echoes in the cold dark. The blueness of the otherworld casts a peculiar slant on the brick of the city.

"It's always New York," Savage muses aloud.

"It's the greatest city in the world," Felicity replies. "It attracts the best and the worst of your kind and ours." The darkness leaches the color from her skin. She looks sickly here, her hair cast black and her creamy skin a haunted white. Two black shadows fall under her cheekbones, her beautiful face turned gaunt.

"Keep your attention at the present, children," Ray says, her eyes big watery orbs scanning the darkness. "Ruses abound."

Savage is fascinated and full of questions, but he holds his tongue. If they find Bishop, if they make their way out of here, he'll ask later. As they continue, he spies a vampire standing under the shallow blue halo of a streetlight. Its mangled jaw hangs open as it stands impossibly still. As they pass, he hears a horrible sucking sound as it pulls air in through its ruined mouth, inhaling the floating remnants of Verity. Its red eyes turn to them, reflecting in the dark like that of some nocturnal animal. Savage grimaces and looks away.

They weave their way through the haunted city, Ray the only light among a world of ghosts and demons. At their right, the bay sprawls out into the night, black and still. No movement in the stagnant air means no movement in the water. It sits like a giant obsidian looking glass, reflecting the blue-black sky above. As Savage watches, something stirs its stillness, cool inky ripples cross the surface. Some foreign shape rises from the water. Then another. And another.

A score of great blue-black horses are born of the bay, the water sliding over their coats like oil. The beasts break into a run, climbing and clamoring over the sea-slicked rocks, heading straight toward them. The clapping of their hooves echoes like thunder along the empty Brooklyn streets.

Ray pushes Savage and Felicity back with a motherly arm, tucking them into the darkness. "Stay here, be silent, and let me deal with these tricksters."

Savage positions himself before Felicity, masking her in the shadows between two streetlights. He glances down at her face, but her eyes are intent on Ray. The pack of horses gallops down the street, and Ray approaches them head on.

The creatures are enormous. Their green kelp manes unfurl behind them as they run. Gaunt and underfed, they pull their lips back over their teeth in indignant squeals, snorting air through their noses in furious nickers.

As they approach Ray, she holds her hands up to them, calmly. They come to a grinding halt, some rearing on their hind legs and kicking into the blue night.

"I am not here for you forlorn creatures. You feast on the emotions of my creations, but I do not rend you limb from limb because it is my belief that all life has merit. Even yours."

In a blink, the horses have transformed into women, naked and dripping wet, standing in the street like lost girls.

"We could smell you from the water," the woman at the front says. "Your presence is an unwelcome one, Earth Witch.

You have no dominion here."

"I claim dominion wherever I see fit. When your *knave* refuses to play by the rules set eons ago, I react accordingly."

The women snicker and laugh, saliva bursting from their lips, like they are still animals.

"*Whore*," one cries.

"*Witch*," the women heckle.

"*Earth bitch.*"

With every slight they throw, they take small steps in around her. Closing in slowly, subtly. Then faster, circling in and threatening to swallow her with their many slick, raw bodies.

"Shit," Savage says to himself, forgetting Ray's instructions to stay mute in his moment of worry.

Felicity covers his mouth with both her hands, a moment too late.

The women turn to Savage, eyes wide and hungry as they move like water toward him, a wave rolling into shore. Slowly at first, then all at once.

They are changing again, their sunken faces becoming full, their algae green hair shifting to a lush black. Their forms elongate and their breasts and hips fill in their missing curves. In a moment, they are upon him, swarming like bees.

"What a beautiful man," one voice says.

"Look how strong you are."

"I bet you taste as good as you smell."

"Come with us."

They push Felicity out of the way, pull at his hands, and claw his skin and clothing.

"Stop," he demands.

"We've something to show you."

"Come. *Come look.*"

"Just here, in the water."

"Yes, come with us into the water."

"Get off me," he insists, covering his face and batting them away.

Ray takes one of the women by her shoulders and pitches her away into the street.

Savage pushes at their naked forms, but his hands pass through them like they are liquid. They rip at his shirt, pull at his coat, attempt to unbutton his jeans. One clenches a handful of his hair and pulls like she's trying to rip it from the roots. He bellows in pain.

They tug at his hands and begin to drag him toward the direction of the bay. Felicity grasps one of their manes and pulls, hard. Some of the women turn on her, morphing back into horses and crashing down upon her with their massive hooves. Savage sees her collapse beneath a heap of the inky black animals.

Ray gasps, and Savage loses sight of Felicity. Something tears inside him.

"**ENOUGH**," he calls out, mustering up the same deep, true voice from the bottom of himself he used to cast the hellhounds from the mall. He follows it with a growl, more animal than man. With some force unknown to him, the entire group of beasts is plucked from the ground and thrown asunder as if with a giant, invisible hand.

The creatures crash into buildings and light posts. They fall on their backs and sides and stomachs, and the trio are surrounded by a circle of cloying women and horses thirty feet in circumference.

"He is not a human for your consumption," Ray calls at them, spinning on an axis so her words reach all of them, her voice quaking with power. "Leave us." She exhales through pursed lips, her breath a great gale that blows the women away and back to the bay.

Savage collapses at Felicity's side. She lies in a dissolved heap, trampled, trodden, and unconscious.

"Felicity?" he coaxes. He lays one hand beneath her dark head of hair, the other over her chest.

Ray kneels beside Savage as the hoofbeats fade into the night.

"They hurt her," he says, his voice breaking like splintering wood.

"Kelpies would not gain anything from harming a muse. She was merely an obstacle in getting to you." Ray places her hands over Savage's upon Felicity's chest. She stares into Savage's eyes, looking down deep to the very bottom of him. He feels vulnerable and safe, and he stares right back. She gives his hand a squeeze in her own, and Felicity gasps beneath them. Ray's inner light flickers, and she nods at Savage.

"Are they gone?" Felicity asks, confused, breathless.

"Yes, child," Ray says, dropping her gaze from Savage to look at the muse. She smooths the hair away from Felicity's face. "They did not harm the Artist."

Felicity smiles weakly at them from the dirty blue ground.

Savage helps her stand. She's lost some of her perfect composure.

"Just a little rough around the edges," he says as he tucks a stray lock of her long hair behind her ear.

"At least my clothing is still intact."

He looks down and straightens his coat over the tattered remains of his black tee shirt. "Kelpies have sharp claws. This is what I learned today."

"They say you learn something new every day." She nods.

"Come, there's little time," Ray says to them, pressing her palms into each of their backs. "We must go onward."

As they continue, the city is a barren hush. Block after block is uninterrupted by the presence of any other foes. The apartment buildings are now interspersed with luxurious old houses, presiding vacantly over the street from dark hills. There are no lights within their windows.

Savage wonders how he was able to manipulate the kelpies and to banish the hellhounds. He'd like to chalk it up to a rush of emotion, of anger, or some aspect of transforming into a reaper he wasn't told about. Perhaps it was the desire to protect, both Felicity and the shoppers in the mall, but no . . . he knows it's something more. He feels something ancient and terrible stirring within him, like a great bird fluttering its wings. He feels it down to his marrow. He's charged from tip to toe. It's intoxicating and terrifying, and he shudders beneath its weight.

Bishop, where are you? he thinks, as he unconsciously runs his fingers over the chess piece in his pocket. *I need your advice. I need your humor.* But no matter how much he focuses on the reaper, how hard he presses the ivory into his palm, Bishop doesn't appear. Savage swallows the concern in his throat.

Something screams in the distance.

"Avoid the banshees," Ray says as she turns her head to them over her cloaked shoulder. He can see it now, her inner glow is clearly dimmer. It worries him, but he keeps his thoughts to himself.

About a block away, one of the houses on the hill emits the only light on the block, warm bright in a sea of blue darkness. It's a huge mansion built into the precipice of a hill. More castle than house. More monument than residence. It's held back by a great marble and iron gate.

"There," Ray says. "Devlin's lair."

"Of course, it is," Savage remarks, flatly.

"Devlin was never one for subtlety," Felicity says.

As they approach the gate, some movement stirs the air about the house. Like a flicker emitted from a Tesla coil, the space around the property is so charged with demonic energy, it crackles with an electric hum. Savage feels the current pass over his skin, and the hairs on his arms and neck shiver in response.

She turns to Savage. "Be wary of what you see inside. Truth and perception diverge in Devlin's presence."

They climb the stairs to the front door and enter the home of the devil.

THIRTEEN

A hooded figure, its face clad in darkness, approaches the trio in the foyer. Savage's muscles tense, his hands clenching into fists. *Is this Devlin?* he wonders.

The house is lavish, well lit, and clean. It seems antithetical for the home of the deity who calls himself "chaos." A marble staircase curves from the foyer to the upper level, and there are fresh cut roses on a table at the center.

Savage eyes the dark being, wondering if there's anything beneath its hood. The creature beckons them to follow without speaking.

The roses in the vase incline their blossomed heads toward Ray as she passes, thirsty for her sunlight.

The creature guides them through a formal living space off to the right toward a set of stairs. Club music is playing on the lower level, and the bass grows louder as they descend. Savage can't decipher the electric vocals.

Low, warm light illuminates a billiard room, an ornate

cherrywood pool table at the center. Cigar smoke lingers around the sconces and light fixtures and sticks in Savage's nose, that cloying tobacco smell of wood and leather and something gone to rot.

A man is leaning his body over the pool table, lining up his stick with the cue ball for a complex shot. He's dressed casually, dark jeans and a tee shirt over his pale skin. The game must be nearing an end, as the pool table is almost clear.

"Devlin." Ray tilts her head in recognition.

"You know, you guys could've knocked," Devlin says after the white cue ball collides with the green six. "Getty said you just let yourself in. That was kind of rude . . ." he says as he lines up his next shot. His voice is slanted with an accent as well, but it's nothing like Ray's. Eastern European, Savage surmises, something vaguely Slavic.

Devlin stands upright and lowers the music to a tenable volume. He picks up his cigar and takes a deep pull, holding the smoke in his lungs. He appears to be a bit older than Savage, in his mid or late thirties. His face and skull are completely hairless and smooth, and he arcs one naked brow as he scrutinizes them.

"What, you were expecting something worse?" he asks Savage, sizing him up with his gaze.

"Not worse," Savage says, shrugging. "Perhaps more impressive."

"Ha," he laughs. "He's funny. But tell the truth, you thought Getty here was me, right?"

The hooded figure that was their escort is standing off to the side, disinterested, hands folded before him.

"He's a creepy motherfucker, I'll grant you that. Born of

Gettysburg, spirit of bloodshed. He might be my favorite of the battle-born." Devlin sets down his cigar in a crystal ashtray on the table. "Wait, wait, I love doing this," he says, as he runs his hands over his bare arms. "Is this more what you had in mind?" He shakes his body to the beat of the music as he passes his hands over his skin. Black tattoos appear in a jumble of ink. He finishes by gliding his hands over his face, exposing a gaunt skull over his pale skin. He winks at Savage.

He now looks more like a traditional embodiment of death than the devil, but Savage keeps this rumination to himself.

"Bet you're wondering about the accent, yeah?" Devlin says. "Americans really like to paint Russians as the bad guy, so I just lean into it. And when I'm in Russia, I speak with an American accent." He turns to Getty, suddenly impatient. "Dude, it's your turn."

The empty hood picks up a cue stick with gloved fingers and leans over the table. The cue ball hits the eight, and the eight hits the twelve, but the twelve misses the pocket.

"I expect better of you, Getty. Strategy," he says, tapping his temple. "*Strategy*. It's, like, in your very soul. Come on, now."

"Clearly we're interrupting something very important," Felicity says, "but do you think you could be bothered to give us your full attention?"

"Ooh. Testy, testy. The next game is yours, okay?" Devlin tells her as he sinks his next shot. He systematically pockets all the remaining balls, finishing with the black eight. "And that, my friends, is how it's done." He dances, bobbing erratically as he shelves his stick and goes back to his cigar. "So, what's new with you guys?" he asks, shrugging his shoulders in a conspiratorial tone, mocking them. "What, meeting me didn't merit investing in a new shirt for the kid?" He gestures to the tattered remains of Savage's tee.

Savage is tired. He's on an endless emotional rollercoaster he doesn't remember boarding. The bass of the Russian club music is thrumming in his head and throat and ears, drilling into his soul and drowning out whatever patience he has left. "Cut the shit, dude," he says. "You know why we're here."

"Ooh, ballsy." Devlin squeals with delight. "I love to be challenged, I don't have to tell you that. So," he claps his tattooed hands together, the cigar wedged like a thick eleventh digit between his fingers, "you want your reaper friend back? Let's talk negotiations. No one ever got something for nothing, least not from me." He taps the tail of ash from the cigar into the ashtray.

Ray drops the hood of her cloak and breathes in, listening. "I know he's close," Ray says. "You may have cloaked this space in wicked energy, but I can feel my counterpoint, and I know he dwells somewhere within this house."

"Good, yes. You are correct, Ray," he mocks. He drops his voice, the humor ebbing. "But even if you are able to locate him, you'll be taking him exactly nowhere unless I get what I want."

Ray falls into a meditative state, closing her eyes and dropping her chin to her chest.

"You're stymying the whole process by keeping him here," Felicity says, placing a hand on Ray's arm. "If he can't do his job, you don't get your souls, either."

"*Smart*. Yes, little muse, I know. Tell me now, truly, are you banging Bishop on the side, too?" He laughs at the repugnance on her face and starts dancing again, bobbing his head to the beat and mouthing the Russian lyrics. "There is something interesting going on here, though," he says as he points back and forth between Felicity and Savage. "Yeah, I can definitely see that. Some sexual tension, some chemistry." He approaches Savage, still dancing. "Too bad I got a piece of him first, eh?" He grabs Savage's groin as he walks past him, giving his privates a quick squeeze.

Savage curses and jumps away from the assault.

At this, Devlin bursts into a cycle of twisting laughter. He goes to the bar at the end of the room and pours himself a scotch as his giggles wane. "Savage? You want a whiskey, buddy? A little glass of rye?"

Savage stays mute.

"Come on, now, I know Bulleit is your favorite."

"How—?"

"Don't entertain him, Savage," Felicity cautions.

"Oh, I know lots of things. *Lots* of things. Probably everything. What about tequila, huh?" He shakes a bottle of Don Julio 1942 at Savage, a brown glass pyramid with a wooden stopper. "You don't need salt and limes when it's this good."

Savage squints at him. "I'm good, thanks. Just don't touch my junk again."

"Why would I want to? I already got what I needed." He replaces the bottle of 1942 to its glass shelf and steps around the bar. "Humans are such simple creatures. I just adore you guys." He sips his liquor.

Ray opens her eyes and lifts her head. "I've located him," she says. The tattoos on her wrists begin to sprout pink blooms on her dark skin.

"Oh, I knew you could find him. But good luck getting that fucker out of here without my say so. I'm going to need something from you all, first."

"I've read enough in my lifetime to know better than to negotiate with you," Savage says. "This isn't a compromise."

"Well, see now, that's a predicament. Because you're not getting your buddy back unless you're willing to trade." He scratches his fingernails against his tattooed cheek. "I mean I want to help you, I really do, but it's tit for tat, see? Both tits and tats will be necessary."

Savage glances to the women on either side of him. Ray's expression is impassible.

"Look, I had to get creative, here," Devlin continues, "I mean, how do you keep death in your grasp? The idea is inherently counterintuitive. You should come see before you start pooh-poohing everything. I'm particularly proud of what we did." He nods, smiling. "To the upstairs, children."

Felicity and Savage catch each other's concerned gaze as they follow Devlin and Ray back up to the first level, through the foyer where the roses emit their funereal scent. They ascend the great marble staircase and walk down a hall to a room with closed double doors. Two hooded figures stand on either side of the entrance.

"Now, no funny stuff. Everybody stays where I can see them, or I'll torch the whole thing, got it? Whole thing, *poof.* Up in flames." He casts both doors open.

Felicity gasps and covers her mouth.

Inside, Bishop is restrained to a redwood that grows impossibly from the floor in the middle of the room. The tree huge and ancient, its roots eating through the marble tile and its height extending upward through the ceiling into the space above. Bishop is bound by shackles of gunmetal steel. He looks tired and tortured, his mouth gagged by a length of fabric. From a far bough of the tree, a young woman is hanging inverted by her right foot. More hooded, faceless creatures flank the interior of the room, arms crossed, silent.

"Told you we had to get creative," Devlin says as he walks to the reaper. He grabs a fistful of Bishop's hair in his hand and pulls the reaper's head back, so their eyes meet. Bishop is breathing hard beneath his gag and muttering incoherent obscenities at Devlin. "What's that now, Bishop? I can't understand you." He laughs and shoves the reaper's head forward.

Upon seeing the girl, Ray's face is stricken with grief.

"No ideas, sister. I'll let the reaper reap her when I get what I want." He laughs. "*Reaper reap her*, get it? Now, Savage, our resident *artiste*. Take a good look. It should look familiar. You got the other ones pretty fast."

Savage looks at the woman. She's unconscious, her slashed wrists slowly raining blood to the floor in two great puddles that reflect the scene like scarlet mirrors.

"We had The Tower, that was the last one. And The Lovers. And first was The World. So . . ."

Savage sees it. He feels his heart thrumming like a bird in his chest and the blood pulsing in his ears. "*The Hanged Man*," he whispers from the back of his throat, his dry lips mouthing the words.

Devlin squeals in delight.

"It was you." Savage clenches his fists so tightly, his

fingernails cut into his palms.

"Oh, *kotyonok*, yes. It was me." He smiles, white teeth against his white skin like stones in snow. "That means 'kitten' in Russian, because you're like a little baby kitten, you don't know anything. But I can't take all the credit, I had help . . . we'll get to that in a second. Let's talk about the reaper, first.

"So, the only thing that can restrain death is life. *Pervasive* life. The manacles," he kneels and points to Bishop's fettered wrists, "are made from metal you blessed, Ray. Do you remember? It was a long time ago. Like, *millennia* ago. So, he's bound *with* life *to* life—that'd be the thousand-year-old tree—and he's watching life slip from the girl, as she is slowly subjected to exsanguination. I like that word: *exsanguination* . . . but he cannot reap her. She's dying but she's not dead, yet. And so, he's paralyzed." Devlin points to his temple. "Genius. But like I said, not all good ideas are mine. Oh, Tarot Card Killer?" he calls. Nothing happens. "Fuck, I knew he was going to miss his cue." He clears his throat and says louder, "*Oh, Tarot Card Killer?*"

The killer enters the room, his face clad in his usual uniform of a black ski mask beneath the white bone and ram horn mask. Savage's muscles act of their own volition and start at the man out of sheer fury, but Felicity and Ray halt him, each tugging at one of his arms.

"Don't fall for the temptation, Savage one," Ray says, "it's a trap to ensnare you."

"What the fuck is going on?" Savage barks at Devlin.

"I am telling you, man. Don't rush the narrative." Devlin squeezes the arm of the killer. "So, this, this is TCK, we're going to abbreviate it from now on because 'Tarot Card Killer,'" he says it with air-quotes, "is a bit cumbersome. He helped me paint this beautiful scene before you.

"Okay, now this goes like an episode of Scooby-Doo in my head. Let's see," he says, "take off your mask, TCK!"

The man removes the bone and horn mask, and lets it drop to the marble floor with a clatter. He removes the black ski mask beneath it, and Savage nearly loses his grip on reality.

The Tarot Card Killer, in all his glory, is Savage.

The man is a carbon copy of himself. The dark hair that annoyingly catches on his long eyelashes over his forehead. The almost-beard. The broad chest. The only difference is the scarred face. Fresh burns cover half his visage in shiny white patches, only partially healed from when he dropped the lighter in Lainey's gasoline-soaked apartment.

Felicity gasps beside him, clutching her hands over her mouth. Bishop moans beneath his gag. The hanging woman's body sways slightly on its cordage.

"What is this?" Savage snarls.

Ray turns to him immediately. "Savage." She takes him by both shoulders. "This is farce. I told you nothing would be as it seems."

"Oh, but it is, sister," Devlin says, standing on his tiptoes to peek over her head and catch Savage's eye line from across the room.

"Savage," Ray repeats, shaking her head. *"It is farce."*

"So, Mister Savage, if you were wondering what you're capable of, this is it." He gestures to the scene behind him. "You sick fuck." He smiles. "I'm truly impressed."

Savage is shaking. He can't look away from the doppelgänger, from his own dark eyes. The mirror Savage smiles, one half of his face pinching into a gleeful grimace, the other immobilized by the burns.

"I told you I was you," the double says in Savage's own voice, somehow deep and nasal, a quality he usually can't recognize from within his own head.

"You are not me," he asserts.

"Oh, but he is," Devlin says. "I made him to be you."

"You made him?" Something inside Savage eases a little.

Devlin senses his mistake. "Yes, but *from you*. From your spunk." He gestures vaguely to Savage's groin. "Remember, three hot blondes licking you from stem to stern? Ringing any bells?" He nods. "I took some of that precious man-seed, and I made him."

"Then *unmake* him," Savage responds.

A wide smile crosses Devlin's face. "Always so eager to unmake."

"What?"

"Savage." Ray pulls at his arm. "Don't listen to him. I beg of you."

"I tell you what. I'll think about unmaking Mister Crispy over here, *and* I'll let the Bishop go. For trade."

"Wait, what?" the doppelgänger says.

"Shh—shut up," Devlin barks to him, perturbed. "Just shut up."

"What do you want to trade, asshole?" Savage says.

"It's not a big thing," Devlin says. "Just a little thing." He walks toward Savage. "A little, *tiny* thing." His voice is flat now. "I want the bishop."

"You already have him," Felicity snaps.

"No, no. He knows what I'm talking about," referring to

Savage. "You know what I'm talking about, don't you?" He's nodding now, his face only inches from Savage's. He's shorter than Savage, and he has to look up at him, but he somehow manages to be condescending even from below.

The ivory bishop still resides in Savage's coat pocket. "I know what you're talking about."

"It's on you, isn't it? I can smell it." Devlin's eyes widen, and an eerie smile curls over his face, a flag unfurling.

Savage stays mute and glances over Devlin's shoulder to Bishop's pained face, trying to discern any subtle clue as to whether he should concede. But the reaper is paralyzed with pain and still gagged at the mouth.

"It's on him," the other Savage says. "He keeps it in his pocket."

"If I give you what you want, how do I know that you're going to return the favor?"

"I'm not unreasonable, man. I only want what I want. I mean, I gotta get this room cleared out, clean up all the blood. Get this fucking tree outta my house. I'd like to get on with my day."

"Yeah, that's not giving me a lot to trust."

"I tell you what. What if I let Bishop reap the girl first for good measure? Because I know that *you* know, if you don't comply, I can do this all over again. I've got an eternity to think of maniacal little schemes. Also, I have a friend who appears to be more twisted than even me. Right? Number two?"

"I have some ideas." The mirror Savage folds his arms over his broad chest, his ugly half a face twisting under his smile.

"Ray?" Savage asks, looking to her.

She shakes her head. "I cannot see any other options . . ."

"Unlock him," Savage says.

Devlin mutters something in Russian and claps his hands together. He walks across the room back to Bishop. "Okay, no talking. Silent," he says to Bishop.

"He has to say her name," Savage objects.

"*Fuck.* Okay." He points to one of the hooded faceless figures. "Stalin, un-gag him."

Savage wrinkles his nose at the name.

"Stalin*grad*," Devlin says. "*Battle-born*, remember?"

Stalin removes the fabric from Bishop's mouth.

Devlin shoots his fingers like guns, and the locks on the shackles pop open. Bishop rushes to the bleeding girl, pulling the gloves from his fingers.

He cradles her inverted head in his hands and whispers her name in his reaper's voice. He blows a breath in her face, grasps one of her blood covered hands, and pulls the spirit from her body. When she comes free, she looks frightened and confused but only for a moment before he escorts her to her gateway. They disappear and the body sways as they go, still hanging like an inverted Christ.

"Always so dramatic," Devlin mutters to himself, scratching at the back of his bald head. "Alright, that's done. Time to give Devlin the piece now."

Savage retrieves the ivory bishop from his pocket, extending it to the devil.

A perverse joy crosses Devlin's face as he withdraws it from Savage's hand. He presses the piece under his nose and inhales deeply.

"If you knew I had it, why couldn't you just take it from me?" Savage asks.

"Free will. I may be the god of chaos, but even I have to play by our rules."

"You didn't have my consent when you sicced your sirens on me and stole my fucking semen."

"That was different because you definitely wanted to fornicate with the triplets. You gave your spunk freely. They just gave it to me afterward." He's quiet for a moment, looking at Savage with appraising eyes. Almost warm. Almost affectionate. "One of these days, it's going to hit you, Savage. Come find me when it does."

"What's going to hit me?"

"The truth."

"I don't think I'll be coming to you anytime soon." Savage scowls.

"Don't be so sure. I'm keeping my options open. You should, too."

"That's quite enough, Devlin," Ray interjects.

"I'm not telling him anything. I *just* said I like the rules. I may like bending them, but I'm not breaking any. I'm only telling him I'm here if he decides he wants to talk."

"What are you two talking about?" Savage asks.

Ray leans into Savage. "I implore you Savage one, ignore him."

"Oh, yeah." Devlin nods sardonically, eyes wide. "Ignore me. I'm clearly lying." He chuckles and walks to the dead woman's body, pressing against her abdomen so the body sways like a pendulum. He laughs.

"Can we get rid of the doppel-fuck now?" Savage asks.

"Ooh, him . . ." Devlin looks over his shoulder at the second Savage's burned face. "Yeah, don't think so."

"What," Savage barks.

"I said I'd *think* about unmaking him. And I did. Think about it, that is. And decided no. Too valuable."

Savage crosses the room to his mirror self, arms flexed. If Devlin won't unmake him, Savage will.

The battle-born are on him like flies, gripping his flexed arms beneath clenched black gloves.

Savage's own ruined face laughs back at him. "Gee," the other him says. "Do you think it'd be a fair fight?"

"I think the party's coming to a close," Devlin interjects. "And what kind of host would I be if I didn't walk you out?"

Two of the battle-born forcibly remove Savage from the room, wrenching his arms. Another two prod at Felicity and Ray.

"Do not place hands upon me," Ray says to the one that approaches her. "We will leave."

The battle-born half drag, half push Savage down the marble stairs.

"Let me fucking go, I can walk," he says.

In the foyer, Devlin opens the door for them. "It was a real pleasure. Let's do this again, real soon, mmkay?"

As the women pass over the threshold of the mansion, Devlin stops Savage, pulling on the sleeve of his jacket. "One more thing. Just a piece of advice. You really shouldn't accept drugs from strangers."

Devlin wipes his hand over his face, changing it as he does. His eyes become a little kinder. His nose, flatter and bigger. His skin morphs from ghostly pale to warm and golden, and a thick head of black hair appears where he was once blanched and bald. The skull tattoo disappears, replaced by screwed up lettering over each of his eyes. Oscar, the graveyard janitor, looks back at him now. "Good thing it was a friend who gave them to you," he says in Oscar's voice as he winks.

"What the shit—" Savage starts.

"Buh-bye, now." His face is his own again as he shoves Savage out. "Don't forget to come back and visit real soon."

With that, the door slams.

Outside, the blue night is still snowing ash.

FOURTEEN

"Can you try to stop birthing critters in my living room, please?" Bishop asks Ray. In Bishop's quarters, Ray is sitting heavily, rubbing her hands over a round pregnant belly. "They tend to crap in inconvenient places," the reaper continues, "and by that, I mean everywhere."

Ray exhales. "I can try."

"Are you all right?" Savage asks her, unable to tear his eyes away from her growing form as Bishop hands him a glass of whiskey.

Ray's stomach is swelling beneath her garments, growing at an impossible rate, as if Savage is watching a time lapse of gestation. Her breath catches in her throat with the pain of labor. Nonetheless, she nods.

"Ray doesn't do well being confined indoors for any significant period of time," Felicity says.

"Especially when she's stressed," Bishop adds as he sits.

Ray inhales sharply, a look of pain crossing her face. She

grasps her knees with clenched hands, winces, and with a pop, a young rabbit springs out from under her gown. Her stomach deflates like a balloon, and the rabbit bounces off through the living room.

The rabbit is not the first.

A young merlin is perched on Felicity's shoulder as the muse sips a glass of wine and smokes a pastel colored dream-joint.

A garter snake tangles itself around Savage's feet.

A wolf pup hides under the coffee table.

"How did he make another me?" Savage asks, recoiling his feet from the snake and shaking it from his ankle. His anger and fear have settled in his throat like bile he can't choke down.

"He didn't," Bishop answers.

"What do you mean? You saw the killer. He was me."

"It's an optical illusion," Ray says.

Savage shakes his head, dubious and indignant. "No. That . . . that *thing* knows my thoughts. He pulled art from my head and twisted it and made it violent. Something I never intended."

"And that's how he's not you," Bishop says. "You'd never do that."

Savage slumps back on the couch, pinching the bridge of his long nose between his fingers. "I don't fucking get it."

"Look, think of a clone. Dolly the sheep's clone wasn't Dolly. When celebrities clone their dogs, they say the dogs look identical but aren't the same dog."

From Felicity's shoulder, the merlin tilts its head left and right as if listening to their conversation.

"So, Devlin made a me-clone?"

"For lack of a better term, yes," Bishop says. "A fucked up-magic-serial-killer-clone."

"Jesus, listen to yourself."

Bishop shrugs. "It is what it is."

"How do we get rid of that abomination if Devlin won't?"

Bishop opens his mouth, about to say something, and finds he has no words. He looks to Ray. Closes his mouth. "I don't know. Not yet."

"Okay, then can we talk about the fact that I know Devlin?"

"What do you mean?" Felicity asks.

"I know him from work. Well, not him, exactly. He was the quintessential devil in disguise. He was just a dude I worked with. A janitor."

Ray grunts in pain and presses a hand to her stomach, flattening it, as if stymying the urge to birth another creature. "I know, Savage one. That's why I was there with you, at the laboratory."

"Why would Devlin bother infiltrating your life just to be a janitor?" Felicity asks. "It's not as if he's known for his love of labor."

"He wasn't just a janitor. He befriended me, or tried to, anyway. And he sold me drugs."

"Drugs? As in—" Bishop starts.

"As in special K. As in sleeping pills. As in, he gave me the magical combination of drugs to help me discover my fucked-up entrance to Narnia."

Ray and Bishop glance heavily at each other.

The wolf pup howls from under the table and bats at the laces on Bishop's shoes.

Ray's face grows anxious, her brows pinched together in concern. Ivy vines begin to grow from between her legs, spiraling out onto the ground around her.

"The question is why?" Savage continues, "I mean, there's no way he didn't know what would happen to me. He did it deliberately. I just don't get why he'd want me to discover this world."

"Remember the sirens, kid?" Bishop says after a long sip of whiskey. "He sent them for you."

"Okay. But still: *why?* Why was it important to have me mouth-raped by a bunch of harpies?"

"Sirens, not harpies. You're getting your myths mixed up. But they're actually succubi."

"I don't fucking care what they are. I care about what the goddamn devil wants with me." Savage lets out an exasperated sigh.

On Felicity's shoulder, the merlin flaps its wings. She squints her eyes but remains still, waiting for the bird to settle again. "Who knows why Devlin does what he does? Maybe it was just to get the chess piece from you?" she suggests.

"But Bishop gave me that well after I met Devlin as the janitor. That's making a big assumption that I would even meet Bishop. Or that he'd befriend me or make me his apprentice. Or give me the bishop piece. Why is that important to him, by the way? What can he do with it?"

"I'm not entirely sure, but it's not good," Bishop says. "It's not just a talisman, it's a piece of me. It was carved from my bone."

"That's . . . creepy. Thank you for not telling me that when you gave it to me."

"Yup." Bishop tilts his glass to Savage.

From her corner of the sectional couch, Ray is looking worse for wear, her skin sagging and aging, her shoulders rounding under the great invisible weight of the world.

"You okay over there?" Savage asks her.

"Nervous," is her only reply.

"Great. Mother Earth herself is anxious. That's not at all unsettling . . ."

"Just let her do her thing, kid." Bishop waves a gloved hand. "She'll feel better once she's back outside."

"Let's not overwhelm ourselves with speculating about the Knave's motivations," Ray says as she gathers the vines and bunches them together in a fistful of flora. "Let's focus on what he's planning next. I think it's time we involve the Engineer."

"No, no, no. I don't want to do that." Bishop shakes his head like a petulant child.

"Bishop, it's time."

"It's always a thing with him. It's never a simple conversation. Like 'Oh, hey, heads up, Devlin's up to something weird. K, take care.' It's a whole diatribe covering every possible outcome of every possible scenario, and we have to talk through all of them. At length. Weighing every pro and con. It is always a thing."

"Bishop," she chides.

He rubs his eyes. "Can you two give us a couple minutes please?" he says to Felicity and Savage.

"That's fine, Bishop. I should be tending to my artists. After the sojourn into the underworld, I need some sustenance." Felicity sets her wineglass on the end table and gently removes the merlin from her shoulder. It flutters in objection. "And I should be checking in with the other muses after Verity's passing." She turns to Savage. "Come walk with me."

Outside the mausoleum, they walk quietly through the graveyard, its paths abandoned because of the late hour. The trees are sprouting leaves and buds in little black filagree of shadows. Giant stone monuments punctuate their walk, their epitaphs obscured by the night.

"Thank you," Felicity says.

"For what?"

She gives a half smile, mirthless. "The kelpies," she responds, as if it's obvious.

"You shouldn't be thanking me. You should be chastising me for getting you hurt in the first place." He takes a deep breath. He has that sinking intuitive feeling that occurs before a breakup.

But this isn't a relationship. It may be deeper than any other connection he's had with a woman before, but that's because she's not a woman. And she's not his.

He stops walking, regards the back of her for a moment, her long auburn hair falling down her back. It's tangled and disheveled from the journey under. He did that. His stupidity broke her. "That's why you wanted me to walk with you, right?" he asks. "You're leaving."

She turns back to him, her eyes bright over her shoulder. "Yes."

Emotion wells up inside him. He cannot fathom doing this, doing *any* of this, without knowing her face. Without tasting her inspiration. Without her laugh or opinion or scent in his nose. "Please," he says quietly. "I'll do better. I'll be better. I'll protect you."

"It's not that." She sighs and looks out into the black night. The lights of New York are hidden here, among the dead and their sepulchers. "I keep thinking about that woman. She did nothing. She was as much a chess piece as the one you gave Devlin. Just a pawn . . ." Her voice trails off as her eyes fill with tears. "I'm not used to seeing that, Savage. My existence is beauty and art. I exist in the songs composed on pianos in the dark. The first paint strokes on white canvases. The idea that wakes the writer in the night and drives them to the page. I can't"—she stifles a sob, her eyes swimming beneath unbroken wells of tears—"I can't process what I just witnessed."

Savage's eyes soften as she speaks. He lets all the air escape his lungs. He thinks about not inhaling. About never filling them again. He steps to her. "But I don't know how to stay away." He runs the tips of his fingers over the length of her arm.

She sniffs her emotion down her throat, pulls away from him and folds her arms over her middle. "That's just the inspiration," she says, composing herself. "You can play 'reaper' all you want, but you're an artist to the bone. You're just addicted to the muse. And I'm going to simplify it for you. I'm taking away the temptation."

"Felicity," he says, feeling her name on his tongue like some delicate fruit. "I need you."

She shakes her head. "You don't." She puts a hand to his cheek, rubbing the space where his skin gives way to his scruff with her long thumb. She holds his gaze for a last, loaded moment before walking off into the night.

"Whatever we're going to do, let's get on with it."

"You're in a splendid mood, kid."

He's woken from a broken night of sleep on the reaper's couch. His bones hurt like he's detoxing from some drug he didn't know he'd been addicted to. "I lost my fucking muse."

"She wasn't your muse," Bishop corrects. He's tying a black tie under the collar of a black suit.

"Thank you for that. That feels wonderful," he replies.

"Sorry. I know you're cranky." Bishop glances over his shoulder at him and offers a grimace of a smile. "I'm waiting on Ray before we go to talk to the Engineer. I'm not dealing with him alone."

"You look very Johnny Cash," Savage comments, dryly.

"I am a bit man-in-black, today."

"Who is the Engineer, exactly?"

Bishop thinks a moment. "I don't know how to answer that question without giving up all the secrets of the universe."

"Well, that's helpful," Savage says as he walks to the kitchen sink. He splashes cold water over his face and combs his fingers through his dark hair. "Is he god?" he asks, water dripping from his lips and eyelashes.

"God? Like The Father, The Son, and The Holy Spirit? Like

Allah? Like Brahma? Definitely not."

"So, what is he?"

"He's the Engineer."

"What does he engineer, then?"

Bishop grunts. "Look, kid, I get it. It's in your nature to ask about the nothingness of being and the everything-ness of being, but I don't have time to go over the intricacies of the universe right now. I need to mentally prepare for the inevitably long meeting we are about to embark upon. Willingly, for some reason."

Savage flops on the couch. He fluffs a red pillow, punching it into submission, and leans his head back, staring up at the ceiling. "Why can I see in full color, now?"

Bishop thinks a moment. "I don't know. Maybe your eyes have been opened."

Maybe I'll ask the Engineer, Savage thinks.

Ray enters the mausoleum with a gust of wind, the hood of her brown cloak fluttering behind her head. Underneath she wears dark pants, a maroon tank, and low doeskin boots. She looks like she came straight from scavenging in the forest, and she smells of earth and warm, sweet rot. "The Engineer is ready for our audience."

"Did you tell him we're bringing the kid?"

"Yes, he knows."

They look at each other a beat too long before their eyes skip away.

More secrets, more words unsaid. Like they're talking in code, somehow. Like they're adults spelling out the bad words in front of the toddler.

He sits up. "Would my coming be a problem or something?"

"No. I just want to make sure he knows." Bishop shrugs.

In Bishop's Toronado, Savage lets Ray ride shotgun.

He wants to revel in his dour mood, but Bishop and Ray's ridiculous banter is making it difficult. He gazes out the windshield as the city moves past them in a kaleidoscope of color.

"You have to turn here," Ray says, flicking her tattooed wrist to the right. Bishop continues straight through the intersection. "Well, that was the turn . . ." she says, looking forward stoically.

"Please don't backseat drive," he tells her. "You always tell me these ass-backwards ways of getting around because you're not familiar with the city."

"Excuse me. I'm familiar," she corrects. "This city teems with life. I have my fingers in every inch of it."

"Yeah, in the rats in the subway and the squirrels in the parks but not navigating a vehicle."

"I have dominion over all living things, Bishop, taxi drivers included."

"Don't get me started on how cabbies drive, woman," he retorts.

She sighs in exasperation.

In a midtown high-rise crafted of steel and glass, the three wait. It's been at least a half an hour. Savage doesn't know. Time has become irrelevant since he stopped carrying a phone and renounced his membership to the human race.

The reaper looks perturbed, leaning back in his chair too far and staring up at the ceiling. The Earth Mother exudes patience. If she's bored, Savage can't tell. She's doing that subtle undulating thing again, rolling slowly back and forth like the tide.

Savage sits forward, his head heavy in his palms. His dark hair falls around his face like a short, black curtain. He's despondent. Detoxing. The onslaught of recent events is weighing on him with crushing density, and the lack of Felicity's inspiration is compounding it. He's not examining the fact that he'll never see her again. It's too depressing to bear.

They're in a conference room, a clear box situated at the center of a sterile office. Everything is black and white, metal and glass.

Bishop teeters in his office chair, tilting on its back wheels with a squeak. He whistles some tuneless melody. "Always takes forever . . ." he mutters under his breath. He sits up a little and reaches into the pocket of the reaper coat.

"Here," he says, extending one of the iridescent bottles of inspiration to Savage.

"What, seriously?"

"A *sip*. A teeny, tiny, minuscule little swallow."

Savage pulls the shrunken cork from the bottle, and puts it to his lips, letting a drop of the liquid roll over his tongue and down his throat.

It tastes like her.

It tastes like color. Sunset and blood oranges. Some sweet wine and orgasm. It explodes off his tongue and ripples through his body. It warms his throat and crawls within him, igniting every inch. He feels the roots of his hair hum with a stinging pleasure. He feels it travel down the length of his body, his stomach, his groin, his toenails in his shoes. It feels clean and alive.

"Jesus," he mutters, handing the vial back.

"Better?" Bishop asks.

"Yes," Savage sighs. But it opens up something morose inside him, too. That this is all he'll get of her anymore, that this is the only way he'll be able to taste her inspiration, feels wrong. He feels sustained and robbed at once.

The glass door to the conference room opens. A beautiful woman—perfect posture in a midnight dress and shiny heals, black hair tied back, hooded come-fuck me eyes—enters with a snicker. "You all make quite the threesome," she laughs.

"Bet you'd like that, sister," the reaper responds, staring off into space, not giving her eye contact.

"What you do in your spare time, Bishop, is really up to you. But please," she adds, gesturing to Ray, "don't fornicate with the Forebearer. I'm pretty sure that will lead to the destruction of the universe."

"Where is he, After? We've been here for like, a year."

"Patience is a virtue. Then again, so are moderation and reverence, and you lack those as well, so . . ." She speaks in a quick, sarcastic tone. "That aside, I'm here to bring you to him. But by all means, let's continue talking about threesomes."

Ray stands, smoothing her hands over her pants. "We are ready," she says.

"He's been otherwise engaged in the subterranean labs, so I thought it'd be a more prudent use of your time if I escort you to him."

"Whatever you say," Bishop says, standing, "let's just get on with it. This one's got a world of species to propagate, I've got souls to reap, and that one wants to continue wallowing."

As the three make their way to the exit and down the hallway, the woman makes a point to shake Savage's hand. "I'm After. I'm the primary assistant to the Engineer."

"Savage," he replies.

"Yes, you are," she says, letting her hand linger in the shake. Her heels make a pleasant clicking sound against the industrial flooring.

In the elevator, After turns her attention to Ray. "This impromptu get-together aside, the Engineer was planning to facilitate a meeting with you. He wanted to show you the fruits of your labors. The subterranean greenhouses you designed together are taking shape quite beautifully."

"That's wonderful," Ray replies.

The elevator descends.

42

41

40

"It's fascinating watching the flora undergo photosynthesis without direct sunlight. Your work here directly influenced the public space known as "The Lowline," crafted in the old Williamsburg Bridge Trolley Terminal. This project is its direct predecessor."

28

27

26

"I suppose it all works out, because now you'll get to visit the gardens today. Our hope is they will continue to flourish, especially entering the warm seasons."

Savage sighs uncomfortably. "As long as the world doesn't dissolve before then," he mutters, hands in the pockets of his coat.

"Excuse me?" After snaps, turning to him.

Bishop stares and shakes his head.

"Sorry. Stupid joke." Savage shrugs.

"Interesting . . ." After replies.

2

1

-

The *dash* blinks a few beats while the occupants of the elevator shift in an uncomfortable silence.

B1

B2

The elevator stops, sliding open onto a strange, dark scene. What was once the massive basement of the building has been remade into a garden laboratory oasis. Somehow sterile but fertile at once. The air has a bitter, peppery smell, and the dense humidity gives the scent further purchase inside Savage's nose.

The darkness of the space is punctuated by pockets of light. Under strange domes of illumination every twenty feet, little islands of plant-life are flourishing. Trees, ferns, tropical plants, flowers. People in lab coats circle the green pockets of light. They type on tablets, the screens illuminating their faces in the darkness. The scientists make sense to Savage, but he didn't expect the muses. They glide among the others, beautifully anachronistic in their delicate silk dresses and bare feet. They commune with the scientists in hushed tones.

Savage's heart skips a beat as he searches for Felicity, his mind dubious that he'll see her, but his heart and stomach with expectations of their own. After is rambling about botanists and horticulturists, but he's lost the thread of the conversation. She leads them around the space, commenting scientifically to Ray, who nods politely in reply. The muses bow at Ray as she passes, or clasp her hands in their own, sometimes offering a familial kiss.

From between two dense groupings of greenery, Savage catches sight of a man dressed in a pressed white suit. The man's eyes find Savage's, growing wide behind his wire framed glasses. They swell with such intensity, it's as if Savage sees a fire light within them. Savage casts his gaze down, uncomfortable. The man makes his way through the underground garden toward their group.

"Ah, here he is," After says, upon the Engineer's arrival.

He offers a hurried hello to Bishop and Ray and takes Savage's hand in his ardent grasp, shaking it without introducing himself.

"I'm Savage," he says in an attempt to dispel the intensity of the Engineer's gaze.

"Indeed," the Engineer answers, his voice soft, confident, thoughtful. "Indeed."

The man who has only been referred to Savage as 'the Engineer' appears to be close in age to himself, thirty-something. He's shorter than Savage, but then most people are. His blond hair and close-cropped beard are almost the same hue as his skin, giving him a pallid complexion. He readjusts his glasses over the brim of his nose when he releases Savage's hand. Grass stains mar the sleeves of his suit.

He turns to After. "Please clear the space for us." It's an order, but he proffers it gently. Assertive but kind.

"Right away," After replies. "Will you be requesting my presence?"

"Not at the moment. I'll keep you informed."

After gives a half bow of her head, and proceeds to usher out the scientists, the botanists, and the muses.

Bishop and Savage lean into one of the sets of flora under its domed light, examining the setup.

"Bishop," the Engineer laughs, "I'm afraid I'm going to have to ask you to keep a distance from the specimens. Wouldn't want you to breathe too heavily and spoil all the progress."

Bishop's mouth presses in a hard line. "Fair enough," he says. "Seems logical . . . as always."

"It's actually quite a simple design," the Engineer says. "The above ground parabolas act as solar collectors, capturing and condensing the photons and channeling them down fiberoptic helio-tubes, where they are dispersed and reflected within the domes, casting the sunlight down upon the plants.

"It'll be useful in the coming years, should climate change continue the way we predict it will. They can be utilized in cultivating underground food sources, should subterranean crops become a necessity in the future."

"Ah," Bishop says. He looks bored already.

"The muses have continued to be of help?" Ray asks, running her fingers over a waxy leaf as if she were absentmindedly petting a dog.

"Indeed. They have been essential in inspiring notions into the proper minds. Without the muses, I don't know where we'd be with the project."

"That's wonderful."

The Engineer keeps looking to Savage as he goes through his scientific explanations and observations, like he's seeking his approval.

Savage nods as if any of this makes sense to him.

"I'm so happy you guys are continuing to improve the world," Bishop interjects, "but we need to strategize about Devlin before he undoes everything, and the world is sucked into oblivion, and all the 'parabolas' and 'helio shoots' won't mean shit."

"What's *the Knave* gotten himself into, now?" the Engineer asks, emphasizing Devlin's chosen moniker sardonically. "Nothing you can't handle, I'm sure."

"I know you usually try to stay uninvolved in his bullshit, but we thought you should be involved."

"You need to be on alert," Ray says. "We don't know what he's scheming, but he's taken something from Bishop. I suspect he'll be coming to you soon, if not next."

"To take something?"

"Perhaps."

"What did he take from you?" he asks Bishop, his brow pinching on itself in displeasure.

"A chess piece."

"Carved of his bone," Savage adds. "Sorry, that seems important."

"Indeed, it is." The Engineer nods at him, again staring with eerie intensity. After a pause he adds, "There was an attempted infiltration of my office a short while ago."

"What? Was it Devlin?" Bishop asks.

"I cannot be sure, but I assume so, as the only ones who already know of this building's existence can locate it. I can't think of anyone in need of something within these walls who wouldn't feel comfortable merely asking.

"Regardless, my property is thoroughly protected, and while the guilty party vanished, they were unable to obtain whatever it was they were after."

"Speaking of *After*, you sure you can trust her?" Bishop asks, a stubborn frown bending his mouth.

"Bishop, not this again."

"I don't like her."

"You just don't like that someone else rivals you in snark."

"That may be true but it's not the whole of it."

"She's been my most trusted ally."

"*I* don't trust her."

The Engineer nods. "I know that. But regardless of whether you approve of whom I spend my time with, she has been my longest and most devoted subordinate, as well as a source of companionship to me after I lost, well . . . what I lost." He quiets for a moment, and stares at Savage again, bestowing on him the same overly intimate and too-long-for-comfort gaze as earlier. "Anyhow, this was clearly an outside job. Had After been compromised, I surmise she could have simply allowed the infiltrators into my personal quarters, but their attempt was thwarted. Ergo, it was not After. And my earthly possessions remain my own."

"Good." Bishop concedes. "Try and keep it that way, yeah?"

"I will try. Thank you for involving me. I don't know that I would have understood the severity of the incident without being included in the dialogue."

"Anytime," Bishop says, clapping his hands together. "Shall we?"

The Engineer laughs, joylessly, as if Bishop's request is absurd. "You're not leaving yet? We should go upstairs and examine the implications of Devlin's actions."

Bishop lets his head fall dramatically to one side. "Of course, we should."

The Engineer's personal office is at the penthouse level of the building. Savage stands at one of the large windows, looking out onto Manhattan with a voyeuristic fascination at the people traversing the shrunken streets. The drop of inspiration has waned in his blood and that irritable flatness is beginning to overtake him once more.

The walls of the office are lined with shelf after shelf of identical books with slate spines. It makes Savage think of Bishop's black notebooks, the records he keeps of the gateways of the dying. He wonders what lives on the pages of the Engineer's books.

Ray and Bishop sit opposite the scientist at his desk. He's making notes with a mechanical pencil in tight precise handwriting. Ray and Bishop have recounted the story of when Devlin kidnapped Bishop. The beginning of the event had piqued Savage's interest, the part he was absent for. How Devlin had managed to capture the reaper was a complex plot, carefully calculated. The Engineer had commented as much. "Doesn't seem much like Devlin, all this forethought" he had said.

The forethought to send in his battle-born—the demonic spirits born of bloodshed and war—to seize the opportunity of Verity's passing and utilize her gateway. Through talking it out, they had realized the flaw that had allowed the battle-born entrance to the sacred space: as Verity was not a human, her gateway existed in a realm creatures of the otherworld could access. Verity, yes, but also the battle-born.

It had never been done before. The unwritten rules had been respected. Bishop had been allowed to reap the souls of countless deities in the past, unmolested. But Devlin grew dissatisfied. His dissatisfaction led to plotting, which led to intervening. The battle-born stormed the space and caught Bishop unaware.

But now, the conversation has moved onto the retelling of the moment of the compromise and the traded chess piece, when the innocent was slaughtered, and he learned of the existence of his twin. His interest wanes.

"Second-degree Savage," Bishop calls the doppelgänger. "Burned to a crisp on one side of his face and not nearly as good as the original."

"Thanks," Savage says dryly from the window.

"He made a clone of the Artist . . ." the Engineer thinks aloud, clicking the end of his pencil. "That's . . . unprecedented." He turns to Savage. "What do you make of this?" he asks him.

"What, me?"

"Yes. What do your instincts tell you? I'm very interested in the point of view of someone of your kind."

"I don't know. This is the first time I've been mind-fucked by the devil."

"Probably won't be your last," Bishop mutters.

"You have fresh eyes with which to view the situation," The Engineer prompts again.

What is that look? Savage thinks, shifting under the gaze of the Engineer. *Longing? Sadness? But also . . . excitement.* Savage takes in a thoughtful breath. "I don't think this is something done on a whim. I think he's executing a plan he's been mulling over for a while. Like where did he get his hands on the metal to make Bishop's handcuffs from? The metal he said you blessed?" He gestures to Ray.

"I consecrated it many moons ago. At the inception of the Earth, when the world was new, and life was beginning. I blessed cooling magma from volcanos across the planet so life might someday take root."

The Engineer breaks eye contact from Savage and makes a note.

"Yeah . . . that's disconcerting. He's been holding onto metal that you blessed before the dawn of man, for what? Just in case?"

"Probably," Bishop adds.

The Engineer bombards Ray with an onslaught of questions pertaining to the specifics of the magma and the metal and the rock, of the precise estimate of time and the particulars of the place, which spurs him into a further tangent concerning the formation of land prior to the presence of water.

It's of little help that Ray's sense of time varies vastly from the Engineer's.

Savage resumes staring out the window.

After a while and with a sigh, the Engineer abandons his pencil, closes his notebook, and sits back in his chair. "It feels extremely satisfying to be in this room with all of you"—he smiles—"again."

"Again?" Savage questions.

The Engineer is staring once more.

"*Us*, again. *You*, first time," Bishop adds, casually.

"No, again," the Engineer clarifies.

"I've never been here."

"Not here, no. But in this company."

"I've never met you."

"Don't," Bishop starts.

Ray is shaking her head.

"Don't what?" Savage asks. "What are you talking about?"

The Engineer turns his attention to the reaper and his foil. "I think it's time to admit this was a failed exercise."

Ray shakes her head more ardently. "This isn't the time nor the place. We're holding on with a tenuous grasp," she says, her quiet calm unraveling.

"In fact, this is a really, *really* bad time," Bishop adds, his words loaded.

"What are you talking about?" Savage steps away from the window, closer to the group.

The Engineer leans his chin onto his hand, his fingers covering his mouth. He studies Savage and says nothing.

"I'm getting tired of these two constantly talking in cagey terms like they know something I don't. And while I know you all know many things I don't, somehow it feels like this pertains to me."

"Haven't you paused to question how it is you're able to

commune with the likes of a reaper and the Forebearer? With muses and demons and timekeepers?"

"Drugs," Savage says. "Drugs the devil gave me."

"And that doesn't strike you as odd?"

"*All* of this strikes me as odd, but I've learned to go with the flow."

"Ambit, *stop*," Ray asserts.

"Ambit?" Savage questions.

"It's my name among friends," the Engineer says. "Do you remember calling me that?"

"I don't know what you're talking about." Savage shakes his head. "What? *What?*" He looks to Bishop. He looks to Ray. He looks to the Engineer. "Just come out and say it."

"*Enough,*" Ray says, standing. She turns to Savage and flicks her hands out at him. She looks incensed, angry in a way he has never seen her.

The silence of the penthouse is gone, a wind blowing in his ears and tossing his black hair about. In a blink, he's been cast out of the building, standing on the concrete sidewalk, down forty floors, a cool spring breeze brushing his skin. He steadies himself, the vertigo of suddenly being somewhere he wasn't, and not of his own volition, making him unsteady on his feet.

He squints up to the glass building before him. It erases from his vision, the space around it knitting itself together until it's gone, like it was never there at all.

"Fucking great," Savage says, buttoning his black coat closed to the wind.

Savage knows the famous library resides at Fifth and 40th, though he hasn't visited it yet. He's been saving it, perhaps unconsciously. Perhaps for today. The grid of the city is easy to navigate, especially around midtown, where the buildings are situated like neatly lined gray teeth.

He climbs the stone steps to the library and walks past the twin lion sculptures. They guard the place like sentinels, their stone eyes disinterested in his concerns of reapers and muses, of the Engineer and the Forebearer.

Inside, he weaves his way up marble staircases and past the wooden walled information booths. The building smells like forgotten things.

The Rose Reading Room is exactly how she described it to him. Writers and students sit at long wooden tables, laptops open, indifferent to the marvelous pink and blue murals of clouds painted above them in the carved ceiling.

Savage paces down the long aisle, glancing here and there for any sign of the muse. The space is charged with something both ancient and novel. Enormous volumes sit open on pedestals, their dusty pages exposed to wandering fingers. He approaches the end of the room where a wooden door gives way to a private research area, and he turns back to face the length of the space. His eyes skim over the people. On the far wall over the entrance, the hands of a massive clock slide over its ivory face.

People read. Others write. Tourists enter the room, marvel and snap pictures of the ceiling, and wander out. A sign at the entrance requests no flash photography to avoid disturbing the readers. Savage pulls a chair out from the farthest table, away from anyone else, its wooden feet scraping over the polished floor, and he waits.

It takes over an hour of watching the internal mechanisms of the room—the artists that power the energy like hamsters on wheels—before she arrives. His stomach contracts on itself at the sight of her, but he remains seated. He wants to savor watching her without her knowing for a moment. He wants a moment of gazing upon her without her pushing him away.

She weaves around the people, like a silent ghost of a dancer. Here and there, she glances over the shoulders of unsuspecting individuals, placing a tender hand on their backs. She's a teacher. A monk. A bird floating on the breeze, the wings of her spirit spread out over her artists. Taciturn and beautiful, she is a universe unto herself. The writers type furiously at their keys as she passes.

She's about a quarter of the way down the length of the room when her posture straightens, and she takes a long, perceptible breath. Her eyes find him where he's hiding. He stands, slowly, presenting himself to her. He can see the dance of her throat as she swallows. Her chest moves like an ocean under her breasts, swelling and falling with the tide of her breathing.

They stare at one another, all the space, the whole room between them, charged with something animal and feline. Instinct and wanting. His breath quickens in his chest, his heart fluttering like the fragile human thing it is.

All else is forgotten.

Some shared, internal starter gun fires, and at once, they

make their way toward one another with confident haste, her light eyes locked onto his dark.

When they meet, it's like some great hand laid its fingers on the keys of a piano, the hammers hitting the strings within, creating a resounding harmony. He takes her face in his hands, looking down into her eyes with searching intensity. She draws in a shallow, trembling breath.

Here, under a painted sky, Savage feels on the brink of epiphany. On the brink of satisfaction and cognizance and climax at once. He unloads all that onto her, his desperate need of her leaks out of his every pore, out of his mouth and into her own.

He feels her resolve breaking down and disintegrating. She clutches to him. She moves with him. She presses into him.

"Now?" he pulls away and asks into her face.

"Now."

In the bedroom of the muse, giant framed Klimt prints flank the bed. The painted women look down with shared lust onto Savage and Felicity as they tangle within and around each other.

He takes her carefully, like he's holding water he fears might spill through his cupped hands. Like he's carrying a flame in the wind. She kisses his neck and bites his ears. She rips off his shirt and runs her fingers over the plane of his chest. He parts her legs like he's Moses and she is the sea. He tastes her. Drinks her. Partakes of her. She has little moles on her inner thigh, like flecks of chocolate melting against the warmth of her skin. She is art itself. It's like nothing he has ever known. She cries in exaltation, tears streaking down her face, before she loses herself completely to the momentum of the moment.

She pulls him inside.

It's minutes or hours but it doesn't matter because time loses all meaning, it unravels and falls apart and is cast aside with the blankets on the floor. When he finishes, sweat stained and exhausted, demanding she come with him, an eternity is born. A prolific endeavor. A perfect oblivion.

Crafted from their consummation, from the break in the block in his mind, an existence of its own catapults him to the edge of his being and springs him back like a slingshot and a trampoline.

He holds her to him, still inside her, and looks down at her. For the first time since his banishment eons ago, for the first time in this life and the many before it, he knows.

He remembers.

INTERLUDE

A whirring sound fills their ears. Soft, like hands run over the back of a bristly-haired animal. Constant. Rhythmic, like the loops of a ceiling fan. In this static, they hear nothing, so they might hear everything.

They sit before one another, cross legged, left palm up, right palm down. Their hands hover over one another's so they're conjoined like pieces of a puzzle, their nebula-freckled fingers stretched out before them.

"Well?" the impatient one demands, throwing his hands up.

They remain silent, as they must if they are to divine anything.

The Knave stalks off, indignant.

The little rectangular windows let in too little light from the street into the cluttered basement apartment. They burn nag champa incense, and the smoke clings to the windows, presses to the glass. The air is warm and heavy.

Here, amidst the dozens of psychics that litter the West Village—the tarot card readers, palmists, and mediums—the Oracles make their home and have since the 1960s. Hiding in plain sight. Vibrating beneath the street.

They fill the space with things they like. Things with energy. Things with buzz. Countless vintage TVs, some displaying gray static screens, some dormant since the 80s, and one that has been converted into a fish tank to house a single rainbow-tailed betta. A young Bengal cat pats at the fish through the glass. Geodes, geodes everywhere. One large enough to sit in, its top cracked open like a giant oyster revealing a purple universe inside. A taxidermic fawn under a bell jar. Blue winged butterflies pinned in a glass box. Big black branches from a long dead tree. Conch shells. Animal bones. A single human skull.

Their own private cabinet of curiosities, lying unseen under Cornelia Street.

Devlin picks up the skull and blows into the eye socket. It makes a hollow sound.

The twin souls sit near the east facing wall, near a strange three-tiered altar. Candles burn from the top level, with long flames on long wicks quivering despite the still air. Bells litter the lower shelves: silver and brass bells on little handles, jingle bells, diner bells, dinner bells, glass bells, silver baby rattles. Above hang lamps crafted of old ostrich eggs, casting a veined amber light over their puffy white hair.

The Oracles close their sightless white eyes and fold their hands in their laps.

"Finally," he says. "What did you see?"

"Nothing," they say together, in one voice.

"What? How is that possible?"

"No—" one starts.

"—thing," the other finishes.

They open their eyes and regard him, the four white orbs unblinking. It's unnerving, even to Devlin. He looks down at the skull in his hands.

"I heard you the first time." He grunts, more to the skull than to them. "Alas, poor Yorick . . ." He sets it down onto one of the old television sets. "Guys, guys. You're the Oracles. You see all the things. All there is to see. Elaborate."

"What you ask us to seek exists outside the scope," one says.

"Outside the scope of time, space, life, death, earth, air, fire, water, plasma, matter, science, art, idea, and consciousness," the other continues, her voice flat.

"Seeing as we are composed of time, space, life, death, earth, air, fire, water, plasma, matter, science, art, idea, and consciousness, it is beyond us."

"We cannot look where you seek."

"Where you seek does not exist."

"But that's the point." Devlin slams his fist down onto the skull, cracking the ancient bone. A few of its teeth come loose. "*Can* it exist?"

"Your question is inane."

"Can humans evolve into cats?"

"Can the continents reform into one mass?"

"Anything is possible."

"Anything can be."

Devlin smiles and clenches his fists triumphantly, the tattoos over his fingers stretching in the exertion.

"However . . ."

"How—"

"—ever."

"It never has. In time, space, life, death, earth, air, fire, water, plasma, matter, science, art, idea, and consciousness, what you seek has never been."

"In every iteration of every possible existence—"

"—in every possible outcome of every possible universe—"

"—it never has."

"That means nothing. This would be none of that. Not time, space, life, air, etcetera, etcetera . . . blah, blah, blah. It would be something *new*."

"New is beyond us."

"We are ancient."

"And we are tired."

"We are everything—"

"—and what you describe is nothing."

Devlin grunts, "This is so fucking frustrating. That's the whole point!"

"What you may take away is this."

"There is a void."

"Voids can be filled."

"It will work," he tells them. "I know it. I *know* it. And I'm so close."

"We are ancient."

"And we are tired."

"And you must go now."

The Knave stands for a moment, brooding. Attempting to be intimidating, perhaps.

The Bengal cat has climbed to a nearby perch and is pawing

at the cottony-white orb of hair of the oracle on the left. She doesn't notice.

Devlin walks through the cloud of incense smoke toward the door and opens it, letting in sharp afternoon light from the street. "Now ladies, this is between you and me, yeah? Don't tell the others what I asked if they come looking."

They blink once, twice and look off into the void.

"They'll be looking."

"But not with us."

"Your visit today will remain unknown to the others."

"Good."

With that, the Knave slams the door behind himself. They see his shoes as he walks past their window.

They see everything.

TEMPERANCE

PART III

TEMPERANCE

FIFTEEN

Things are fuzzy. Of all the words in all the languages, *fuzzy* is such a cheap word, but that's what Savage thinks. Things are fucking fuzzy. The moment of sharp clarity with Felicity has softened, and his two realities are coalescing into one. The massive amount of information is difficult to process with his human mind.

The Engineer's building is easy to find now that he has been reminded of his true self. It tries to hide from him, to conceal its existence. But it's like a kid playing hide and seek, he can see its toes sticking out from under the door. He pulls away its protective layer like he's casting a curtain aside.

He adjusts the collar of his long dark coat. How strange that after all this time, after all these incarnations, he would find himself in the garb of a reaper.

The door opens under his hands, the metal bending to his will, the atoms impressionable and fluid. The lobby is dark, but light illuminates the doors of the silver elevator. It chimes and opens, though he doesn't recall pushing the button.

Up.

Ascending.

He had to leave. Felicity knew. They were puddles of emotion, the great realization visible on his face, betraying his thoughts. But she already knew.

They shared a long silence, reveling in the moment. She broke it with a hoarse whisper.

"This is why I didn't want to persist," she had said, as she slid a lock of his hair out of his eye.

"How long did you know?" he asked her quietly.

"From the first night we met. There's a reason why you taste like nothing else I have ever known in this world."

He had stayed quiet for a long time. "Why didn't you tell me?"

She shook her head. "It wasn't my place."

He kissed her hair, and dressed, and told her he needed time.

The elevator chimes again, and he's at the penthouse office, stepping into the grand space on the forty-second floor.

The Engineer is still sitting behind his desk. Savage wonders if he's moved at all since earlier that day. Ray and Bishop have long since left.

It's late and the office is dim, but a small desk light illuminates the space before the Engineer, where he pours over his notes and makes occasional annotations. He's absorbed, spinning, his lips moving with his thoughts. The sleeves of his shirt are rolled up to the elbow.

"Ambit," Savage says, approaching the desk.

The Engineer looks up, surprised.

"I know," Savage says, condensing his world of thoughts

and scope of emotion into two small words.

Ambit furrows his brow in sadness and hope. "You remember?"

"I remembered everything. Everything." Savage exhales. "For one instant. It grew into an eternity. And it all became clear to me. I knew . . . but now the instant is done and gone, and I am so confused."

Ambit sets down his pencil. "Savage," he says, "you know."

"We are the creators."

"Yes."

"We are gods."

"Before the known universe was created, another analogous universe existed, one with creatures of varied talent. Massive and ageless. Blithe and ingenuous.

"Among these creatures, there existed four companions. Friends who wished to work together on an artistic endeavor, one of infinite balance and justice, to witness the effects of a macrocosm spun solely on equilibrium. They each brought a unique perspective and talent to the project.

"They preoccupied their existences with this undertaking. At first it was just hypothetical, the idea-drunk musings of creative spirits. But the more they talked about it, the more substantial it became. This idea became a manifestation. This manifestation became a reality. And this reality became a universe.

"Bishop, as he was not known then but is now, was

morbidly curious at the idea that an entity could cease to exist. His kind—*our* kind—was doomed, if you will, to live forever. Bishop wished to bestow the peace of passing through the veil of night upon his creations.

"Ray was preoccupied with the inverse. She wished to watch things grow. To mature. To know a beginning, as she had none of her own. Bishop would bring the end and Ray would proffer the start. Ray's beginning and Bishop's end created time.

"Then there was the artist and the architect. You, Savage. And me.

"While you were fascinated with the beauty of all things—the quiet subtleties and artistic particulars—I was concerned with the science. Thus, you are the reason why the world looks the way it does, and I am the reason why the world works the way it does. Down to the molecule, down to the *atom*. We once worked together to create the entire fabric of this universe.

"Where Bishop and Ray created time, we created space.

"This world is a marriage of our work, where beauty meets science. Happenstance and designed coincidence. We are in the Fibonacci swirls tucked into every corner of the universe. We are the golden ratio. We are why chlorophyll reflects green light. We are why a rainbow is the result of sunlight through a prism.

"To put it another way: Pythagoras once said, 'There is geometry in the humming of the strings; there is music in the spacing of the spheres.' I am the geometry in the humming of your strings; you are the music in the spacing of my spheres." Ambit presses his lips together and watches his words take purchase.

Human emotions evade Savage. He's beyond the comprehension of his mind and body. Ah, but his soul. His soul knows this story. It's his history.

"And Devlin?" he asks, remembering. "We needed a fifth."

"Yes. Our concept was being crafted with so much warmth and positivity. But we were striving for balance. We each had a foil, Ray to Bishop and you to me, but we needed a foil for our four selves.

"Devlin was a comrade, though not quite a friend. Not as close to us as we were to each other. He was a sensitive soul. Thoughtful, pragmatic. We approached him with the idea and posed to him our problem. He took the literal weight of the universe on his back in obliging the favor we asked of him. To bring the ultimate balance to our world. To bring unrest to our utopia. He was our Atlas.

"With Devlin, we had our five. No major decisions would be made without a majority vote. We were the original oligarchy.

"But the world of hate and anger and evil long ago corrupted Devlin. He's no longer the benevolent spirit we once knew. He's something different now . . . though I suppose we all are. Perhaps striving for the equanimity we sought was the true great flaw in our plan."

Ambit lets the words hang in the air, intangible but vivid, like prisms. He stands and approaches Savage. "Brother," he says, arms extended. Savage looks at him for a moment, remembering the depth and breadth of their history. He hugs the Engineer, breaking.

Tears swell in his human eyes, as if to remind him of when he created them. He is the reason why tears exist. Why emotion has a tangible manifestation to display on the face in undeniable candor.

"How long was it?" he mumbles into the shoulder of his friend. "How long before I changed my mind?"

"You didn't change your mind, exactly," Ambit replies. He pats Savage on the shoulder and returns to his chair.

Savage sits heavily across from him, burying his mouth into his palm, gripping his face. The desk light reflects in Ambit's glasses creating two golden orbs over his eyes.

"You didn't wish to scrap the design entirely," Ambit continues, "you merely wanted to start over. You, the eternal perfectionist, thought we could do better. That we *should* do better. That we owed it to ourselves and the likes of our creations to achieve perfection . . . though that meant erasing existence as they knew it."

The past dances its horrible truths over Savage's bones. "You banished me," he says from behind his hand, the memory of rejection a bitter fruit on his tongue.

Ambit takes off his glasses and looks squarely into Savage's eyes. "Yes. It was not a decision taken lightly. Our thought was if you could be sentenced to human life, you would grow to appreciate the minutia of the beauty you yourself had created."

"But I didn't."

"I don't know that that's true."

"I was supposed to be subjected to human life. *One* human life? I've been a human for a dozen lifetimes. Clearly, I haven't learned my fucking lesson. Did you forget about me?"

"No. That's not it. It wasn't time."

"*It wasn't time?*" Savage barks. "What arbitrary

measurement are you using to dictate my banishment? Ambit, you robbed me of myself."

"I know it, Savage. I know. I have regretted that decision for centuries. That's why I had to find you. Why I gave Devlin the drugs that would break down the barrier to our world."

Savage starts to speak, but his words are trapped in confusion behind his lips.

"I had tried and tried to convince Bishop and Ray it was time, but they wouldn't listen. They claimed I wasn't to meddle in your human life, that they could sense if you came back to your divinity, you would still choose to start the universe over." Ambit shrugs his shoulders. "But I didn't care. It wasn't worth it to me, anymore. I missed you. I have been acutely, *painfully* lonely. And incomplete. I wasn't supposed to exist in this world without a foil. Why do you think science has exploded in recent history? The Industrial Revolution, the Information Age. The Internet, Savage. The fucking Internet."

"It looks like you've had yourself a nice Renaissance, brother."

"That's just it. There's no balance. Do you remember the Renaissance? Do you remember DaVinci, Savage? We were the hands that pushed that man to paint the Last Supper, to conceive of his hydraulics and his flying machines. His Mona Lisa and his Vitruvian Man. There's no art now, Savage. No balance. There are no DaVincis."

Savage swallows, the taste of nostalgia mixing with the brine of his anger.

"Please," Ambit continues, "don't harbor resentment toward us. We were just trying to do what we thought was best." He picks up his glasses and runs a cloth over their lenses.

"You aligned with Devlin?" Savage asks.

"It's not something I'm proud of," Ambit replies, replacing his glasses on his face. "Desperation breeds necessity."

"But now Devlin wants to unmake the world . . . Aren't you worried that in bringing me back, you've just irrevocably fucked the universe? Doomed its inhabitants?"

"No," he says, quietly. "I think you've changed. Your mind, that is. You're still very much the same Savage I've always known, though your moniker is new."

Savage tries to remember the centuries that preceded his human existences. "What was my name before? I can't remember."

Ambit looks at him, his eyes earnest. "I can't remember either. It's like you were always 'Savage.' Maybe you always were . . ." They're quiet for a long time before Ambit says, "I need to ask you this, Savage. I need to know. Do you still feel like we ought to strive for perfection? That we should eradicate all flaws, all defects? Do you feel that the human experience is a jumbled mess of excrement, and we should dispose of it and start over?"

Savage thinks for a long moment. "I don't know."

"You'll need to decide soon."

"Why? We've had this debate a hundred times over a thousand years. Why now?"

"Because I've discerned what Devlin is scheming at."

"What?" Savage asks. "He wants to unmake the world to claim its souls?"

"No." Ambit shakes his head. "He wants to make his own universe. Without us."

SIXTEEN

That scheming fucker is already two steps ahead. Savage walks down the darkened streets of Brooklyn to the part of Brighton Beach where the subway clatters overhead. Bits of litter caught in the wind scamper down the sidewalk before Russian storefronts. The night is bitter. His spirit might be learning he's beyond this body, this time, this world, but his skin still feels the cold. He's turned up the collar of his jacket, and he strides with ire and purpose, a plague unto himself. A wraith. A myth.

He may not remember everything, but his once and future glory brims within him. He is a god spurned, and someone is going to feel his wrath.

Ah, yes, this is the shit hole. It looks different and it looks the same. He remembers the confusion his human mind underwent, stumbling down the stairs like a child as he arose from the blanket of the succubi's sick magic.

The glass door yields to his touch; he tells the mechanisms

inside the lock to dance and twist like they're moving for a key.

Up the stairs.

C fucking 7.

He gathers himself, buttons up his anger, and slides into the room silently.

Some hairy beast of a creature is plowing into one of the blondes, her legs and arms splayed and jostling like the limbs of a marionette. The other two are biting dutifully at his ears and kissing his chest. The beast grunts in a way that is part howl of a dog and part snort of a pig.

Savage settles into a moth-bitten armchair in the corner of the red room. He embraces a casual affect and waits a few moments.

He lets out an audible sigh.

The sirens stir, frightened.

"Look, you creepy little shits. I'm going to need you to stop fucking this wildebeest." He gestures. "It's time to answer for what you did."

The women scamper, reaching for sheets and clothes.

"Don't bother," he says. "I've seen you far more indisposed. Or did you forget?"

The beast is puffing his chest out in anger. If possible, he's even uglier from the front than the back. He's grunting in a tongue Savage doesn't condescend to be able to discern, but his intent is clear. He's complaining about either the fee paid to the sirens or the massive blue balls he now suffers from.

Savage is unamused.

His newly remembered deity status may be going to his head, rendering him cocky, but it feels delicious. He lets the beast mutter for a moment, casting his gaze aside in apparent boredom. He stands, straightens his coat, and interrupts the creature mid-argument, evoking his divine voice. "I **DON'T FUCKING CARE.**"

Concise, if not altogether holy.

The creature quivers beneath the weight of the voice of a god. The sound dangles him from the edge of his sanity. He cowers and cries out, clutching his head and running for the door. His erect member slaps back and forth between his legs as he flees the room, in a manner Savage finds both disgusting and amusing. The door slams shut behind him.

"Damn straight."

The triplets are frightened, but they muster their courage to stand together like one three-headed unholy creation.

"Leave this place," they say in their echoing singular voice. "You have no dominion over us. The Knave is our only master. You cannot harm us."

"You want to test that theory?"

The blondes blink in response, the cogs turning in their collective brain.

"Right." He rolls the sleeves up on his jacket, calmly, and lunges. He grabs one of the sirens by the arm and tosses her against the crimson wall of the room, single-handedly, where she collapses like a sack of potatoes. He takes her sister and repeats the process against the opposite wall. Then he takes the last blonde by the throat and drops her on the bed, her breathing collapsing under his grasp. "You gave something to him, didn't you?"

The siren gasps. "We don't know of what you speak."

"*Lies.* You gave it to him."

She swallows for breath, her eyes watering.

"Admit it." He loosens his grip to allow her to speak.

"Yes. We gave the Knave your seed. Please, show mercy. We merely followed instruction."

"What did he do with it? Where is he keeping it?"

"We do not ask questions."

"Of course not." He pauses for a moment to think.

One of the sirens on the ground has stirred and lunges at his back, attempting to throw him off her sister. She scratches at his face. He gasps and growls and pulls her off like an insect, throwing her onto the bed next to the other. Their heads knock together with a hollow thud.

"I should end you now for what you did to me. I should shrivel you to nothingness."

The third has stirred, but she learned from the mistakes of the others. She crawls to the bed and cloys to her sisters.

"Instead . . ." Savage takes one of the blondes by the face, almost tenderly, holding her cheeks in each of his great hands, rubbing his thumbs over her skin.

She looks up at him. Expectant. Confused.

He exhales a deliberate breath in her face like he's trying to make the flame of a candle dance but not go out. She presses a palm against his chest, and he lets her go.

The succubi cry out simultaneously, tumbling into inconsolable sobs. He hasn't harmed them. But he's broken them. What he did to one spreads to the others, as if they're connected through an invisible root system.

Their skin falls from age, mottled, cancerous, and weather worn. Their hips grow too wide and their breasts sag. Their fingernails yellow and thicken. Their teeth grow crooked, some fall out by the root to the floor. Their hair loses its artificial curl and luster. No longer Marilyn Monroes, but tired old women.

Playing the reaper has changed his divinity. He cocks his head at them, marveling at the way the death on his breath has manifested itself on their faces in a perfect marriage of his reaper talents and his artistic sensibility.

Each sees the disease of age on her sisters' faces and bodies.

They cry.

They weep.

They reach for him, imploring him with wordless sobs to reverse the process.

"I'm sure you were growing bored of your existence. Now you'll have a challenge. Have fun collecting seamen now."

He leaves them to stew in their lack of beauty.

He walks. He walks to think. He can bounce into existence wherever he pleases, but he walks to allow the movement of his body to turn the wheels of his brain. Morning is upon Brooklyn, the metal grates on the storefronts whisking upward in melodious clatters as he passes by.

He heads north from Brighton Beach through the neighborhoods of the borough. Through Midwood with the Orthodox Jews in their black, flat brimmed hats. Through Prospect Park South, past its lavish colonial houses. Through a waking Park Slope, where parents push strollers with fidgeting babies inside. Through Gowanus. Through Cobble Hill. Through Brooklyn Heights.

He crosses the Brooklyn Bridge, a silhouette among the tourists who are amassing for a prime photo-op. Their vapid smiling faces flanked by a dynamic New York sunrise to post to their social media pages. This is living, evidently. This is what has become of art without his presence. He's a windswept aberration in the background of the pictures.

He reaches lower Manhattan. The smell of warm stroopwafels sweetens the air from a nearby Wafels and Dinges stand. Morning joggers brush past him to cross over the bridge. He tires of walking. His brain has turned enough.

He shudders. It's different than traveling was as a would-be reaper. As a reaper, he felt like he was leaning into a whisper to fall through space. But as himself, his true self, he can comprehend the *greatness* of space, the fibers of which he, himself, created.

He mentally folds the space onto itself infinitely, until he steps through and emerges at the door of the mausoleum. He remembers this traveling, this deep comprehension of space, as if he never forgot. The whirl of sound and air in his ears is a comforting reminder of his divinity. He pushes the door to the crypt back and lets himself inside.

Bishop isn't home. Savage puts a log in the fireplace and ignites the wood. He picks out a Wynton Marsalis album and lays the vinyl on the turntable. The space still smells of sandalwood and incense, some cross between masculinity and church. He pours himself a glass of whiskey for old times' sake, Bulleit over a fat cube of ice. He lets the liquor roll over his tongue before swallowing it down. It tastes like his life. His sorrow and his boredom.

A few minutes pass as he ruminates on his retired humanity

before he turns his concentration to thoughts of Bishop.

He can see him now, as if the reaper were before him. He's escorting a soul to a gateway, in that tender way that is a pure reflection of his spirit.

Savage had planned to let him finish before interrupting. But something in Bishop changes, like he caught Savage's scent on the breeze. He looks right to him. Through space and thought, he sees Savage seeing him. The reaper's eyes well with emotion, and a small smile crosses his lips. Bishop finishes helping the soul depart and with a blink and a rustle, he stands before him.

"Savage," he says quietly. "You remembered?"

Savage nods.

Bishop folds him into his arms like a son, like a brother.

"You understand I couldn't," he says into Savage's shoulder. "I couldn't tell you. I wanted to, so bad. I knew it right from the start, I knew it was you. I hadn't seen you in so long, and I've missed you something fierce." He pulls away. "But I couldn't tell you."

"I know," Savage says. "I'm pretty sure I wouldn't have believed you anyway. I had to come to it on my own." He sits down, and Bishop follows. He picks up his whiskey and swirls the liquor over the ice.

"When I saw you that morning with the sirens, I thought, maybe . . . maybe you'd remembered, that you were yourself then. But it was clear you had no idea." He's quiet for a moment. "Are you angry?"

"Yes."

Bishop hangs his head.

"But I'm also happy to know myself again." Savage studies his friend.

Bishop smiles. "I'm happy about that, too. It's been too long. I was trying to bring you out of it, in my way. That's what all this apprentice-reaper stuff was about. I was trying to show you the beauty of what we created in the only way I know how." He regards Savage for a long moment. "Did it work?"

Savage lets out a weary sigh. "Ambit asked me that, too."

"Motherfucker, you went to Ambit first?"

Savage grimaces and looks into his glass.

Bishop scoffs.

"Look, it was my first instinct."

"Yeah, yeah . . ."

"I was confused. I *am* confused. There's thirteen billion years of history I'm trying to cram into my very human brain."

"No, it's fine," Bishop says, though it's clearly not. "I see how it is."

"Look, I needed to get the facts. Who better than the record-keeper?"

Bishop perks up a little. "Does Ray know yet?"

"No."

"I need to be there for that."

"Honestly, I'm not sure how she's going to react." Savage sets his drink down, the ice clinking against the glass. "She was the one most ardently opposed to my reclamation of myself. I mean, she threw me out on my ass when Ambit tried to tell me."

"Yeah, sorry about that. I wanted to handle it a little more gracefully." Bishop scratches his facial scruff. "She's just afraid you and Devlin are going to kill everything she loves."

"I'm not going to do that."

Bishop straightens. "You're not?"

"No. I'm not going to let Devlin manipulate me. I'm not fond of being the unwitting pawn."

"Aaaaand?"

"And?"

"'And you're a genius, Bishop, king of reapers, master of the macabre, for showing me the error in my ways and the beauty of the universe.' That's what you meant to say."

Savage laughs. "It's true. I tip my proverbial hat to you. Thank you for the window into your world. I might never have truly appreciated the art of what you do without this apprenticeship, for lack of a better word."

"So, now, should we tell Ray?"

"Yes, let's call a meeting of the four. Ambit's made some discoveries and Ray needs to be on alert."

"Yeah, I really don't like that he's your go-to buddy now."

"You wanted to be my go-to buddy?"

"You appreciate my humor. Ray, god love her, but she can be intense . . ."

Someone knocks on the door of the mausoleum, and before Bishop can open it, Ambit lets himself in.

"Good god, I never thought I'd see the day," Bishop proclaims. "The Engineer? Here? In my dirt-covered abode?"

"I cleared my schedule. Some things are more pressing than—"

"Helio-tubes?" Bishop jests.

"Yes." Ambit smiles. "Some things are more important than helio-tubes." Ambit looks strange in his crisp white paleness against the rich tones of the reaper's quarters. "It's not so bad," he remarks.

"Did you think I slept in an actual tomb?"

Ambit bites his lip. "I didn't know what to think."

Bishop throws his hands up in dismay. "This guy . . ."

"Off to see the Forebearer, are we?"

"Watch out, kid, he's in your head already."

Savage smiles. "That's kind of always how it was."

"We were going to give you a shout, but since we're all here, shall we?"

"Savage," Ambit asks. "Do you think you can pinpoint her?"

Savage thinks of their missing piece, of Ray. In some ways, she still feels a stranger to him. His corporeal self cleaves to its memories, and corporeal Savage doesn't know Ray as well.

He concentrates. He remembers her from the days before there was time. She was sultry and warm, like wood on a fire. She was tenacious like fresh earth under fingernails. She was the breath of their group; she was its rhythm and its reason. She was the color to Bishop's shadow.

"Feel her," Bishop says, placing a hand on his chest, "from here. Not from here." He taps his temple.

"I'm trying. It's hard . . . I don't know her like I do you. I am still this self. I may have been a dozen other selves, and I may have been the big self in the sky, but it's confusing to be all that at once." The unruly lock of hair falls into Savage's eye, as if his human body was trying to remind him it still exists, it still has a say.

"It's not just that," Bishop says. "Ray's always difficult to pinpoint, even for me. She's everywhere, she's in everything.

It takes some getting used to."

Savage closes his eyes again. "She feels farther away . . ."

Ambit nods in agreement. "She's constantly shifting, traversing the world. One moment, she'll be camped by the Rio Bueno in Chile, the next, among the rice farmers in Laos. She's everywhere."

Savage closes his eyes again and catches a glimpse of her over the miles, her features illuminated by an orange glow. "She's by a fire."

Bishop nods. "You got it now."

"She's . . . she's in Tahoe." Savage opens his eyes. "You all spend your time in New York, and Ray's in Tahoe?"

"Says something about what we value doesn't it?" Bishop smiles a big, broad, avuncular smile. "You're starting to feel like your old self, again." He pats him on the shoulder. "It's good to have you back. Let's do this."

Savage wills space onto itself like an infinite accordion and pushes through the layers. He steps out onto a snow crusted mountain, the cool dark shadow of the lake down below. The air is so crisp, it cuts through his nose and fills his lungs with pine-scented oxygen.

Ray is stoking the logs of the fire, a young rabbit and a fawn nestled around her feet.

"Savage?" she asks, when she sees the trio approach. She stands and removes the hood of her cloak. "You've remembered." Tears begin to well in her big eyes, catching in her lashes.

"Yes," Savage replies.

"I hope you won't feel like a stranger to me, Savage," she says. Her tears break free and stream down her face. "I've known you in ways no one can understand. I've seen you without shape or form. I am no stranger."

"I'm sorry. I'm still reacclimating. But you're . . . you're not angry? You practically threw my ass down forty stories before, when—"

"I was fighting a losing battle. Clearly. You were meant to remember now, and so you have."

Savage says nothing.

"He's still feeling spurned from his banishment." Ambit breaks the silence.

"You must understand," she says. "We did what we did for the good of all life in this world. Our every godly whim cannot be executed. I was protecting my children."

"I know." Savage nods. "It doesn't mean it didn't hurt."

She steps toward him. "I'm sorry I hurt you. I have been very sorry to be without you. But I would make the same decision again."

Savage smiles at her candor. "I know you would."

She takes his hands in her own. "The question is, would you?"

"We've all been pestering him about that since he's remembered," Bishop says.

"I don't think so," he says down to her face.

"No?"

He sighs. "No."

"Then it was not for naught." She embraces him, pulling him in with her strong arms. He feels her tears saturating the shoulder of his jacket. He returns her embrace and lets her cry. She smells of witch hazel and moss.

"I remember my motivations," Savage says, pulling away

from the embrace.

The group sits around the fire. Bishop puts his arm around Ray. She clears the emotion from her sinuses with a great breath in. The rabbit trembles in its sleep, its long white ears flicking in the glow of the flames.

"Part of me still feels like we can do better," Savage continues, "but I've tasted the spectrum of the human experience. From life through death."

"So, what you're saying is, I tipped the scales," Bishop prompts.

"You jest, but it's true. I couldn't unmake all those souls. I've seen their hearts. It's not in me anymore. That's not even mentioning Devlin. Fuck if I'm going to let him lay claim to the world of humanity. Do I think we could've done better? Yes. But it's too late to try now." He sighs.

Savage looks down to the lake below at the little amber lights illuminating the shoreline.

"Speaking of Devlin," Ambit says, "I've sussed out what his plan is."

"First, you need to tell them," Savage says.

"Tell us what?" Bishop asks.

"No more secrets, I can't fit that all into my brain."

Ambit sighs, giving Savage a loaded look. "I gave Devlin the way to bring Savage back."

"The drugs?" Bishop asks.

"Yes. We located Savage together, and I calculated the precise cocktail it would take to summon Savage to this world."

"No," Bishop barks. "You almost killed him."

"But I didn't."

"You were perilously close, my friend." He shakes his head.

"Ambit," Ray says. "That was not your choice to make alone."

"You say that, but I thought it was time. *Beyond* time." He picks up a stick from the ground and prods the flames. "But my plan has backfired, slightly. I thought Devlin's ulterior motive was to bring Savage back and side with him in the unmaking of the world. But when I realized he kept Savage's semen—"

"Which is fucking gross," Savage interjects.

"—and he plotted to get Bishop's bone, and the attempted infiltration of my personal artifacts, I realized what his actual plot is."

"Which is what?" Bishop asks.

"He wants to craft his own universe. That's the only reason he would need a piece of each of us."

"What did he try to steal from you?" Savage asks.

"I keep vials of my blood locked away for research purposes. Though I've fashioned this corporeal body, I'm curious as to the effects divinity has on DNA."

"Fascinating," Bishop says sarcastically.

"You're sure he wasn't able to access it?" Ray asks.

"Yes. All the vials are still in place. As his scheme to steal them failed, I presume he'll be coming for you next," he says to Ray.

"Do you have anything of yours that he could access?" Savage asks. "A bit of you? Some flesh or bone?'

"All my creations are of my flesh and bone."

"Well, that makes it difficult," Bishop says.

Ambit scratches at his upper lip. "It would need to be more specific. An actual piece of your body."

"If he can utilize any piece of my flora or fauna, he would have had a necessary piece of me long ago." Ray worries.

"No, I think Ambit is right. It can't be that nebulous. He didn't just take some piece of art and call it good from me. He took my *cum*." He grimaces. "And he wants Ambit's blood, he didn't just grab the Wi-Fi code from his building. He didn't grab any MacBook Pro. He needs something off your body. Your corporeal form."

"I will remain on alert," Ray says. "As should you," she adds to Ambit.

"Indeed. I've already increased my security measures on my personal quarters and limited access to only necessary personnel. *Trusted* personnel."

"I've got some reapings I need to attend to. Will you be all right without me?" Bishop asks Ray, patting her thigh.

"I typically flourish without you."

"*Was that a joke*?" Bishop mocks disbelief. "I think that was a joke," he says to the other two.

"You're ruining it," she replies.

"I'm good at that."

"So, what, we'll all just stay on alert and wait for Devlin to make his move?" Savage asks. "I don't like that."

"I don't like it much either, but I've been unable to anticipate the specifics of his next move, other than singling out Ray."

"We'll stay together," Ray says, gesturing to Ambit, "and be vigilant to make sure our body parts and excretions stay our own. In the meantime, Savage, you should go to Felicity."

"Why would a muse help?" Ambit asks.

"She's the reason he remembered," Ray says.

"How ... she ... how did you know that?" Savage asks, confused.

"She must have been. I doubt anything else but a connection with one of my daughters' daughters would reawaken your divinity. Only that or one of the other original five lifting your banishment and allowing you to remember." She looks into him, her gaze intense, the flames reflecting orange over the brown. "We need you to remember yourself as much as possible."

Savage nods. "You're right."

With a swirl of color, he leaves the mountain and finds his muse.

INTERLUDE

From a dark hallway, Felicity peers into the studio. The room beyond is lit by big paned windows, displaying the city at large, which ebbs in swells like a concrete and metal ocean below. The hem of her gown brushes the hardwood floor as she enters. There's no music, only the sound of the dancer's quiet grunts and her feet as they hit the ground.

"One, two, three, four . . ." she counts as she pirouettes.

The dancer can't concentrate. In midtown, the blare of taxi horns is as ubiquitous as bird calls in the forest, and she just wants them to shut up. She wears yoga pants, a sweatshirt, and her broken ballerina shoes, and she feels a fraud.

Felicity feels this. The dancer's frustration, her ire, her self-doubt permeates the space in a thick fog of negativity. But when Felicity enters the room, she swallows it all in one wicked tonic, absorbs it, and replaces it. She replaces it all with inspiration.

The dancer stops and takes a breath. She closes her eyes

and bathes in Felicity's light. She doesn't know it, but she feels it. It washes over her in great warm waves, a pool of inspiration and confidence. Of self-worth and beauty.

The dancer takes off her sweatshirt, panting in exertion. She walks to her phone where it's plugged into the stereo system. She smiles as she cues up a song.

The beginning chords of The Velvet Underground's "Oh! Sweet Nuthin'" plays over the speakers, and the ballerina starts a new dance. She has no choreography but what is born of the moment as she begins to whirl across the studio in low sensual movements.

The dancer stole the song from Felicity's heart. Since the night she met Savage, the song has been playing somewhere in the back of her mind, on a slow sweet loop.

Felicity sighs. She's trying to reclaim herself. To leave her mark upon her artists, but Savage keeps creeping in.

She was wrecked. The night he left, she fell into broken uncontrollable sobs, burrowing into their love-stained sheets, prepared never to rise again. Ashamed and vulnerable, her perfect composure abandoned. She had released her strong two-handed grip on the world and spiraled into a sweet oblivion. A sweet nothing.

How do you keep yourself together after losing yourself to a god? she had wondered.

You don't.

The music picks up, and the ballerina increases the pace of her dance. She spins and leaps, the energy of the muse inspiring a hectic, magic interpretation of the song.

Felicity let go. She let herself be empty so she could be new. All his wonderful artistic energy, she thought it had robbed her, but it didn't. It fed her. It overdosed her. Felicity is nothing if not resilient, and her cup runneth over. So, she has wandered the world, doling out the surplus of inspiration and talent to whomever she can bestow it upon. She'd rain it down on New York if she could. She'd bathe the entire city in his art. But she's only one muse. She's no god. If she must hand out all this artistic genius one soul at a time, so be it.

Felicity drags her fingers over the barre that lines the mirror, its worn wood slick under the ripples of her fingers.

Savage hasn't returned. She can only imagine what he's going through, the weight of the universe crashing over his head in an avalanche of celestial information. But damn if she was going to stay in bed forever while he figured it out.

She wonders if he'll return at all. If the innate inner artist in him, the *king* of all artists, needed a hit of pure inspiration to unriddle the answer to his cosmic questions, and now he's done with her. She wouldn't blame him. She feared as much, and now it might damn well be true.

In some ways, she's thankful. Even if he never finds his way back to her. If he's so overwhelmed by the enormity of his being that he can't be bothered with her any longer, she's still thankful. She's the purest form of herself she's ever been. Alive in ways she's never known, illuminating the inner artist in every spirit who crosses her path. She made a businessman compose a song on the subway. She made a chef scrap his entire menu and craft a new cuisine.

Part of why Felicity loves this studio is because it's close to home. Across the avenue, the large paned windows of her own apartment mirror this one.

The song is reaching its climax. The guitar spinning into

a solo. The bass holding down the rhythm. The background singers echoing like an angelic choir. The dancer spins and spins and spins, teetering like a beautiful top.

Felicity reaches to the window.

The dancer finishes behind her and breathes heavily in triumph.

In her apartment, standing at the window, Savage watches, his tall form and tousled black hair visible from where she stands. He was waiting for her, and he looks at her now, somehow both patient and eager.

Her tiger pout unfurls into a smile and in a whirl of color and prisms, she joins him.

SEVENTEEN

"You left," she says.

"I didn't want to. If I had my way, we'd never leave this bed."

Felicity's hand is on his chest, circling the bristle of hair that lives there. The inspiration comes off her in waves. As she inspires him, he inspires her, and they make a warm synergy so strong, it smells of ozone.

Her bed is like a womb.

"We can arrange that."

He kisses her in that warm, open-mouthed way born of postcoital familiarity. "You think?"

She nods. "Yes. I'm fairly confident you can run the universe from this very spot." She lifts her head from the pillow and reaches to a side table, where she fetches one of her dream joints and lights it with a match. "I think you've earned this," she says, passing it to him.

"I think you're right." He sits up and takes a hit, exhaling a puff of pastel smoke. "Oh wow," he sighs. "The sandmen do their job well." He snuggles down into the golden covers.

"You know I talked to Reve about you."

"Did you? What'd that dreamy bastard say?"

She hesitates. "He said that you had a history of killing your sandmen."

"What?" He leans toward her on a propped-up arm.

"It seems something about your godly nature made their job a little more difficult." She takes another puff.

"So, I've had trouble sleeping my entire adult life because I kept killing off any sandman who deigned to help me? Did they know who I was?"

"I think they could only sense something wasn't right, not exactly who you were. You wore them thin."

"That's fucking awful. They were just trying to do their job, and I killed them." He gasps, but the joint is doing its job, and it comes out half as a yawn. "Walt. I killed Old Walt."

"Who's Walt?" Felicity asks.

"Sandman," he mutters. "He tried to warn me. Poor Old Walt . . . I wonder if I've been an insomniac in all my human lives . . ."

He lays back down, gazing at the atrium ceiling above her bed, the glass glazed over by the cool night and obscured by a rainbow of smoke. Felicity clicks off the light.

He breathes in and out and feels a peace he hasn't experienced in this lifetime. He drifts off.

It's before there was time and before there was space, but he looks like his current self. He wears the body of Ryan Savage, because he's become attached to it.

It feels like a dream, and it feels like the past. But that's how it was then. Vacant and dreamy, empty space and possibility. He lets himself surrender, though he knows that time is gone. He indulges his subconscious and acquiesces to the dream.

Bishop is making him laugh, ever the jovial reaper, and he feels like himself in a way he hasn't in centuries. In eons.

Now there's music and there's beauty. He's dancing. He's in a golden dive bar, the jukebox playing a sultry sixties tune. Felicity is before him, wagging her hips, all satin shape and form. They laugh as they dance, and he pushes her hair over her shoulder and kisses the back of her neck through smiling lips.

Ray is dancing too, buoyant in a way he hasn't seen her in longer than he can remember. She pulls down the hood of her cloak and spins beside them on the dance floor. Her tattoos are swirling over her wrists in brilliant pink blooms.

Bishop toasts them with a vial of Felicity's inspiration as they dance. "To art!" he says.

"To art!" they repeat.

"*Savage,*" a voice whispers behind him.

He ignores it and continues his spin. He's alive and things are simple and beautiful, like the promise of possibility and the possibility of promise.

"*Savage,*" the voice says again. It's in his ear this time, but there's no form, no body, behind it.

Behind the bar, Devlin is pouring drinks. "A shot of tequila, brother?" he asks. He is Oscar and Devlin at once, the tattoos dancing over his skin in a revolving picture show.

"Tequiiiiila," Felicity ruminates.

"**SAVAGE**," the voice shouts. He gets a glimpse of the face this time before it disappears, like a blue Judas in Mary Magdalene's ear at *The Last Supper*.

"What!" he asks, but no one is there to answer.

Ray freezes before him, her face falling.

Felicity is still dancing, but now, the music has stopped. She twists like a marionette on tangled strings.

"What the fuck," he says.

Devlin jumps the bar in a swift motion and pulls out a revolver. But the gun isn't made of steel and bullets. It's built of words. Words crafted from Ambit's tiny precise handwriting. A billion words etched together in length and coils, coalesced into a weapon. He raises it and puts it in Savage's face. Devlin is blue and black in the golden bar. "I don't need you anymore," he says. There's no hint of his usual, playful Russian accent.

Savage's hands are up, defensively. Felicity falls to the ground, still undulating like an overly wound toy.

"You do need me," Savage replies. "We need each other."

"Bullshit," Devlin says.

The battle-born emerge from the shadows and from corners, their darkness absorbing the amber light.

Bishop looks to Savage as two battle-born flank him. "I couldn't tell you," the reaper says, distraught.

"It's fine, Bishop. I know now."

"I couldn't tell you," he repeats.

Devlin cocks the revolver, a bullet slides into the chamber. It sounds metallic though it's made of letters and punctuation. "Say goodnight, pilgrim," Devlin says.

"**SAVAGE**," the voice yells. Savage recognizes it now. It belongs to Ambit. The Engineer is beside him.

"What?"

"It's time," Ambit replies.

Devlin pulls the trigger.

Savage wakes, covered in dream sweat. Felicity is safe and unconscious by his side, her hand draped over his chest. Beneath her painted fingernails, his human heart feels like a crazed metronome in his chest.

"Felicity." He rouses her.

"Mm?" She wakes.

"Devlin is making his move. I need to go. It's time."

EIGHTEEN

Ambit's quarters exist like a cavity in Savage's mouth. He can feel the space, the void where something ought to be, but he can't press himself into it. He can't close the hole. Spacetime in and around the tower has been manipulated, and every time Savage attempts to place himself in the penthouse office, something bounces him out.

He must enter on foot.

He passes through the glass doors of the building. The lights are dimmed, and the EXIT signs cast an eerie red glow over the lobby and the unmanned reception desk. He presses the button to request an elevator. The doors are polished steel, and Savage watches his tall, distorted reflection split down the middle as they open with a chime.

Inside, he presses 42, and the elevator abides.

Savage thinks about Felicity, about how the space between her eyebrows knits itself together both when she's frustrated and when she's writhing in pleasure. They had knit together before he left, as she chastised him. "You're foolish to go alone."

Savage had gathered his clothing from where it was scattered around the muse's room. "I know Devlin, Felicity. He's maniacal. By very definition, he's chaotic. I won't subject you to involvement."

"I'm already in the thick of it, the least I can do now is help."

Savage shook his head as he buttoned his pants. "He will tear you to shreds without a second thought if it will expose my underbelly. You may want to risk yourself, but I won't."

"I'm already at risk solely because I exist. If he doesn't use me as a tool to manipulate you today, I guarantee he'll get to it tomorrow."

"If I'm focused on you, I won't be able to focus on helping Ambit." He ran his fingers through his dark hair in exasperation.

"What's happened to Ambit?" she asked.

"I don't know, exactly. I can't sense him, but I can feel a void where he should be. I don't have time to continue arguing, so here's what you can do to help. I'm going to the high-rise now. Can you find Ray and Bishop and send them to me? I don't want to waste any more time, and I will need them."

She had agreed and dissolved into a flurry of color like a Technicolor snowstorm.

In the elevator, Savage watches his reflection in the stainless-steel doors. He regards his form, this form he'd been born into. His too big ears and his electric face. The things he'd judged once and often. Now, it's the face he'd pick if he were given the choice. It's the face he wore when he remembered himself, and therefore, it's the face of god. Ears be damned.

At the 38th floor, the elevator loses power. The lights flicker and go out.

Savage lets out a sigh.

In the dark, something sighs back.

Savage thinks of fire, the thing the gods allegedly gifted unto man, and in a cupped hand, he summons a flame.

The blackness stirs around him in eddies like a silent tornado of night. From inside the cyclone, the hands of darkness reach for him, and tousle his hair and clothing as if the wind had fingers. The wind increases in speed, and the hands grab at him more aggressively, until they force themselves into his ears and eyes, up his nostrils and down his throat, suffocating and deafening him. The shadows stub out his flame as he struggles against them.

He's swallowed into a perfect deafness, a weightless black chasm where no feeling and no thought live. No bothers, no future, no past. Only darkness.

How long he lets the shadows take him, he can't be sure. How many minutes he let them grope him and lick their black tongues over him. How long he let himself be swallowed by their great, dark throats. It feels like perfect supplication. Like drowning.

It brings to mind another black and sightless time. A time before time.

A time when he *created* time. Time and space. When he was god.

God?

He's a fucking god.

God doesn't get suffocated by shadows.

God brings light. Light and wrath.

He thinks of fire again. The perfect marriage of light and wrath. The supposed gift. If it was a gift, it was his first, his to give. He summons a fire within him, and lights himself up like a torch, a blazing effigy against the darkness. He explodes his divinity back into form.

The elevator doors burst open, birthing a wave of black water out onto the 38th floor, Savage's body within it like a babe in the sac. He gasps life back into his lungs, sputtering up ink-dark liquid. It reminds him of water from a rinse cup, when he would paint and swirl his brushes around in an old dirty glass. The water would darken and darken in grays and blues until it was so black, he'd have to swap it out for a fresh glass.

He gets to his feet and the inky water evaporates with a hiss from his clothes into a dark mist. He sucks in air through his nose and coughs out a black cloud.

This floor of the building is empty. The vast space spreads out in an unfinished construction zone, all darkness and exposed structural pillars. Savage wonders what Ambit is planning to build here, but for now, it's nothing.

Savage jogs the length of the floor in search of the stairwell. He makes the rest of the journey upward on foot, climbing the stairs two at once.

The door to the 42nd floor is unlocked and unbarred. Devlin wouldn't be so foolish as to think a lock could keep Savage out.

But there is a creature—*a woman?*— Savage wonders in the darkness on the office floor. In the distance beyond, he can see the glass cube that is Ambit's office, but the blinds are drawn over the windows.

The creature is bare, pink skinned, and hairless. Tall and lean, its hands and feet tapered to points like a deformed ballerina. It turns its head to Savage as if catching his scent, and lifts itself off the floor, spider-like. It stalks toward him, its eyes stitched closed, its jaw hanging open, broken and unhinged. "Help me," it rasps.

Savage doesn't reply.

"*Help me*," it repeats through its ruined mouth as it slides closer.

"With what?" he responds, guarded.

"I'm starving." As it gasps air into its laboring lungs, the birdcage of its ribs undulates with the tide of its breathing. "He's starving me."

"Devlin?"

"*The Knave.*"

"Why?"

"He needed me," the broken thing inhales sharply, the strain from speaking visibly exhausting, "to be ravenous. Ravenous at the right time." It edges closer to Savage, carrying its ovular head heavily.

Savage is torn between empathy and caution. "What do you need to sustain yourself?"

It rasps for a moment. Shuddering inhale. Broken exhale. "It once was beauty."

Savage watches it from under his furrowed brow.

"Beauty. Creativity. Art."

"You're a muse?"

"No, that was long ago. Too long. Too long ago, now." It's within arm's reach of him. "He broke me. Too starved. I need something stronger." It extends its pointed hands before Savage, as if warming frigid fingers before a fire. "I don't need your art."

"What do you need?"

It shivers before him and musters the remainder of its strength to force its eyelids open, ripping the black stitches through its skin to reveal the bloody orbs that once were eyes. *"Your fear."*

It grabs Savage by the throat, knocking him on his back and throttling him. As it squeezes, it places its broken mouth over his and sucks in like it's huffing fumes from his lungs.

As the creature feasts on him, he is immobilized. His eyes roll into his head and in the darkness, terrible fear overcomes him. Every anxiety. Every embarrassment. Every phobia. Every bout of depression, every nightmare, every moment of terror. Every time adrenaline rushed into his veins. Every time his stomach dropped from under him. Every fear-ridden incident of his mortal life compounded and replaying simultaneously inside the theater of his mind.

He is twenty, walking into his apartment to find his roommate unconscious from overdose, foam and vomit erupting from his mouth in a volcano of sick.

He is fourteen and processing the news of his parents' death for the first time. It hits him repeatedly like a Mack truck colliding into a wall, the news crashing into his brain over and over on a loop.

He is five and awake in the night, reveling in terror of the thought of ghosts at his door and creatures under his bed.

He sees Felicity dead, dismembered, hanging, bleeding, and crushed.

He is blind.

He is paralyzed.

Half his body is numb due to stroke.

He cannot create or sketch or paint.

He stands with a rope around his neck, facing execution.

He stands with a rope around his neck, resigned to suicide.

The bottom comes out from under him, and he feels his neck snap.

This is where he wakes.

He's in the lab in Vegas sitting on a chair under fluorescents, having fallen asleep face down on the counter. The clock on the wall reads 3:30.

"What?" he says aloud. "No. No, no."

He knows he's not here. This is some manifestation of fear he's fighting. He stands, runs across the lab, the eyes of the dogs in their cages following him as he reaches for the steel door handle. His hand passes through the metal, and he cannot grab purchase. "What?" he utters in confusion as he paws at the door.

And then he's asleep in the chair in the lab, waking under fluorescents. The clock on the wall reads 3:30.

Was he dreaming? Something is wrong. Something is right? He was doing something of terrible importance. Or else he was dreaming that he was. He stands and walks to the door. As he reaches the door handle, he cannot grab it. His hand passes through the steel over and over like he's a ghost.

Frustrated, he cries out and goes to punch through the door.

And he's waking in his chair in the corner of the lab, the fluorescents, the clock. 3:30. Big, brown canine eyes watching him sleep from their Plexiglass containers.

How many times has he done this?

He's dreaming. One of those fucking continuum dreams, he's sure. He does not stand this time but stays seated in his chair and looks around the room. There are two dogs in Plexiglass cages, one some kind of spaniel mutt, the other a terrier. The terrier wags its tail when he looks at it. There's a metal sink in the counter near him. A yellow biohazard trashcan.

The steel clock ticks on the wall.

3:31.

He stands and goes to it, reaches up to its metallic face. It looks down its nose at him like a judgmental adult admonishing someone else's hysterical child. He tries to rip it from the wall.

It *ticks* in defiance. He digs his fingernails into the damn thing, scraping at the drywall it's fixed into. It *tocks* obstinately. His fingernails begin to rip up, coming loose from their beds and trailing crimson blood down his hands and on the face of the clock.

He pauses. Blood. Red.

He remembers red.

He stands back from the wall, smiling to himself.

"You done fucked up," he says, his fingernails pouring blood onto the polished linoleum, pooling like pictures from a true-crime murder scene. "It was a nice try. A good effort. But you screwed the pooch."

He takes a deep breath and reaches out his pillaged hands in front of him, cracking his knuckles and stretching a bit from side to side. He closes his eyes, centers himself, and mentally calls his consciousness back to his body—not this body in the lab, *this* one is a mirage.

He wakes with a gasp. Prostrate on the floor, his mess of black hair obscures most of his face. The broken former muse is suckling at his mouth like a babe from the teat. Someone else is tugging at his jacket, trying to pull it off his sleeping form. They both startle away as he stirs back to wakefulness, the second form skittering back and stumbling over its feet, the muse staring slack-jawed into his dark eyes.

Savage pulls the muse's hands from his throat, prying its fingers from his flesh. He casts the ruined thing away with a growl. It sits crumpled in a corner, its belly swollen from feast, pregnant with his terror. It licks at its fingers like a child.

"You're awake," the second creature says.

"Yes. And you know why." Savage stands.

"I overlooked a minor detail," the joiner says, a little bored and a little cocky, as he rubs his thumb over his fingernails. He's a sandman—a sharp looking creature clad in a three-piece deep amaranth suit, with well coifed hair and a close-cropped beard. Little flecks of gold catch the light in his hair as he moves.

Savage recognizes him, not at first, but it comes to him after a moment. The day Savage overdosed on ketamine, Ambivalen, and rye whiskey, this sandman stood over him imploring him to stop taking the sleeping pills.

Savage gets it now, understands that which made no sense

to his drug addled mind before.

"It was more than a minor detail," Savage chides. He pauses for a beat, studies the sandman who has betrayed him. "What did he give you? I assume it would take a lot for you to betray a charge."

The sandman sighs. "Do you know what this is?" He lifts his hand to reveal its contents to Savage. It's a crystal suspended in a glass orb, reflecting rainbows back upon itself in infinite fractals.

"I'm willing to bet that's a continuum dream."

"Yes. Quite rare indeed." The sandman holds up the orb to better appreciate it. "Sandmen craft all kinds of dreams. Recurring. Lucid. Prophetic. Nightmares. Night terrors. We even have sway over daydreams. But helping teenagers and toddlers wet their sheets—albeit for different reasons—is a tedious existence. At least for me. I wanted the opportunity to create something unique. Each continuum dream you experienced spanned out for an eternity. *Ad infinitum*. It was enough to keep me entertained . . . at least for a while."

"Remy," the former muse says through its mangled mouth. Savage and the sandman look to it. It shakes its head. "You speak too much."

"Methinks the jig is up," Remy says. He throws the continuum orb to the ground, smashing it into bits of crystalline dream and puffs of pastel colored gas. "Are you going to end me?" he asks Savage, earnestly.

"The sandmen were half my domain, once. Bishop and I made you. The art that comes from the mind in the little nightly deaths . . . but it seems like you all have been self-governing for quite a while. And you've gone off the rails without leadership."

"There is chaos, too, in the dreaming mind," Remy adds.

"You're right. Devlin had a hand in your creation as well."

"I didn't know how to refuse him," Remy says. "*How do you refuse him?* If it's any consolation, when Devlin told me of the arrangement, I didn't know. I only knew that there was something different about you . . . I wouldn't have manipulated your dreams had I known who you were. Who you *actually* were." The sandman looks to Savage and sighs. "I've been so tragically, terribly bored."

Savage thinks for a moment, rubbing his hands over his face. "You'll have to pay penance, but as for how, I can't decide now. I have bigger fish to fry tonight. Besides, I think I'm the one who earned the continuum dreams."

"What do you mean, 'earned' them?"

Savage laughs without joy. "It's a metaphor for my existence. In the dreams, I wake to a mundane moment over and over. I've been doomed to die and wake to a mundane life, time and again. Never accepting my origin. Never learning from my mistakes. But this time, *this life*, is like that last continuum dream you gave me. I get it. Finally. I can see the color now."

The door to the stairwell opens, and Ray and Felicity enter the floor, disheveled and looking worse for wear. "Savage," Felicity says as they rush to him.

"Did the shadows get to you?" he asks.

"They tried," Ray replies, tossing her long dreadlocks over her shoulder.

"Why are you with a sandman?" Felicity questions in his ear.

"He's *my* sandman. Or he was. Remy, the myth, plaguing my human existence with insomnia and continuum dreams at the behest of Devlin."

"You tampered with a dreamer?" Ray asks, incensed. "That's a capital offense."

Remy bows his head a little before Ray. "I'm aware of that, *madame*. It was a fool's endeavor and one I am sure I'll pay for, dearly."

"We can deal with him later. Besides," Savage adds, scrutinizing Remy with a deep gaze, "I think he may be of use to us."

Remy swallows, hard. *"C'est la vie.* My fate awaits. But what are you going to do with that thing?" Remy gestures to the beast in the corner. It's drunk on overindulgence, still writhing as it holds its distended belly.

Felicity gasps in horror when she sees it. "Oh, sister, what have you become?"

Ray kneels beside the naked creature, reproach and sorrow in her eyes.

"Can't we turn her back?" Savage asks.

"No," Ray answers. "And if we leave her, she'll evolve. Into a vampire." She puts her hand on the hairless forehead of the creature. "I'm so sorry, my child." She utters something low and magic, in her own worldly tongue. Her words lilt and roll and Savage thinks it must be a prayer.

The bleeding eyes of the former muse flutter and roll back into its head, and it falls into unconsciousness.

"I wish what I give I could also take away, but I need Bishop."

Through the doorway to the stairwell, Bishop tumbles in.

"Sonofabit—oh good," he interrupts himself. "You guys are already here."

"Right on cue, buddy. What happened to you?" Savage asks, offering the reaper a hand. "Shadows?"

"No, Dev's got this place guarded from floor to ceiling. I had to come from the roof. The friggin' battle-born were crawling all over the place. You think if we spritz bug spray under their hoods, it'll do anything?" Bishop catches sight of the unconscious creature, the no-longer-muse. The not-yet-vampire. "Oh no." He points to her. "What have we here?"

"A Devlin trap. For me, it seems."

"She needs to move onward," Ray pleads.

"I don't think you should leave," Savage says. "What if there's a trap at her gateway like there was at Verity's?"

"True." Bishop nods. He closes his eyes for a moment, and with a rolling curl of smoke, Rook appears before them, marble-eyed and silent.

"Buddy," Bishop says to him. "Look, I know this is above your pay grade, but I'm going to need you to take this poor creature to her gateway."

Rook blinks.

"You *are* ready. This is what we've been training for."

Rook blinks again.

"Alright, that's what I like to hear," Bishop says, clapping the raven-headed reaper on his small shoulder. "You can do it. Be on alert, and if anything seems fishy, *you get the hell out of there*, you hear?"

Rook kneels before the broken muse and puts his dark head near her pink one. In a little, raspy, reaper voice, Savage hears the crow mutter "TRINITY." It's the first time he's ever heard Rook make a sound. Rook pulls the long-buried spirit from the broken body.

The spirit looks little like the dead form on the ground. Trinity is as beautiful and pure as every muse, golden and glowing, with haunted blue eyes. She looks to each of them and whispers "Forgive me" as Rook escorts her soul away to the next life.

Remy sniffs in, uncomfortably.

"Yes, child. Let that be a warning to you," Ray says to him.

As they approach the glass walls of the Engineer's office, they can see some light is flickering off the blinds from inside.

Savage leans against the door to open it, but something leans against it. He and Bishop push hard to clear what bars their way. The body of a slain timekeeper has been abandoned on the ground. The albino creature's wrists have been slit right through the middle of his twin hourglass tattoos, and sand spills to the floor from his veins.

"Dear god," Bishop says.

"Devlin's completely out of fucks to give," Savage says, as he and Bishop place the body against a wall.

"What does that mean," Felicity asks, "that Devlin's killed a timekeeper?"

Ray goes to the albino creature and says the same foreign prayer over his body, one hand placed over his chest, the other over her own.

"It means he's fucking with spacetime," Savage answers.

In the center of the Engineer's office, a four-sided structure has been erected of glass. Static blinks across the surface, like it's made of old, fading television screens. Savage approaches the box.

It's massive—ten feet tall and ten feet wide and ten feet deep—and it claims a majority of Ambit's office. Savage touches his hand to the glass screens, and they blink in a succession of ones and zeros, infinite code covering the surface.

"Binary?" Bishop asks. "This is too sophisticated for Devlin."

"Not too sophisticated," Remy remarks casually, the last to enter the office. "Just too technological."

"Potato, potato," Bishop says, using the same pronunciation twice.

"Is it though?" Remy asks, squinting. He makes himself comfortable behind Ambit's desk, reclining back in the Engineer's chair.

"Shh," Savage says to them, leaning into the box. He removes his hand from the glass and the ones and zeros fade back to static. "Ambit's inside."

"The box?" Felicity asks, confused and concerned.

"It's not a box," Savage corrects. "It's a cage. Some kind of Faraday cage."

Bishop and Ray approach, each laying their hands over the glass.

"I can't tell if he's alive or dead," Ray says. A vein of fear pulses over her forehead.

"That's the point," Savage replies. "It's Schrödinger's box, and Ambit's the cat."

"What does that mean?" Felicity asks.

"It means he's both alive *and* dead. Because both possibilities are equally probable."

"He can't be dead," Felicity scoffs. "Devlin can't murder a god."

"On a full and complete level, you are correct," Ray answers, as she runs her fingers over the glass. "Devlin does not possess the power to kill him on an ethereal level."

"But . . . ?" Felicity remarks.

"We each created human-like forms for ourselves," Bishop answers. "To walk the earth. Our 'boots-on-the-ground,' so to speak. And Devlin *can* kill that."

"And the corporeal shell that houses the god," Savage continues Bishop's thought, "is trapped in this cage."

"How do we fix this? How do we get him out?" Bishop asks.

"If we could see into the box, that would push Ambit into one existence or the other," Savage answers, "but I don't know how to do that."

Felicity goes to him. "This is where I come in handy." She pulls a vial of inspiration from her gown and hands it over. "Drink," she says.

He uncorks the little bottle and downs the substance. As he waits for it to kick in, she places her hand to his temple and looks into his eyes to help. The warmth of Felicity's inspiration passes over him, from his throat and stomach, out to his fingertips. He feels her swimming in his bloodstream.

His eyes go wide with an idea.

"Magnet," he says, quietly at first.

"What was that?" Bishop asks.

"A magnet." Savage turns to the box. "This is a computer."

"A computer?" Remy questions from behind Ambit's desk. "Sorry, trying not to get involved." He throws up his hands.

"Yes, a computer. Ambit is like the motherboard. And computers are vulnerable to magnets."

"Look kid, I may not know a lot about technology," Bishop comments, "but I'm pretty sure we've evolved past the days of floppy disks getting erased from contact with a refrigerator magnet."

"I'm not talking about a refrigerator magnet," Savage corrects. "I mean an EMP. An electromagnetic pulse."

"And where are we gonna get one of those?"

"You're looking at him."

"What?" Ray and Felicity say, incredulous and in tandem.

"I'm a fucking god, I can change myself on an atomic level. Rearrange, reconfigure, fuse. Divide . . ."

"No, no, no," Bishop starts, putting the pieces together before the others. "No nuclear fission, Savage. You're going to blow New York off the map!"

"Not necessarily," Savage responds. "If I split an atom inside me and only emit the gamma rays—"

"Damn, you sound like Ambit right now."

"Good. One of us needs to. Felicity's inspo mixed with being in Ambit's quarters is helping. If I absorb the explosion and emit only the gamma rays," he reiterates, "the molecules in the atmosphere will ionize and emit an electromagnetic pulse."

"'Absorb the explosion'?"

"You're going to kill yourself." Felicity censures.

"Possibly," he replies. "You guys should clear the area. I'm confident I can contain the explosion, but it might still . . ."

"Blow our hair back?" Remy speculates.

"Kid. This is not *the* idea, this is just the first idea, and *the* idea will surely follow."

"We are on a time crunch. We don't have the luxury of waiting for ten more ideas." He turns to the muse. "Felicity—"

"I'm not going anywhere."

"Please?"

Felicity pivots around the desk to stand beside Remy, who hasn't moved. "There."

"Yeah, this desk will definitely protect us from nuclear apocalypse." Remy knocks on the surface. "Oak."

Savage sighs, not wanting to waste any more time. "Bishop, if I can't control the detonation . . ."

The reaper is shaking his head.

"*Listen.* You have to, you're the only one who can. Reap my spirit, but take my body, too. If you get me to a gateway quickly enough, it should stop the repercussions."

"We're not doing this."

"Yes, we are. Get ready."

Savage focuses on his earthly self at the atomic level. He burrows within, where time slows. Down deep inside, swimming in the abyss that is nothing but molecules and energy, he picks an atom, any atom. He wills it to come apart, but it slips through this mental grasp like an eager fish. Then, there. At last. Nuclear fission.

Where there was a vast darkness, light forms. And heat.

It explodes out from the center point, slowly, slowly. Rippling through the nearby space. Bigger. Brighter. Out and out.

He feels the heat and pressure consume his earthly form. It starts as a glowing heat he can manage, an expansion he can control.

This body. He didn't choose it but, would again and again into infinity. Savage will always be Savage. This body, at once equally strong and fragile, begins to crack at the seams.

The explosion begins to rip him apart.

Bigger.

Painful.

Intolerably painful.

Dear god, why is it so painful?

He places his hands on the screens of the Faraday cage, which bend and refract light in broken rainbows, before the glowing within overtakes him. He watches in slow motion agony as his hands ignite and burst into impossible pieces, the magma within cresting the fissures and bleeding their nuclear power out into the world.

"Savage . . ." Bishop calls from somewhere that feels very far away.

I am a savage.

He looks to Ray across the room, her muscles tensed to spring. He looks to Bishop, his face frozen in the middle of falling. He's pulling the gloves from his hands to reap Savage.

In case he fails.

In case . . .

Savage feels like he's beginning to fail.

Panic unfurls within him, the echo of his godly confidence from before seemingly immature bluster now.

What have I done?

He turns to Felicity as he loses his tenuous grip, to see her radiant face once more before they're wiped off the map along with the tri-state area. Her eyes upon him look not frightened, not equivocal. She squints in determination and looks at him with pure confidence. *You've got this,* her eyes say, before his own become two ruinous things exploding in the pillory of his skull. He cries out with a broken voice that sounds like an eruption in his throat, all gravel and growl and fire.

It is a heat and a pain unlike any he has ever known. He feels like he's birthing all the pieces of himself into the world at large in a fiery nuclear labor. And soon, the world will be nothing but these many fragments of Savage, silent and burning. Dust and ash.

Just as his earthly form explodes into a million billion atomic pieces and nothing more, he calls it back.

He remembers his purpose.

He remembers his nature.

And he pulls it all back like a pendulum swing.

He grunts out in exertion, calling his shards back, back. Back to him. Back into center. But he feels the magnetic pulse vibrating out like a manic heartbeat. He lets it go, he lets the energy go but keeps the explosion inside.

With a final scream, what's left of Savage's wasted body knits itself back together and falls to the floor.

NINETEEN

Someone is shouting.

"Bishop, *he's dying.*"

Savage opens his eyes. From the floor of the office, he stares up at the concerned faces of the muse and the mother. Felicity is covering her mouth.

"I won't do it," Bishop says, pacing the length of the office. "I'm not reaping him."

"Well, it's too late now," Remy remarks, gesturing to Savage's open eyes.

The smell of scorched skin and electricity is thick and caustic. The main lights in the room have burned out, the emergency lights casting an orange glow like halos around the heads of the women.

Savage blinks his eyes, hard. "It's okay, Bishop. Remy's right, you missed your opportunity." He feels his body, wiggling his fingers and swallowing with his scorched throat. "I should be dead."

"Yes," Ray says simply.

"I couldn't do it, kid," Bishop says. "I knew you'd be able to handle it."

Savage sits up. "You cut it a little close, there, buddy." His teeth are singing in his mouth and every time he blinks the lids over his eyes, it feels like sandpapery anguish. "While I'm not complaining that you didn't reap me—"

"I just couldn't do it. And since no one else can . . ."

"Whenever your earthly forms have passed," Ray says, placing a hand on Savage's arm, "Bishop has always been your reaper. No one else *can* reap you. Are you quite well?"

Savage makes a grunting sound as he runs his hands through his hair. He feels like someone assembled his parts backwards.

From his seat behind Ambit's desk, Remy points to the Faraday cage. "You might want to take a look at that."

The group snaps their attention to the box.

Inside is Ambit. And Ambit. And Ambit. And Ambit.

And a million more, stacked on top and beside himself, over and over again, occupying every square centimeter of the space. It reminds Savage of the old Microsoft version of solitaire, where a victory would yield dancing duplicates of cards bouncing and visually echoing off themselves.

The box contains the multiverse of Ambits in every imaginable state.

There's a smiling Ambit.

A laughing Ambit.

An Ambit giggling maniacally.

One is thoughtful.

One is sobbing.

One is writing out equations on the glass of the cage in what appears to be his own blood.

One Ambit is in deep debate with another Ambit.

One is pulling out his own hair while screaming.

One is rocking back and forth on the ground in the fetal position.

One is bloody, one is reciting pi, one is banging on the glass walls of the box.

But that's only the live Ambits. There are piles of Ambit bodies littering the cage, either dead or unconscious. Savage can only guess.

The noise the many Ambits produce makes an unpleasant hum of mania in the Engineer's voice.

"Holy shit," Savage says with his dry and ruined tongue.

"At least now you have a spare?" Remy comments, dryly.

"Which one of them is the real Ambit?" Felicity asks, "Or are they all the real Ambit?"

"They all are." Savage runs a hand over his head. Inside, a headache is raging like the tolling of a bell. "I'm trying to think like Ambit ... and to think like Devlin. Somehow, Devlin has magnified quantum mechanics inside this box to a human scale."

"What does that mean?" Ray asks, at his side.

"Ambit's acting like a particle and a wave."

"Again," Bishop says, "that's too damn sophisticated."

"He had Ambit's help," Savage utters.

"What?" the group echoes, confused.

"I don't believe it," Bishop says, shaking his head.

"Not directly. He trusted that assistant of his with too much knowledge, it seems."

"Dammit, I *knew* it. I never trusted that little punk."

"Who? After?" Ray asks.

"It *had* to be her," Bishop says, reveling in the victory of his righteousness.

Savage nods and the tolling increases. "Devlin must have purchased her loyalty somehow. Like he did with this one." He gestures over his shoulder to the sandman. "This is all a distraction while she's off helping Devlin to those blood samples. We need to hurry."

Ray is passing her hands over the glass trying to comfort the many Ambits, to no avail.

"I don't think he can see us," she says.

"Maybe the glass walls are one-way mirrors," Felicity suggests.

"How do we release him?" Ray asks.

"I don't know." Savage presses on his temples. "And I can't think with all this chatter."

"Wait, if we can hear him, can't he hear us?" Bishop realizes. "*Ambit*," he shouts.

The pale faces all turn to the sound of Bishop's voice.

Savage goes to the glass. "Ambit," he calls. "We need to know how to get to your samples."

"*Where am I?*" the many voices say at once.

"You are trapped," Ray replies.

The Ambits appear to see their confines for the first time.

"*What is this? Where am I? Get me out,*" the voices say. They put their many hands to the glass like an Aryan centipede. "*Savage? Get me out!*"

"We're trying, Ambit. We're trying."

Many of the Ambits start to panic, banging on the glass,

screaming, and hyperventilating.

"We will get you out, but you have to help us. Where are your samples? We need to get to them before Devlin does," Savage shouts through the glass.

"*No, no, no, no,*" the Ambits cry. They shake and shudder and freeze, like a computer glitch.

The sound of thunder calls from across the city, startling Savage and pulling his attention to the window of the tower. A heinous purple storm is beginning to brew, swirling with hints of a cyclone. Lightning explodes from the center, touching down over the Manhattan skyline as thunder erupts overhead.

"Shit," Savage mutters. "Ambit, focus."

"*Let me out. Let me out. Let me. Let me. Out. Out. Let me out.*"

"He's losing it." Savage looks around for something heavy. He settles on the base of some art nouveau statue that sits on a shelf against the wall. He strikes the glass. It bounces the statue back but doesn't break.

"Savage, that won't work," Ray says as she goes to the window. Outside the storm is escalating. Lightning touches down to the city in pulses every few seconds.

"*Out. Out. Outoutout. Out. Outout,*" the Ambits stutter.

Bishop picks up a chair and helps Savage, beating against the glass.

Inside the ecosystem of Ambit's office, the world begins to unhinge. Little objects like paperclips and pens and the ends of Ray's locs begin to float.

Savage and Bishop alternate, striking the glass again, and again. The box cracks under the assault.

Larger objects, books and plants, release and float around

like bits of flotsam in the ocean after a shipwreck. It's as though Ambit has turned the knob down on gravity. Savage is mid-swing, when the statue comes free from his hand and launches away, spiraling into space like a satellite in orbit.

Savage feels his feet lift from the ground, hovering close to the glass cage.

"Christ. What now?" Remy scoffs as he drifts upward, out of Ambit's chair.

"Ambit's verging on mania," Ray responds.

"*Ouououououououououou . . .*"

"Gravity is failing. Physics is failing." The water in the floating potted plants begins to evaporate into steam, as matter begins to break down, the molecules speeding up and changing from liquid into gas.

The air sparks and crackles in purple bits of plasma that pop in tiny bursts of lightning.

The five float as though the office is a spaceship far off in a star-speckled night.

"*Ooooooouuuuuu . . .*"

"Is it just us in here?" Bishop asks as he struggles with the floating tails of his long coat.

Remy is hovering by the window and twists his body slowly to look outside. "So far."

As Savage drifts, it's almost peaceful. His headache is subsiding, and he takes in a deep, thoughtful breath as he watches the many Engineers glitch in their cage in every state imaginable.

A multiverse of Ambits. Every Ambit ever.

Something clicks.

If Ambit is in a multiverse, he exists in all states at once.

And if he exists in all states at once, he exists both inside and outside the box.

That's it.

Ambit is outside the box.

Savage attempts to focus his mental willpower onto the thought, *Ambit exists outside the box.*

It works.

Gravity kicks back into existence, releasing the inhabitants of the room to the floor, and with a painful thud, Savage meets the floor with his wasted human form. Remy lands crookedly in the office chair, and it pitches him to the side. Ray, Felicity, and Bishop land with loud exhalations, as papers float to the ground in a scholastic blizzard.

Outside, the storm over the city dissipates as quickly as it began.

Ambit is singular once more and does, in fact, exist outside the box. He readjusts the glasses on his face, looking exhausted and wane. "Savage." He extends a hand, helping him from the ground. "How did you do it?"

"You were existing in every state," Savage says with his pained voice. "And if you existed in every state, that meant you existed both inside and outside the box. Once I knew you existed outside the box, that affirmed your existence. Like Schrödinger's cat, once you see whether the cat is alive or dead, it pushes it into one existence or the other."

Ambit smirks. "That's true. I'm glad you were able to root out the solution, I was spinning so badly. I couldn't have done it."

The Engineer wavers on his feet and Bishop grabs him by the arm.

"Whoa, buddy."

"No time to rest," Savage says. "You need to take us to your samples."

"If I push myself in this state, the fabric of the universe could unhinge itself."

"Suck it up, man," Bishop shouts.

"I assume," Savage says, "you need to be present for us to access your samples."

"Yes. You're right." Ambit sighs, resigned. "In that bookcase you'll find a copy of *The Origin of the Species* on the third shelf down. Toward the left."

Bishop spots it.

"Pull."

"That's amazingly cheesy," Bishop says as he tugs on the book and the shelf swings out. A dark tunnel extends beyond the bookcase.

Savage turns to Felicity. "Can you stay here and keep an eye on our traitorous little buddy?" Savage eyes Remy, who throws his hands up in a dramatic shrug.

"I can do that." She goes to him. "Be careful."

He leans his forehead into hers. "Thank you. You'll be safer here."

She rubs her fingers over his cheek. He kisses her briefly, a strong solid kiss on the mouth. "Not goodbye," he says.

"I wouldn't have it."

The gods head through the bookcase to the tunnel beyond.

"Why do I feel like I'm underground?" Savage asks.

"Not underground. In a mountainside," Ray says as she runs her fingers along the wall of the dark cavern, as they make their way through.

The air is bitter, a biting cruel cold, and Savage tucks his long black coat tighter around himself. "Fuck, it's cold," he says through fogged breath. As his teeth chatter, the vibrations renew his headache.

"You adjusted the spatial spectrum?" Ray asks Ambit. "Or perhaps the temporal?"

"Both. I created a wormhole. This vault exists in an unnamed mountain on an island off the North Pole in 1913."

"Why the past?" Bishop asks as they walk.

"World War II brought an onslaught of liabilities, what with the Manhattan project and the atomic bombs. The world was a safer place prior to the First World War. I discerned this was the superlative space and time for me to hide my most valuable valuables."

"As long as we keep Savage-the-A-bomb from detonating again," Bishop says.

"I don't think I could make a repeat performance anytime soon."

They follow the path, twisting farther into the girth of the mountain. Overhead, yellow bulbs in black cages illuminate the tunnel. Their footfalls echo off the space in infinite loops before and behind them.

Bishop leans into Savage. "You're not looking so good, buddy."

Savage shakes his head, and it rattles as if broken. "We should hurry," he says, pulling at his limbs, urging them to hasten. "But I can't force myself to go much faster." His body feels like a sack of stones in water. He thinks of Virginia Woolf again, with river stones in the pockets of her overcoat, consigning herself to death. His perspective has changed a million times over since he last thought of her. Because sometimes death feels like family. And the breaking leads to something better, something beautiful. He feels truly ancient for the first time since remembering his divinity, he feels every one of his billion billion years. He longs for rest. But he presses on.

Bishop claps a hand on his shoulder, and Savage winces. "Ooh, sorry." He frowns. "We'll fix you up soon."

"We're almost there," Ambit says. "The first door is just ahead."

They approach the heavy steel door. It sits in the icy stone of the mountain and looks like the door of a safe.

On a keypad, Ambit enters a long code. "Bishop, help me," he says, turning to the reaper.

Together, grunting, they turn the spoked handle of the heavy door. Inside, the air is slightly warmer as Ambit flicks on a series of fluorescent lights above their heads.

The room is long and narrow, lined with mirrors that reflect the bluish fluorescence back and forth a million times. At the opposite end is another door with a series of black screened computers situated before it.

Ambit sits at a stool in front of a steel table and picks up a pencil and notebook.

"What are you doing?" Bishop asks.

"Always so dubious . . ." Ambit mutters. "I need a few minutes. I have to work out the mathematics of making a new symmetrical figure."

"Not for funzies, I assume."

"It's part of the security," Ambit says, not taking his eyes from the paper as he rapidly works through long form equations. "Highly advanced mathematics to deter the errant wanderer. Once I enter this information, it can't be used twice."

Bishop begins to pace. "K, just make it fast . . ."

Savage goes to the mirror and studies his broken form. His hair is grayed and frazzled from the strain. His lips are dry and cracked. His eyes are bloodshot to the point of ruin. His appearance is beginning to resemble the antiquity within. Ray is studying her own form beside him, rubbing her fingers along her full lips. They make eye contact, Ray to Savage's reflection, Savage to Ray's. They smile sadly at one another.

"Alright, done." Ambit sets his pencil down and takes his paper with him as he walks to the end of the space, waking the screens with a tap of his finger. He types the long sequence of numbers into one of the computers.

The Engineer takes a white electrical skullcap off a hook on the wall, cords trailing from it like a little white squid, and plugs one end into another of the computers. He places it on his head and cues up a program on the screen that flashes images at him in rapid succession.

One of the computers is capturing his brainwaves in black and white hills and valleys.

After a moment, the images stop and a green light is generated above the door, which beeps to indicate they are cleared to proceed.

Ambit places his hand on the door to push it open. "'Once more unto the breach, dear friends.'"

The guarded space is an expansive cave, dimly lit with a vaulted ceiling extending into the mountain and cragged stone walls. The assorted things Ambit most values are situated along the perimeter, and a spotlight illuminates each item.

Here is an unknowable creature, long dead and submerged in liquid.

There is a gray speckled meteorite hovering on some magnetic plane and spinning on an axis, glinting little sparks of light every now and again.

A plant that grows without a vessel, roots dripping into the space beneath it.

A glass box with golden spinning cogs—humanity's first attempt at an analog computer.

Another glass case with vials of blood, one of which is currently being removed by a thin woman in a blue suit.

"Shit," Savage says as he enters.

The doppelgänger—Second-degree Savage, as Bishop had called him—is standing behind After, arms folded and brooding.

"Oh good," the clone says. "Right on schedule. Which, in this case, means late." He grimaces, his scarred face pulling at the corners. "And looking a little worse for wear. Did you get in a fight with a microwave?"

"Better than a blowtorch."

"After?" Ambit calls to his associate. She flips her glossy black head to him like an obsidian coin. Her eyes go wide, and she drops her gaze to the floor, shielding herself from the glare of her god.

"What a pair you two make. I knew it," Bishop says to After. "This whole time, I *knew* it. I knew you couldn't be trusted. I'd be giddy if I weren't so disgusted."

"So dramatic," she sighs.

Savage interjects, "You're right. The theatrics can end because there's no way we're letting you leave with that."

"This?" she asks. "I was going to keep one for personal use." She shrugs and tosses the vial to Bishop. He catches it in his cupped hands. "Devlin already took one. You guys took an absurdly long time."

"Did I not give you enough?" Ambit asks her. "I trusted you with everything, with the secrets and inner workings of the universe down to the molecule and out to the cosmos. What could you possibly gain?"

"My own chance to be a creator." She lets her face soften, a modicum of empathy coming from her heavy eyes. "I respect and treasure everything you've given and taught me. But, sir, you are my glass ceiling. I'll never be more than this because I can never be more than *you*. Devlin has offered me the chance to help create something new."

"He'll never let you be an equal," Ray says to her.

"I know that. But I'll get a chance to spin the physics of a new universe, crafting something new and my own, and

I'll no longer linger in the shadow of the Engineer. *I'll be* the Engineer. Who would pass on that?"

"I knew it." Bishop shakes his head. "I could smell the hunger on you."

"You feel . . . different," Ray speaks to After. "You've changed something inside your form. What have you done to yourself?"

"I had to rearrange some of my internal makeup to mimic the biometrics of the Engineer." She shrugs. "Otherwise, I wouldn't have been able to get in."

"Now we're down to the end." Devlin's ghostly face emerges from the darkness of the vault. "Don't bother looking for the vial. I've already relocated it."

Savage looks to Ray, who looks back at him, wide-eyed.

"Shit." He realizes.

It's a trap.

"Ray, *go,*" he says.

"She can't just whisk out of existence," Devlin says, wiggling his fingers in the ether. "Not here. This is the past, friends. If she tries, she'll dissolve the universe as we know it. And while that is what I want, I'm pretty sure that's not what you all want. You have to make your way back the way you came. And I think you know," Devlin says to Ray, taking a step closer, "we can outrun you."

Second-degree Savage eases slightly closer.

Bishop, Ambit, and Savage sidestep toward Ray, enveloping her in a protective circle.

"What about the rules?" Savage asks. "I thought you said you like playing by the rules? What are you going to do, pin her down and steal her fingernail? Force a buccal swab?" He shakes his sore head. "I don't believe you want it to go down that way."

Devlin smiles from his corner of the dark vault, the golden light shed down on the suspended plant illuminating half his face. "This is getting a little ridiculous. You all know if I want something, I get it." He darts toward Savage, grasping his pounding head between his pale hands. "So, you have remembered, my friend."

Savage winces, the tolling in his head almost unbearable. "And you've changed your mind." Devlin shakes his head. "Such a pity. It could have been great you know. It could have been *perfect*."

Ambit and Bishop close in tighter around Ray.

"Go," Savage says to them. "You can make it. I'll hold them off."

The burnt twin laughs, walking closer to Devlin and Savage. "*How?* You're so broken, I'm now the more viable incarnation."

Devlin presses his palms into Savage's temples.

Savage grunts in pain. "Bishop wouldn't reap me before. I don't think he's going to be so keen to do it now. I can take the pain."

Devlin puts his face right next to Savage's. He breathes in, and they're so close, Savage can feel the air move as he pulls it into his lungs. "It's not your pain I want," Devlin whispers.

Second-degree Savage lunges forward and rips Savage's reaper coat off his body. Savage stiffens, not knowing what to expect.

"What, you're going to strip me?" He smirks through the pain. "Knock yourselves out."

Devlin drops his hands from Savage's head, and the clone hands the devil Savage's coat. "No need." He tosses the coat over his shoulder and he, After, and the burnt Savage blink out of the vault.

"What the hell just happened? I thought he said we couldn't leave."

"Clearly, he was bluffing," Ambit replies, putting his hand on the wall. "I should've known she altered the temporal state back. This is the present. We're no longer in 1913."

"Why did he take your coat?" Bishop asks. "I thought he needed something of Ray?"

Ray stiffens. "And so, he has gotten it."

The men look at her, confused. "On the mountain, in Tahoe. When you told me you had remembered, I cried my mortal tears into your shoulder. Onto the wool of your jacket."

The gods look to one another, realizing their error.

"We have to go," Bishop says, "*now*."

TWENTY

The quiet of the underlands belays a false sense of peace. As the group approaches Devlin's quarters, they hear voices. A chant echoes through the perma-night, voices reciting something together like the beat of a single drum. The words aren't yet decipherable, but the voices grow louder the closer they get.

Nothing good can come of this, Savage thinks.

The air smells like the moments before a storm, the smell of electric ozone and damp concrete floods Savage's nose in an olfactory onslaught.

They pass through the gate and discover a massive assembly of Devlin's finest in front of the property. There's a bonfire in the center, burning tall and bright, the orange of the flames stark against the blue world. Devlin stands beside it, shirtless with a stern look on his tattooed face. He speaks in a low voice to one of the battle-born, but Savage can't hear the exchange.

Another half dozen of the hooded battle-born circle the flames.

The blonde triplet sirens are present as well. Naked. Supple. Devlin must have undone the havoc Savage wreaked on their beauty. They writhe on the ground, thrusting their hips and dragging their sensuous forms in a slow circuit just outside the battle-born. They pull themselves forward, twisting and arcing through the dirt, streaking mud down their stomachs and over their creamy breasts. Their feet and fingers blacken in the effort.

Beyond the succubi, the vampires assemble. They tilt their tall albino heads down at a sickening angle, puppets on drooping strings. Their mouths hang open, and their chests swell and fall with the current of their breaths.

Then, there are the hellhounds. They run in a counterclockwise circuit.

Past the hounds, the kelpies trot clockwise in their green-black horse form. Lines of kelp trail from their black manes, their lips pulled back over their bluish teeth.

Savage smells the sick magic. He feels the charge they create. They're winding up for their lord, turning the mechanisms of the great clock of his spirit.

On the street, cockroaches click in a hasty march to the scene of the ritual. Rats stream from the gutters in gray and pink rivers, and fat black flies swarm inward.

Across the property, other dark figures are in attendance, hands folded in prayer or concentration, Savage can only guess. The mouths of the many creatures move in unison as they chant.

Savage can decipher the words now. He can hear the spell.

"Medicine, marquee, basement, October,
Forceps, Frankfurt, sheepskin, cross over."

The voices speak in such clear and precise unison, it sends waves of goosebumps over Savage's entropic skin, the prickles standing out from the tattoos down his arm.

"Edelweiss, elephant, pomegranate, Dover,
Sugarcane, Sri Lanka, telephone, disorder."

After and Second-degree Savage exit the front door of the house. The burnt twin is wearing Savage's black reaper coat over his bare chest. It sickens Savage to see it on him. It was a token of his life as Bishop's apprentice. His twin is carefree and nonchalant in a way Savage himself is certain he's never appeared. The copy is laughing at something After has told him. She turns her dark head over her shoulder, flirtatious, and the twin touches her casually as if they have a history of contact. It's odd to see himself this way. It's like watching a home video of a memory long gone. The copy catches Savage's eye and nods to him, a self-satisfied smile crossing over the half of his face that works. He pops the collar of Savage's coat as it lays over the muscles on his chest, as if to say "This? Yeah, it's mine now."

Savage clenches his fists in anger. "I fucking hate that thing," he says to the others. "It's an abomination."

The doppelgänger and After weave through the circles of creatures and stand beside Devlin, waiting for their cues. The twin leans into Devlin's ear and whispers something, gesturing to Savage and the others.

Devlin looks up to his four fellow creators at the gate of his property. He waves, comically overzealous. "Hey guys!" he shouts. "So glad you could come!"

Savage is done. If it weren't enough to want to stop Devlin's ritual, he wants to rend that fucking copy limb from limb. He wants to throw it on the fire until it's nothing but ash. He wants to swallow it back into himself, absorb the evil and the misdeeds, and vomit what remains into the night.

Without thinking, he makes for the circle. Ambit, Ray, and Bishop follow his pursuit. They approach the kelpies making their chase to nowhere. The rhythm of their run increases a notch, the internal cogs of the circle a beat or two faster than a moment ago.

"Stop," Ray declares, placing her hands on Bishop and Savage's backs. "Don't cross the circle."

They turn back to face her.

"Why?" Savage asks.

She's shaking her head. "There is strong and sinister magic at play here." She breathes in, deeply. "It smells . . . backward and . . . electric. I don't know what will happen if you cross the threshold, but I surmise it won't be pleasant."

"We have to try," Savage retorts.

"He just lowered his guard to let After and the other through—maybe it's still down," Ambit sputters. He runs to the threshold of the circle. A jolt of electricity blasts him back from the epicenter. He calls out in pain as he lands ten feet back, crumpled in on himself like a discarded bit of refuse.

"Are you okay?" Bishop asks as Savage helps Ambit to his feet.

"It's electric, but it's not *only* electric," Ambit says, his white suit sullied from the blast. "There's something else there. Something out of place . . ."

"Order." Savage realizes, turning back to the circle. "The god of chaos, of *disorder*, is using order. Look, the movements of his demons are precise. Methodic."

The words continue and increase in speed. As the rhythm of the chant accelerates, so does the momentum at which the circles spin.

"Bangkok, barometer, fault line, fluke,
Chimney, criminal, syncope, transmute."

Devlin removes his pants and casts them aside. He stands naked, brazen, spectral in the darkness. He steps into the flames.

"Quell the fire," Ray says. "We have to quell the fire."

"How?"

"It's pointless," Devlin says to them, the flames all around him licking his pale skin and wrapping around his torso and arms. He's as impervious to their burns as a carved piece of marble. His voice rings in their ears like he's standing at their shoulders and not across the yard. He looks at them intently over the crowd, his gaze unwavering, all humor and jest gone. "This is my time."

Ray closes her eyes and spreads her dark hands before her. She shakes in concentration as if she is lifting something beyond her strength. Her hands blanch from exertion. White spreads from her fingertips and up her arms. The vine tattoos on her wrists shudder in an unseen wind.

Savage realizes as the lack of color climbs over her, she's

not turning white, she's turning silver. She's turning into *light*. She radiates like the moon. She begins to hover off the ground. A breeze stirs the stagnant air, twisting her cloak around her, whipping it like a flag unfurling.

Savage hears it before he sees it—a roaring din in the hollow night. It rolls in, down the dead suburban street, looking more like a blackened shadow than anything else in the bluish haze. It's fifty, a hundred feet tall. Ray's glowing hands are above her head.

She has summoned a tidal wave.

As it approaches the house, the roar of the water mutes out all other sound.

"I'd be worried if I were you," Savage says to Devlin. Despite the sound of the water and the distance between them, he knows Devlin can hear him.

Undeterred, the assembly maintains its chanting, still circling their Knave. Devlin watches, almost in appreciation, as the tidal wave approaches. He cocks his head up in the last moment before it drops, half smiling, welcoming.

The wave comes down in a torrent. It covers and consumes everything, dousing it all in a hundred million gallons of water. It spreads over the property, splitting through the gaps in the fence and crashing to the street below.

Ray hovers above the chaos the wave has wrought, her three fellow deities dry below her in a protective ring.

The water crashes into the walls of Devlin's massive house, and curls back in on itself in a mini tide.

It takes several moments for the water to dissipate, spreading down the street and through the yards of the empty shadow-houses that flank Devlin's. As the torrent clears,

Savage sees the invisible barrier that domes the creatures spiraling the fire. The water slides over it as if there were a glass bubble protecting the ritual.

"Goddammit," Savage says.

The creatures are undisturbed, the fire still lit, the voices still chanting.

The horses and hounds run at breakneck speed now, in a whir of blackness and panting.

Another wicked smile flashes over Devlin's face.

"My time," he says again and nods.

The voices rap on, rattling off the incantation.

"Death, darkness, gunpowder, broker,
Ophidia, fellatio, paragon, cross over.
Shadow, shaman, Andromeda, ox heart,
Suppression, regression, possession, impart."

The chanting comes to an abrupt halt, the last of the voices resounding like a low key played on a piano, the note left to linger in the air until it dissipates into nothingness.

At this, one of the battle-born—Savage assumes it's Getty, but the demons are identical—steps into the innermost ring of the ritual. The hooded figure goes to the six position of the circle. One of the sirens moves to the twelve position. After and Savage's twin shift and situate themselves at the nine and three positions.

Devlin looks to Savage. "Last chance, pilgrim," his voice a hum in Savage's ear. "You wanted to unmake this world once. Care to make something different with me?"

Savage doesn't hesitate. "No, Devlin. You lost your purpose

a long time ago."

"I haven't lost anything."

"You let yourself become corrupted. You lost yourself to the thrill of evil instead of the joy of balance. Of equilibrium. You're not who we started this journey with. I may have forgotten myself, but I was never lost." Savage shakes his head. "Nothing I'd bring to your new world would be allowed to be beautiful at all."

"Fair enough. I'll have to make do with the charred version." At this, he places his open hands out in front of him, like he's in meditation. He closes his eyes for a moment, and the flames twisting about his body grow. A malignant odor wafts into Savage's nose, something like burning plastic mixed with the static off an old TV.

Savage's twin strips the reaper jacket from his bare chest and folds it over his arms, the orange glow reflecting in the parts of stretched, fresh scars where his skin was melted. He smiles at Devlin. Savage winces at the deranged version of himself. His talent turned sick. His face spoiled.

"What do we do?" Savage asks no one in particular.

"I don't think there's anything we can do," Ambit answers.

"Let him go," Bishop says, with something like an idea crossing his face.

"What?" Savage demands. "Are you fucking kidding me? You all banished me for far less."

"Exactly," Bishop says, pointing to Devlin in the flames. "Look, he thinks he's figured it out. He thinks he's thought of everything. But there's no spark of life. There's no Ray to coax spirits from womb to world."

Ray's face twists into a grin. "And no kind reaper to cull

them back into darkness."

"I'm not getting it," Ambit says.

"He can take our cast offs and our forgotten pieces," Ray says. "But he will not be able to generate life."

"This," Bishop continues the thread, "will be his banishment. He can have his world. But let's see how chaos manages to reign a world when there's no one to populate it."

Devlin speaks now, in his divine voice. Savage has heard it from himself, he has heard it from Ray and Bishop. But Devlin's god voice is twisted. Dissonant, like a record in reverse.

"**FIRST, THERE WAS TIME**," he says.

Getty throws something small into the flames, as Second-degree Savage tosses in the black coat. The items ignite and send a ripple of orange up Devlin's naked form. The fire changes from orange to yellow.

Bishop cries out as if someone has stabbed him. "The chess piece." Bishop winces. He falls to his knees and keens in pain.

Ray calls out like a wolf, her pain echoing through the hollow night, all animal aching, as tears stream down her face.

Devlin continues, "**THEN THERE WAS SPACE**."

Ambit and Savage glance to one another, bracing for the pain.

After and the siren throw their goods into the fire, and a glint of light reflects off the siren's hand, catching Savage's eye. It looks like an abalone shell. He has time to wonder, idly, if the sirens stored his semen in a shell before the pain stabs through him.

It starts at his groin, a white-hot pain like needles through his most private places, and spreads to his stomach and down his legs. It advances to his chest, to his fingers, to his head. It beats like a heart, and it feels like Devlin is inside him, echoing through the hallways of his veins, reverberating in the room that is his brain.

He feels Devlin's sick joy inside him, his gleeful exaltation, as the devil steals something sacred from within his innermost self.

Savage opens his eyes. He wasn't aware he had closed them. Ambit is on his knees, clutching his wrists into his chest. Ray's howls are still echoing in the blue dark.

The flames around Devlin's body have changed again, from yellow to white. "**THERE WAS ORDER. AND THEN,**" he takes a deep breath, "**THERE WAS CHAOS.**"

At this, the flames burst up around him, turning to a sick, hot blue. Finally, he catches. The fire eats through his flesh, consuming the body of the devil.

Savage can smell the terrible burning from where he stands.

Devlin speaks through his smoldering flesh as his mouth falls to ruin.

"Fire, earth, air, water.
Salt, seed, blood, bone.
Be as one,
act as fodder.
Take this flesh to craft my own."

His flesh is gone, sacrificed to his cause. A burning skeleton stands amid the blue flames, and a howl escapes from his empty jaw. It starts as a high, piercing note, and evolves to a low cry, like a foghorn in the night.

Savage watches as the bones shudder in on themselves and collapse into the pit of the fire. The flames flare up, consuming the last of him.

For a moment, there is perfect silence.

Then, the explosion.

A supernova ripples out in a whirl of energy and sound, razing all the demons and creatures, stubbing them out like candles in a gale.

Savage feels himself launched, propelled into the darkness, a disk on the wind.

A horrible sucking sound accompanies a sudden loss of light, a vacuum stealing everything around it. The world goes silent, and somehow the silence feels louder than the explosion.

Consciousness falls through Savage's grasp like water through his fingers.

He succumbs to a complete emptiness, dampening even the impossible black-hole sound, lost to a crack in the world.

Swallowed by the night.

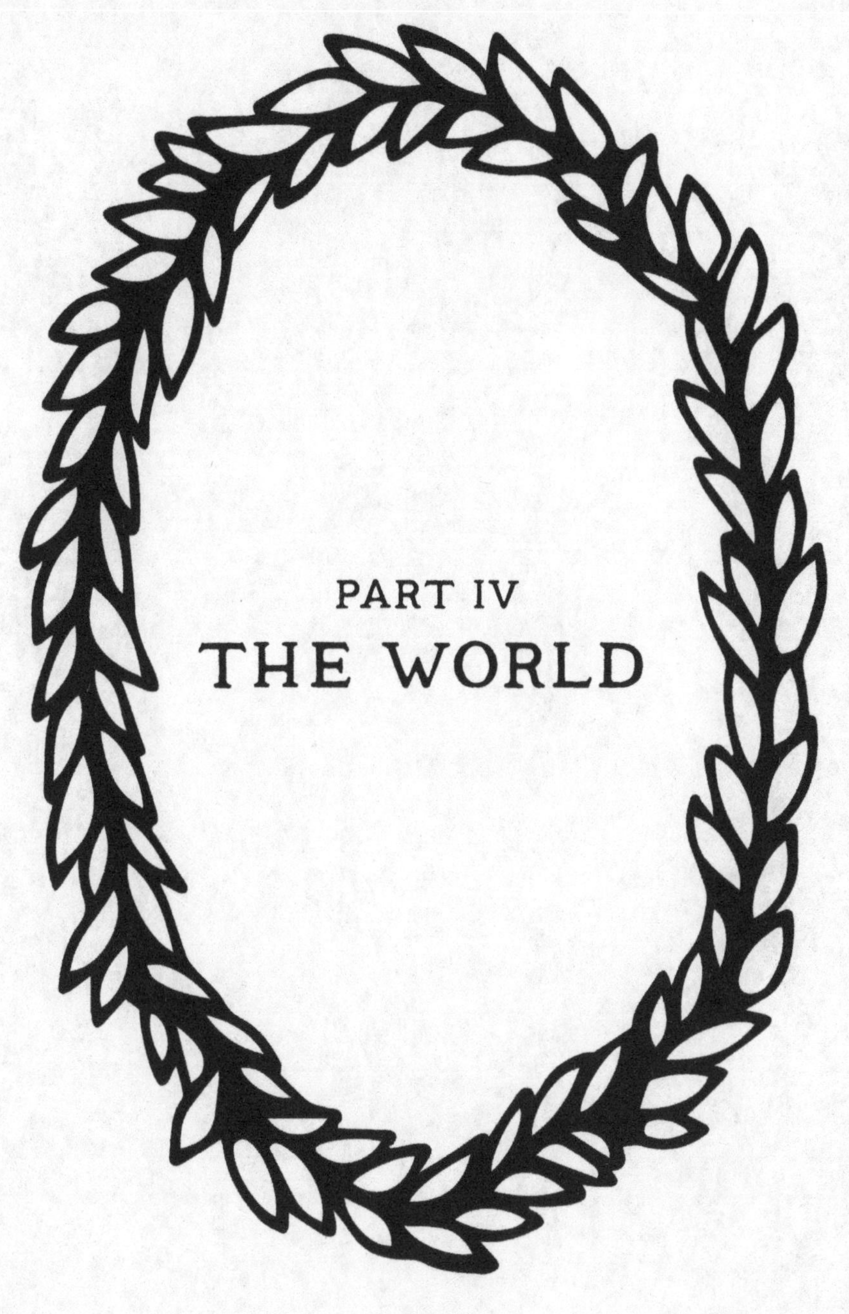
PART IV
THE WORLD

INTERLUDE

There is nothing.

Savage looks down to his dirty, bare hands.

One hand is shiny, burned, healing. The other looks like it always has. The tattoos on his arm formed into a twisted aggregate of ink from when they were burned in the gas fire at the high rise.

He regrets being the second Savage. He likes to think of himself as the first. Certainly, the better. But now, finally, he is the only. It is him and no other because this is the new frontier. The new universe.

Except the new universe looks a lot like fucking nothing.

He draws in a deep, thoughtful breath. Maybe they failed. Or maybe the rest succeeded, but he got cast out or lost along the way because he was the thing that was never supposed to exist.

But wait, here's something. After. She's coughing into her hand, covered in soot and dust, her normally glossy, smooth

357

hair a disheveled mess.

The landscape unfurls before them, a dustbowl. A great, barren firepit, charred to nothing but cinders and soot.

Getty is dusting himself off. The siren is crying streaky tears down her smudged face, bracing herself against the blackened ground.

"Get up," the only Savage left says, coughing at her.

"My sisters, my sisters . . ." she wails, as she clutches herself tightly into a ball.

"Leaving your sisters didn't occur to you before you made the agreement?" After laughs, looking to Savage with pure bemusement in her eyes. She coughs again. "Where do you think Devlin landed?"

Savage squats to the ground and rubs his finger through the ash. A bone protrudes from the dirt, and he cleans away the excess to free it. "Not sure," he says, lifting the bone from the ground. It's black and blue and from no animal that exists. "Huh. I think I found him."

"Look, here's another one," After says, pulling a second bone from under the crying siren. "Get off."

The bones pull themselves from After and Savage's grasps and clink against one another like magnets. From across the wasteland, the pieces fly together until Devlin shakes himself into form, a blue-black skeleton and nothing more.

"Wha, what is this?" skeletal Devlin screams.

"Sir?" After asks.

"*Spread out*," he barks. "Find the souls."

Getty, After, Savage, and Devlin each walk in different directions, searching the nothingness for something resembling a soul. But as they make their way farther apart, they begin to approach each other again and wind up knitted together, in a circle, around the crying siren.

"*Again*," screams the bones.

Again, they walk apart but again, they end up circled around one another.

"Pull one," Devlin says.

"Sir?"

"Pull one from the ether. A soul. Pull one into existence and let it be born so I might begin my world."

After grimaces. "What, me? You're assuming because I'm a female I can propagate your world?"

"I cannot concentrate with all that noise," Devlin screams, turning to the siren. In a blaze, her crumpled form ignites and is reduced to ashes.

"Oh good," the only Savage says. "Now we're down to four. That'll make it easier."

"Fix. This." Devlin says, his bones trembling and clicking against one another.

"We may have made a miscalculation . . ."

"Goddammit," Devlin says.

"I think," Savage replies, "they already did."

TWENTY ONE

There is nothing.

No form.

No fingers or teeth or back or dick.

No hum or music or breathing or laments.

No hurt.

No pain.

No thing.

Nothing.

There is only a perfect and complete void.

Savage feels as though this ought to bother him, but it doesn't.

He feels peaceful.

Peaceful and potent.

Since the moment he became a creator, he's been on an endless loop, a carousel of time. Existence is rising and falling and reaching for a brass ring. Lungs expanding and releasing. Hands spinning tirelessly on the face of a clock.

But not anymore.

There is no loop. No line. No shape or geometry. No science at all.

No sound.

No stirring.

No vibrations on the string of the instrument of the world.

No sand slipping through a fissure in an hourglass.

The glass has been broken. The sand is scattered everywhere. Nowhere.

But . . . there is a speck. One speck of sand. How did he not notice it before? It's the only thing. It exists in this perfect nonexistence. How odd.

What are you? Savage thinks with a brain that doesn't exist.

What is this tiny insignificant thing sending ripples through his perfect void?

He looks closer, he dives deeper.

Oh.

There it is.

The universe.

The thing he once carved and crafted and shined and studied.

This is it, this infinitesimal thing.

His child, his creation. He examines it like the tired coin it is.

It's growing. It's beating. It's fluttering and breathing.

It hovers before him, begging for his compassion.

It beats within his great nonexistent hands like a bird, its feathers on his skin. Its wings tremble against his fingers with its silken existence. With smooth permanence. With hollow little bird bones holding the whole damn thing together.

Savage gets closer, pulls in infinitely.

Here's the eye of the storm on a massive planet, a great red hurricane thousands of miles wide. He looks closer. Lightning touches down to the planet's surface every second or two. The rhythm of the storm is like a piece of music. The wind is a swirling broken thing, the thunder calling back and forth to itself across miles and miles. He listens to it for a moment. He listens for an eternity.

He pulls back, and pulls back in, somewhere else.

Here is an ocean. Vast. Blue, black, gray. A universe unto itself. It rolls and swells and falls and repeats. It tastes like baptism. Like the yield of Trappist monks. It's the wine of creation. It's quiet, and it's deafening.

He pulls back again and examines things at random.

Here is a dying star.

Here is a moon.

Here is the earth.

Here is a bridge, spanning a great brown river.

Here is a pile of pink insulation, like poisoned cotton candy.

Here is a tick on the back of a dog.

Here is a person. Their lungs and hands and heart. Their freckled back. Their spine hiding beneath like a piece of rusted rebar. Their marrow a sweet, spongey mess within it all.

Here is a crack.

Here is a molecule.

Here is momentum.

Here is a moment.

Here is everything.

Savage spins a new form for himself. He wills it into existence, pulling atoms from here and there across the universe. He makes something that looks a bit—a lot—like how he used to look. Black hair and too big ears and deep-set eyes. Electric faced. He recreates the tattoos on his forearm as a playful reminder of the forces of the universe. Death, The Sun, The Hanged Man.

The cemetery in Brooklyn has changed. The leaves are dying on the trees, and dust motes dance in the afternoon sunlight. Savage passes the angel of death statue, its bowed head guarding the remains of a long-ago mayor.

To human ears, it would be quiet. But Savage hears everything. The beating of wings. The rustling. The breathing. The chalk white roots slowly growing, reaching through the damp earth like fingers pressing into the graves below.

He finds Rook by the pond. The fountain is raining a soft mist skyward in the autumn afternoon. The crow-headed reaper sits like he always does, a bit like a child and a lot like an animal. He cocks his head as he watches Savage approach, blinking his great glassy eyes.

"Savage one," he says, though his beak doesn't move.

Savage can hear him now, his little bird words that flutter into his ears on black wings. Savage can hear everything.

"We wondered where you had gone," the crow says.

Savage settles into the grass beside him.

"I forgot myself for a moment."

"It happens," Rook says as he shifts his gaze back to the water.

Savage takes a deep breath into his new lungs. The air smells like burning wood in a hearth somewhere close by. He can taste the carbon on the back of his tongue.

The two sit in silence for a moment, Savage reveling in the nothingness of being. In time and shape and space. He lets the hush sit on his tongue and dissolve like a communion wafer.

"Where is Bishop?" he asks, breaking the quiet.

"He went."

"Went where?"

"To the shadow place." The reaper sits forward and fidgets, running his black gloved fingers over one another.

"Why?"

"Why what?"

Savage clears his throat, smiling at the way the crow's mind works. "Why did Bishop go to the Shadowlands?"

"His new job. In the low place. The shadow place."

"New job?"

"Yes. For balance. There has to be five. There was always five. Except when you were gone. But there were still five. Four and one lost still make five."

Savage nods. "True." He places a hand on the reaper's shoulder. "Thank you, Rook."

"Thank you, Savage one."

"For what?"

The crow gestures before him, spreading his fingers out as if to indicate *everything*.

"Ah," Savage says as he stands. "You're most welcome."

Savage walks through the empty streets of the Shadowlands. There's no breathing or beating or stirring. The quiet echoes and bounces off itself in an infinity of nothing. But Savage notes it feels different than it did before, like the moments before dawn, no longer perpetual midnight.

He thinks about Devlin's Big Bang. About where he is now. About whether he's stewing in his banishment.

When he arrives at the place where Devlin's mansion once stood, he finds nothing but a crater and the faint odor of forgotten smoke.

No Bishop.

Nothing.

He turns around, thinking, wondering where to go next, when the silence is broken with a clang followed by a crash. A hammering. Another crash.

He follows the source of the noise.

The weak predawn light reveals Remy, standing on a ladder, pulling metal siding from a house and throwing it into a pile. His brown and gold flecked hair is more disheveled, more unkempt than Savage has seen it before, and he wears laborer's clothing, paint speckled coveralls and big dirty boots.

At the bottom of the ladder, a satchel is overflowing with a rainbow of sand, the stuff of unfermented dreams.

"Remy?" Savage calls.

The sandman looks down to him. "Ah, the Artist. Maybe you can help." He climbs down the ladder and pulls off a pair of work gloves. They're covered in remnants of the sticky dreams.

"Help how? What are you doing?"

"The r—well, *Bishop*, as I guess he's not the reaper anymore. Bishop has requested I energize this place a little bit." He picks up a handful of the sand and swirls his hands around each other until they form the cotton-candy-like substance that is dreams.

"By removing sheet metal from a random house?"

"Yes. Well, first I remove the old, and then I—" at this Remy takes the fluff and blows it over the house with a great breath. The space he had been working on recreates itself almost exactly, but with a slightly livelier appearance. There's luster and color. "It's better. Not too much pizzazz, I've been explicitly told. Not too much fucking pizzazz. It's still the Shadowlands, just spruced up a bit. One piece at a time." He sighs.

Savage looks down the block and notices the nearest few houses. Their roofs and yards and trees all look less haunted. Different, new.

"Is this your penance?"

Remy nods. "My flagellation. One square foot at a time." He grabs another sprinkle of dust and adds it atop the same space he was working on. "There we go." He rubs his thumb over a small smudge on the wall and buffs it out. "You weren't around to figure out what to do with me, so Bishop took it upon himself."

"I see that."

"It's actually not so bad." Remy claps the dust from his hands. "I was bored. That's the whole reason I fell in with

Devlin in the first place. And now I get to do something new, my own work, one small piece at a time. It still needs to be an echo of the world topside, but Bishop wanted something his own style. Just not too much pizzazz . . ."

Something in Savage's head clicks. The Shadowlands are an echo of the real world, as Remy just said. And Savage remembers. He realizes.

"Remy," Savage says to the sandman, "I forgive you."

The sandman falls mute. His mouth opening and closing, unable to find a response. He looks uncomfortable with the sensation.

"Keep up the good work for Bishop," Savage continues, "I'm sure he appreciates it."

"I-I will. I mean, I have to, but I will."

"Good." Savage claps Remy on the shoulder, and the sandman climbs back up the rungs of the ladder to further resurface the earth under the earth.

Savage returns to the cemetery, but the echoed version. The bottom-side version.

The Smithe family mausoleum exists in the under-land, just as it does in the world above. The door is ajar, and he lets himself in.

Bishop reclines on his sofa, his shoes propped up on the cushions. His hands are bare, and he's concentrating on reading a dark blue notebook, mouthing the words to himself.

Savage steps into Bishop's line of sight.

A flicker of a smile crosses his whiskered face. "I can't make sense of any of this," he says. "It's like he *prided* himself on being disorganized."

"He was the god of chaos."

"He didn't have to take the job so literally." He tosses the book onto the coffee table and sits up. "Whatcha doing, kid?"

"Oh, you know." Savage shrugs. "Reacquainting myself with existence. The usual. You?"

"Just trying to meet my new job expectations."

They look at each other for a long moment. Bishop breaks, smiles, and stands.

"Come here, you." Bishop pulls Savage into a big hug. "It's good to have you back," he says into his shoulder as they part.

"How long was I gone?"

"A couple years."

"*Years?*"

"All drops in the bucket, buddy. We knew you'd find your way back."

"Years . . ." Savage mumbles to himself. "And I was the only one?"

"I mean, we all got knocked off our block for a bit after the Big Bad Bang, but we returned soon thereafter."

"So . . . Devlin succeeded?"

"In *un*making our world? No. But in making his own? Yes. It was the only way." Bishop sits, forearms to knees like he's waiting for the bus. "It's been a long existence, kid. We've been cycling through the motions for millennia. It's okay to change every now and again. We work with what we have. Even when we don't have something essential . . . like you. But you're here now."

Savage sighs and runs his fingers through his hair. "I don't understand. Why am I always the vulnerable one?"

"You were still corporeal, kid. You separated from your body and spun out into godliness without the memory of how to return. But it seems you figured it out."

Savage flops on the sectional opposite the former reaper. "So, what happened?"

"What I realized was the only thing that could happen. It was better for Devlin to spin out on his own. Now he's got his own sick creation to toy with, and he took his demonic little beasties with him. But—and here's the kicker—there's no life there. There can't be. And however long it takes for him to figure that fact out, well," he draws in a deep breath, "that'll be the duration of his banishment."

"And you?"

Bishop smiles around the glint of sadness in his eyes.

Savage shakes his head. "Bishop . . . you didn't have to do this."

"Yes, I did. Gotta have that balance, baby. I'm the new god of chaos."

"But you weren't designed for it."

"No," he sighs, "and I miss my vocation. My true vocation. Also, I'm inclined to be far more orderly than chaos requires. But I'll exist in a little minor distress to keep the pendulum of the universe swinging. And maybe join a reaper at a gateway every now and then."

"I'm sure Rook would be happy to have the master at his side from time to time."

"Nah, I think he's enjoying his promotion." Bishop smiles again, pride welling in his eyes. He looks down. "I couldn't do both, as much as I want to. Death and unrest are equally pivotal, but I stretched myself thin trying to master chaos and reign over death. So, I let Rook take the wheel."

"I am so sorry," Savage says. "I know how hard that must be for you."

"All part of the karmic balance. Maybe I'll get to go back to it someday. In the meantime, I've gotta make this realm feel more like home."

"That reminds me," Savage says. "I ran into the traitor. I see you've got him hard at work."

"Who, Remy?" Bishop laughs. "It seemed like a good punishment. If I have to be down here day after unending day, it might as well look a little less like Chernobyl."

"What about the others? Ray? Ambit?"

"Flourishing. They're working to mend this planet we choose to call home. Science. Life. They're quite simpatico these days."

They sit in silence a moment, Bishop gazing at Savage with an avuncular glint in his eye.

"Why don't you ask me about her?" Bishop questions.

Savage sighs. "Because I'm on my way to see her next. My worry for you and for the fate of the universe was more pressing than my desire to see Felicity. That should tell you how much you mean to me, you grim bastard."

"Ha! Not so grim anymore."

"You never really were. But also, I want to savor that moment. When I see her. I've been inhuman for a hot minute, and it's taking me some time to acclimate."

"I think we should go now, friend."

"We? I don't think—"

"Yeah, no, I'm coming," Bishop says through his grin.

"Alright, just don't be pissed when I tell you to beat it."

Bishop only smiles in reply as he stands. "Shall we?"

Ambit is squatting in his crisp white suit, the ocean waves soaking the hems of his pant legs. His eyes are squinting beneath his glasses, from sunlight and from concentration.

Nearby, a toddler is digging with a plastic spade. She's building a sandcastle, giggling as she flicks wet clumps of sand over her dark skin and into her curly hair.

"This is not good," Ambit says to the little girl, who lets her face fall to mimic his.

Ambit shakes his head.

She shakes her head in response.

"Ray?" Ambit calls.

Ray is standing in the water, waist deep, hand in hand with Felicity. The women are meditating with the ocean, the water lapping at their breasts and arms. They have their eyes closed in the afternoon sunlight, and the current of the ocean is rocking them back and forth.

In the distance, the New York City skyline sits like a fragile, faraway thing.

"Ray?" Ambit calls again.

"We are trying to commune with the ocean," Ray replies, mildly exasperated.

"But the waterline is definitely eroding. There's an almost imperceptible shift, infinitesimal, really. But it will be measurable within, say twenty-four months?" Ambit stands, clapping the wet sand off his hands. "You'd think she'd care more about this," he says to the little girl. He glances inland and spots the two dark figures against the sand.

Savage and Bishop approach, like afternoon shadows.

"*Savage*," Ambit expels.

"Savage?" Felicity echoes. She and Ray turn around to face the shore. "*Savage*," she cries again when she sees him.

Savage smiles at her. His being is fully actualized for the first time since touching back down into this universe. He was not himself, not entirely, until he saw her again, rocking in the water, her gown floating around her like a Mucha print incarnate.

She's the closest thing to perfection he has known.

She makes her way toward him, stumbling in the current a little. Ray holds onto her with a maternal hand. As she comes out of the water, Savage sees her form is swollen and bursting beneath her soaking sea foam dress.

"What?" he gasps. "You're pregnant?"

"She's not with child, if that's what you mean," Ray says to him as she helps Felicity up the shoreline. "She's with creation. She's with *universe*."

Savage embraces Felicity, holding her delicate face in his hands and regarding her changed form. "What? What does that mean?"

"When her gestation is complete, she will not birth a human babe, but a fledgling universe, born of beauty and teeming with whatever life you choose to populate it with."

"It was by chance," Felicity says, "but it means you and I created something. Something beautiful."

Savage cries out in shock and joy. "But I-I've been gone so long?"

"This isn't a normal incubation, love," Felicity says to him. "I've been waiting for you. Waiting for your return."

Savage absorbs the information, lets it sit on his tongue. Settle in his mind. He looks down at Felicity, at her comely face between his hands. A smile unfurls there. Together, they revel in this one flawless moment. They are sanguine and full of promise for the changes to come. Here, together. On the precipice, toeing the tide. Not yet over the edge. Not yet in the water.

She brings her face to his and kisses him. "I've missed you," she says.

He pulls back and wraps her in his long arms.

"We've got you covered here, kid," Bishop says, stepping forward and patting Savage on the shoulder.

"What does that mean?" Savage asks, wiping tears from his eyes.

Bishop takes a deep breath. "You don't have to stay in this world. You and Felicity can go on to tend to your new creation, and our universe won't suffer for it."

"How, exactly? Won't that throw off the internal pendulum we were just talking about?"

"It would if we didn't have a replacement for you," Ambit says, smiling.

"Replacement? But . . . who?"

"Verity," Ambit says, looking down at the chubby legged toddler.

"I will take care of this world, Savage one," she says as she sets down her shovel in the sand. "Go on and rage your art into the darkness."

"Verity?" Savage asks her.

"I took a new form," she says in her sweet, high voice. "Fresh. Invigorating. But I will be ready. The Oracles didn't give me false prophesies after all. I may have misinterpreted them, but their words proved sacrosanct. You are the renaissance, Savage one. I'll tend to your creations, here. Worry not."

"The balance here will stay intact," Ambit says, nodding. "Much has changed, Savage. Much had to. But we're nothing if not industrious. And we're all excited for your new beginning."

"But . . ." Savage lets his mind turn over for a moment. "How will our new world be balanced?"

"It doesn't have to be," Felicity answers. "Not exactly. It can be whatever we choose."

"Oh." He lets the truth of this sink in. It's been a long existence of living in this universe with its rules and boundaries and balance. "This universe was an experiment in balance," he begins.

"And ours can be an experiment of our own devising," she finishes, threading her fingers through his.

"A creation built on creating," Savage says.

"An invention of inventiveness," Ambit suggests.

"A macrocosm of inspiration," Ray adds.

"An aesthetic . . . somethin' somethin'." Bishop clears his throat. "I'm not as good at this as you guys are."

Ray turns to Felicity, placing a tender hand on her shoulder. "Are you ready, child?"

"Now?" Savage asks.

AUTHOR'S NOTE

The scene in which Bishop takes Savage and Felicity to eat Indian food in The Village is based on a real restaurant on Bleecker Street called Ghandi Cafe. My husband and I joke it was 80% of why we moved to New York in 2015. Go eat there. For my last meal in this world, I'd love nothing more than a big bowl of chicken tikka masala, hot and fresh from Ghandi. And, fuck it, throw in an order of their homemade garlic naan and poori. If I'm about to die, gluten will be the least of my worries.

—ESH LEIGHTON, MARCH 2025

ACKNOWLEDGEMENTS

As we all know, writing can be a solitary experience, but I'd like to take the time to express gratitude for the wonderful humans who had a part in bringing *Journey Man* to fruition.

My sweet William. I gave Savage your colorblindness because I wanted to see the world through your eyes. Words always seem to fail me when expressing the magnitude of my love and appreciation for the generous, beautiful, hilarious, fucking genius man that you are. Thank you forever for the insane amount of support that you continue to give me in all things but especially those related to my craft. Books may not be your thing, but I love that you love that they're mine. I'm so stupidly lucky to be in the same universe as you.

So much love to my family by blood and by marriage, thank you for your years of support, unfailing optimism, and encouragement. Especially to my parents, from whom I inherited your unique and disparate ways with words. When I was a teenager and decided I wanted to pursue a creative career, individually you each told me, (paraphrasing here) "Go knock 'em dead." Not every kid gets such a supportive set of parents.

I owe such gratitude to my writing community, both online and off. My sweet Nixie Pixie, Nix Damon. You are such a unique spirit—I'm so grateful to have your friendship and your advice. I hope *Journey Man* had enough violence for you. Alex Knudsen and Charlotte Zang for being early readers, fellow basset hound enthusiasts, and serious couple goals. Special appreciation to Erik Harden, who was not only an early reader and steadfast cheerleader, but who gave me a writing prompt over a decade ago in a bar (not entirely unlike *Clover's*) which merged with the technicolor hellscape that was floating around in my head. You helped provide *Journey Man* with the inkling of an anchor.

My j'eatjet? family: it may seem small but when I told you all I was setting out to write a novel for NaNoWriMo in November of 2016, never have I felt more supported by such a lovable group of weirdos in my life. Brooklyn got dimmer the day j'eatjet? closed her doors.

Special thanks to my many friends in the multitude of cities I've breezed through in the last fifteen years. I have been so fortunate to know so many beautiful souls in this life.

It would be impossible to tell a story about an artist without the help of many actual artists. Much appreciation to each of the craftspeople who contributed to the final product. Julia Scott, my formatter, for embracing the vision and bringing your artistic talent to all the little details—I want a tarot reading when this is done. To those at Ebook Launch for beautifully creating the first impression Savage and the world of *Journey Man* have on readers: Dane Low, my artist, and Alisha, project manager. To Emma Endicott for your sharp eye and meticulous final pass.

To my dogs. You guys didn't help, but you're cute so I'll include you. Our OG Three (rest in peace) and our Fab Four. Dogs make life better, guys. Go adopt one.

Lastly, to Madeleine, the woman in the high tower. I owe you a debt of gratitude I will never be able to properly repay. Years ago, I asked you to read some of my work on a whim, which you probably now know is an aberration. But I could see your sharp wit and your impeccable taste even in the fledgling friendship we had then. Over the years, you have evolved from an early reader to critique partner and close friend, to a champion and confidante, and now: publisher. I'm so happy that while our books may not live in the same universe, they get to sit on the shelf beside one another. Profoundly, proudly extra.

ABOUT THE AUTHOR

Credit: ESH Leighton and her iPhone

ESH Leighton grew up in Nevada, where she kept herself entertained making potions, penning rhymes, and imagining alternate worlds in the safety of her backyard with her faithful dog sidekick. That love of language and fantasy evolved and birthed the novel you are now holding, *Journey Man*, her first. Her work has been featured across many literary journals, both in print and online, and she released her first collection of poetry in 2020 entitled *Backwards Births*. When not working on her craft, she can be found doting on her many dogs, watching hockey with her husband, or attempting to teach herself a new skill. After many moves across the country, she has finally settled in San Antonio, Texas.